HOW TO BECOME A
SEER

HOW TO BECOME A
SEER

MARTY REEDER

MART-OLOGY PUBLISHING

AN IMPRINT OF M.O.P.
SMITHFIELD, UTAH

ISBN 13: 979-8-9932435-0-4

Published by Mart-Ology Press
Smithfield, Utah
www.martyreeder.com

Cover design by Edgar Lipsey
Cover design ©2025 by Mart-Ology Press

DEDICATED TO BONNIE—A NATURAL BORN *SEER* WHO DISCERNS THOSE HALF-HIDDEN FROM THE EYE AND HAS HELPED ME TO DO THE SAME.

Prologue
FORESEER

The priest sensed something. Something to come. His eyes snapped open, and he looked up.

The jungle teemed with so much rainfall that purposely creating a hole in his section of roof could only mean a lot of unnecessary soakings. But the priest had felt no burden shifting his sleeping mat under the roofed portion of the temple's living quarters anytime the moisture began to fall and trickle out the sloped entryway. The reward for this inconvenience came any time the night sky remained clear and revealed the inky expanse dotted with silver specks. Better still, anytime the moon chose to march along the track beyond his roof, the priest could contemplate the power within these moving celestial objects.

This night, with his eyes adjusting to the darkness above him, he noted that the moon was not yet out, but he knew it would be soon. Stepping out of his hut, he walked towards the top of the temple, oblivious to the soft sounds and smells of the night jungle and the slumbering village below him. Instead, he went to the stone where he had previously secreted the materials that he had created for just such a moment as this.

With the stone hefted up, the priest reached into the cavity below and removed the brush and lidded pot. He looked towards the tree-top-lined eastern horizon and noted the hazy, silvery glow that emitted from it. The moon was almost ready.

The priest quickly secured the ropes to anchors and lowered the plank hanging from either end down the back wall of the temple. Then he secured himself and gripped his equipment in one hand while scaling delicately down a rope ladder.

He had carefully chosen this spot to record his vision long ago, and now that he could sense it coming, he balanced calmly in front of it. He removed the lid to the pot. The dark and viscous liquid substance still held the same consistency since he first created it just for this purpose. The priest gripped the brush and waited.

Before he could have second thoughts about his precarious position, the moon left the horizon, and the vision occurred. Furiously, he painted. The substance that had simply reflected the black night moments before the moonrise, now shimmered a faint silver. With fluttering eyes that seemed to be both seeing and guiding the movement of his brush-wielding hand as well as staring through the wall in front of him to some distant scene, he took the dreamlike images from his mind's eye and transferred them to crude hieroglyphics on the stone face in front of him.

There was no way for the priest to know how long he hung there across the back of the temple, walking back and forth along the plank, bending up and down, and using each brush stroke to inscribe row after row of quixotic yet perfectly prophetic images. All he knew was that when the final image fluttered past his mind and his hand came to a conclusive stop, he blinked several times and then felt immediately exhausted.

The moon had tracked a large distance during this time, but its light allowed him to review his work. It all focused on a girl. A girl who must be a seer, but a seer unlike any the priest had ever known or even heard of. A powerful seer, but apparently ignorant as to the extent of her power.

The priest wished he could meet this seer. He wanted to find her, to tap into her power. But the face—especially the eyes—had been hidden from him, as dreams will do sometimes. Besides, the priest's sight showed only things to come—and it was clear that this seer came from a very different world, far ahead of the cycle of his current world. Yet, he thought, she still had a connection to the one he currently inhabited.

A brief survey of the images brought the priest to the final hieroglyphic, and the vision that inspired it weighed over him. He took a moment longer to add some finishing touches.

Whether I meet this seer girl or not, he pondered to himself, *she will be faced with more than the challenge of understanding her seeing potential.* His eyes probed deeper into the final hieroglyph. *She will be faced with traumatic loss—one that may very well undo her.*

PART ONE

NATURAL BORNAPPERS

Chapter 1
APTITUDE TEST

The puffs of steam escaping Eric's mouth into the frigid night air accentuated his heavy breathing. Having reached his destination, he stationed his bike on the edge of the empty parking lot, which sat on top of a steep hill surrounded by some quaint, small businesses and offering a vista of the city below.

But Eric did not come for a view of the city. Instead he kicked the snow off the curb which outlined the parking lot and sat, staring at the black surface in front of him.

He did this every now and then. Not often, but any time he felt out-of-place he found himself gravitating towards the parking lot where he met up with Charlotte a few months back. The place where they held hands, gazed into each other's eyes, and . . . and he got transported to another world (literally), hunted down a pair of pirate twins, and killed a natural born pirate. He smiled. The world he remembered remained so starkly different from this one: warm tropical air instead of frigid temperatures, the thousand smells of the ocean, the tug of the wind against the tightened sheets and lines of the boat. He sighed. Eric did not regret his decision to come back, but sometimes he could not help but think of what might have been.

His thoughts were interrupted by some voices echoing off the front of one of the businesses sitting on the other side of the street adjacent to the parking lot. There, he spotted two forms, teenagers from the looks of it. When they crossed the street on their way to the parking lot, they traversed under a street lamp and he immediately recognized them both: Tina Ortiz and Luke Bateman.

What are they doing here? Eric thought. It was a school night, and most of the businesses were just closing down. Unless they were coming to reminisce on pirate hunting exploits of the past, as he had, there was really no good reason to—

A man that Eric had not noticed before peeled himself out of the darkness and intercepted the duo as they stepped onto the surface of the parking lot. "I apologize for the mix up. The building owner was supposed to have it unlocked, but I suppose you saw my note since you are here." Eric could not see the man's face, but something in the man's tone suggested that his apology was more manufactured than real.

Luke glanced over to Tina, whose no-nonsense expression had jarred teachers and administrators in high school, let alone a fellow junior peer like Eric. She directed her gaze towards the man. "Well, where are we meeting now, Mr. Neech? You can't possibly hope to give your presentation in a parking lot."

The man named Neech paused. "That is not my intent, Ms. Ortiz. In fact, if you don't mind waiting here for just a moment longer, then . . ." Neech glanced across his shoulder to the night sky. Eric followed his gaze and saw that the waning moon was about to finish its ascent into the sky from the far horizon. Something in Eric clicked. *Wait a second*, he realized. He stood up.

"Excellent," Eric heard Neech's voice announce. "Now, you will see what I have to offer you."

Eric started forward just as Neech's head swiveled back to Tina and Luke. Before Eric could say anything, Neech's eyes met with Luke's. The boy vanished.

Tina Ortiz gasped as she stared at the empty spot next to her. "What just happened?" She turned to look at Mr. Neech, "Did you see what happened to—" Before the rest of the sentence could leave her lips, Tina Ortiz also disappeared.

Neech immediately turned around and headed for the dark corner of the parking lot where he first appeared, but Eric finally found his voice. "Wait! Stop!"

Neech pivoted in Eric's direction, clearly not expecting anyone else to be nearby. Eric ran up to him, noticing his sharp features, slicked-back blond hair, and the cold blue eyes of an adult probably in his late twenties. Eric recognized him. "You were at the school earlier today," he stated out loud.

Neech squinted in the small light from the street lamp. "Yes," he said thoughtfully.

Eric's indignation fired up within himself. "You're a natural born seer. Only a seer would be able to look someone in the eyes once the moon came up and make them disappear. You just sent those two to the worlds where they can realize their natural born potential."

Neech's eyes widened momentarily—clearly it was rare for someone who was not a seer to know about them. After a moment, however, Neech seemed to relax. "Yes, I am. I would offer to send you to a world of pirates, but if you know about seers then it appears that one has already done that for you. Sadly, that seer brought you back as well."

"Sadly? That seer sent me and brought me back after asking me for permission. What you just did is—"

"'Natural bornapping' is what some people distastefully call it. I prefer to call it 'affirming,' since I'm simply affirming the natural order by sending them to the place where they most naturally belong rather than wasting their time living a mediocre existence here and now."

Eric thought it strange how calm and reasoned Neech seemed to be in spite of his recent action. "I don't care what you call it," Eric replied, "It's wrong."

Neech looked at his watch. "Now, look. I'd love to have this philosophical debate with you, but I couldn't send you back to the world of pirates until, well, through to the next phase of the moon, so you're really just wasting my time."

Eric peered more closely at Neech, seeing his slicked-back blond hair shimmer in the faint light. "How did you know which phase of the moon I—"

Neech waved his hand, "Look, I've still got something else to get done tonight, so why don't you just run along. If you still feel really concerned, why don't you call the cops on me or something?"

Even though they were nearly the same height, Neech patted Eric condescendingly on the head and then walked towards a black corner of the parking lot where Eric noticed a small car. Just as he got in his car, Eric saw Neech remove a cell phone, make a call, and say, "Phase One complete. Onto Phase Two."

Eric pulled out his own cell phone, briefly considering calling Neech's bluff. Then he realized that it was no bluff. What would he say to the police if he called them? "I just saw a man send two teenage kids to another world?" No. There was only one person for him to call: another seer.

A moment later, "Charlotte? It's me, Eric."

Calling Charlotte about a meddling seer forced Eric to consider an interesting conversation they shared only hours earlier that day in school.

"I think it's funny," Eric had told Charlotte during their lunch period.

Charlotte's ponytail bobbed dazzlingly. "That what's funny? That you go on police ride-alongs and want to tell them to drop anchor instead of park?" She loved making any reference to his natural born pirate hunting ability any chance she got.

Eric never could get the best of Charlotte so instead he ignored her. "I think it's funny the way that you won't look into other people's eyes anymore when you first meet them." He deliberately looked into her sparkling blue eyes. "It makes them uncomfortable."

Charlotte's eyes turned from Eric's. She nibbled on her sandwich.

Not wanting to embarrass his best friend, (in fact, not even knowing he was capable of it) Eric tried to coax her face back to his. "I didn't mean it was funny like 'cats-on-the-internet' funny . . . just more like the 'I-think-that's-interesting' funny."

Eric's ploy worked. Charlotte's face swiveled back to him and her eyes renewed their sparkle. "You think cats on the internet are funny?"

Now Eric had to take a second to reconsider. "Well, I guess I . . . no, not really. Actually, have you seen that one where the lady dresses her cat up like Zorro and he—"

"It's none of my business," Charlotte stated, interrupting.

Eric raised his eyebrows. "None of your . . . you asked me if I thought watching cats on the internet was interesting so I—"

Charlotte smiled in amusement. "Not the cats-on-the-internet thing," she said, "other people's natural born abilities are none of my business."

"Oh." Eric fell silent for a moment. He knew how Charlotte had been slightly withdrawn about her role as a natural born seer ever since they returned from his stint as a pirate hunter. He simply had not known how to bring it up with her since he was so used to Charlotte being the one to give *him* the pep talks, not the other way around. In every other sense, Charlotte was the same, confident, fiery person he had known since the day they met, but when it came to other people's natural born abilities and her own as a seer, she had been strangely reserved.

Charlotte must have noticed Eric's pensive state and sensed the discomfort creeping in. "Tell me about that french fry grease fire fiasco again. You know, that story with the meatloaf you told me on the day we met when you gave me a tour of the school."

Eric heard her but still stayed in his own thoughts for a moment longer. "Charlotte," he said, "I'm glad you made my natural born ability your business."

17

Charlotte's eyebrows cinched together, and she seemed about to say something, but then she paused, as if changing her mind. Her eyebrows shifted back, and she smiled while saying, "Well, lunchtime is almost over."

Eric nodded. "Right. Well, I'll see you after school then? Or is your dad picking you up?"

"You'll see me next hour," Charlotte grinned.

"Next hour?"

"Remember, all juniors are supposed to go to that meeting with their guidance counselor next hour. Since we're both with Mr. Pickney, we'll be in the same classroom." Charlotte observed Eric's bewildered face. She shook her head, amused. "I think the school would have better luck getting you to remember things if they used signal flags from the top of a mast."

Eric smiled. "Now that makes sense. All this mumbling over an intercom while I'm trying to study old Caribbean maps . . . ridiculous!"

"Alright, Pirate Hunter, we'd better go. I've got to drop stuff off in my locker first."

"If I even *am* a pirate hunter . . ." Eric countered casually, teasing about the possibility that Charlotte might have actually designated him as a pirate hunter rather than pirate because she felt it fit his personality as well as skills better than a pirate.

Charlotte squinted back at Eric. "Watch it, buddy, or you'll be wishing you were in a hurricane before I'm through with you."

As long as he had his friendship with Charlotte, it really did not matter to him what his official natural born title was. Eric smiled back. "I don't doubt it for a second."

Just after the lunch bell rang, they worked their way to the classroom where they were to meet with Mr. Pickney, their guidance counselor. The balding counselor's mustache wavered above his lip as he spoke, causing Eric to think of a flag in a breeze. That made him reflect on signal flags, which reminded him of Charlotte's tease about him not paying attention. "Listen," he chided himself.

18

"Students, we have a very special privilege for you today," Mr. Pickney announced.

"This is going to help us with scholarship opportunities, right Mr. Pickney?" Tina Ortiz, seated in the front row, did not even bother to raise her hand.

Mr. Pickney nodded, "Yes, Tina, as I promised you. But it's also so much more than that."

Charlotte leaned forward, since she was sitting behind Eric, and whispered, "Look at Mr. Pickney. He's actually trembling. Have you ever seen him this nervous before?"

Eric noticed Mr. Pickney's hand visibly fluttering. "No," he responded, "Just frustrated with students who haven't planned out their life through to retirement . . . you know, like me . . . or anyone who isn't Tina Ortiz . . ."

Mr. Pickney continued, "The eminent psychiatrist Doctor Leonard Corinth from the acclaimed GIA research institution has generously offered to conduct free aptitude testing for our students here in Nibleton High School with a brand new, state-of-the-art, simplified aptitude system designed to give the most valuable, quick, and effective feedback."

Eric's eyebrows rose. He turned and whispered to Charlotte, "Um, can you find us a Natural Born Translator . . . 'cause I don't think that—"

"He's a seer," Charlotte mumbled, almost to herself.

Eric looked at the man standing in the corner. A broad-shouldered man with short, silver hair leaned against the wall and adjusted his thin glasses as he carefully scanned the room. "You saw his eyes?" Eric queried while still gazing at the man. "I thought that was none of your business . . ."

Eric saw that the man's gaze had started to sweep in their direction. He turned to Charlotte and saw her face drop. "I didn't see his eyes," Charlotte responded.

"Then how can you know that he's a natural born seer?" Eric asked. Out of the corner of his eyes, he saw that the man's eyes dwelt on him and Charlotte as they whispered.

Charlotte's face stayed firmly down. "An eminent doctor who developed a new state-of-the-art aptitude test with quick feedback? Anything 'aptitude' reeks of a natural born seer. Combine that with the fact that he happens to come to give it personally? I'd be willing to bet if he were not personally here, those tests would not be nearly as accurate."

Dr. Leonard Corinth was now invited to come forward to address the students. The professor strode to the center of the room, removed his glasses, and smiled in a disarming way. "Why, Mr. Pickney, that was a highly flattering introduction. I appreciate your exaggerations of my accomplishments, but really I am not here to talk to you students. I'm sure the last thing a high school student wants to do with only an hour or so before school lets out is listen to some stuffy academic drone on and on. So we'll just administer these tests and then just bring the test to me when you are done and on your way out. I'll wish you good luck with your life's journey, and you can pick up results from Mr. Pickney tomorrow."

Dr. Corinth replaced his glasses then turned his silver head to Mr. Pickney. "If you wouldn't mind helping me pass out these tests . . ."

"Of course," Mr. Pickney announced, jumping forward fast enough that he stumbled and jarred one of the desks. After grabbing a handful, he started to head down the row where Eric and Charlotte sat.

Dr. Corinth held out a hand. "I'll . . . uh . . . I'll take this row, if you don't mind starting on the other side of the room."

"Absolutely, Dr. Corinth! It would be an honor that—"

"Thank you," Dr. Corinth smiled curtly.

Out of the corner of his eye, Eric saw Charlotte playing with the eraser on her pencil, eyes carefully zeroed in on her innocuous duty. Dr. Corinth placed the small booklet down on Eric's desk and Eric looked up to thank him, but he saw the Doctor's eyes adamantly fixed on Charlotte.

"Here you go, young lady," Dr. Corinth voiced as he placed the test deliberately on her desk, his eyes scanning her head, waiting for her face to turn up towards him.

"Thanks," Charlotte replied blithely, and quickly grabbed the booklet, writing on the top without looking up at him.

Dr. Corinth lingered a moment longer, but then moved farther down the row.

After waiting for Dr. Corinth to slide down a few desks from them, Eric swiveled. He brimmed with unasked questions, but now that he faced Charlotte, who looked back at him with a strange expression that he did not recognize, he could not think of anything to say. Eric turned around and zipped through the test, barely thinking about anything that he wrote down. Then he sat and waited. Around him, other students wrapped up their tests, packed their stuff, and then took the tests to the front of the room, where Dr. Corinth smiled cordially, shook their hands, and accepted their tests, marking a piece of paper before filing each of them away in a file folder.

If there were any doubts about Charlotte's supposition before, they vanished. Clearly, Dr. Corinth had everything set up to look people in the eyes as they handed him their tests. The man was either a natural born seer or someone with an unhealthy fascination with personal contact. Still unclear to Eric was why Charlotte was so set on not looking him in the eye. She had already told him that she had often spoken with other seers—it was how she got most of her secondhand information about natural born abilities. Besides, it was one thing to not look into other people's eyes because it was none of her business. But this . . . this was another seer trying to look into *her* eyes.

Charlotte had also seen Dr. Corinth's system for turning in the tests. Eric could sense her mind churning. She caught his attention, and he turned his face subtly towards her. Charlotte whispered, "Can you turn in my test for me?"

Eric looked back up to the front. "Sure." He was not positive that would be allowed to, considering the system Dr. Corinth had set up, but he could claim ignorance easily enough. "But I don't know if they'll just let you walk out of the room."

Charlotte's eyebrows scrunched together. Mr. Pickney manned the door, thanking each student as they left. One word from Dr. Corinth would convince his adoring fan, Mr. Pickney, to hold back any student that Corinth might need to "chat" with.

Hmmm, Eric thought. Then he decided to reason his way through the situation in a way that made sense to him. A narrow channel was being closely watched by a patrol ship. The harbor they sat in could be easily monitored by the fort sitting at the front of the room. What Eric needed was something that would clear out the patrol ship and distract the fortress. A fire ship would do the job, but Eric knew how much trouble a false fire alarm would get him into. But a false something else . . . Eric smiled. "I've got an idea," he whispered to Charlotte.

Eric tapped the shoulder of Dave Gardner sitting in front of him. Dave's buzzed, black stubble head swiveled around. His relaxed Filipino countenance appeared ready for anything other than the test they were taking. "Hey, what's up, Eric?"

Eric whispered into Dave's ear, and Dave grinned quixotically. "No problem, man!"

Dave packed up his stuff and turned in his test. He nodded to Mr. Pickney as he left the room. "Get ready," Eric told Charlotte while he eyed the door.

"Ready for what?"

"Every ship in this harbor is going to clear out into that channel in just a few moments."

Charlotte smiled. "I should've suspected you put your pirate hunting mind to this task!"

Eric had no time to respond. In the hallway beyond the classroom door a voice rang out, "Fight, fight, fight!"

Immediately, the silence in their classroom broke as students first looked at one another and then all stood up. Mr. Pickney seemed torn between trying to get the students to sit down and going to investigate the ruckus in the hallway. "Dude," the voice continued, "no shots to the face! That's not a fair fight . . ."

This tipped the scale. First Mr. Pickney exited the classroom, and then the students all inquisitively made for the doorway. "Now," Eric said and grabbed Charlotte's hand.

Eric kept Charlotte on the leeward side from Dr. Corinth as they left. Dr. Corinth hopelessly scanned the mass of faces as they streamed past him and hit the heavy current at the doorway.

Once out the door, Charlotte and Eric detected Mr. Pickney down the hallway speaking with Dave Gardner. Dave seemed pretty excited and pointed towards a bend in the hallway, Mr. Pickney and the mass of students charged towards the intersection. Eric kept hold of Charlotte's hand and led her the opposite direction and down some stairs.

Eric halted in the middle of the stairs. "Wait a second," he turned to Charlotte. "We left your test. He knows which desk you were in." Eric's mind raced. "Once he figures out your name, he might be able to have Mr. Pickney call you in and—"

"That might be hard to do considering the name on the test is Samuel Wesley," Charlotte told Eric.

Eric smiled at her subtle nod to their buddy from his old ship, the *Rosemary*, in the world of pirates. "Brilliant! Now let's get you out of here so you can explain what—"

A figure came streaking towards the stairs above them, lightly hopping onto the railing and half-sliding, half-springing down to where Eric and Charlotte stood. Once level with them, Dave Gardner jumped off the railing, sailed over their heads, and landed adeptly a couple of stairs below them. He was laughing.

"Man, you shoulda seen Mr. Pickney run around that corner. He looked like a dam was about to break and he needed to go stick his finger in it! It was awesome—almost as awesome as the rush of a good parkour run!"

Even though this was not the first time Eric had seen Dave's casual acrobatics, he still managed to be thrown off guard. "How do you do that? I trip just thinking about skipping a stair when going up in a hurry."

Dave nonchalantly ran up a wall and around a corner while he walked with them—not to show off, Eric realized, but simply because the wall was there and he knew he could do it. "That's your problem, Eric. When doing parkour, thinking kills it. You've just got to move first and then trust that your body will figure out the rest!"

Eric shook his head at Dave's incomprehensible passion. "Well, I don't know about trusting my own body to not crash and get broken in a dozen places, but I trust you. Speaking of that," Eric slapped Dave on the back, "I'll pay you tomorrow for the distraction."

Dave glided along their side. "Forget it, that was too much fun to get paid for. Plus, you got me outta finishing that boring test thingie. Tell you what, how about you come with me for an evening of parkour, and we'll call it even?"

Charlotte smiled. "I think he'd love that, Dave."

Eric eyed Charlotte critically but answered in the affirmative. "Sure thing. Sounds fun."

"Great! We can head downtown to hit the alleys behind the theater and bookstore—they got a wicked fire escape that you can flip off onto the rim of a dumpster," Dave offered.

"Alleys? I didn't even know Nibleton was big enough to have alleys . . ." Eric hedged, the image of him awkwardly flipping into a full face crash on the side of a dumpster caused him to wince involuntarily.

"If you love parkour enough," Dave grinned, "you have a talent for sniffing out a good alley. I'll give you a tour tonight."

"Tonight? Isn't it too cold for a parkour run?" Eric asked while Charlotte held back her snickering.

"Once you get moving, you warm right up. Trust me, it's a blast!"

Charlotte nudged Eric playfully. Eric sighed. "Okay, but I'm still not sure about tonight. I . . . uh . . . I'm swamped with some stuff. Next week might work best."

Dave returned Eric's slap on the back. "Deal! But I'll still be going tonight if things free up for you . . ."

"Are you kids just leaving from taking the aptitude test?"

By this time Eric, Charlotte, and Dave were crossing the foyer of the front entrance. A man at a booth set up in the middle of it had called out to them his query.

Dave turned toward the man. "Yep, it was the most exciting aptitude test I've ever taken." He winked at Charlotte and Eric. Eric turned to Charlotte and noticed that she had her eyes averted.

The man with blond, slicked-back hair and a black jacket covering a white collared shirt eyed them carefully. "Well, I'm here to give a scholarship and college-readiness presentation. It'll be tonight and tomorrow night. I'm signing people up right now."

Dave approached the man and grabbed a brochure. "College? I hear their campuses are great for parkour."

The man smiled as he faced Dave. "That they are. We will actually be discussing campus layouts in tonight's presentation. You, especially, should come."

"Right," Dave said. "Where is it?"

"I put an address on the brochure. It's a small venue so I'm afraid we only have room for students and not parents. Make sure you're not late."

Dave laughed. "Dude, I haven't been late to anything since 3rd period. You can count on me!" Dave turned to Eric and whispered, "Unless parkour is going good tonight . . . ya can't interrupt a solid course run, ya know what I mean?"

Eric nodded, even though he unequivocally did not know what Dave meant.

"I didn't get a chance to ask your other friend. Do you want to grab her and bring her over here to see if she'd be interested?" the man said, his blond head bobbing in the direction of the doors.

Eric looked to his side and realized that Charlotte was no longer there. He searched past the front entrance and saw her walking swiftly towards the parking lot.

"Uh, right . . . I'll, uh, grab her. Later, Dave! Thanks again!" Eric sprinted outside until he caught up with Charlotte, who had a look of concern on her face.

"What's going on?" Eric spat out as he tried to catch his breath. "You didn't look *that* guy in the eyes did you? We weren't in danger, were we?"

Charlotte shook her head. "I didn't look at him. I'm just ready to get out of here, that's all. Can I get a ride?"

"Sure," Eric said, glancing at her with uncertainty.

While they drove towards Charlotte's house, the car stayed quiet . . . a rarity anytime Eric did anything with Charlotte. As he took the last couple of turns towards her house, Eric ventured a query. "Anything going on that you want to tell me about?"

Charlotte paused for a moment before saying, distractedly, "Well, it's just that . . . I . . . well, for the first time in my life, I actually don't want to move."

Eric slowed the car down. "Wait, are you moving?" He had become so dependent on Charlotte in the last couple of months that he hated to fathom returning to his old life before he knew her.

Charlotte touched his arm reassuringly. "I'm just saying that all of my life, my family and I have moved so often . . . and I never cared. In fact, I looked forward to new places and new people . . . seeing new abilities." She smiled. "But now, I'm realizing that, for the first time, I don't want to move anymore. I'm happy here."

Eric smiled back. "Good. Cause the last time you left me, I had to kidnap a pirate just to get you back. I can't imagine what I'd have to do this time!"

Charlotte laughed. Eric pulled into her driveway. She squeezed his arm and stepped out of the car. "See you tomorrow. Let me know how parkour goes . . ." Her smile turned into a mischievous grin.

Eric shook his head. "I'll get you for that one, by the way!"

She found great joy in his threat, closed the door, and jogged up the driveway to her house. Just as Eric put the car in reverse and was about to pull out, he saw Charlotte wait before entering her home. Her fingers paused as they touched the doorknob and she seemed to be contemplating something. Finally, she took a deep breath and entered.

Eric thought for a moment himself before sliding out of the driveway and thinking that for all he did not know, one thing he did know: Charlotte was hiding something from him.

Chapter 2
BODYGUARD

Sally's Scribblings

Dad is hogging the TV again because of some important basketball game that he needs to watch, which means I can't watch any of the movies I want to see until he's done. Honestly, doesn't Dad realize that unless it's a championship game, there's no point in watching it. Where's the suspense? I started to tell him that but he gave me that one look—you know, the look that makes you think he's holding back something mean but he won't be able to hold back much longer if I keep talking—so I decided that I'd better write about it instead. Maybe he'll read about it later when he picks up my Scribblings Diary to see what's in it, but I'm pretty sure that won't happen either. He's a lot like Eric. I've left the Scribblings Diary out in plain sight for Eric to pick up for weeks on end hoping he'll read about all the stuff I write about him, but he's not even tempted. If I could get him to believe it had a secret treasure map, he might give it a second look (since he's such a big fan of pirates lately), but I don't think he'd fall for it.

Speaking of Eric, I thought I heard the side door open. Give me a second to investigate . . . Okay, it was Eric. He's doing that mysterious disappearing thing again, and I'm going to find out what he's up to. If I can't watch a movie, I can at least try to act like I'm in one! Stay tuned. I'll bring this with me and take notes.

. . . I should have known! He's with Charlotte. It took some work to catch up to him because he's got a nicer bike than I do (not because he's better at biking!). I don't know why he chooses to ride to this blasted parking lot. That's a big hill to come up. And all they're doing is sitting on a curb in the parking lot. I swear, if they kiss, I'm going to be so mad. This is, like, the least romantic place in the whole world. I mean, I'm happy that he's with Charlotte, because she's so cool, but he's got to do better than a parking lot in the middle of winter for a kiss.

Wait a second. I think there's someone else here. I heard something behind me and . . .

Charlotte stepped into a street lamp's soft light and walked towards Eric. She seemed thoughtful, demure. Her ponytail still had the same bounce and her gait reflected her forever confidence, but the twinkle in her eye seemed—well, not gone, but delayed.

When she reached Eric, she got straight to the point. "Where were they when he ferried them?"

Eric had to take a second to think. "Fairied? Like, used his magical fairy powers?"

Charlotte remembered her audience, someone still new to the world of natural born abilities. "Sorry, seer talk. Ferried, like ferry boats who take people from one side of a river to another. A seer ferries people to and from worlds—from this world to the place and time where their abilities are the most useful."

Eric nodded. "Just right over there." Eric took his hand out of his pocket, where he had guarded it against the cold, and pointed towards the middle of the parking lot.

This seemed to be something Charlotte expected because she only nodded and then sat down on the curb. Eric, who had stood to welcome her, joined her.

"Is there anything we can do? I realized what was happening but only moments before he . . . uh . . . ferried them."

Charlotte stuck her hands in her jacket pocket and shivered. "Yes. Seers can ferry people and bring them back without actually going with them." She turned and smiled at Eric. "When I sent you, though, I just wanted in on the ride."

Eric nudged her playfully. "Or you wanted an excuse to hold my hand," thinking of how she gripped his hands just before the moonrise in this very place only a few months ago.

Charlotte's smile did not go away. She shrugged before returning to the topic at hand. "The problem is that the person has to return to the same spot they were ferried to by the time the moon reciprocates to the phase they left with."

That was a mouthful to anyone unfamiliar to the world of seers, and even Eric—still a novice at this seer business—had to recall some of the mechanics of switching worlds to make sense of what she just said. A seer needed to look

29

someone in the eyes while near their birthplace during the same phase of the moon in order to send them to the time and place of their natural born ability. To come back to the home world that they left, they needed to return to the spot where they were "ferried," as Charlotte put it, on the "reciprocal" phase of the moon—fancy seer talk that meant the phase of the moon opposite of the one that brought them.

Charlotte had come with Eric when they ferried, so she only needed to join him to the spot where they entered the pirate hunting world, and they returned together. Though two weeks had passed for Eric and Charlotte in the world of pirate hunting while they waited for the moon to reciprocate, it was still the same night back in their home world by the time they returned, just a couple of hours later.

After Eric recalled all of these points, he tried to restate what Charlotte had just told him, "So if Luke and Tina don't know that they need to return to the spot they got ferried to by the time the moon reciprocates, then they might be stuck in that world."

Charlotte nodded. "Exactly. Luke and Tina probably have no idea where they are or what's going on. They are wandering around in their new worlds, but they have no idea how or when they can return from it."

Eric put his face in his hands. "Oh no. This is horrible. They're gone! What will their families think? What will happen to them?"

Charlotte reached out and patted Eric on the back. "Now you get a sense for why I am not eager to re-enter the realm of seers. With you, I got a sense for how real and dangerous the fallout can be."

"But this is different," Eric replied, his face still down. "They had no idea. It might as well be as if they died since they are never coming back."

Charlotte did not respond for a while. "Eric, you tend to despair a bit too soon. There's always hope. Maybe they stayed put or maybe they'll wander back to their starting point within a couple weeks of that world's time. If so, just by me being here tonight, they could be ferried back."

"So as long as you are within the vicinity of where they disappeared, you can ferry them back?"

"We have until the moonset. If they don't reappear by then, well, then I'm afraid we've lost them." Charlotte's face reflected a self-seriousness uncommon to her.

They just settled into a comfortable silence, when they heard the scraping of steps coming from behind them. For a brief moment, Eric wondered if Luke and Tina were somehow returning, but as he and Charlotte turned around, he instead saw the silhouette of a very large figure walking beside a diminutive one.

Charlotte recognized the large figure far before Eric, saying, "You found someone, Dad?"

Eric's eyes widened, "That's your dad?" he said. "What's he doing here?" Eric had met Charlotte's parents a few times but in the darkness it was difficult to make out any defining characteristics, except that Charlotte's dad was a large, brawny figure.

"He insisted on helping," Charlotte responded as she stood up and turned around to meet her father.

"Wait," Eric followed suit and stood up, "does he know about . . . about your ability?"

Charlotte smiled at Eric's question but did not have time to respond. Instead, a deep voice interrupted. "I found someone, but not a natural bornapper. Just a girl who is probably up past her bedtime."

The forms drew close enough to the lamplight by this time that Eric recognized the smaller figure just as she spoke. "Actually, my bedtime is kind of flexible because my mom and dad let me read after I go to bed. I know I don't have a book with me, but I was reading the street signs so maybe that could—"

"Sally," Eric felt unsure of whether to be frustrated or amused, "do Mom and Dad know that you're not home?"

Charlotte smiled. "Sally!"

Sally grinned, "Charlotte!" The unkempt hair of Sally led the way into an embrace of the one person in the crew who seemed happy to see her, or at least tolerant of her presence.

Sally glanced over at her brother, "I told Mom and Dad I was going to follow you and see what you were up to, and they thought it was a great idea! In fact—"

"We're just sitting in a parking lot," Eric sighed. "You can go home."

Sally clung to Charlotte's hand. "That's okay. I'd rather stay with you guys." If Sally noticed Eric's impatient eyebrow-raising, she subtly ignored it. "Besides, I'm nearly a teenager now so Mom says that you need to put up with me more. Not that anyone has to 'put up' with me because I'm pretty easy to get along with and—"

"You are very easy to get along with, Sally. We'd love to have you stay with us," Charlotte blithely remarked, much to Eric's exasperation.

Sally grinned and sat down between the two on the curb, grabbing both of their hands and ushering them to sit down next to her. The force of her movement caused them to plop down before Eric could offer his dissent.

The burly voice of Charlotte's dad sounded out to the side of them, "Charlotte, I'm going to make another round, but I'll be within hearing, so call if something seems off or you're able to ferry either of the kids back." With that, the large form of Charlotte's dad glided away from the lamplight and melded with the darkening night.

"'Ferry either of the kids' . . . I guess that answers my question of whether your dad knows about your ability," Eric said as he looked back to the black spot where Charlotte's dad had disappeared.

"What ability?" Sally asked, determined to make sure she was not forgotten in the conversation. "I mean, you've got plenty of abilities but which one is—"

Eric did his best to ignore his little sister. "I don't think you've told me what your dad's natural born ability is . . ."

"Sally, Eric is talking about how I can see other people's natural born abilities." Eric almost interrupted since he did not think that was something Charlotte should be telling just anyone, let alone his little sister. Regardless, Charlotte continued before Eric could say anything. "And my dad is a natural born bodyguard."

"Bodyguard?" Eric and Sally asked at the same time.

"Yes," Charlotte smiled at Eric. "You can imagine why I didn't tell you before. I don't want to scare away all the boys that like to hang out with me."

"I won't lie," Eric responded, "that is a bit intimidating."

"A bit awesome is more like it!" Sally squeezed Charlotte's hand. "You have your own bodyguard! I'd love to have an exciting enough life that I could have my own personal bodyguard."

Eric rolled his eyes and tried to slide his hand out of Sally's. "Sally, you do realize that would mean your bodyguard is protecting you from people who are trying to hurt you, right?"

Sally kept a firm grip on her brother's hand while still looking at Charlotte. "Not necessarily, Eric. A lot of bodyguards just protect people from, like, the paparazzi or adoring fans. What is he guarding you from right now, Charlotte?"

"Sally," Eric replied, "it's time for you to go home."

Charlotte continued, thoughtful. "Well, Sally, our friends got taken away, and we're trying to get them back. My dad is just making sure that we don't get taken too."

Sally looked around. "We're trying to get them back by sitting on the curb of a parking lot?"

"Sally," Eric said, "it would be too much work to explain it all to you, but trust me—"

"Not only can I see other people's natural born ability," Charlotte charged forward, "but I can ferry them back and forth between worlds where they get to put their ability to use. The person who stole our friends is someone like me who sent them to another world. I'm waiting here to see if I can bring them back."

Sally looked carefully at Charlotte. She started to say something, then stopped. She turned to Eric with inquiring eyes. In spite of his irritation at having his sister still around, Eric softened and then smiled. "Congratulations, Charlotte. You've managed the impossible. You made Sally speechless." He took a second to soak it in, then said to Sally. "No, she's not kidding. This is real, Sis."

33

Sally turned back to Charlotte. "But . . . but how? How did someone else do that? How can *you* do that?" Her hands tightened their hold on Charlotte and Eric's hands as she awaited a response.

Eric again tried to squirm his hand out of hers, but her grip only hardened.

"Well," Charlotte looked up at the moon and locked eyes on it. "I just sense it."

"How though?" Sally persisted.

"The same way that I knew how to hunt pirates," Eric threw in, "The same way that you know how to be annoying."

"What do you mean the same way that you knew how to hunt pirates?" Sally questioned.

Before Sally could follow up, Charlotte interrupted, still fixed on Sally's query about how she ferried people. She murmured while searching the face of the moon, "Something nudges me, and it's like I can see them through a misty mirror, and I tug at them with my mind and they come through the mirror."

Sally's eyes widened, her voice lowered, "Can you see them now?"

Charlotte shook her head very slightly, "No." She paused before continuing. "But I *am* sensing something. I've not felt this before."

Eric studied Charlotte, observing her trance. "What's happening, Charlotte? Should I call your dad over?"

Charlotte's eyes slowly lowered from the moon. "I don't know, Eric. It's . . . it's like I can track the moon's path up the sky. I can sense where it was earlier, and it's like . . . it's like there is a hole in the sky somewhere, and I can almost tell what happened when it was in that spot . . . a spot that looks like a—well—a portal."

"A portal?" Sally's eyes brightened. "Holy cow, you guys, if this is a prank, it's one of the coolest ones I've ever been a part of!"

"Is there just one hole, er, portal in the sky?" Eric asked. "There should be two."

Charlotte squinted. "No, there's just . . . wait. I see. There are two that overlap, almost completely . . . more like a circle that has been stretched slightly, probably because Luke and Tina got ferried at nearly the same time." With eyes still scrutinizing the abyss above, Charlotte asked, "Which did you say went first? Luke?"

"Yes," Eric nodded.

Charlotte stared for a moment. "I can sense his world. I can see his path. I can—"

"I'm going to call your dad over," Eric said.

"This is so cool!" Sally threw in.

"Eric," Charlotte said, "I think I can actually . . . well, if I focus hard enough, I feel like I could—"

Before Eric could respond, an extraordinary unseen force hooked them, the world around them sporadically began to wink out, and—incredibly—through it all, the moon reversed its upward movement in the sky, actually blurring backwards until settling into a previous spot. The pull was as irresistible as it was inevitable. Eric's second-to-last thought before giving himself completely over to the supernatural tug was fairly simple: *We're being ferried!*

His last thought was, *I knew I should've sent Sally home.*

PART TWO
CHICLERO

Chapter 1
QUIET LUKE

The rope that supported Luke Bateman up the trunks of the last four sapodilla trees had served him well. That is why he did not suspect that this time the rope had been surreptitiously slit halfway through. As soon as he wrapped it around the tree in front of him, each renewed pressure he gave it while ascending the trunk bordered on snapping the rope and causing him to fall.

Thus unaware, Luke quietly trusted his rope while glancing up the trunk of the sapodilla tree, his fingers pressing the soft, moist bark covering the hard trunk beneath it. *This should be a good one,* he thought.

Two days ago if someone had told him he would be in a jungle finding trees to tap sapodilla and turn the collected sap into chicle—once the prime ingredient for chewing gum—he would not even have laughed. He would have walked away and wondered if someone had misplaced their medication. Yet now it was hard for Luke to explain. After the panic passed, after the confusion settled, once he was given a gathering sack, a machete, and pointed into the dense rain forest, Luke not only felt calm in this situation. He felt comfortable. More than that, he felt as if he were thriving.

The sharp machete only took a few swings to carve an angled line in the soft bark and then reverberate against the tough wood of the trunk. Luke tied the canvas bag to the trunk, tucking the lip of the bag under the lowest scar in the bark so that the white, latex-like sap from the tree could trickle into the bag. Luke's eyes traveled up the trunk. *Plenty more where this came from.*

With the damaged rope around the tree and himself, Luke placed his feet on the trunk and pushed the rope tight so that it supported him in the air.

The split part of the rope strained but momentarily held. Then, while using the pressure from the spurs on his feet digging into the trunk sides to hold himself up, his hands worked with the machete to carve more lines in the tree, making angular "v" marks that would lead in a zigzag pattern all the way down to the bag.

As he thwacked the bark of the tree, revealing the red and fibery wood underneath, Luke's thoughts wandered.

The aptitude test administered by the silver-haired guy with glasses made the afternoon unique, but it was the other guy in the school lobby—the one with slicked-back blond hair and sharp blue eyes—who said that he had some scholarship opportunities for Luke that changed everything. While his parents already had Luke looking at several "unique-to-his-situation" scholarship opportunities, Luke realized that this particular man seemed like he could offer something more—something he extended without knowing anything about Luke's personal life. That was intensely appealing to Luke.

So Luke went for it. Then he saw Tina at the meeting spot. They noticed the sign saying that the meeting place had been relocated to another venue across the parking lot. They shrugged and started through the parking lot before the very man they were looking for interrupted them. After Tina and the man exchanged a few words in the dark, the man's blond hair shimmered as he glanced into the sky, then back at him, his cold blue eyes suddenly reflecting the recently risen moon. The next thing Luke knew, everything fell away except for that same, low, bright moon.

Back to daytime, and as a reminder of one of the many bizarre changes that had happened since then, the oppressive tropical heat and his working caused the sweat to trickle down his face. There had been snow on the curbs of the parking lot! Now he could see the tropical mists closing in on his position, which meant that the daily rains were about to start.

Luke shifted his position by digging the spurs higher into the tree trunk. Then, he slid the rope around his waist up the trunk and tightened again by leaning back—a motion that felt natural to Luke. The fibers at the split of the rope slowly started to wrench apart with this renewed pressure, then it stopped and held once more.

Oblivious to the fraying of the rope, Luke continued his methodical hacking at the sapodilla bark, which allowed him to continue considering his unique situation.

For most of the night after his arrival, he assumed this was just some sort of weird dream. He tried to sleep it off, but any time he would lie down, the details of the branches, roots, undergrowth and vines were far too real to remind him of any dream. Eventually, he made his way to the top of the ridge nearest to his position until he caught sight of a black smoke drifting up through the tropical trees. He could not explain where he was, how he got there, or how this all seemed so real, but he sensed that going towards the smoke from the fire might get him some answers.

When he broke through the clearing four Latino-looking men, two on the ground and two standing near them, stared back at him in surprise for quite some time before one of them looked at his companions and then stepped forward. The man was not speaking Spanish to him, though he must have been using a dialect because it was difficult to work out what he said, but Luke understood the basics: Who are you and what are you doing here?

Luke countered by saying that he was from the town of Nibleton, but that got little reaction. He looked around at the jungle. Though it seemed strange to say, he clarified that he was from the United States. He followed up by asking if they could help him get home.

The man he spoke to turned to his companions. They muttered something that Luke could not make out. The man turned back to Luke and told him, again using his strange dialect, that a boat would be coming up the river for them in a week's time and that the boat would take them back to the coast, where he could find out about getting home.

A week?! Luke thought, but considering the situation it probably was his best option.

Luke nodded his appreciation to the man, who then continued to explain that if the boy wanted a ride in the boat, he would need to help them gather up some . . . something. Luke could not quite understand what it was . . . some *thing*, some word that he was unfamiliar with.

Luke readjusted his position on the sapodilla tree, shifting another couple of feet upwards. Another filament layer of the rope gave way but it still managed to support his weight. That meeting was two days ago. Eventually, he pieced together what the man said. He said something to the effect that the men were short on their quantity of "chicle" after two of them became injured when a man fell down from a tree onto his companion. The astute leader of the group gave Luke a quick training on locating and gathering chicle and told him to not come back until he had gathered five bags worth of the white, milky sap—his price for a ticket on the boat down the river.

Luke took a moment's break. The jungle floor lay about twenty feet below him. Resting against the trunk of a towering ceiba tree sat three full bags of chicle that Luke had collected already. Soon he would have this tree tapped and would only need one more bag. That was after only two full days. The man thought it would take Luke most of the week before the boat arrived to gather up the required amount of chicle, but Luke satisfied himself with the thought that he would probably be able to return to the base camp by tomorrow evening.

After wiping the sweat off of his forehead, Luke shuffled up the trunk another couple of feet, his eye looking warily at the gathering rain clouds through the canopy above him. A small part of him seemed to feel as if the space between himself and the tree trunk had increased, even if only by the slightest amount. But instead of dwelling on that inexplicable thought, he amazed himself by the fluid movement of the machete in his hands to the bark on the tree before him. He realized, the more he thought about it, that he could actually sense by the texture and protrusions of the bark where the tree was most vulnerable to giving up the maximum amount of sap. *How could this be?* Luke thought. *I've only known this task for, well, not even 48 hours . . .* Yet as Luke chopped, stepped higher, searched the bark, and chopped again, a small part of him realized that he would be sad to finish that last bag of chicle and return to the camp to figure out how to come back home.

Now almost thirty feet up in the air, Luke glanced up and down the trunk. Seven more feet would bring him to the main branches of the tree and to an end of this tree's store of sap. *Just a couple more movements upwards*, he gauged, *and just in time to finish and avoid the rain*. Luke stepped up the trunk, slid the rope up and leaned back, machete at the ready.

As he put his full weight into the rope support, a sickening feeling coursed through his body like a lightning bolt. It was as if the rope had suddenly disintegrated because nothing checked his body's backward momentum. Wildly, Luke's head swiveled backward and in a split second saw nothing but over thirty feet between him and the jungle floor below. His rope, the loop severed and frayed on two ends, fluttered downward between him and the ground as a grisly precursor to his own fate.

"What just happened?"

Although Eric and Sally made the query at the same time, their tones differed drastically. Eric asked as if he had an idea but needed clarification. Sally asked as if she wondered whether she had suddenly died and was experiencing a weird sort of afterlife.

The canopy of a humid and dense tropical rain forest blocked any semblance of direct light from the stars or moon above. It took a minute or so before they could start making out the forms of each other among the dense undergrowth.

Charlotte remained quiet, but Eric picked out her poised form on the other side of Sally. "Did you just ferry us?" Eric asked. "Are we in the world of pirates?"

Charlotte turned her head towards him but made no response.

That did not stop Sally from doing so. "I mean, I didn't think you guys were kidding around, but I didn't really think it was *real* real . . . you know? I mean, I guess I believed it but it didn't occur to me that—" there is no knowing how long Sally could have gone on if Eric did not interrupt.

"But it wasn't my phase of the moon, Charlotte. How could you have possibly . . ." Eric did not know how to finish his sentence.

Finally Charlotte spoke. "I don't think this is the world of pirates, Eric. I think . . . . I think . . . I ferried us to Luke's world. That's what it felt like, but I can't say for sure."

Eric's eyebrows raised. "But Luke wasn't even there! Is that possible? Is it possible to ferry to someone's world without even having them there?"

Charlotte's tone sounded thoughtful. "I don't know, Eric. This is all new to me. I haven't even *heard* of this sort of thing before. All I know is that as we looked at the moon and talked about them being ferried, it was as if I could retrace the moon's path and reset it to where Luke's ferrying happened. The next thing I knew, here we are."

Eric considered this. "That's amazing, Charlotte. And you haven't even heard of this sort of thing happening before? What about in your conversations with other seers? This sort of thing never came up?"

"Those conversations were always short," Charlotte answered. "We talked through the basics of it but never got past that."

"Oh," Eric replied, "I always thought you would meet and discuss over days or weeks. Seems like you could get a lot more information that way."

Charlotte's response was curt. "Never had the chance. My family moved too much."

"Not that I don't love it here," Sally saw a gap to jump into, "but what do we do now? It seems like there was something important going on when we were in the parking lot and now we're just sitting here while you two chat away and—"

"The minute I get told by my younger sister that I chat too much . . ." Eric threw out under his breath.

"We find Luke," Charlotte answered. "Though how we do that is beyond me." Her head swept back and forth so that her eyes could catch a glimpse of a small opening in the canopy above. "Look at the phase of the moon, Eric. It's slightly different from the one that we entered at."

Eric shifted his head to look. "You're right. Not by much but enough that it is different. What does that mean?"

Charlotte thought about it, "I feel as if I was able to trace back to the ferrying point to his world, but a couple days have passed for him here—maybe because we ferried here a little bit later than he did and a half an hour back home is the equivalent to a couple of days here. If that's the case, he could be anywhere."

Sally summed up. "So let me get this straight: We've got to find Luke, but he has a couple days head start in a jungle that we've never been in before in the middle of the night." She paused for a breath. "How much time have we got?"

"Until the moon reciprocates," Charlotte said. Then realizing Sally was still picking up that lingo, she followed up. "Until the phase of the moon is opposite of the one that Luke used to enter. So twelve days or so. "

Sally nodded. "Eric, can I borrow your cell phone?"

Eric mechanically reached into his pocket and felt the phone. "Wait," he said, "what for?"

Sally kept her hand out, "Not to be a downer, but twelve days is an awful long time to be gone when I told Mom and Dad that I was just going to drop off something I borrowed from Celia Boatwright. We should at least call Mom and Dad to tell them the situation."

"Call them?!" Eric exclaimed, "First of all, we're not getting reception here for too many reasons for me to explain." He pulled out his phone and showed her that there were no bars. "And second of all, I thought you told Mom and Dad you were coming to check on me!"

"First of all," Sally countered her brother using his same tone, "I figured that it wouldn't hurt to at least see if the phone worked. Second of all, I *was* coming to check on you, I just didn't tell Mom and Dad that's where I was going because I'm pretty sure they would've wanted you to be left alone . . . but then I wouldn't have been able to figure out what it is that you were—"

Before Eric's outburst could interrupt Sally, Charlotte jumped in, "Don't worry, Sally. Remember that when we return through a reciprocated phase of the moon, we are ferried back to the same time that we left . . . well, at least to within a few hours depending on where the moon was in the sky when we left and where it is when we return."

Sally nodded. "Oh, yeah, I forgot. I still say that it makes no sense, but it tells me everything we need to know: what we're doing and how long we have to do it and that Mom and Dad probably won't freak out. Will twelve days be enough?"

Eric spoke past Sally. "Charlotte. Do me a favor and don't ever look into Sally's eyes once there's enough light to do so. The last thing we need is her analyzing one more thing to death like her own natural born ability." Sally about protested, but Eric continued. "As far as whether twelve days will be enough, well, I've hunted pirates in a tropical setting similar to this, I'm pretty sure I can hunt Luke . . . and I doubt I'll need twelve days to do it."

Charlotte whispered in Sally's ear. "Three months ago, your brother would've plopped down on the ground and declared his own uselessness. Now look at him."

"I guess I should thank you," Sally responded, "Except that since then he's not been afraid of speaking his mind around me. Of course, I always speak my mind, but I guess I don't like it as much when other people do it to me, especially if they think I'm far too talkative and won't—"

"If I were Luke and this were my world," Eric spoke through their whispers, "I wouldn't stay put for too long. I'd try to get some more information. We're on a slope right now. I think we'd better go upwards to get to the top of the ridge and then rest and see what our next move will be in the morning."

Eric started working his way upwards, weaving in and out of the undergrowth, still gripping his little sister's hand, who in turn still held on to Charlotte.

"Not to stop our progress," Sally offered, "but would it be more comfortable if I went to the back so that you could hold Charlotte's hand instead?"

The only response she got from Eric was a sharp tug that took her through some palm fronds. Charlotte trailed behind with a smile on her face.

Eric proved as good as his word. The next morning they saw the same smoke that Luke had seen. They met with two injured (and confused) Latino men in a chiclero camp who told Eric, Charlotte, and Sally—in a creole English dialect—the direction Luke had headed and what he was out doing. Eric led them through the forest where they came in and out of contact with the river and stumbled across three chicle trees that had been tapped for sap.

Towards the evening of that first full day, they came to a point where Eric said they needed to cross the river, since that was where Luke probably had gone. They snacked on some of the cassava bread the chicleros had given them at the base camp and some mangos that Eric found while they discussed their next move, and Eric continually tried to quiet his younger sister . . . with only minimal success.

They worked up the river until finding a tremendous fallen tree spanning across the deepest part of the river with the top branches touching the shallow part on one end. After some convincing of Sally, they bridged the river and hopped into the shallow far side, wading to the bank.

Eric then led them deeper into the jungle, where he saw some leaves peaking out among others that appeared to belong to a sapodilla tree. With the sun going down, and some mists closing in from the south, there was a sense of urgency as they pushed forward, their already tired legs exerting final efforts as Eric assured them they were near their destination.

In the moment that they broke through the undergrowth and found themselves staring at the expanse of a tall sapodilla tree, they heard a cry and their eyes shot upwards. Horrified, the three witnessed a rope fluttering downwards and Luke falling head first towards the ground.

But he did not drop from the tree. Instead they saw that his legs still gripped the trunk of the tree using the help of some sort of spurs attached to his feet. These kept him from tumbling into the air while his body swiveled awkwardly down the face of the tree trunk, his hands gripping bark desperately. For a moment he held still, body sprawled against the trunk with his head downwards more than thirty feet above them.

"Oh no!" Sally cried out. "Luke, hold on! We can help—don't move!"

Eric and Charlotte, on the other hand, just got to work. "What can we do?" Charlotte looked to Eric, all business.

"We can get some of these vines and break them off at the bottom and pull them towards Luke. He'll be able to grab it from up there and then slide down."

Eric and Charlotte scoured the clearing under the tree and found a vine that seemed to match the task at hand. They broke off the bottom and started to tug it towards the sapodilla tree to get within reach of Luke.

Sally, still in a frenzy, called out, "Luke, Eric and Charlotte are trying to bring you a vine that you can hold onto. We'll let you know when you can reach out and grab it and—"

"Sally," Eric said, "it's no use yelling up at Luke like that. When he sees the vine, he'll grab it."

Sally could not believe that Eric would take a time like this to nitpick with her. "Eric, it doesn't hurt to tell him what we are doing. He needs to know that we're going to help him."

Charlotte gave another hard tug to free the vine from some others higher up. "That's not what Eric is saying, Sally. It's no use yelling at Luke because he's deaf. He can't hear you anyway."

For the second time in as many days, Sally was rendered speechless. Then everyone paused as they saw movement on the tree. Amazingly, Luke was able to hug the trunk of the tree so powerfully, that he released his spurs and then delicately bent his body at an angle no one thought possible while his feet came along one side of the trunk. They slid past his head until before jabbing the spurs back into the trunk and he could work his way right side up again. He took a second to catch his breath and then, with arms still lingering around the trunk, he stepped down carefully, spur over spur, until reaching the ground.

Once he was stable, he took a deep breath and turned around. His eyes grew wide. "Charlotte? Eric?" he said, his voice tinted with the lack of tonal perception.

"Luke," Charlotte said, making sure her lips moved carefully. "We've been looking for you. This is Eric's sister, Sally, and we're here to take you back home."

Then it began to rain.

Chapter 2
NIGHT WATCH &
RETREAT CUT OFF

After they found some semblance of shelter under the ceiba tree, Charlotte took some time to explain the technicalities of this bizarre situation Luke found himself in. Had he not been in a jungle and felt the natural ease of seeking out chicle, he would have thought his lip reading was way off. It did not help that the sun had gone down sometime during the downpour and Luke was losing his ability to see what Charlotte was saying.

The girl named Sally kept on trying to jump in and eagerly join the conversation, but Eric mercifully put her off and said something about getting rest and continuing tomorrow when the sun was up. Luke offered to stay up for the first watch, explaining that there were dangers this far out in the jungle.

Eric nodded in agreement. They found a cavity under the giant, folding layers of the ceiba tree's ground-level roots and secreted themselves as far into them as possible. Though not perfectly dry, the gap protected them from the largest droplets that increasingly found their way through the canopy.

After everyone had laid down, Luke picked something up and fingered it thoughtfully. His rope. The one that supported him to the top of the tree but then snapped and nearly caused him to drop head first, thirty feet to the ground. With light fading, he could not examine it quite as closely as he would have liked, but his finger detected that part of the rope seemed to have been cut clean while the rest frayed. The questions remained: someone cut the rope partially through before he climbed up that last tree . . . but who?

After a few hours, Luke woke up Eric so he could take his turn on watch. Eric rubbed his eyes and moved out of the black cavity. Once at the entrance, Eric turned his face into the moonlight shimmering down through the branches and nodded to Luke, who was just laying down. Before Luke closed his eyes, he saw Eric examining the rope he left at the entrance. "Cut?" Eric's lips queried with enough moonlight to allow Luke room to interpret.

Luke nodded.

Eric looked around before turning back to Luke. "That's why you thought we should have a watch?"

Luke's chin affirmed the statement, and he drifted off to sleep.

A few hours later, Eric woke up Charlotte. Not because he was tired or because he did not want to take her vigil, but because he knew that she would be furious with him if she woke up discovering that he had let her sleep through her turn on watch.

Eric stayed with Charlotte at the entrance for a moment, and they both remained quiet as Charlotte shook off her sleep.

"Not tired?" Charlotte asked after a while.

"Just thinking," Eric replied.

"About getting us out of here and back to the ferry landing tomorrow? Or Tina?"

Eric looked at Charlotte for a while. "Nah."

Charlotte's eyebrows rose. "Then?"

"When you talked about moving, back when we were in . . . well, back in our world, it scared me."

Charlotte smiled. "Why?"

49

Eric's eyes fell to the ground. "You know why, Charlotte." If she did know, she remained maddeningly silent. Eric took a deep breath and continued, "Because you are my best friend, because I owe who I am to you, because I . . . I . . ."

Charlotte opted not to torture him anymore. "I have no plans of moving, Eric, so you can settle down."

Eric stayed quiet for a moment before speaking up, "You see, that's the thing with you. You don't say anything straight out: am I a natural born pirate or pirate hunter? Are you really going to move or do you just not have *plans* to move?"

"If you really want to know the pirate/pirate hunter thing, then I will tell you. I'm not trying to hide anything from you, I'm just—"

"I don't care about that," Eric interrupted her. "It makes no difference. The experience you gave me is what matters."

"Can't that be the same with whether I have plans to move or not?" Charlotte responded.

Eric paused. "No. Because I don't want my experience with you to move away with you." He then got up and worked back into the cavity with the others.

Charlotte's previous smile faltered. She watched Eric fall asleep before turning back out to monitor the darkness.

Early in the morning, before daylight had arrived but after the deepest darkness of night had dissembled, Sally woke up and stretched. She saw Charlotte at the mouth of their shelter and crawled over to her, blinking and yawning.

"Don't I get a turn at watch?"

Charlotte looked at Sally and smiled. "You're our mascot, Sally, we get to pamper you and let you sleep all night."

Sally looked around. "What are you staying up to look for?"

Charlotte shrugged. "Honestly, I don't know. Those boys seem to think this jungle is a lot more exciting than it really is."

"So, Eric is a natural born pirate hunter. You are a natural born seer. Luke is a natural born . . ."

"Chicle gatherer . . . or chiclero . . . something like that."

Sally nodded. "I noticed that you didn't tell me what I am naturally born to be."

Charlotte patted Sally on the arm. "I guess I'm not too eager to meddle with people's lives anymore. I used to be super involved as a seer, and natural born abilities were my main focus." Charlotte took a deep breath. "But . . . when I took your brother to the world of pirates . . . there were some close calls. I just can't help thinking what if things had not worked out the way they did? What if something had turned out differently, and I would've had to come back and try to explain to you or your parents why Eric was gone . . ."

Sally felt the weight of Charlotte's responsibility pushing down on her. "Would my natural born ability get me killed?"

Charlotte put her arm around Sally and tugged her close. "It's not all about that. It's that I used to think I had this super special power that connected me with other people. Now, I can't help but think that it's a curse that can possibly hurt other people. I kind of wish that I *couldn't* see other people's natural born abilities at all. I just want to connect with them in normal, non-seer, ways."

"Except that you ferried us to Luke's world . . ." Sally pushed.

"That's exactly my point. That other seer guy—Neech, I think Eric called him—meddled in someone else's life where he shouldn't have. So, even though I want to remove myself from the world of seeing, I feel that I am duty-bound to fix this problem. Still, if it weren't for seers trying to interfere, Luke wouldn't be in this situation in the first place."

"Well, I don't know if it was visiting the world of pirates or something else," Sally responded, turning to look at the sleeping forms behind her, "but my brother sure has changed since he met you. He used to always be so quiet and drawn in and . . . well . . . just, gloomy, you know?"

Charlotte chuckled, "Well, I'll tell you, at one point when we were in the world of pirate hunting he got pretty down on himself just because he was too stubborn to accept the help he earned—it kept him from recognizing his full potential. I finally had to give him a little bit of a forceful push to snap him out of his funk."

Sally laughed. "Well, I'm glad you pushed him. I push him all the time, and it hasn't done anything!" Sally ventured one more comment. "Just so you know, I'm guessing you'll have to be the one to push him to admit that he has a crush on you too . . ."

Charlotte glanced sideways at Sally, whose eyebrows raised shrewdly. Charlotte repressed a snicker and gave Sally a warm side hug. The two went quiet for a while and Charlotte yawned.

Sally gauged the growing light. "Well, I'm awake. You might as well sleep for a little bit while the boys do. It's light outside so I don't think there is any danger."

Charlotte glanced around to the peaceful jungle floor laid out in front of them. "You're probably right. Okay, mascot, you're in charge!"

Sally thought she was awake, but the harder she battled to keep her eyes open the more they weighed down on her. Her head nodded and she jerked herself back to an upright position.

"Sally, you can go rest. I'm awake now."

Sally's head swiveled behind her, and she saw Luke stretching as he smoothly exited the cavity to sit next to her. "Luke! You're awake." She did not realize that his face was down as he adjusted his position next to her. She repeated the statement after he settled into his spot and looked up at her.

"I've found I don't need as much sleep here as I might at home," he explained.

Sally noted that his voice was just a smidgen off from the speaking tones she was used to hearing, further reminding her of his hearing loss condition. "Luke, how can you understand what I'm saying right now? I mean, I remember trying to lip read when the principal was speaking at an assembly and the sound system went out. After a couple of sentences, I just gave up because it was impossible to tell what he was saying."

Luke nodded. "You have the luxury of giving up because you know the sound system will be fixed the next time he speaks. If I want to understand, there is no waiting until next time. I *have* to be able to read lips unless they give me an interpreter."

"Why would you need an interpreter if you can just read lips?"

Luke smiled. "Even if you've learned to speak Spanish, you probably prefer to listen to something important in your native language. Signing is the *best* way for me to understand something."

Sally nodded. "Oh, I see." There was a short pause. "Luke, I'm sorry that I didn't know you were deaf. Your little sister is in my grade but she never told me that you couldn't hear."

"I guess she just sees me as an older brother who gets annoyed with his little sister, not as someone who is deaf," Luke replied, smiling. "And that's the way I like it."

"I think Eric sees me in the same way you see your sister, but I don't like it!" Sally said, but Luke had turned back to check on the others after detecting some movement. When he looked back at her, she almost repeated herself, then she changed her mind. "Don't you worry that you sometimes miss out on stuff if you can't see what someone is saying?"

Luke shrugged. "It can be a little lonely at times, but I've found that 90% of the things people say don't really matter that much—just filling up dead space. If something is truly important, I find out one way or another."

Sally thought about this before replying, "Don't tell Eric about that 90% thing . . . he'd totally agree with you and then bring it up any time I said anything."

Luke laughed. "Maybe Eric and I both need to be nicer to our little sisters!"

Eric shuffled up next to them, rubbing his eyes. "Careful, Luke. Don't say something you might regret later!"

Charlotte joined them. "I can't believe I'm the one that's going to say this, but are we going to chat or are we going to go home?"

Minutes later, Luke led them back through the trails of the jungle towards the river crossing they had taken the day before. The forest teemed with the sounds of insects, birds, and scurrying forms in the undergrowth. The heat of the tropical sun took the moisture from the downpour the day before and intensified it into a heavy humidity that oozed into their bodies, heating them up through their walk.

After a short time, they heard the surge of the river through a screen of trees, and then they finally broke through and saw the river in front of them.

"This isn't the same crossing we made yesterday, is it?" Charlotte asked as she scanned the scene in front of them.

"I don't think so," Eric replied. "It doesn't look familiar."

Sally jumped in. "Of course not! Remember, we crossed on a fallen tree? There's no tree here." She looked around. "In fact, is this a different river? I don't remember the river looking this brown or this fast. I thought it was more of a black or dark green. And wasn't it a kind of slow river? This one is too fast to be the same one."

Eric scrutinized the bank on the other side. "Wait. The hole in the ground where the pulled up roots were yesterday looks the same as where the tree was that we used to cross the river yesterday."

Charlotte saw where Eric pointed. "True. And I think I remember that big boulder on the top of the bank next to it."

"That's right. I stood on the boulder to look at the river before we crossed. What is going on here?"

Luke leaned against a tree, casually taking in the scene. "It's the rain. The rain flooded the river."

Eric kept his gaze on the fast-flowing, brown current in front of them. "You're right. That's exactly what happened. The water level rose and sped up and then washed away the tree we used to cross."

Charlotte looked from their river bank to the opposite side. "We can't cross back this way. Even if we tried to swim, we'd be swept away with the current." She eyed some of the carnivorous rapids downstream from them. "How are we going to get across?"

"Is there a bridge?" Sally asked, hopefully.

Luke calmly and naturally climbed up the trunk of the tree he had been leaning against only a moment earlier. He looked upstream for a while before descending. "We add an extra day to our hike by going upstream."

"The opposite direction from where we're supposed to head?" Eric asked.

Luke nodded. "There are some hills up that way. I'm guessing the river narrows up there and we'll have a better chance at getting a crossing."

Charlotte looked back and forth between Eric and Luke. "I'm not opposed to more walking, but couldn't we just wait for the river level to come down?"

Luke glanced over at the river. "We could, but the storm system from yesterday seems to be moving in the direction of the head of the river so it might be a wait of a couple of days. And if another storm rolls in while we're waiting, we'll be out of luck and have to find an alternate way around the river anyway."

Charlotte nodded. "I hate sitting anyway. Let's go to those hills!"

Luke started hoisting the bags of gathered chicle on his shoulders as they prepared to hike upstream. Eric caught his attention with a wave of his hand. "You're not really planning on carrying that chicle with you, are you? Charlotte will ferry us home so you don't need to return those to the chiclero camp."

Luke readjusted the straps on the bags around his shoulder. "I know," he said. "But the chicleros were in a fix and it'd be a shame for these bags to be wasted. The camp is along the path back to the ferrying point so it wouldn't hurt for me to drop them off anyway."

Eric grabbed one of the bags still on the ground. "Good point. So hopefully you won't mind if I carry some with you."

Charlotte smiled as she shouldered the final bag. "You boys are so much more than your natural abilities."

Sally leaned in to Charlotte and whispered, "For the record, Charlotte, so are you!"

Chapter 3
WRESTLING MATCH

Adding to the diet of mangoes and cassava bread were the results of Luke's fishing skills. With equipment from the chiclero base camp, he found a spot on the overflowing river and within minutes had a couple fish on the bank.

Charlotte opted to start a fire and Sally offered assistance, while Eric and Luke gutted the fish. After they had finished and Luke was about to take the fish over to Charlotte and Sally, Eric held him back.

"The person who cut your tree harness," Eric barely even spoke out loud, knowing he did not have to for Luke to understand him, "which side of the river were they on?"

Luke eyed the girls stoking the growing fire. "I'm not sure. It would probably have to have been while I slept the day before you found me."

"That last sapodilla tree was not very far from the river, which means that you slept on the opposite side before crossing and tapping the tree the next day. So the mysterious harness slasher must have been on the opposite side of the river then . . ."

"Yes. But I can't be sure that he didn't follow me across, just to see if it worked or not."

Eric tossed the fish guts back in the river and rinsed his hands off. He turned back to Luke. "Is that why you suggested we hike upriver to find a crossing, so that we can throw off any potential pursuers that might be stuck on this side of the river with us?"

Luke nodded slowly. "That was one reason that sitting in one place did not seem like the best idea. Still, the others I mentioned are just as valid."

Eric put his hands in the air, "I never doubted that. But I did want to know if the whole act of returning the chicle to the base camp . . . well, maybe you're interested in checking out who is surprised by your return or which chicleros are still missing from the camp . . . ?" Eric prodded.

Luke paused a moment before responding, "I truly do want to give them the chicle I gathered." He looked over towards Charlotte and Sally. "But I'd be lying if I said that I don't suspect one of those chicleros of sabotaging my tree sling."

After they finished eating, there was still light left in the day. Charlotte proposed that they keep going. "We've got to be close to those hills, right?" She glanced up river but the trees from this angle blocked a view of anything more than fifty yards. "The sooner we cross the river, the better."

Luke nodded. "The river is getting narrower. I think we could reach the hills and a crossing point before sundown."

Their subsequent hike took them weaving through the undergrowth, with the river in and out of view. They could tell that they were moving in an upward direction by the slope of the trail. That and the heat added to their fatigue.

Within an hour, however, they found themselves as a crossing point. Boulders lined the river as water crashed past them. They could tell that during normal river level times, this area was just a succession of large pools of river water. Now, the pools were submerged and only the larger rocks were visible under the strong current. Luke found an extra long vine and chopped it down, then he held onto one end while Eric and Charlotte anchored the other in case he lost a foothold.

Their precaution was wise but unnecessary. Luke danced from one boulder top to another with ease before reaching the other bank. He found a sturdy tree to wrap the vine around, and Eric and Charlotte did the same on their side. Using the vine as a stabilizer, and with Eric helping a not-wanting-to-be-helped Sally, they found themselves on the other side.

Luke took a quick swing at the vine with his machete and it fell into the river's current.

"We could've kept it up," Charlotte noted. "If someone else were in the area, it might've helped them cross."

Luke and Eric looked at each other. "I know," Luke said.

Charlotte noticed the look. She gazed across the river bank curiously, then back at Luke, then Eric. Luke started to lead them up a gravelly rockslide that would clear them of the river entirely. Charlotte let Sally follow before turning to Eric, "I saw that look and I know that—"

"I'll tell you tonight," Eric said. "For now, let's find ourselves a place to camp."

Charlotte had expected a struggle to get the information out of Eric so she sputtered for a second. "Um . . . okay. That's, uh, a good idea."

Eric laughed. "You may know me pretty well, seer, but I know you pretty well too!"

The two scrambled up the slippery embankment and found themselves at a high point overlooking the river and the lowlands beyond where they had just come from. For miles and miles, all they could see were leafy canopy after leafy canopy stretching along the horizon.

"It almost looks like an ocean of leaves," Eric muttered.

"So it's almost like home to you," Charlotte put a hand on Eric's shoulder.

Eric reached his opposite hand across his body and rested it on hers. "Well, more like summer home. I still have my regular home in Nibleton . . . just like you." He looked at her.

Charlotte caught his inference, "Yes. Just like me."

"Hey, I hope you two aren't kissing or anything, because I think you should come check this out!" The voice belonged to Sally, who was ahead of them through a screen of trees, farther in from the tall embankment.

Eric shook his head. "Next time she needs a ride to a friend's . . ." he threatened under his breath, "she'd better hope her bike is in good condition because I am *not* going to—"

"Let's go, Pirate Hunter." Charlotte grinned.

Once they got through the screen of trees, they saw Luke crawling up a huge, plant-infested, mound. "This must be one of the hilltops that Luke saw from where we first got to the river crossing," Charlotte observed looking up at it.

"Doesn't it look funny for a hill, though?" Sally asked.

"What did you expect a hill to look like," Eric asked, "flat?" He was still a bit perturbed by her jibe moments before.

"No, she's right," Charlotte said. "It's all covered with undergrowth and some trees, but it has . . . well . . . a kind of . . . symmetrical look about it. Almost angular."

Eric shifted his position. "Huh. That's true. In fact—"

"True when Charlotte says it, but not when your little sister says it!" Sally interrupted.

Eric ignored her as only older siblings can do. "In fact, it looks like it is in the shape of a . . . a pyramid."

Charlotte, Sally, and Eric all looked at each other with a shared awe. "Do you mean, this is some kind of ancient Egyptian pyramid?!" Sally asked.

"Not Egyptian," Eric said. "That's the other side of the world." He started to follow Luke.

"Which world?" Sally responded in a low breath.

"That would make this pyramid . . . what? Aztec? Mayan?" Charlotte asked as she caught up to Eric.

"We're in the jungle," Eric responded, "so probably Mayan." They both inspected the beginning part of the pyramid.

"You can see the stone steps through the earth and crumbling rocks," Charlotte said. "This has got to be pretty old."

"Hundreds of years," Eric nodded.

"Are you two just going to stare at the ground or are you going to climb to the top?" Sally stated, running past them.

Even though her run only lasted a few seconds before she had to stop and rest, it was enough to get Charlotte and Eric to follow her. The climb to the top was not as easy as they thought it would be. The pyramid was over one hundred feet tall, and it was more than 45 degrees in angle climbing up. When they made it to the top, there was just enough sun left to splash a burningly beautiful twilight vista across the sky.

Emphasizing the age of the pyramid, trees covered it from bottom to top, having gained root in the crevasses of stones hundreds of years earlier and eventually shooting upwards, crumbling the rocks below them with their expanding roots and layering the pyramid structure with leaf after falling leaf, which disintegrated and became a shallow covering of earth, grass, and weeds. Over the course of a few centuries, the man-made structure converted into a cleverly disguised, natural-looking hill in the jungle. Nature's crowning camouflage came in the form of a medium-sized sapodilla tree extending out from on top of the large altar at the very peak of the pyramid, the roots seeming to swallow the altar as a squid would its prey before reaching down to the flat space at the top of the pyramid.

Luke had already tied his final chicle bag to the trunk of the sapodilla tree by the time they joined him. Eric waited for him to turn around and look down at him before speaking. "It's going to be dark any minute now. Even you can't be that fast at tapping this tree for chicle."

Luke shook his head. "Just getting it ready for tomorrow morning."

Charlotte waited for Luke to climb down from his perch at the top of the altar. "If I would've known we were just following you up here to watch you tie a bag to a tree, I might've saved myself the energy!"

Luke smiled, catching Charlotte's tease in her eyes. "Nothing like pointlessly climbing a steep hill after a long day of hiking." He signaled their attention towards either side of the pyramid. "But it may not have been completely pointless. There are some roofless walls over there that might have been the living quarters of some priests, or temple workers, or a king or . . . well, whoever lived here."

Luke's companions turned and saw over the edge of both sides of the flat top of the pyramid, the sides had been carved back to make room for a few twisting walls, which must have divided up some rooms or storage areas.

Charlotte stepped closer to investigate. The walls set aside space for little more than a wide hallway, but they seemed fairly secure from outside threats in spite of its roofless state. "Well, it's not the Taj-mahal, but it should work pretty well for us tonight."

In the diminishing twilight, they cleared out some space in one of the rooms and tried to make it as comfortable as possible. As Sally tried to gather enough leaves to make a comfortable resting spot, she asked Charlotte. "Do you really think the priests slept up here? Wouldn't that be amazing to sleep hundreds of feet above everyone else and be able to look down at the town below and see the people walking around and stuff?"

Charlotte smiled. "That'd be pretty neat." She lay down. "But I think trekking up and down every time I had to go to the bathroom wouldn't make it worth it."

She did not see Eric smile, but she knew that he did.

Charlotte was not sure how much time had passed since she fell asleep, but she felt rested when her eyes snapped open. She stared up at the star-crowded sky above. They experienced only glimpses of the night sky up until that point thanks to the smothering canopy of the jungle, but on the top of the pyramid, only the scraggy branches of the lone sapodilla tree managed to blot out a small corner of the vista.

The tops of the ancient walls around them seemed to shimmer with a pale glow. Charlotte's eyes searched the glow curiously, and suddenly a statement embedded deep in her mind rose to the surface: "We do not take the moonlight for granted. It is like the snow or like the dew on a July morning. It does not reveal but changes what it covers."

A seer once shared that quote with her from some book she had not heard of, some book about rabbits or something. The seer was making the point of the special nature of the moon's mystical qualities—and who more than seers could recognize that about the moon?

"It does not reveal but changes what it covers," she mused. What better example of that than their presence here, in a different world, different age, in the thick of an endless jungle on top of an ancient pyramid . . . all because of the changing light of the moon? *I'll have to find the book from that author when I get back. I'm betting whoever wrote it was a seer!*

A new thought occurred to her, and she was not sure where it came from, but it felt natural and real. *What if this view I have right now is the same view of a priest who lived here centuries and centuries ago?* Not only did she feel sure that it was a priest who lived here and that this room had a view through the roof into the sky, but at the same moment, she realized that the priest who lived here, at the top of his world and underneath a wide expanse of sky, was a seer.

Charlotte stood up and wound her way through the small, walled divisions back to the top of the pyramid. Eric sat in the moonlight, overlooking the jungle around them.

"Charlotte," he said when he recognized her. "you've got another hour before it's your turn to watch."

Charlotte walked past him with hardly a nod.

"Charlotte?" Eric asked, haltingly standing up and following her. "Are you sleepwalking?"

"The moon just came up," she said, walking towards the far edge of the pyramid, past the altar and sapodilla tree, over to the opposite side from where they ascended.

Eric looked out across the muted glimmering along the jungle canopy lit by the recently risen moon. "Yeah. Just a minute ago. Why?"

"Something has changed," Charlotte said.

Eric followed behind her until she came to the edge of the pyramid. The back side of the pyramid had a far more perpendicular decline than the side they ascended, which caused Eric to instinctively reach out and grab Charlotte's hand when they got there. "Careful, Charlotte. I'm still not sure if you're awake or not."

Charlotte barely heard Eric. He tried again. "I mean, if you have to go to the bathroom, this is definitely the fastest way down, but it may cause other problems as well."

"I need you to lower me down this wall," Charlotte suddenly turned to Eric.

She saw Eric check over the edge and then look back to Charlotte. "What are you talking about? We can just go over to the stairs if you want to get down."

Charlotte shook her head. "There is something on this wall and I need to see what it is."

Eric attempted to pull Charlotte away from the edge. "Well, we can check it out in the morning while Luke is gathering chicle. Come on, you should sleep for an hour more."

Charlotte resisted. "The moonlight is shining on this side of the pyramid, and something has changed because of it. If we wait until morning, it will be gone."

Her eyes scoured the wall below them before she turned to Eric. "I'm awake, Eric. And I'm telling you that a seer was here long ago. And he left something here for me to find, but I need your help."

Eric must have been able to sense the sincerity in her plea. "I saw some vines on the opposite side of the pyramid from where we were sleeping. I'll go find the sturdiest ones and we'll double you up on them to make sure you're secure."

"Thank you," Charlotte squeezed his hand before he let go and went to secure the vines.

A few minutes later, Eric was burdened with a large load of vines, which he dropped at the feet of Charlotte, along with his machete which he used to cut the vines. Then he took two ends of the vines and dragged them over to the altar, wrapped them around and returned to where Charlotte stood. He made a loop with the end of both vines and tied a tight knot. He delicately slipped the loop over Charlotte's head and worked it down to her waist.

"Any chance you'll reconsider this?" Eric searched Charlotte's face, who was still staring at the wall-face below.

Charlotte turned to Eric and gave him the warm, confident, and irreplaceable smile that he knew. "Any chance you would've backed down from the Willard Pirate Twins?"

Still nervous, but conceding the point, Eric smiled back. "Okay, seer. Keep your legs out and against the wall, and have your hands holding on tight to the vine. I'll lower you down until you ask me to stop."

Charlotte scooted to the edge of the pyramid so that the tension on the vines tightened. She looked up at Eric, paused, then stepped towards him and planted a kiss on his cheek before quickly going back and stepping over the edge.

She moved down so quickly, she barely got a glimpse of the look of absolute bewilderment and amusement on Eric's face, but she heard him mutter, "Maybe I'm the one who is sleepwalking."

As Charlotte slid down the back wall of the pyramid, she kept her eyes melded to the stone face in front of her. This side of the pyramid had far less vegetation on it due to the perpendicular slope, but she still had to scrape away some hanging mosses and spider-webbed weeds to get a look at the stone face beneath it.

After Eric lowered her about fifteen feet, she found a slight ledge. She stepped past it and continued down before telling Eric to halt. Protected from the elements by its position underneath the ledge, but still within view of the moonlight, the stone face displayed a complex array of strange characters of hieroglyphic-type writing.

"I found something," Charlotte called up to Eric. "Can you tie off the vines there? I might be looking at this for a while."

After a couple of vibrations in the vine, Eric's head reached out from the edge of the pyramid top. "All set. What do you see?"

"Some writing," she answered while scrutinizing the figures in front of her. "You don't happen to read Mayan hieroglyphics, do you?"

"Dang," Eric responded. "I shouldn't have taken up class time drawing sailing ships during my advanced Mayan hieroglyphics course; otherwise, I'd totally be of use to you."

It went quiet for a while as Charlotte studied the strange forms in front of her. "Well," Charlotte eventually announced, "these characters may have been put here by a seer, but not in any way that I'd understand."

"What if I tossed you down a pencil and paper and you tried to copy them?" Eric proposed. "That way we could look at it during the daytime and without one of us hanging over a ledge a hundred feet above the forest floor."

"There's far too many of them," Charlotte shook her head while looking at the wall-face before her. "I'd need a couple volumes of paper to copy it all. In fact," she used her legs to slide over to the side, "this part of the wall here has even smaller characters than the rest so that it can fit more in this square space that . . ." her voice trailed off.

"That what? What about the square space?" Eric asked.

"Sorry, I just thought that I—" Charlotte's voice faltered as she looked carefully at the hieroglyphs in front of her.

"What is it?"

Charlotte's fingers traced the figures painted onto the stone centuries ago. "It just looks like . . . well, it looks like there is a picture of someone hanging down the back of the pyramid looking at the figures."

"What?" Eric's voice could not have sounded more lost. "What are you talking about?"

Charlotte blinked and looked closely at the rough form. "I don't know. It just looks like . . . well . . . like a pyramid, and there is a rope or a vine and a figure with a large eye at the end of it hanging down from the vine in front of some small characters."

"Maybe that's a record of how they created these hieroglyphics," Eric offered.

Charlotte's eyes traced the character-filled wall upwards. "Eric," she said suddenly. "Maybe get me that pencil and paper after all."

"What is it?" Eric asked.

"I think it's better if I show you. Can you find a pencil and paper?"

"I'll be right back," Eric called down. "Don't move."

Charlotte started looking at all the figures filled within the square space that contained the glyph of the person hanging down the pyramid. The square was the size of three pyramid stones by three pyramid stones, and each stone was the equivalent of a medium-sized TV set. A rough estimate indicated about fifty glyphs within that space.

After a while she felt the vine vibrating. Then she could hear some scraping above her. "Eric?"

"I thought I'd hand deliver it," Eric answered, climbing down the vine as if it were a halyard on a sailing ship. Once he got to the ledge, he set his feet down.

"Paper and pencil?" Charlotte asked with outstretched hand.

"I was looking around for stuff to write with, but then I thought of something better," he answered. "I just remembered that I have my phone."

"It's got a camera," Charlotte realized.

"It's not a great camera, but it should be easier than trying to scratch copies of ancient hieroglyphics."

He handed Charlotte the phone, and she focused the camera on the square with the smaller hieroglyphs in front of her. In order to fit it all within the camera's frame, she had to push herself out and slightly to the side.

Eric was able to stabilize her as she reached out with the camera arm and clung to the vine with her other hand. "Ready?" she said to Eric.

"Ready," he answered, holding the vine with one hand and her waist with the other as he lay flat on the ledge.

The face of the wall lit up with the flash from the phone's camera. "One more for luck," she said and pressed the button again. This time there was no flash. "What did I do wrong?" she asked.

"It just takes a moment for the flash to charge," Eric replied. "Give it a second, and it should flash for the next one."

"Okay," Charlotte said. "Are you fine holding me like this for another second while—"

Suddenly there was a strong vibration and a jerk on the vine. "What was that?" Eric asked.

Charlotte's voice trembled. "A jaguar."

Eric looked at Charlotte but saw that she was not looking up. Instead she stared at the moonlit wall. "What do you mean a jaguar? How can you—"

"It's a jaguar, and you are going to save me from falling."

"How can you possibly—"

A second jolt zipped through the vine, and before Eric could finish his question, Charlotte started to plummet downwards. With one hand still holding the vine, Eric clamped down on the retreating vine while his other hand joined it. He spread his legs as much as he could on the ledge and managed to bring the vine to a stop.

Charlotte's eyes connected with Eric's, and they both took a second for a sigh of relief. Then, they heard from above and beyond the edge of the pyramid, a heavy purring sound mixed with a half growl.

"A jaguar!" Eric hissed while gripping the vine. "You were right."

"Shhh!" Charlotte whispered. "I'm not sure if it knows if we are here."

Seeming to recognize the wisdom of Charlotte's statement, Eric nodded. But the advice came too late. A second later, Charlotte saw a silhouette with slitted eyelids peer curiously and menacingly over the edge.

Because of the concentration of holding onto Charlotte, Eric could not turn his head upward, but he must have sensed from Charlotte's look what she was seeing. "You somehow knew I would save you from falling," Eric muttered through clenched teeth. "Can you tell me if we survive a jaguar attack?"

Charlotte's eyes scanned the wall in front of her before she looked back to Eric. "We do."

A moment later a voice above them cried out causing the crouching jaguar to jump away from the edge. A metallic clanking sound followed, which prompted a fierce reply from the panther with a screaming cry that made the hairs on the back of their necks stand up.

Luke's mom flitted in and out of his subconsciousness. Once again, he just wanted to go lock himself up in his room and play videogames or cry as he contemplated his pitiable position in life and the friends that he would never make or connect with. But his mom held him back from his retreat. She watched his desperate plea in sign language to be left alone, that he had a hard enough life and he just wanted to be left alone.

Luke's mom listened kindly, compassionately, and with a pain in her eyes that rang of the sting of the injustice of life. But when he finished, her eyes steeled over and she signed back to him that they were going to practice his speaking sounds. In spite of his complaints, she insisted, and he practiced vowel-sound after vowel-sound, then consonant-sound after consonant-sound. His mom constantly directed the improvements, at times even using her fingers to physically adjust his tongue in his mouth to the correct spot before having him try again and again. Just when Luke thought that he could not stand any more practicing, and felt that he had to have gotten the sound at least close to right or never would . . . she told him to do more.

The image of his mom ordering another fifteen minutes of practice for the same sound he had been working on for an hour faded away and another image took its place. He sat in the truck in the parking lot of the community recreation center and his dad signed to him that he would pick him up in an hour. Luke sulked, refusing to move. His dad tapped him on the shoulder, but Luke kept his head down. His dad reached across the cab of the truck and turned his face towards him. Because he could not sign with one hand holding on to Luke, he made sure to pronounce with his lips carefully. "I know that you don't like wrestling, but you also didn't like practicing sounds with Mom and now you can speak clearly without help from sign language or an interpreter when you need to."

Luke tried to turn his face away, but his dad held firmly onto his chin, so he looked his dad in the eyes and replied, "Maybe, but why does that mean I should throw myself into a sport where people have an excuse to beat me up everyday without getting in trouble for it?"

His dad let go of his chin, but Luke stared him down, demanding an answer. His dad nodded. "Wrestling was my idea, and I'm sorry you think it's an excuse for people to beat you up. But I got the idea after something your mom said. She said that you had done so much work to just get by in this world without an interpreter, but she felt that you were so much more talented than just someone who could survive, that you could thrive if given the right opportunity."

Luke's eyes faltered, but his dad continued, "And I knew that you had been working a lot on grandpa's farm and were physically fit, and I thought that wrestling could be that opportunity for you. You have an ability to notice things that others don't, you're strong, and you have already proven to yourself that you can do hard things when you need to."

Luke turned away momentarily, but he found himself drawn to his father's gaze once more in order to face a closing statement, "You weren't made to just survive in this world, Luke, you were made to thrive. I'm sorry if you don't feel like you belong in it and that the world is against you, but if someone has you on your back, you've got to stop thinking about how to lift your shoulders off the mat but how to get your opponent on *their* back. If you think there's something better for you than wrestling, I'm happy to hear it, but until then let's give it another fifteen minutes . . . and then another . . . and then another." His dad smiled at his own reference to the unyielding training of Luke's mom. Luke did not smile back, but he did exit the cab of the truck and trudged over to the entrance of the recreation center.

This image swirled into a mesh of shifting memories, which floated in and out of focus until he found himself engaged in the wrestling match that would determine the region championship. Luke faced Austin Phillips, an opponent who had outmatched him for years on end as Luke settled into the sport of wrestling. This year, however, Luke seemed to grow into his own. He had wrestled to the top of his weight class on the school team, and he had surprised himself with some early wins that season. He suffered some difficult defeats in the middle of the season, but he learned from them. And now, at the region championship he felt strangely confident as the ref rested his hand in the air between Austin and him.

Everything slowed down, and by the time the referee's hand lifted up, Luke saw the position of Austin's feet and his observant mind knew that they rested slightly on the heels, meaning Austin was expecting an attack. Luke obliged, almost. He feinted an attack, which made Austin unexpectedly release the tenseness of his defensive stance and opened up the possibility of a real attack. Luke's second lunge fired for Austin's legs and caught one quickly. He felt Austin reaching for balance with his other leg and knew that he needed to be quick, so he lifted up and shoved his shoulders into Austin's torso, throwing them both onto the mat. The only problem was that Luke's speed caused confusion when they both sprawled onto the mat, and the next thing he knew, Austin had a hand wrapped under his armpit and around the back of his neck. Luke tried to bring his leg around to stabilize himself but before he could do so he was wrenched across the mat and onto his spine. It only took a moment before Austin plastered his full weight onto his chest. And Luke could feel his shoulders sagging, nearing defeat on the mat.

Just like that, Luke managed to take down Austin Phillips, only to have the tables reversed and leave him within moments of the event that would signal the end of his efforts, an end that would promise that all his work really did not matter. And he could sense the worthlessness of pretending he had a say in his own destiny in this harsh world, a world that yelled at him when he could not hear, and a world that laughed without him in sounds he would never register as he retreated alone to be smothered slowly but inevitably—as he was now.

Luke's eyes followed his head downward towards the mat. Before they reached the bottom, something caught the corner of his eye—his mom and dad watching from the bleachers. He expected to see their faces anticipating his failure, sorrowfully preparing to comfort him.

But he did not see that.

Instead Luke saw the look on his mom's face which both accepted the injustice of the world but which also chose to fight back. "Pin him!" she yelled, or mouthed, or something. She was not telling him to get off his back. It was like his dad told him, she was telling him to not just survive but thrive. He almost laughed. His shoulders were less than an inch away from signaling his loss, and she was telling him how to win. She actually believed he could win. *Don't you get it, Mom?* he wanted to scream. *I can't do this! I've got to accept that I'm a failure. You have to accept that your son is broken, that he can't win.*

His mom's intensity refused to relent, however, and Luke suddenly noticed that Austin's weight, in its crushing certainty, leaned a bit over and above the center of his chest. Luke also felt Austin's knee touching his own leg instead of being straightened out perpendicular to his body. *Maybe*, he thought, *just maybe*, a burst of strength by pushing up with his chest might throw Austin off and give him a new chance.

Luke lifted his knees slightly in preparation for such a move. *Maybe*, he thought. *Maybe.* Then his knees lowered slightly. *And if I do? Then what? He'll find another way to pin me. His coach will yell instructions that I won't understand. He'll hear my ragged breathing, and in the end he'll outmaneuver me because he has had all the advantages and none of the challenges in his life that I've had. And after we're done, he'll hear me congratulate him in a voice that's different from everyone else's.*

Luke's knees lowered all the way down until his straightened legs fully hit the mat. He turned his eyes so that his periphery could no longer see his parents. His shoulders sagged the final immeasurable distance to the mat and, as the final signal of his defeat, the referee's hand slammed down on the mat, a movement Luke felt through reverberating waves where his body connected to the mat. Strangely, the vibrations did not die away, but they built on each other, gaining strength and magnitude until everything else slid out of mind except for the strong, low pulsing feeling that overcame all other senses.

Luke's eyes snapped open. His chest still registered that weird, low but strong, vibration. But this did not come from a hand hitting a mat in a dream—it was real. He grabbed his machete and carefully tip-toed out of the walled-in sleeping area.

As his eyes adjusted to the moonlit scene before him, nothing seemed to stand out. Suddenly, he caught a movement over on the altar. He took his breath in. It was not what he could see, it was what he could *not* see that troubled him.

Crouched upon the altar and leaning against the sapodilla tree was a blackness deeper than any of the shapes and shadows surrounding it. The movement he noticed was the dark form of claws reaching out and scraping against the trunk of the sapodilla tree. From that spot, that form, the vibrations originated, and Luke knew that he was looking at a large jungle cat. Even though he could not hear it, he could feel the vibrations of the animal purring contentedly while sharpening its claws on the trunk of the sapodilla tree.

Where was Eric? Luke thought. Then he realized that Charlotte had been missing when he left the sleeping quarters.

The scraping claws suddenly snapped a vine wrapped around the trunk and altar. *That vine wasn't there when I wrapped the chicle bag around the trunk*, Luke thought. Just as the vine snapped, the jaguar's ears perked up, and it glided effortlessly down from the sapodilla trunk to the back edge of the pyramid. Luke saw the vine trailing loosely on the ground and leading over the edge of the pyramid, just where the jaguar stalked. Then he noticed the large animal crouching at the edge.

While he did not have all the details, Luke realized that the vine must have been used by Eric and Charlotte for some reason. Now, the large beast must have heard them because, gauging by its crouched and tense position, it was preparing to make a strike downward.

In a split moment, a thousand thoughts washed over Luke. What were Charlotte and Eric thinking? How did they end up cornered off the side of a pyramid against a full-grown jaguar. What could he do to help them? He was no match for a full-grown jaguar, cornered or not. His recent dreams registered in his thoughts as he realized that he couldn't even beat Austin Phillips in a fair fight. This was a predator in its element, and if he lost it wasn't an awkward car ride home with parents trying to reassure him that he would certainly win next season . . . losing here meant death.

And suddenly Luke remembered how he got here. How, after losing the region championship, he simply wanted to disappear. He started looking at colleges far away where his parents could not impose their high expectations on him and he could fail in quiet solitude. Then the man had an offer of a scholarship not based on his disability or the sport for which he had lost his passion. He went to meet the man and instead of getting college offers, he ended up far away from his parents and their high expectations . . . gathering chicle of all things. And instead of failing, he was a success, even when someone tried to sabotage him. Even in a totally different world, Luke could not escape the feeling of his mom telling him to keep working, believing he could thrive.

Here, Luke found himself in a world he finally felt he belonged to . . . that he actually felt he thrived in. Help for Charlotte and Eric in this situation would be him or no one at all. While Luke had long since become accustomed to failure for himself, he knew he could not stand by as long as that failure stood a chance of hurting someone he cared about. Luke dashed aside his inhibitions, jumped up to the pyramid's flat top and rushed toward the animal.

Unsure of how loud he would need to be to catch the jaguar's attention, Luke expelled more from his lungs than he might normally use, just in case. It must have been enough. Shocked by the noise and not expecting an approach from the side, the jaguar's sinewy muscles jolted it nearly a dozen feet upwards and at least as many to the side.

After the landing, the jaguar eyed its adversary and its dark face warped into a contemptuous snarl. Luke swung the machete low, causing sparks to fly off of the pyramid's stone, hoping to scare the intimidating mass of muscle, teeth, and claws before him.

The jaguar, instead of running off as Luke hoped, embraced the challenge. It crouched again and faced Luke head on while opening its mouth into what must have been a fearsome battle cry. For Luke, however, it might as well have been a yawn. "Sorry, cat. You're going to have to go back to purring if you want me to catch anything you say."

If Luke was disappointed that his machete causing sparks on the rocks did not scare off the jaguar, the jungle cat seemed equally disappointed that its fierce cry had not seemed to have any effect on Luke. The two slowly circled each other, watching each move carefully, muscles tense, eyes glaring. One part of Luke panicked, asking him what in the world he was doing. This animal, he realized, could tear him to pieces in a matter of seconds and would have no qualms doing so. He could sense the machete held out in front of him shaking almost imperceptibly but uncontrollably.

The other part of Luke, however, welcomed this test. He had been hurt and lonely for so long. He had tried and failed so many times. As he circled around, his feet carefully picking up and setting down in an ordered succession, he could not help but feel as if he were in another wrestling match—albeit one without referees, mat, or rules—a wrestling match that would determine once and for all if Luke could ultimately succeed or not.

As Luke thought about this, it made him realize that he did not want to have any doubt afterward. He almost wanted the jaguar to have all the advantages in this battle, as in life, just like Austin Phillips had. Luke wanted a win so complete that he would never doubt himself again. Or, he thought grimly to himself, a failure so final that he would never have to face the long drudgery of repeated failures for the rest of his life. For that reason, he took one last look at his machete . . . and tossed it out of reach of their circling.

Luke Bateman, then, faced a full-grown, furious jaguar . . . with his bare hands.

The jaguar's patience lagged, and Luke knew by using the moonlight to watch the animal's muscles expand and retract underneath its black fur that it was preparing to strike. In the midst of his thoughts, something clicked in the cat, and it sprang at him with more speed than Luke would have considered possible. It was all he could do to drop backwards to the ground and throw a foot in the air above him.

The foot landed a strong blow against the spot where the jaguar's belly met its front leg. The jaguar must have cried out, but Luke would not hear it. He remembered striking a blow against Austin Phillip's leg and landing on the ground before suddenly finding himself on his back, so he immediately scrambled to his feet and flipped around to face the animal. Luke saw the panther stamping its front right paw up and down while its face snarled in irritation.

Before Luke settled back into his defensive crouch, the jaguar attacked again. This time, instead of pouncing, it hopped forward and struck out with its good paw. Luke parried a claw by the side with his arm as wrestlers do when their opponents reach for their heads. It was enough to save him from getting gashed, but the jaguar pressed purposely forward. Luke edged backward. A few more strikes from the claws and a few more parries led Luke backwards in some controlled shuffling. He tried to not completely panic in the face of this large animal, but he also started to feel a bit overwhelmed.

Then his back leg lost its footing and he had to use his free hand to stabilize himself on the ground. He risked a glance backward and noticed that in the circling and the attack, his back had been towards the pyramid's drop off. Unknowingly, he had retreated to the very edge, a drop of at least a hundred feet looming behind him. Before he could even register that in his mind, the jaguar struck at his arm and succeeded in gashing his shirt with its razor-sharp claws, causing him to cry out.

Now Luke had an enraged jaguar only a few feet in front of him, a precipitous drop off less than an inch directly behind him, and only his bare hands to fend off the inevitable attack. This is what he feared, but also what he suspected. Even in a world where he was good, it was not good enough.

While there was some intense scowling and shuffling up above, Eric dug deep and hauled in the Charlotte-laden vine until her fingers appeared on the edge of the outcropping where he lay. He held out his arm and their hands simultaneously grabbed the other's arms just below the elbows in a firm grip that allowed Eric to then release the vine and use his other hand to reach under her armpit. With Charlotte's help, he managed to swing her on top of the ledge.

They did not have much time for rest. Up above, they could hear some grunting and then some scraping immediately above them. Charlotte helped Eric to his knees. "Your machete," she said urgently, "throw it to Luke!"

Eric mechanically checked for the machete's handle sticking out of his belt, and slid it off his waist. "But how will he know that—"

"We don't have time! See that foot?" she pointed to a foot that dangled over the edge of the pyramid, "throw it just above there. Now!"

Eric knew better than to second-guess Charlotte. He put the machete in two hands and tossed it, handle-first, as far upwards as he could. The machete soared to a point just behind and to the side of where the foot stuck out from the wall. It seemed to hover in the air for a moment, and Eric watched for an arm to fire back and snatch it.

But nothing happened. The machete dropped back down the way it came, and Eric thoughtlessly caught it by the handle. He looked over to Charlotte and saw her baffled look. "I thought he was supposed to grab it. Wasn't I supposed to throw it to him?"

Charlotte looked at Eric, then the machete. "Yes," she mumbled, "I'm sure of it."

"Then . . . but . . . well, what now?" Eric replied. "Do I toss it up there again?"

Charlotte started nodding as she considered his proposal. As she nodded she looked up and her nodding stopped. Then she turned her face back to Eric. "Never mind." Then she pointed upwards.

Eric followed her finger back to the edge of the pyramid. The foot was gone. Not only that, but they soon heard scuffling and the whiny cry of a jaguar in retreat.

Luke was not despairing. He was out of options, with one foot hanging over the edge of what would be his doom, but he almost felt matter-of-fact about his situation. In the back of his mind, he knew that this was a possibility of his engaging with the jaguar, and he accepted, with a distressing certainty, the result. He worked hard, not just in this battle, but for all his life. And for what? Just one failure after another, one almost-victory-crumbling-to-defeat after another. Luke saw the jaguar tensing its muscles to prepare for a definitive blow, and he tucked his head to the side in anticipation of the swat.

At that moment, he saw something rise out of the corner of his eye just above and to the side of his head. It was a machete.

Luke had given up, but down below, Eric and Charlotte were sending him a message. Fight! Thrive!

Luke could not help but think of a different time, on the brink of another defeat, he saw out of his periphery a couple of people who believed in him more than he believed in himself. Back then it was almost enough to fight back, but—certain of his own inferiority—he never did discover how complete his failure was . . . or was not.

This machete in the air offered the same challenge as his mom telling him to pin Austin, and Luke knew that he owed it to his mom and dad—and to

Eric and Charlotte—to struggle until he was pinned due to forces completely out of his control. I still have some control, he thought, and as he thought it, the machete in his periphery started to adhere to gravity and make its descent.

Instead of reaching out for it, however, Luke realized that—trapped at the edge of the pyramid with dwindling options—he still insisted on overcoming this challenge, or succumbing to it without any advantages. Luke Bateman ignored the machete and, on the edge of a hundred foot precipice, turned to face the jaguar's oncoming strike.

Cornered enough that he could not dodge to the left or right, Luke watched as the lightning-fast paw shot for his face. While a dire circumstance in the first place, the edge of the pyramid also offered him an option he did not have previously. By allowing his foot to drop down behind him, all the way past his knee, Luke could dodge lower than usual, plus still have the ability to keep his head up for his next move. With renewed certainty, Luke's foot slid down behind him, and a split-second later the jaguar's paw grasped at the empty air above his head.

In that moment, with the extension of the jaguar's front leg, Luke saw the animal's vulnerable underbelly. Luke's foot that still rested on the edge of the pyramid caught purchase and flung all of his weight into the exposed body of the jaguar. As his arms wrapped around the animal's torso, Luke could feel the surprised jungle cat trying to squirm into a position so that its teeth could turn into Luke's shoulder. Instead of panicking, however, Luke now had his other foot back on the pyramid, and he gave an added surge to his original push until, just as the jaguar's mouth came within inches of his shoulder, Luke managed to grind his foe's body onto the hard stone surface of the pyramid.

With the flopping on the ground, the jaguar seemed to have had its sense of equilibrium knocked out of it—unsure of how it had gone from four paws on the ground to none. In a frenzy, the animal squirmed with the hope of gaining some sense of a foundation. The large animal's incredible strength fought against Luke's grip and frantically burst in unpredictable directions, while the mouth and claws flailed everywhere in hopes of catching flesh and extricating this menace.

Luke, however, knew that he would not be extricated for anything. With each powerful volley of the jaguar's movements, Luke used his tough tree-climbing arms to squeeze the muscle-encased body even harder. *You may want to get to your feet again, cat, but this fight is everything for me.* Luke made a sudden realization. *And I am not in this world, or any world, to just survive. I'm here to thrive!*

This final thought resulted in a formidable squeeze to the jaguar that would not relent. The pent-up frustrations of a whole life's worth of suffering and adversity seemed to flow from somewhere deep inside of him and find itself circulating through his arms, compressing the jaguar with a vice-like certainty. And as the jaguar made its final, exhausting, retaliation, Luke's mom and dad, and all the teachers, family members, neighbors, and Eric and Charlotte—the people who fought for him and believed in him—impelled one last culminating thrust into the ground. In fact, so empowered was he that once the jaguar's body went limp in submission, Luke had to mentally stop himself short of crushing the animal's ribcage.

In a surreal moment, Luke realized that he had won, he was victorious—utterly and completely. Slowly, he stood up and took a few steps back. Before him, he could see the up and down breathing of the jaguar and he marveled that such a large, dominant animal had been subjected to his force. For half a minute neither the jaguar nor Luke moved as both assessed what had just happened. Then, slowly, the jaguar rolled to its stomach, heaved in a few breaths, and warily returned to its feet. It eyed Luke through slitted eyes, but the fight was gone. A moment later, the animal slinked off towards the opposite end of the pyramid, swallowed up in the night that matched its sleek fur.

Luke took one more moment to allow the feeling of complete satisfaction, of freedom from a lifetime of self-doubt, to wash over him. He smiled. And then the moment passed, on the surface. Underneath, however, Luke knew he would never be the same.

By the time Luke got the vine reattached to the sapodilla tree, the jungle seemed to have already forgotten that a teenager just wrestled a jaguar to the ground with his bare hands. Once Charlotte made it back to the top of the pyramid, Luke had nearly forgotten it himself.

"Thanks for the machete," Luke told them as soon as they found their footing.

Eric looked at Charlotte and then back at Luke. "But you didn't even use it," he protested.

Luke shifted himself so that he could see their faces in the moonlight. "I used it. More than you know." And before Eric could follow up on this enigmatic statement, Luke queried, "What were you doing down there?"

"Wait," Eric gasped, "Luke, you just took on a jaguar by yourself. How is it that you're okay? I don't even see a scratch on you!"

Luke did not immediately respond, and Charlotte could tell that Luke was not as much interested in his own exploits as he was theirs, so she responded, "We were just looking into the future."

"We were?" Eric turned to Charlotte. "I think both of you owe me an explanation."

Chapter 4
SIGNS OF A FORESEER

I just had the worst dream!" Sally came stumbling towards them, rubbing her eyes. "There was this terrified lady shrieking about something over and over again—like that one lady from that movie with the banshee—and anyway the lady . . ." She looked at the three of them standing together. " . . . and what is everyone doing up so early, anyway?"

Charlotte and Eric looked at each other and were about to respond when suddenly there was a deeply sickening, horrendous, grunt-like howling sort of sound that echoed from the jungle below them. All but Luke flinched at the noise and surveyed the top of the pyramid, alarmed.

"What?" Luke intoned, seeing their movement but not hearing the sound that caused it.

They did not respond for a moment as they waited for the noise's echoes to drift off. Suddenly, the sound renewed its strength with such energy that seemed to surround them. They flinched again and instinctively cowered.

Luke glanced around following their second reaction but noticed nothing out of place. "What are you hearing?" Luke asked again calmly.

"I'm not sure," Eric finally responded. "It's some kind of animal. It doesn't quite sound like a jaguar, but it sounds big and predatory."

Luke's eyes made another circuit of their location. "I don't sense anything dangerous nearby."

Charlotte held her composure, but she clearly felt rattled. "It sounds pretty dangerous to me. I can't even imagine what kind of animal would make that sound."

"I think we should get out of here," Eric said. "Let's get our stuff and go now."

As they moved towards the rooms to gather their stuff, the beast-like croaking crescendoed over the jungle expanse again. They quickened their step. Within a minute they had everything gathered and headed towards the steep steps of the pyramid.

Luke held them back. "I left a chicle bag tied around the tree on the altar." Eric almost told him to forget it, but instead he just nodded.

Luke returned momentarily and Charlotte said, "Sorry, you never got to gather chicle for that final bag."

Luke smiled. "It's not that important. Still, though, I actually got a pretty decent batch of chicle from that tree."

"When did you have time to do that?" Eric asked.

"I didn't. But the jaguar that sharpened its claws on the tree managed to release a good amount in just the right spot above the bag . . . before clawing your vine in half," Luke replied.

Eric almost laughed at this, but the spectral and looming animal noise surged into their conversation. They all turned towards the steps and, with as much speed as caution would allow, made their way down the pyramid's crumbling face.

Once at the bottom, Charlotte asked Luke which way, and he pointed them towards the river. They had not gone a dozen yards, however, before the unnatural booming grunts pounded all around them. Eric pulled out his recovered machete, which caused Luke to do the same.

"Where is it?" Eric asked Charlotte and Sally.

Because the noise seemed to come from all around them, they at first shrugged, but with the next onslaught of bellowing Charlotte finally pointed behind a small mound facing the pyramid. "The other side of that is my best guess."

Eric nodded. He turned to Luke. "You go around that side and I'll go around this side."

Luke needed no further instructions. He strode quickly towards the left hand side of the mound.

"I wish I couldn't hear the blasted thing. I might be as fearless as Luke," Eric muttered before warily heading towards the right side of the mound.

Once he rounded the back side of the mound, which he guessed was really some kind of jungle-engulfed Mayan structure on a smaller scale than the pyramid, Eric felt overwhelmed by the guttural screams. Every step he expected to find a large beast waiting on the other side of a fallen tree or screen of vines. He did his best to subdue his trembling as he worked farther around, cowering below each ferocious cry.

Finally, Eric saw movement in front of him and froze, gripping his machete handle as if it kept him from tumbling down an abyss. Before his imagination could run away with him, the movement materialized in front of him. It was Luke.

Eric's relief lasted only until the savage sound burst out as if from right next to him. By the time he lifted himself up from his crouched position, he saw Luke as calm as ever, grinning at him.

"How can you possibly . . ." Eric started, but he was fairly sure that Luke could not see his face to read his lips in the darkness so he stopped. Instead he saw Luke take his machete and point it above his head.

Eric looked up, but just saw the dark canopy of the jungle. He quickly slinked over to Luke's side under a new barrage of cries from all around him.

Once there, Luke tapped his shoulder and pointed upwards again. "Is that what you're so worried about?"

Eric's gaze went upwards again. Silhouetted against the moonlit sky, a small animal, no taller than Eric's knee, sat on an elevated tree branch. Eric just about informed Luke that he was crazy, that the sound they were hearing could not have come from something so miniscule, but he was interrupted.

The deafening noise started again, building on itself until culminating in a roar. And, as if a trick of sight, Eric watched as the small animal on the branch moved in sync with every belting sound that he heard. The noise that they had been so scared of . . . came from that tiny, harmless creature.

Eric looked over to Luke and simply nodded sheepishly.

They soon made it back to Charlotte and Sally. Eric explained what he had seen, including the generosity of Luke managing to not full-out laugh in his face.

Sally listened attentively and then quipped, "Oh yeah. Of course. It's a howler monkey."

"How do you know that?" Eric asked, irritated.

Sally either did not notice or ignored his irritation. "We saw one on our class field trip to the zoo. Those little guys were the loudest things in the zoo!"

"You couldn't make that connection while we were on top of the pyramid?" Eric asked.

Sally shrugged. "For some reason it sounds a bit different in the jungle than in a zoo."

Further solidifying Eric's annoyance, Charlotte laughed. "What a bunch of ninnies we are!"

Before Eric could respond, Luke corralled the group towards the river. "The sun will be up soon. We're all awake. We might as well get going. We'll take a rest this afternoon."

They silently agreed and filed after Luke. As Eric took the final spot in their traveling group he realized that, while he discovered what had been making the creepy noise in the jungle, he still had some questions for both Luke and Charlotte that remained unanswered.

Their stopping point that early afternoon took them to the first sapodilla tree that Luke had tapped for chicle. Once they set down their chicle bags and found some comfortable spots in the underbrush, Luke went off to get some water and fruit to go with their cassava bread, which he knew were close by from his first visit to the spot.

Eric found Charlotte swatting at some buzzing insects while pulling out Eric's phone. "We need to talk," Eric said.

"I wondered when we were going to have this chat," Charlotte said, not looking up from the cell phone.

"Of course you knew I was going to ask you about seeing into the future," Eric nodded while sitting down next to Charlotte. "Do we even need to have this conversation or would I be wasting your time?"

Charlotte chuckled. "I knew we were going to have this talk because I know you . . . not because I saw into the future."

"But you did see into the future, didn't you?" Eric asked.

Charlotte looked at Eric. "Kind of. Look." She pulled up a picture on Eric's phone and then used her fingers to zoom in on it. "Remember that picture I told you about with the figure hanging down the back of the pyramid? Well, immediately following it was . . . hang on . . ."

They both looked at the picture. Eric felt he might as well be looking at a blank wall. "How did you see anything on that wall? I can barely tell there are scratches on it."

Charlotte's finger scrolled up and down on the picture. "This isn't what it looked like," she said. "There were images that were pretty easy to pick out."

Eric's view picked out nothing. "Like?"

"Next to the first image of the figure hanging down the back of the pyramid, it showed another image with a second figure, one with a weird mast and sail coming out of its back, holding onto the rope or vine connected to the first figure, the one with the big eye."

"The figures represented us?" Eric ventured. "A sail for a pirate hunter and an eye for a seer?" He considered it a bit more. "That's how you knew I would catch you," Eric mused, though he could see nothing of that on the stone face reflecting off the cell phone screen. "Well, I believe you because you

86

totally called what happened. I assume the next frame showed me tossing my machete up to a third figure in front of a jaguar?"

"Exactly," Charlotte confirmed. "I mean, the images weren't amazing or anything . . . they were pretty crude. But once I figured out the first one, the ones after it were pretty easy to interpret." She shook her head with her eyes still on the screen. "But this isn't showing any of it."

"Did you see any others?" Eric asked.

Charlotte nodded. "Those images were only the first part of the first line. That's why I was excited to see what else was there." She chewed lightly on her lip.

"You do realize what this means, right?" Eric stated after a pause. "It means that someone hundreds of years ago knew that we would be at the pyramid and knew that we'd be attacked by a jaguar."

Charlotte nodded slowly.

"But how is this even possible?" Eric followed up. "I mean, I know I'm saying this while in another world after being ferried here by someone who can see other people's natural born abilities . . . but how could this seer have known about us?"

"He was a foreseer," Charlotte determined quietly.

"A what?"

"All seers can at least sense some aspect of the future because we detect natural born abilities that are in the future," Charlotte explained, "but some have that skill enhanced and can actually see people and events in the future."

"You gathered this info from other seers that you've met?" Eric asked and then followed up before she could respond, "Have you met a foreseer?"

Charlotte shook her head. "Foreseers are very rare so I've just heard about them, and even then only briefly. I couldn't tell you what exactly they can do and what the limits to their abilities are."

Eric looked at the phone and then at Charlotte. "Well, they can apparently tell what specific things happen hundreds of years in advance." They both fell quiet. Then Eric said, "Kind of makes me want to see what else that foreseer saw."

Charlotte's lips pressed together and she seemed to be thinking. "I'm going back."

"What?" After their intense, early morning adventure with the jaguar and then the scare with the howler monkey, Eric had not even considered retracing their steps. "What are you talking about?"

"We've got about a week before it's time to ferry Luke back home when the moon reciprocates. Instead of waiting at the ferrying spot, I'm going to go back to that pyramid."

Eric took a deep breath. "Hang on. Let's not be rash."

Charlotte eyed Eric assertively. "Like when you raced off to face a natural born pirate alone? At least I have the decency to tell you about my rash move beforehand."

"Fair point," Eric conceded, "but wasn't that the main reason that you wanted to stop using your seer skills? Not being able to account for the danger of my rash actions?"

Charlotte went quiet for a moment. "That is when it was dangerous for you." Eric let her sit on this thought. She then added, "This is different. I don't mind being responsible for my own safety."

"Okay," Eric agreed, "so maybe you can realize that I was responsible for my own safety when I faced Jedediah Willard."

Charlotte gave a wistful smile. "I appreciate what you are doing, but it's still different. You never would have been up against him in the first place if I hadn't told you your natural born ability and ferried you to that world."

Eric nodded. "Fine. I don't really have a big problem with you going back as long as I can join you. But, if you think that this is only affecting you, don't forget that there are three people relying on you to be ferried back to the world they came from."

Charlotte caught her breath. Her eyebrow furrowed. "I never should have told you I was planning on going back. You were smart enough to leave me out of your plans because you knew I could talk you out of it!"

Eric lifted his hands up. "It's not that I—"

Suddenly Luke strode briskly up to them. "I might need your help," he said to Eric as he pulled out his machete.

"Another jaguar?" Eric stood up.

Luke shook his head. "The jaguar cut your vine. This is the guy who cut my harness."

"What?" Charlotte said, but Eric had already pulled out his machete and the two threaded their way into the undergrowth.

Sally could tell that Charlotte and Eric were engaged in a deep discussion that she would doubtless fail to understand. Since the obvious alternative was to just sit by herself and try to sleep, she decided to follow Luke instead. She had to scurry at first, but eventually she came up behind him and almost started chatting before she realized he would not have heard her come up behind him.

Luke worked through the undergrowth and pivoted to climb up a short incline before reaching a spot where water trickled down some rocks. As he reached out with their water flasks, he turned towards Sally, as if he knew she had been behind him the whole time. "Sally, you want to help fill up the other flasks?"

Sally raised her eyebrows and grabbed a couple flasks. "How did you know I was behind you?"

Luke smiled. "Superpowers." Then he paused. "And I saw you out of my peripheral vision when I turned up the hill."

The two were quiet as they filled the flasks, then afterward Luke moved forward, still farther up the slope. "There's a papaya tree up this way. You can help me gather some and bring them back."

They walked quietly for a minute or so, not of Sally's accord, but because she could not place herself in a position for him to see her talking while she

HOW TO BECOME A *SEER*

followed him. The trail flattened and Luke came to a halt in front of a single, skinny-trunked tree loaded with papaya fruits just a couple body lengths upwards. Luke barely hesitated as he gripped the branchless trunk and worked his way up to the first fruits. Squeezing the trunk between his legs and using a tight grip with one hand, he probed the fruits with his other hand until he picked four of them and delicately tossed them to Sally.

Once he slid down and inspected them further, he seemed satisfied. "Do you know what Charlotte and Eric were doing on the backside of the pyramid?" he asked as they packed up the fruit. "I mean," he followed up, "did they talk about it as we walked this morning?"

Sally shook her head. "Nope. It was super quiet on our walk. I tried to talk to them a couple of times. Eric ignored me like he always does, and Charlotte just gave short answers."

Luke nodded thoughtfully and started walking back the way they came, but he slowed up so that Sally could walk next to him. Sally took advantage. "What would they do on the side of the pyramid? And at that time of night? Were they trying to keep it a secret from us?"

"Not sure," Luke answered. "They didn't seem too secretive, but I had just wrestled a jaguar and you guys heard a howler monkey shortly afterward, so we were all pretty distracted at the time."

"You just wrestled a jaguar?!" Sally responded, realizing for the first time that her dream from that morning actually connected with real-life events. "What in the world were you—"

Luke put his hand over her mouth and then put his finger in front of his lips. Sally's voice gurgled to a stop. Just between some foliage, she could see two large animal ears sticking in the air. As they carefully stepped closer and it came into view, she saw that it was a donkey, tied to a tree, nibbling on some nearby plants, and loaded with chicle bags. Luke took the scene in for a moment before he motioned for Sally to carefully follow him.

They retraced their steps back down the path they originally followed up the slope, but once Sally heard the trickling of the water where they filled up their water flasks, Luke turned a different direction. They awkwardly worked through some heavy underbrush for a moment before managing to creep up to a large fallen log.

Luke motioned for Sally to look carefully over the top. Only thirty feet or so away, they now had a view of two men at the trickling spring, filling up their own water flasks, washing their faces, and drinking while talking in low voices further disguised by the trickling water. The darkness of the jungle in the spot they just crawled to kept them entirely hidden, while the spring, in contrast, was lit by some gaps in the canopy above, making it easy to observe the two men undetected.

Sally found it interesting for a moment, but then wondered what they were doing secretly watching from a distance when they could just go up and speak to them.

"Is my voice too loud or too soft when I speak to you like this?" Luke asked in a strong whisper. Sally was confused by the query so Luke tried again. "Can you hear me?" She nodded. "But I'm not speaking so loud that those men might pick up the noise of me talking?" Sally suddenly understood. Luke could not hear his own voice so he was checking with her to regulate it before talking too much.

Sally nodded. "I can hear you, and you're quiet enough that they can't hear us. The water is loud so I can't hear them, and I'm sure it keeps them from hearing us as long as we don't talk real loudly."

Luke nodded. His eyes went back to the two men. "The one closest to the spring is saying something about the injured men back at camp not recovering very well . . . something about those men not gathering any more chicle till after getting in the boat and going back home."

Sally wanted to ask Luke what in the world he was talking about, but suddenly she realized what was happening. He was translating. She may not be able to hear their voices from that distance with the background noise, but nothing was keeping Luke from reading their lips. She watched the discussion between the two men with renewed interest.

Luke continued. "Now that same man is asking about the new . . . something. Ah, I think he's saying 'boy' . . . They speak with a weird dialect because their lips are a bit off from what I'm used to seeing." Luke squinted

91

his eyes in thought. "I think that he's talking about me. These are both men from the chiclero base camp, and when they were showing me how to find and tap chicle trees, he kept calling me 'new boy.'"

At this point, Sally saw the other man respond. She waited for Luke to pass along his interpretation. It came barely a moment later. "He says that he followed me for the first couple of days. He says that he was surprised at how I was finding trees that they missed and gathering quite a bit of chicle in a small amount of time . . . a lot faster than they were expecting."

Sally watched the man turn to sit down, which paused Luke's interpretation, but once seated, the man turned back around and Luke picked up where he left off. "He says that he knew he had to do what he did with the others because . . . some guy's name . . . would reach his required amount of chicle and more if he didn't do it."

The other man said something in return, but by this time he was facing the other direction so Luke could not read his lips. That did not stop Luke from interpreting. "The other guy is agreeing."

"How can you know?" Sally tugged at his sleeve so that he would read her lips. "You can't see his lips . . ."

Luke registered her question and answered it after turning back to the scene in front of them. "His body language. He is not tense and he's leaning toward his comrade with his shoulders hunched. It shows that he's not trying to confront him."

Sally noticed these small details only after Luke's explanation, and she shook her head at this whole world of communication that she had taken for granted. She became so dependent on speaking that she had no clue how many other ways to communicate there were.

The other man responded. "He says that he sneaked into my camp one night and . . ." Luke's lips pursed and his fists clenched.

"And what?" Sally asked, not even bothering to face Luke so he could see. She did not need to. He knew what she would have asked.

"He's the one who cut my rope." Luke's eyes melded onto the man in front of them. "Now he's saying that he followed me across the river to make sure that it worked. Then he said that he watched from a distance as I ascended the next chicle tree." There was a pause, and Luke's eyebrows fused together with an intense anger. "He's talking about how surprised he was when I managed to keep myself from falling . . . and then said that a group of young people showed up so he took off in case they found him nearby."

The other man, with his back facing them, responded. His head bobbed and he waved his hand behind him. Sally got Luke's attention. "Is he telling him about us—about Eric, Charlotte, and me? Is that one of the guys we met in the camp, and he is waving his hand towards camp to talk about when he saw us?"

Luke's fiery eyes lit for a moment. "That's my guess. Good job reading body language."

The man facing them continued. "Now he's saying that he couldn't do anything that night because the group set up a watch." The man wiped his face with his hand, disguising the following words, but Luke picked up after that. "He's saying that he followed us back to the river, but we went upstream because of the flooding. He chose to stay and wait for the river to go down. He is thinking that we got lost in the jungle or will be held up for days and miss the boat."

The other man said something that Luke and Sally missed, but then Luke picked up once more on the man facing them. "He is saying something about that . . . that one guy's name that he mentioned before . . . that the one guy will be short on his chicle quota for this trip, and the chicle company will fire him for sure." The other man responded and the man facing them continued, "He says of course the company would choose one of them to take the . . . the one guy's name . . . spot. They were the only two who would have brought a good amount of chicle back from the expedition." The other man nodded. The two men said something else that Luke did not interpret. And then they laughed, and the one man stood up.

Luke turned around and put his back to the log. Sally saw the two men conversing a bit more, but she could tell that they were now wrapping up the discussion, something Luke must have noticed before her. She turned to join Luke.

"What are you thinking?" she asked.

Luke breathed in strongly from his nose. "I'm thinking that they're not getting away with this." He stood up and started to purposefully, though not brashly, work his way through the jungle, away from the two men.

Sally ran to catch up. After some time she caught up to him. "But they're the other direction, where are we going?"

Luke only caught a few of her words since he was so focused on moving forward, but he picked up enough to figure it out. "I think Eric might want to be in on this. These men are pirating some chicle, and Eric's a pirate hunter."

They found the spot where Eric and Charlotte sat against the tree trunk. Luke set down the water flasks and papayas and then approached Eric and Charlotte, pulling out his machete and calling for Eric to join him. Luke did not even need to break his step. Eric hopped up and pulled out his own machete before Charlotte and Sally could even ask each other what was happening.

"Come on," Charlotte said after taking a moment to recover.

"Are we following them?" Sally asked.

"Only after we get something that will save them," Charlotte responded.

Chapter 5
EXPLOSIVE CHICLERO
POLITICS

Dante put more firewood under the boiling vat of chicle. The cloudy white substance bubbled slowly and ponderously, and as it did, Dante thought of how small of an amount it was compared to what he needed. He thought for sure they would be able to reach their chicle quota on this trip, but some freak accidents cost him two of his laborers and the chicleros were only able to gather a minimal amount.

Grabbing his stick, Dante put it in the cauldron and stirred the chicle, creating a small path that slowly disappeared everywhere the stick passed, reminding him of the fleeting nature of success and failure out here in the jungle.

One moment he thought he was doomed with the loss of two laborers, and then the next he got a new shot of hope when that strangely dressed boy popped out of the jungle and seemed willing to help gather chicle only in exchange for passage to America. Sure, the boy seemed to be a bit slow understanding them, but any foreigner to their parts usually struggled understanding their English creole, which sounded like an abridged form of standard English.

Regardless, the boy was a chicle-gathering wonder. He picked up the intricacies of chicle gathering as if it were second nature, even though he claimed never to have even heard of the job before. Almost, Dante was insulted by the ease with which the boy picked up the duty of something that had been carefully passed through generations of his own family . . . but he could not afford to be insulted. If he did not provide the quota of chicle demanded by the company, he would certainly be fired as supervisor, possibly as gatherer, and his family—already struggling to get by—would be in the most dire straits.

Dante made another pass with the stick and watched the thickening chicle surge up to fill in the void created. That hope he held for the boy now started to fade just as surely as the chicle's surface went flat again. They had not heard anything from the boy for days and the man who volunteered to keep an eye on him had not returned either. Knowing his luck, Dante wondered if both had been lost in some other accident.

The braying of a donkey jolted Dante out of his thoughts, and he looked up hopefully towards the path where the sound came from. It was Felipe and Carlos. He looked hopefully towards the burden on the donkey and saw only one sack of chicle.

"Dat all?" he queried, tiredly.

"Dis all we gonna find," Felipe nodded slowly. "These trees be all tapped out, Dante."

Dante accepted the bad news with resignation. "And the boy? Any luck?"

Felipe shook his head. "I followed the boy wandering around for a day. He give up and take off. I guess he's gonna get himself lost or be knocked down dead by a jaguar."

Dante's eyebrows knit together. "I thought he had so much promise. Sure, he was green in some ways, but that boy seemed to have a knack for the job."

Felipe shrugged and started untying his bag of chicle.

"I'm surprised you chose to untie that bag rather than cut it."

Dante, Felipe, and Carlos turned to see someone emerge from the deep shade of the jungle, face set and machete held cautiously to his side.

As soon as Dante recognized Luke, he looked to Felipe. "What once was lost, but now is found!"

Felipe's face went gray. He looked from Dante and Carlos back to Luke.

"Do you want to tell your boss about the accidents or should I?" Luke stepped farther into the clearing.

Dante felt bewildered by this sudden appearance and obtuse accusation. He looked back at Felipe, who seemed to be considering options. Finally, Felipe nodded meaningfully at Carlos and both of them took out their machetes. Felipe turned to Dante and said under his breath. "I wasn't gonna tell you, cause it woulda distressed you, but I found out that the boy'd been following us for days. He cut de harness o' Muñoz so he'd fall on top of Barrow, which knocked him down so neither could help harvest. I confronted him 'bout it after you sent him off, and he took off in the bush. I thought that was the last we seen of him, but now we'll take care o' this once and for all!"

This seemed like far too much information for Dante to take in all at once, and compounding the problem was the movement of Felipe and Carlos towards the boy. The two struck an intimidating picture as they fanned out so as to be able to approach Luke on two sides.

Rather than being nervous, Luke smiled. "Why would I spy on your camp, hurt your workers, take off, and then come back to camp again?" Dante was surprised that Luke heard what Felipe said, since he had been careful to whisper. Luke continued, "Why don't you just admit that the reason you're doing this is to make sure your boss doesn't get enough chicle to—"

Before Luke could finish his statement, Felipe took a swing at Luke, who easily sidestepped the attack.

"You got good ears to hear what I jus' said to Dante, but you gonna need better skills with a machete if you don't wanna get knocked down by Carlos and me," Felipe snarled.

Dante watched in awe as Luke shook his head in response to Felipe's statement. "I don't need skills with a machete." Luke looked to Carlos and then back to Felipe. "Because I'm not going to use one." He then tossed his machete behind him and lowered into a careful stance with hands in front of him, facing Felipe.

"You one crazy boy!" Felipe almost laughed. "Maybe you think you can take on one of us even without your machete, but ya can't take us both on."

Dante almost stepped forward to stop the massacre from happening, but Luke shook his head again. "I'm just taking on you, Felipe."

Felipe snorted. "I disagree." Then he gestured for Carlos to move in.

Dante looked to Carlos, who took an eager step forward until something materialized out of the jungle to his side, bringing him to a halt. Dante shifted to get a better view and saw that another boy had exited the shadows of the jungle and was holding a machete pointedly at Carlos's chest. "I disagree with your disagreement," the boy said.

Felipe growled and mentioned something about how it didn't matter anyway before leaping towards Luke with a ferocious swing of the machete. Luke stayed low, let the machete fly above him and then attacked Felipe's vulnerable side, keeping an outstretched hand gripping onto the upper part of Felipe's machete-wielding arm and using his other arm to wrap around his torso, pick him up, and drive him to the ground. He slammed into the moist jungle floor face-first and before he could even respond to such a move, Luke adjusted his grip on Felipe's arm and started throwing it up and down against the ground until Felipe was forced to drop the machete.

Dante thought the struggle might end at that point, except that Felipe shifted so that he could use his other arm to land a fist on Luke's face. Luke, however, was prepared for such a move, and in a flash managed to link his arm around Felipe's legs and wrap his other arm around the back of Felipe's neck and rock him back against the ground so that he was scrunched up in a tight vice of Luke's trunk-clinging arms, effectively taking away any momentum or movement for a counter strike. A couple of times Dante noticed Felipe try to wrench himself free, but he might as well have been stuck in a boa constrictor's coils. After a couple of futile jerks, Felipe went limp, trying to cuss through his restricted breathing.

Dante then saw a sudden movement where Carlos stood. The sour-faced chiclero flung his machete upwards and smacked the other boy's machete away from his chest. "Now we see how you fight, boy, when you're not sneakin' up on someone!" he grunted between teeth.

The boy seemed strangely calm. "Fair enough. You can have the first shot."

Carlos did not seem pleased with the polite invitation. With a growl, he flung his machete towards the boy. Dante could hardly tell what happened next. There was a flurry of movement, and hard crashing of metal on metal. The boy was in the air charging towards his attacker one moment, and Carlos was knocked down to the ground the next. The boy then held both his and Carlos's machetes in his hands.

Luke, who had been observing from his position on the ground, loosened his hold on Felipe, who was too exhausted or too subdued to move.

Within a short couple of minutes, the whole landscape of the scene had changed abruptly, and there had been several accusations, none of which Dante knew quite what to do with. What he knew was that his fellow chicleros had been expertly taken out within a matter of moments by two boys he barely knew. As a precaution, Dante reached to his hip and pulled out his revolver.

"Don't kill my men," Dante warned, "or I'll hafta kill you."

The boy with the machetes tossed them behind him into the bush, and Luke spoke out. "Put the gun down, sir. These men are the ones that are causing the problem. They're the ones who are sabotaging this trip."

"That's what you say," Dante responded, nervous and suspicious, "but Felipe says that you are the one doing the sabotaging, and you certainly look dangerous to me!"

Luke shook his head slowly but assuredly, and Dante seemed even more conflicted.

"Listen to him, Dante. His talking has always been off. There's something not right with that boy," Felipe mumbled pathetically. "Besides, you saw what they did to us—dey're killers. If ya don't shoot them now, they could kill you in a heartbeat."

The scene of the two boys' efficiency in taking out Felipe and Carlos ran through Dante's mind, and, even though something about Felipe's story did not add up, a rush of panic ran through him. He wondered how quickly the boys could close the gap with him and finish their job before he even knew what happened. Without thinking, Dante shifted the gun until it leveled onto Luke's chest.

"Before anyone does anything drastic, I think you might find these bags of chicle that Luke gathered illuminating!"

Dante kept the revolver set on Luke, but his head swiveled to the trail leading from the jungle where two young ladies approached, both of them loaded with chicle bags. "Where did you get the bags o' chicle?"

The girl smiled. "I didn't get them. The person you are pointing that gun at got them—for you. Even though those two clowns over there did everything they could to stop him, including cutting his tree harness."

Unconsciously, Dante lowered his revolver. Then, he looked over to Felipe, who seemed beaten enough by this point that he did not even have the energy to dispute the claim. Dante glanced behind him to where his other two, injured, men were before turning back to Felipe and Carlos. "Ya chauncey me, boys!" he cried out angrily. "You'd sabotage yer own crew!"

Both of them averted their eyes, but Dante continued. "I see now. Felipe, you want my position as supervisor. You'd sabotage me so ya can take my pay and the position I worked so hard for." Once again, the revolver started to rise, but this time towards Felipe.

Luke shifted so as to be in the path of the revolver. "Enough people have been hurt. Shouldn't we be preparing the chicle?"

Dante glanced back over to the bags of chicle that had just rescued his livelihood. The revolver lowered once more, but this time for good. He holstered it.

While they tied up Carlos and Felipe and brought the chicle over to the cauldron, Dante heard the girl say to Luke and the other boy: "Silly boys. You're in such a hurry to go fix things with machetes and fists, you don't even think that sometimes all you need is a bag of chicle."

That was when they all heard the distant sound of an otherworldly explosion.

Chapter 6
FERRY, COMPLICATED

Sally's Scribblings

Well a lot has happened since I last wrote something in here while spying on Eric and Charlotte in the parking lot. Um. A lot. And it's crazy. Really crazy. I'll have to write a lot more later, but for now I'll just throw down some short moments from some of the days out here so that I can remember them and use them to write more later.

. . .

Day 4
A few hours after the explosion, we figured it was a volcano somewhere pretty far to the south of here. Even though it was far enough away that we couldn't see it, the smoke and ashes filled the sky by nighttime. And now, even though it's the next day,

things are pretty hazy and it feels like the sun never really came up—like on a really cloudy day. It reminds me of that one movie, The Vampires and the Volcano, where the volcano explosion blocks out the sun, which makes it so the vampires don't have to hide during the daytime anymore. Cool idea, but the story goes nowhere. The vampires are scary but dumb. If they would've made some of the vampires smart and got some of the main characters to have to deal with their own friends or family turning into vampires instead of just getting killed, then it would've been more intense AND given you something to care about. Besides, having a silver grenade instead of a silver bullet to finish off the last vampires in the final scene—wow. The dumbness was oozing off the screen. I guess Mom and Dad were right in telling me not to watch it, but Angie really wanted to watch it and her parents didn't care so I guess this just makes me second guess Angie's choices—but not in friends, just in movies.

Day 6
We helped the chicleros finish turning the chicle into blocks (so boring, and they were not in the mood to answer any of my questions about the way they talk!). Then the boat showed up on the river after lunch time, and they all took off. Dante kept telling us to come and he'd help us get back to the states, but we kept saying no thanks. He was pretty

confused, like, what are you going to do here in the jungle? And I wanted to tell him that we were going to just hang out and wrestle jaguars, but I didn't think he would get the joke. These guys don't seem to get jokes very much. The other two mean chiclero guys were super sour-faced getting on to the boat. I think if they hadn't been tied up, the one guy would've tried to punch Luke. I would've loved to see him try! Luke is crazy strong and smart. He found a way to get more sap out of a couple chicle trees close by that had been tapped already. So he got another batch of chicle before the boat came. Dante was pretty stoked about it. He said it was definitely going to save his job and family. It was a pretty sweet scene. I could tell Luke wasn't too comfortable with it by the way he squirmed when Dante complimented him. I'm pretty sure Luke understood 99% of it too.

Day 12

Sorry I haven't written. It's been a weird few days. First of all, if I have to eat another piece of cassava bread, I'm going to strangle a monkey. Second of all, instead of being happy to hang out in the base camp and chill and talk until the moon "ressiprakates" (fancy seer talk), Charlotte had a bee in her bonnet about going to see the pyramid again. The pyramid wasn't my favorite spot, and it was so far away, so I voted against it. But apparently this little group is not a democracy because no one even voted, and when they packed up and left, I had to just hurry and catch up.

Side note: I don't think movies do justice to how many swarming, disgusting, and disturbing bugs there are in the jungle. All. The. Time. It doesn't stop! Take me to Snowy Nibleton, and I'll run barefoot around Wahlquist Middle School three times just to show my appreciation for our climate which doesn't allow for armies of pests 24/7!

When we got to the pyramid, Charlotte waited for nighttime to check out some symbols on the steep backside. I found plenty of writing on the stairs and walls near the top, but she wasn't happy until she could hang like a spider off the back and try to take pictures with Eric's phone. Because of the volcano explosion, the nighttimes have been super dark and she's been using up the battery on Eric's phone just to have a flashlight. So you can imagine that she was pretty frustrated because she never could see the images she saw earlier.

We spent a couple of days there, heard some more howler monkeys (but didn't freak out this time), and listened to Luke tell us about his wrestling match with the jaguar. Um. Wow. It was amazing, but he needs to work on his storytelling skills because he just told the bare facts and left out all the emotion. After three nights of failure and the days and nights just getting darker and darker with the ash, we finally headed back to base camp.

We took our time and did some extra camping and fishing on the way. Luke found a few more chicle trees and tapped them, and left the bag hanging from the tree for someone else to pick up—just because. Everyone's pretty quiet. Except me. Which is kind of awkward.

Day 14

Tomorrow morning (early!) we hike back up to the ridge where we first came into the chicle-hunting world. I will not miss the bugs! I will also be excited to see the sun again. This gloomy sky filled with ashes is starting to get on my nerves! I don't think I'm the only one bothered by it. Charlotte and Eric have been pretty quiet for the last little while. So has Luke, but he doesn't like talking much anyway, plus I think he's a bit sad about leaving the world of chicleros. Just this evening I thought I heard a motor on the river, and I told Luke and he seemed very excited about the idea of meeting some chicleros . . . but by the time we made it to the river to check there was nothing there. Luke suggested that maybe I was hearing howler monkeys again. That's right, the deaf kid was making fun of the hearing kid about what she heard. At least Luke's not so gloomy that he can't make a little joke!

Day 15

Well, I don't care what world you're in, early mornings stink. Still, everyone is awake and we are about to go. Luke is cleaning up some final things in camp and getting the chicle stored for any chiclero that comes back. I'm a bit nervous to ferry. Last time it caught me by surprise so it was no big deal. This time, I've been expecting it for a couple of weeks so it makes me—

"What are you writing about, Sally?" Luke asked as he and the others gathered at the edge of camp.

"She likes to jot down all her secrets in there," Eric waved Luke's face away from Sally to respond.

Sally moved back within Luke's line-of-sight. "Not that Eric would care to read them even if I did. Besides, it's not secrets so much. I just like good stories. This is a pretty cool story we're a part of and I want to remember it."

"Well, then you won't mind if we read it out loud then?" Eric suggested.

Sally scrunched her face in response. She knew there was no dealing with Eric when he was in this sort of mood. *Where was this attitude when I left my diary sitting in the bathroom for weeks waiting for you to read it?!* She closed her diary and slid behind Luke, ready for the hike up the ridge.

Luke gazed around the camp for a moment longer than they would have expected. Sally heard Charlotte behind her quietly say, "You sure about this, Luke? You don't have to go home, you know."

Luke paused for a moment and Sally thought he was going to have a long, thoughtful speech. Instead, he just nodded and disappeared into the undergrowth.

Sally took one last glance at the camp, swatted some bugs for good measure, and started after Luke, though not before wondering if she saw a shadow shimmer on the opposite edge of the camp. She knew better than to bother Eric about it. Within moments the whole group found themselves hiking through the jungle lowlands towards the ridge where they all first arrived.

Sally was out of breath when they reached the clearing just below the ridge where they first ferried into the chiclero world. "A lot easier going down than coming up," she tried, but Luke did not see her say it, Eric ignored her, and Charlotte gave her a pity smile.

Luke looked over at Charlotte. "Will this work even if we can't see the moon through these ashes?"

Charlotte nodded thoughtfully. "Before, I really needed an unobstructed moon to be visible. But it's weird lately because I've been able to, well, *feel* where the moon is. In fact, it is rising right now and I'm pretty sure that whether we can even see a pinprick of moonlight through this gloom or not, I shouldn't have any problems ferrying us back."

It was a lot to say, and even though Eric turned his flashlight on her while she spoke, it was unclear how much Luke understood. Sally could tell, however, that he got the takeaway: she could still ferry them.

"Do we have time for a quick bite to eat?" Sally asked, breaking yet another awkward silence. It was a thankless job that she had been tirelessly accomplishing their entire time there.

Charlotte nodded. "Sure, if it's fast. I mean, we don't have to ferry right when the moon comes up, but I'd like to get back sooner rather than later."

"Sally, I didn't pack food because I didn't think we would need some for a short hike up the ridge," Eric said.

"Forget it," Sally waved her hand in the air. "I'm sorry I asked."

In a strange moment that defied his brotherness, Eric sighed and said, "But, I did see some pineapple plants just off the side of the path we took coming up. I'll go grab a couple."

Luke missed their exchange so Sally was about to explain to him, but he kept his eyes curiously following Eric as he stepped into the gloom. A moment later there was a strange grunt and a cry before a thrashing could be heard in the undergrowth. Eric's voice called out, "Someone's coming!"

Sally could tell that Luke could not hear it, but because his eyes had been focused on the area where Eric had gone he was the first to see the dark figure tumbling into the clearing, barreling in their direction. Before Sally could

107

even make out who the grunting form belonged to, Luke sprang in front of him and pressed him to the ground.

Some crashing followed and Eric jumped into the scene. "Who was that? Is everyone okay?" He looked down and saw Luke smothering someone at his feet. "Luke, who is it?"

Sally saw that Luke's face was downward. "He can't hear you, and I don't think we know. It's too dark to—"

"Ya wanna know who this is?" a voice sputtered out of the darkness. "I had to escape and fool someone into telling me all the way back up the river, just so I could try to hunt down this boy that ruined my life! I found you at the camp and was gonna attack in the morning, when everyone would be fast asleep, but you got up and went up this ridge before I could. Then, as I was tryna catch up to you, this other boy tripped right into me and knocked me down!"

"Felipe," Eric muttered in realization, "you really have to let this go."

"No, this boy gotta let *me* go. He's gonna crush me!"

Eric tapped Luke's leg. Luke loosened his hold on Felipe and lifted his head up. Eric signaled that he could sit up. Luke rolled to a sitting position, and Eric squatted, taking his phone out to light up his face and explain what happened.

Almost as soon as the light fell on Eric's face, Sally saw something move behind Luke. Before she could call out, an arm wrapped around Luke's neck from behind and a pistol found itself hovering at his temple.

Luke's hands had reactively shot up to cling to Felipe's arm, wrapped around his throat. Though taken by surprise, Sally saw that Luke's face was calm, though intense. Eric immediately raised his hands up in the air. "Easy, Felipe. You need to calm down."

"All I want is the boy. Leave him to me and go." Felipe's voice slithered across to them from the gloom behind Luke.

Eric shook his head slowly. "We're not leaving our friend, and if you let go of Luke right now, we'll forget this happened."

"I mean it!" Felipe raised his voice. The pistol rattled.

Sally noticed Eric's muscles tense and Luke's eyes narrowed. The grip of his hands on Felipe's arm tightened.

"Blast," Charlotte muttered just loud enough so that only Sally could hear her, "these boys are going to get themselves killed." Sally felt the tension mounting and wondered what could possibly be done about it. Suddenly she felt Charlotte grabbing her left hand with her right.

"I'm gonna ask you one more time. Leave the boy and go!" Felipe's voice maintained a level of ardor that highlighted his instability.

Sally saw Charlotte reach down with her left hand towards Eric. They must have connected and Sally heard Charlotte whisper, "Eric, slowly reach out and touch Luke's foot. Squeeze my hand when you do."

Eric said nothing, but Sally noticed, out of the corner of her eyes, that he shifted the light from the cell phone so that it shone away from his other hand, which then dropped down towards the ground.

Sally held her breath. And then it happened.

Feeling a slight tug to her hand, Sally noticed the gloom that surrounded them transitioned to a more clean and crisp blackness. Stars pricked into view, and a silver moon welcomed them to the receiving end of the ferry.

Because they had been gone for so long, it was almost incredible to Sally that they could now be suddenly back home. The blacktop of the parking lot formed a stark contrast with the spongy undergrowth of the jungle. The frigid air bit at her skin, unlike the damp and warm tropical atmosphere. But one thing Sally saw stayed the same: Felipe had ferried with them, his arm still wrapped around Luke's throat, his pistol still inches from Luke's temple.

The treacherous chiclero's eyes widened and rolled back and forth wildly. While his mind could not fully grasp what had happened to him, he suddenly had some clarity as his hand renewed a grip on the pistol and his finger extended to the trigger.

"Luke!" Sally screamed in panic, even though she knew he could not hear her.

A second later, the pistol was engulfed by a large hand, propelled backwards, and then ripped out of Felipe's grasp before being tossed a dozen yards across the parking lot.

The figure who accomplished this feat immediately addressed himself to Charlotte. "Everything okay?"

"Yeah, Dad. Thanks."

Felipe's grip on Luke's neck released, and Luke turned his face upwards to see the large form of Charlotte's father standing above him and Felipe. The intensity in his brow released, and he turned back to the group.

Eric smiled at Luke and nodded towards Mr. Reeves: "Natural born bodyguard."

PART THREE
AQUEDUCT ENGINEER

Chapter 1
TINA'S TROUBLES

Tina Ortiz watched in horror from her high position on the northeast tower of the proposed aqueduct to Cordovia. She had been taking measurements and making calculations for the other piers forming in-between her tower and the southwest tower. Things were looking good, and after nearly five days in this strange, inexplicable experience, she actually felt competent and at ease.

But now, not only were the towers being brutally dismantled, block by block, by the nightmarish-looking marauders below, but she also knew that their chief engineer, her mentor, was down there. And from the looks of things at her vantage point, the Visigoths did not seem to care about showing any mercy to those captured.

"What am I doing here?" she thought out loud as she watched months' worth of work being dismantled before her eyes. Though she only came in at the last five days of it, the wanton destruction still felt like a personal sting. "Where is my family? What happened in that parking lot? How can this feel so real? And if it is real, how can it be?"

Marcus Oleas Lectorius found her, as she knew he would, and told her that they needed to retreat back to Cordovia. She looked at him, and he recognized the meaning behind it. He shook his head. Tina groaned. The chief engineer was gone.

She took one last look at the sprawling architectural feat before her and then turned to join the centurion with a small guard of Roman soldiers as they followed the aqueduct channel that had been built up from this point to Cordovia for another seven miles.

The heat of the day was intensifying, putting a dull glint on the view of the Iberian landscape before them. Not only did the small ridgeline they travel on give them a decent view of the surrounding countryside, but it also enabled them to see, on the main road below, several scattered groups of laborers, craftsmen, and support personnel from the aqueduct building crew trying to make a chaotic retreat back to Cordovia as well.

"That is what I feel like right now," Tina thought to herself as she saw the amorphous clusters streaming along.

If dispersed groups of people in disarray represented how she felt now, five days ago it would have been some strong columns of supremely disciplined soldiers marching in complete lockstep. Tina, at that point, had life figured out.

Ever since entering high school, she mapped out her plans of becoming an international lawyer (the most prestigious thing she could imagine) with such meticulous detail that it would have put her guidance counselor to shame. Each class she took, she made sure to do whatever was necessary to get the coveted "A" grade. She signed up for all the right clubs, which would have the desired effect in the college admissions office. When registering for classes, she strategically gave herself the rigor that would separate her from other high-achieving students when it came down to selecting the valedictorian. In fact, her preparation for a successful legal career seemed to reflect the careful placement of piers built to support a channel on a massive, beautiful aqueduct.

That, however, was the great disconnect. As carefully planned as her future had been, she was not happy or even excited about it. All of her actions hinged on each piece working out perfectly, which meant that she could never lose focus and her life always operated beneath an oppressive layer of stress. Yet, when some strange, mystical force caused her to come and experience the most random and remote occurrence possible—to witness and then be part

113

of an aqueduct-building team—Tina could not express how absolutely thrilling it was for her.

Five days ago, she went from a parking lot to a foggy glade and spent one of the most miserable nights of her life attempting to figure out where she was and what had happened. Then, at the break of dawn, she saw that she had wandered around all night in the cleft of a hill. Once she saw a large holding basin built of stone at the mouth of the cleft, she had hope that civilization could not be too far away. As soon as she approached the holding basin, she saw a conduit leading out of it and a stone channel heading on a very slow gradient down the slope of the hill. A mile later, she stood mesmerized as pillars suddenly pushed down from the channel and to reach the floor of a small valley. There the channel stopped, as the structure was incomplete, but in her mind she could see the webbed stone arches in their completed form coming together to create a sturdy support for a water pathway—an aqueduct.

When Tina was younger, she had been absorbed by her 6th grade unit on the Romans. She spent weeks afterwards still looking at pictures of Roman architecture, especially aqueducts, and studying their features and purposes. But that was a long time ago. Life caught back up to her and other things took precedence, like her goal to be a prestigious international lawyer. As soon as she saw the aqueduct, however, everything came spilling back to her recollection. She had to figure out what had happened to her, yes, but she also had to figure out more about this aqueduct and this crew of people who were building it using ancient tools and equipment.

The city of Cordovia loomed closer and Tina inwardly recoiled. She felt that the closer she got to the city, the sooner she would have to face the reality of this desperate situation: she was in a time and place unfamiliar to her with no means for returning, and she could no longer find comfort in being part of the building of the aqueduct since it had now been dismantled by the Visigoths. For all her careful planning, Tina found herself hopelessly without any future prospects at all.

"What happened?" Charlotte's dad queried. "How did you ferry there?"

Charlotte shook her head. "I don't know. He wasn't even at the ferry point. I could just sense where the moon was when he was ferried and the next thing I knew, the moon returned to that spot and we went."

"Where are we? What kinda voodoo is this?" Felipe remained on the cold ground of the parking lot, looking around desperately. "Who is this person that is—"

Mr. Reeves said nothing in return. He simply towered over Felipe until his trembling mouth stumbled to a halt. Then he turned back to Charlotte. "And this fellow?"

Charlotte looked at Felipe. "He pulled that gun on Luke at the ferry point, and I just trusted you would be able to help us if we ferried."

Mr. Reeves nodded. "We'll figure out what to do with him later. For now, why doesn't everyone just come with me to our house and we'll sort this out and make sense of it."

No one moved or acknowledged his statement. The large man scanned the group, then rested on Charlotte. "Well?"

Charlotte glanced at her companions then back at her dad. "We still need to get Tina."

"Of course," Mr. Reeves affirmed. "I thought we could go home, get everyone back to their homes, figure out what to do with this guy, and then come back here."

Eric shifted uncomfortably. "If it's all the same, Mr. Reeves, I'd like to go help find Tina."

Luke had been sitting with his back to a street lamp, which helped him to see their faces well enough to get the idea of what they had been saying. "I'm coming too," he pitched in.

Sally, feeling left out, jumped in at this point. "Me too!" Though she added, only loud enough for Charlotte to hear, " . . . unless she's in a place with lots of bugs because I am tired of bugs."

Eric pushed back. "No, you're not. You're going home."

Sally perked up indignantly. "I am too coming with, Eric. And if you think you can—"

Mr. Reeves raised his hand in a motion of silence before their conversation could escalate. The group fell silent and knew that whatever Mr. Reeves decided would be what happened. His physical presence alone demanded that sort of respect. "Can you ferry us immediately to her world like you did with this one," he pointed to Luke, "without waiting for her to return to the ferry point?"

Charlotte paused to search her senses. Sure enough, the power of the moon and her connection to it glowed within her. "I'm confident I can."

Mr. Reeves looked at the entire group. "The more people that come, the harder it will be to protect all of you. I'm used to protecting just one person."

"We won't be a burden," Eric offered. "We'll be helpful. Luke and I already got us out of a couple scrapes."

Charlotte couldn't help but toss in, "I only needed to get them out of a couple too."

Eric almost protested before he realized that it was technically true. His mouth clamped shut.

"And you, little miss?" Mr. Reeves nodded towards Sally.

Sally eagerly took to her own defense. "I wasn't a problem at all. And whenever I wanted to complain, I just wrote in my diary. And even when Eric was mean to me, I didn't fight with him too much."

"Do you know where this ferrying will take us," Mr. Reeves faced Charlotte again.

"Yes, I remember Tina's ability from the first time I met Eric," Charlotte said. "She is a natural born aqueduct engineer." There was a pause. "So . . . it should be low-key enough."

Mr. Reeves nodded. "It's never quite as low-key as one thinks, but an aqueduct engineer should be better than a natural born viking or something like that."

"Should we go, then?" Charlotte asked.

Mr. Reeves shook his head. "One more loose end." He nodded towards Felipe. "We can't just leave him here by himself. Who knows what kind of trouble he would get himself into."

Charlotte frowned for a moment. "We can send him back to his world right now."

"You're not going back to that world," Mr. Reeves frowned, "especially considering the way you just came from it."

Charlotte shrugged, "Well, Luke could hold onto you and you could hold onto Felipe. I could just send you three there, you can toss him in the jungle, and then I could bring you two back . . ."

Mr. Reeves's frown deepened. "You and I were separated by worlds once tonight. I'm not going to let that happen again, especially not with a natural bornapper on the prowl."

Charlotte chewed on her lip for a minute. "We can just take him with us."

Mr. Reeves tilted his head. "Then I'd be babysitting another person."

"Without his gun, he's harmless. Luke can take him down before the guy can finish a sentence."

Mr. Reeves looked at Felipe, who appeared to be a pathetic mess, then at everyone else. "Aqueduct engineer, huh?"

Charlotte nodded. "Let's tie up these loose ends, Dad."

Mr. Reeves mulled for a moment longer before finally announcing, "We need to do the right thing, and the right thing is to undo what this natural bornapper has done." Charlotte smiled, and her dad continued. "But, Charlotte, you realize what this means, right? All this will have brought some attention to us by other interested natural born . . . cohorts. Even if no one actually saw that you were a seer, it wouldn't take much to guess, and especially to figure out how special of a seer you really are considering what you've already done tonight."

Charlotte's smile disappeared. Eric looked back and forth between the two curiously. Mr. Reeves continued, "In fact, your mom and I already talked about it before I brought you over here. She is doing her thing right now."

Charlotte kept her face down for a moment, and then slowly nodded. Eric seemed to be about to ask her a question, but she suddenly lifted her head up. "Well, let's go."

She grabbed Sally's hand firmly, then more delicately offered her other hand to Eric. He quickly took her hand in his. Luke stood up and grabbed Eric's free hand. Mr. Reeves forced Felipe to his feet, who was still recovering from the first ferrying, then took Luke's other hand while gripping Felipe's shoulder on the other side of him.

With everyone connected, Charlotte took a deep breath. She glanced over to Eric. Eric had questions in his eyes, but he simply squeezed her hand. She squeezed back. Then she turned her face to the sky, focused on the moon, and mentally tugged on it. As before, the moon slid back down its path, but instead of going quite as far as it did with Luke, it settled into the spot immediately before that.

The last thing she heard from their world was an odd scraping sound, then the fading stars, the vanishing parking lot, and the frigid air gave way to an enveloping darkness with only the moon as a constant.

Chapter 2
REBUILDING

With our water supply from the north cut off, we cannot hold Cordovia against the Visigoths without the completion of that aqueduct," Cordovia's proconsular magistrate explained. The council remained quiet.

One council member finally piped in. "Then is it a lost cause? Our garrison can't protect both the city and the construction site. Do we abandon this great city solely because we can't get water here?"

As a centurion, Marcus Oleas Lectorius had remained quiet in a corner, leaving this to the council, but at this point he finally felt justified in speaking out. "Not a lost cause. Our soldiers might be stretched, but the Visigoths are stretched too. They are drawing off of their barely supported outpost on this side of the Pyrenees Mountains. One legion could take care of this problem."

The magistrate turned to Marcus. "You know how Rome works. If we do get a legion, it won't be for another year. The city can't last that long. If that aqueduct is not completed within the next few months, we will have to evacuate Cordovia. People have already started to leave on their own since we've rationed the water supply."

The councilmen murmured to each other as they considered the dire circumstances. Marcus sighed. "I could bring the whole garrison out of the city to protect the construction site until they finished. It would leave the city open to attack, which is a great risk, but if the Visigoths don't think to attack Cordovia, then that should be enough soldiers to hold off them until the aqueduct is completed. Once done, it should be easier to protect, with far fewer soldiers."

The magistrate turned back to the council. Several of them started nodding their heads. One of them said, "If they don't attack the city, then we will have our water supply. If they do, well, we can arm citizens. That might slow an attack on the city enough to evacuate."

The magistrate nodded, but lifted a finger. "You're overlooking something." The room went quiet again. "You may be able to protect the construction site, but the chief engineer has been killed. It will take months to get a new one sent from Rome or somewhere else with a competent aqueduct engineer."

While the council mulled over this difficult point, Marcus shifted. He seemed to be considering something. Finally, he said in a voice loud enough to interrupt the doubtful whisperings that had filled the room. "Perhaps we don't need a new engineer."

"What are you talking about?" the magistrate replied. "Building an aqueduct is a very delicate matter. You can't just hand the job over to a talented mason or carpenter."

"The chief engineer's assistant might be up to the task," Marcus pushed.

"What assistant? He had no assistant. There was only one engineer in the whole crew."

"I don't know where she came from, but she—"

"She?" the magistrate interrupted. It was repeated by a few of the council members.

Marcus took a deep breath. "Look, if you want to just abandon the city, then I will be the first to help organize a retreat. Of course, the political positions that you all worked so hard to gain will be meaningless in other cities." This jab caused some uncomfortable fidgeting. "But if you want to give this idea a chance, then there is a girl who showed up some days ago, and as of yesterday she was recalculating and fixing some of the chief engineer's figures for him. The reason she didn't get killed in the attack is because he sent her up to retake some measurements after she pointed out a possible way to adjust the pier heights in a more effective way."

The council members looked at each other, surprised. The magistrate burrowed his eyebrows together. Marcus continued, "I don't know if she can do it. But she seems talented enough to me, and if you want to give her a chance at rebuilding that aqueduct, I don't think we have very much to lose."

After a brief moment of consultation with the council members, the magistrate turned to the centurion. "Where is she?"

Even though she never left the ground in the first place, within moments Sally suddenly sensed gravity exerting its influence on her again. A new world started to materialize around her and she felt more things than just Charlotte's hand. Curiously, the moon that had been so clear moments earlier vanished. The stars did not resume their spots in the night sky. And then her feet felt heavy . . . no, wet. Then her shins. Then knees. Thighs.

In a panicky moment of realization, she cried out, "I'm sinking! Help! I'm sinking into something."

Charlotte's hand, now above her rather than level at her side, tightened at her exclamation. Now Sally found her waist starting to dampen. She caught her breath and wondered why she had agreed to travel to yet another world. Mainly pride, she realized, not wanting Eric to have his way and keep her out of the adventure. Now, she'd do anything to be back in that dry, lighted, parking lot.

All of a sudden, Sally felt herself splurching upwards and outwards. Two giant arms had taken her under the armpits and effortlessly slipped her out of the wet trap she had been in and onto dry ground right next to Charlotte.

"Thanks, Dad," Sally heard Charlotte say to the large figure next to them. "I wasn't really sure what was going on and—"

"He's gone," Charlotte's dad replied.

"What?" Charlotte asked.

"That was all it took for him to make a break for it," Mr. Reeves said. "The second I let go of him to get to Sally, he slipped off."

"I'll get him," Eric offered. He let go of Charlotte's hand and sprinted into the darkness. "Get back here, Felipe!" Eric yelled. There were a couple footfall-caused splashes. "Felipe!"

Mr. Reeves seemed to consider a moment before deciding, "We need to stay together as a group." He cupped his massive hands around his mouth. "Eric! Come back." Silence. "If you haven't caught him by now, he's probably still sprinting a half mile away."

Seconds later, they heard the deliberate steps of Eric returning to be with them. He shrugged. "He got away."

Sally remembered her specific words of appeal to come along on this adventure: "I wasn't a problem." Now, within seconds of arriving, she happened to help Felipe escape. "Sorry," she squeaked.

Surprisingly, it was Eric who pitched in to minimize Sally's blunder. "Well, no big harm done. Felipe has sealed his own fate. He'll now be stuck in this world for the rest of his life. Hopefully, it can make use of an out-of-place chiclero!"

"I'm not so sure that he's gone for good, Eric," Mr. Reeves mused, but he did not dwell on it. "Now what?"

"Well, it's foggy and there is apparently a marsh or something surrounding us," Eric volunteered. "I suggest we find a dry spot and wait until morning."

Tina took a deep breath. She should be studying for the ACT she was scheduled to take next Saturday. Instead she found herself surrounded by a group of skilled laborers, the survivors of the Visigoth attack on their aqueduct work crew, all of them waiting to hear her instructions.

While the centurion had to convince the council members to give her a chance at this desperation job, these laborers had seen her work with the chief engineer already. They saw what she could do, and they trusted her. Yet that only made Tina more nervous. If this was about how to best approach composing a college-entrance exam, then she would have no problem pointing them in the right direction. However, they were expecting her to give them direction in completing a complicated architectural enterprise. This was so far out of the realm of her comfort zone of excelling in the world of the syllabus, quiz, study session, and grade computation that she momentarily froze.

The laborers looked at her expectantly as she stood in front of one of the remains of the aqueduct's crumbled piers. She felt a warm breeze pick up the dust of pulverized limestone where the masons had been custom-shaping stone pieces. She noticed the shadow of the pier curve before the broken arch. She fingered the dioptra tool that helped her sight and calculate levels and angles. Tina realized that though she was new to this world, she was not unfamiliar with it. For some reason, everything here seemed to be a part of something deep inside of her. She took her second deep breath, and then she began to speak.

"The damage is extensive, but we are lucky it is not worse. The Visigoths tore down the scaffolding, but did not destroy it. The original foundations are still here and the stones have only been displaced, not broken." As Tina spoke, she started convincing herself that they really could do this.

"Within a couple of days, we will be back to where we were before the Visigoths came if we all work hard and help speed up the process. We'll start by having the masons scavenge the scattered stones and organize them by size and purpose. The carpenters will reinforce the scaffolding and reassemble the arch pieces. Once this is done, the construction should go quickly."

The plan was a solid one moving forward. This is what Tina liked, a careful, meticulous, well-thought-out strategy. The laborers seemed to like it too. They held new purpose in their eyes, and her specific, pointed instructions gave them something to do. They were ready to go . . . almost. Tina saw a few of them keep on gazing past her towards the hills to the north.

"And you can work at ease for your safety knowing that we now have the whole centuria of soldiers from Cordovia protecting us against any future attacks," Tina looked over towards the centurion, Marcus Oleas Lectorius, who stood erect to the side of their gathering. He did not move, but his calm dignity lent credibility to his ability to protect them, especially considering that his soldiers were already dispatched to their positions and making patrols of the area.

With that said the last of the laborers stood ready to continue, eager even. Tina released them, but held back the several supervisors to impart some more detailed instructions. After they dispersed, Marcus approached.

"Lady Tina," he said, "I'm not sure why we deserved to receive your miraculous company, but I can tell you that it is most timely."

Tina nodded uneasily. Whether someone commented on her brilliance at school or in a field of Roman era Hispania, she never knew how to respond. "Hopefully, we can finish what the chief engineer started."

"Indeed. Though, I'm hoping more that we can finish what you adjusted from what the chief engineer started. The night before the attack, he told me how he could not explain your impressive ability to see things that he could not, even though you seemed to have no formal training with building aqueducts or even some of the most basic terminology for the equipment or methods." Marcus paused and noticed that he made her uncomfortable.

He looked away and said, "Well, I must be on my way now. The patrols will be coming in all this morning to report and resume patrolling. Goodbye, Lady Tina. And please let me know if you need anything."

"Qui sunt?" The soldiers held out their spears menacingly.

Mr. Reeves stood in front of Charlotte and the others with his arms outstretched. "Anyone catch that?"

That morning they found some type of rock basin and followed the channel that had been built leading out of it. They barely got one hundred yards before a group of a dozen Roman soldiers burst over the crest of a hill and formed a threatening semi-circle around them. Now, one of them kept on yelling at them in gibberish that went well beyond the English creole they experienced with the chicleros.

"Anyone speak Latin?" Charlotte turned to the group hopefully.

Surprisingly, it was Luke that pitched in. "I don't speak Latin, but he is asking us who we are, and if we don't give him a good answer soon, we'll be in trouble."

Sally felt like she should explain. "Luke is basing this off of body language. In fact, you'd be amazed how much we can understand about what someone is saying if you take into account the expressions that—"

"Thanks for the lesson, Sally," Eric interrupted, "but we need to stick to Luke's most important point: how do we get these guys to not poke us?"

Charlotte frowned. "You don't think anything bad like this happened to Tina when she got here, do you?"

"No," Eric decided. "This is her world. I'm fairly certain nothing bad would have happened to Tina."

"Yes but—" Charlotte started, but before she could say anything else, the soldier speaking to them lowered his spear.

"Tina?" he repeated. "Concis Dominam Tina?"

Luke took over. He stood forward and nodded. "Tina." He lifted his hands as if to say, "Where?"

The soldiers consulted for a moment. They lowered their spears. The one in charge motioned for them to line up in front of them and then pointed down the slope they stood on.

Mr. Reeves looked at the soldiers skeptically, but Luke said, "I don't think they're tricking us. They actually want to take us somewhere, probably to Tina. I say we get in line and start moving."

Mr. Reeves nodded and then organized them so that Luke was in the lead, followed by Eric, Sally, then Charlotte and himself. Then, they started down the slope, keeping the stone channel to their left and avoiding the dust that their tramping feet kicked up as they moved.

Within a short amount of time, they found themselves entering a field between two hills with dozens of workers swarming all around them. The skeleton of an aqueduct rose up to the side of them, and all around they heard the sounds of masons chipping away at stones, carpenters assembling scaffolding, or supervisors barking orders. Most were too engaged with their current duties to pay any attention to them, but those who managed to see them stopped and gaped. Charlotte figured that they rarely saw a group of people dressed like them.

Soon, they found themselves approaching a tent structure towards the middle of the field. Charlotte saw a figure at the tent opening, pointing farther up the field and giving instructions to a couple of men. Two soldiers stood warily at her side. Luke must have seen it too because he broke into a run with such enthusiasm that the bark of the soldier behind them would not have stopped him if he could have heard it.

The soldiers at the tent heard it, and they immediately shifted in front of Tina and held out their spears. Luke came to a stop in front of them, and before either could figure out what to do, Tina shoved the soldiers out of the way and jumped over to Luke. The two of them hugged each other tightly, which Charlotte found interesting as she shared a couple of classes with Tina and knew she was not a gushy person by nature, nor did Charlotte think she really knew Luke all that well. Yet certain circumstances remove any sort of reserve people might feel towards another. Here was a person from the world she knew.

As if to confirm this, as soon as Tina gazed over Luke's shoulder, she saw the rest of them approaching. "Eric! Charlotte!" she called out. "I can't believe . . . what are you? . . . what am I . . . ? How did you . . . ?"

After Eric and Charlotte took their turns giving her a hug, Charlotte lightly held Tina's hands in hers. "We need to talk."

Tina, by this time, had regained most of her composure, though her eyes shimmered with suppressed emotion. "Yes. Yes. That is an understatement." She waved off the soldiers still standing guard and those who had escorted the group there in the first place, and she ushered everyone into her spacious workplace under the shade of the white-canvassed tent.

Some time later a long pause settled over the tent. "Wow," Tina finally said. "That explains so much . . . and so little at the same time!"

Charlotte nodded. "The crazy thing is that I only understand half of it myself."

"But you do know that we can go back, right?" Tina asked.

"Yes," Charlotte replied firmly. "That much I'm sure of."

"In another . . . let's see, it's been six days so . . . nine days?"

Charlotte nodded. "I trust your math more than mine, but that sounds right."

Having maintained a laudable silence for the whole time of explanations, Sally finally took a moment to voice her thoughts. "So what are we going to do for those nine days?"

Charlotte saw Tina look from Sally and then to her. "I'm hoping that I might help get this project on the way to completion," Tina asserted. "Even if I can't see it finished in nine days, it would be nice to help these people out. They're in a pretty tough situation."

Charlotte smiled. "Just let us know how we can help."

Tina nodded appreciatively to Charlotte. "I'll take you up on that."

"But first you'll have to explain to us how you speak Latin," Eric interjected. "I mean, I know you've always been a good student, but since when have you been doing secret Latin courses?"

HOW TO BECOME A **SEER**

Tina knit her eyebrows together. "Good question . . . . and I don't exactly know the answer, either. I guess it just turns out that, when they speak, I hear that it's not English . . . but I understand it *as* English. And when I speak back to them, I think of it as English, but I'm not speaking English. I'm not sure how else to explain it."

Charlotte nodded. "I don't know how to explain it either, but I do know that when seers ferry people, they are sent to a place where they are able to experience their natural born abilities. They would not be able to experience it very well without speaking the language. That skill is somehow provided for them, or it's embedded deep within them somewhere and released once they enter the world that belongs to them."

Tina nodded. "Well, it's not perfect. If I see a tool or something that I've never seen before, I have to ask someone what it is. But I understand their explanation and I'm fairly quick at being able to use the real name soon enough."

"That's true," Eric said. "I didn't know all of the terminology for sailing or ships, but they immediately made sense when I asked about it."

"Exactly," Charlotte said. "You have natural abilities, but you still need to learn some of the basic working language of the skill."

Tina smiled. "One basic working language term that you look like you could use would be 'water' . . . you all look parched. How about I get you some food and water? You can refresh yourselves here for a little bit while I check on the progress of the aqueduct, and then we'll figure out some different ways that you can help out. Because you'd better believe I'm going to put you to work over these next nine days. The people of Cordovia are relying on you for it."

As soon as Tina left, Charlotte saw Sally smiling. "What have we done? She's putting us to work? Maybe we should've waited up at that marsh for nine days and *then* come to get her!"

Charlotte's dad, who had been sitting cautiously at the entrance to the tent, turned to face the group. "If what Tina said about the Visigoths last attack is true, then laying low for nine days is not a bad idea at all because I'm fairly certain we'll see another attack before nine days are out. The problem would be getting Tina to agree to lay low with us."

Charlotte considered her dad's point for a moment. "It's true. She seems pretty invested in sticking around here." She thought a moment longer. "I guess we'll have to be careful then. Maybe, as part of the work that we do for Tina, we can keep a special lookout for the Visigoths? It probably shouldn't be too hard to see a large band of raiders coming this direction, and if we do, we can always grab Tina and make a retreat to somewhere safe."

Charlotte's dad nodded. "Not too hard, no." He seemed as if he could have said something else but held it back.

Charlotte wondered if he was thinking the same thing that she was: besides the Visigoths, there was still a rogue chiclero wandering around somewhere nearby. He might be more difficult to see coming than large roving bands of raiders.

Chapter 3
THROUGH THE
LOOKING GLASS

Facade firmly held her hand over the man's mouth after she shoved him down on the spongy ground. She could not see much, but she did see that his eyes were wide in fear and he was ready to either faint or scream. She hoped for the former, but just to make sure he did not scream, she brought her face nearly up to his own and began to breathe, deeply, rhythmically, and calmingly. It was not hypnosis, exactly, but it had much the same effect. The man's breathing slowed and his eyelids lowered somewhat.

Suddenly she heard someone running straight in their direction. "Get back here, Felipe!" a voice cried out. The running abruptly stopped and Facade, looking carefully to the side, noticed someone's shoes no more than a body length away from them through the dark, misty night. The shoes shifted and then held still, allowing the owner of them to listen. She could almost see him cocking his head to an angle to catch any last sound wave heading that direction.

She knew that at any moment the boy could step in her direction, or—if he had good eyesight—simply look and see her and the man's dark forms plastered onto the ground. She quickly clasped her lips together, tightened her chest, and used her tongue to create a small sound vaguely representing a couple distant footfalls splashing lightly through water. By keeping her mouth closed, it gave the impression that the sound came from somewhere beyond them.

"Felipe!" the boy yelled, his feet turning towards the perceived sound, away from where Facade huddled on the ground.

One foot moved forward before a deep, intense voice interrupted. "Eric! Come back." The footstep stopped. "If you haven't caught him by now, he's probably still sprinting a half mile away." To Facade's relief, that was enough. The feet retraced their steps and returned to the place they came from.

Facade strained her ears to listen to the conversation taking place once the boy, Eric, returned. Eric mentioned that Felipe was now stuck, and he called him a "chiclero" . . . whatever that was. She heard some mention of finding a dry spot.

"That's our cue, chiclero," she whispered to Felipe. "Let's move before they decide that this is the dry spot they are looking for."

Felipe did not put up much resistance. The guy had just been ferried twice in one night without any warning. She could probably slap him without getting much of a response at this point. She tugged on him and then they silently made for a point in the opposite direction of the sounds of the group.

As they moved, Facade considered the unusual events of the evening. Neech had just told her to keep watch at the building with the note by the parking lot in case that third kid they were expecting showed up. Instead it was a different boy—the one called Eric—and that girl, Charlotte. The seer. Then Eric's little sister. And then, the seer's father.

Her eyes narrowed. The father made her nervous. He was large and intimidating, yes, but Facade had dealt with many of those types. No, this man was also sharp, careful, and dangerous. She would have to be extra cautious around him. Back in the parking lot, she watched him making a perimeter of the area when he and her daughter first got there. Facade had melded herself pretty neatly into a dark shadow that most would not have taken a second glance at, but the meticulous way he scouted out every nook and cranny, she was not sure she would have avoided his scrutiny. Fortunately, he discovered Eric's sister just before getting to her hiding spot, which gave Facade time to slink over to a corner that he had already checked.

"Are you a witch, girl?" Felipe suddenly whispered. He had gathered enough of his senses to finally form some words.

Facade sighed. "I'm a street magician. Now clamp that mouth shut." She found a place on the other side of the mound right before a bigger slope where they could settle in to wait out the night.

Felipe eyed her curiously. "Street magician?" He looked like he was going to ask more, but her glare cut it short. Felipe looked at the mist gloomily hovering around him for a few minutes and then finally shrugged, closed his eyes, and fell into a heavy sleep.

Facade watched him carefully. She was very uncertain about her choice. What would Neech say? But she also had very little time to figure out what to do. After the girl—Charlotte—and Eric and his sister had disappeared, the large man stepped back and looked around for a little bit, probably shocked, but his body language only showed some restrained shifting and that was all. He checked his watch and then angled around to a different position near the same spot, his hands opened, ready. After a few minutes, the whole gang materialized, just in front of where the large man stood.

This time it was Facade's turn to be shocked. They had returned with two new figures, one holding a gun to the other's head. Facade cringed, never liking violence regardless of the side it came from. To her relief, and a bit consternation by the cool effectiveness of it, the large man stepped forward and wrenched the pistol out of the hand of the man holding it as natural as picking up a penny from the ground.

After that, she saw that the person who had the gun to his head was the boy named Luke, the one that Neech had "affirmed" earlier that night. *How had Charlotte ferried to Luke's world without him there?* She assumed that Charlotte had ferried to Eric's world, or Eric's little sister's world, but clearly she had gone to Luke's world and brought him back. Facade was no expert on the seer world, but she knew most of the basics, thanks to Neech. This, however, was something new to her.

132

Facade barely had time to process this before she saw some sort of discussion. If she felt out of the loop, she at least found comfort in recognizing that nobody in that group seemed too confident about what was happening either. As the group conversed, Facade started to wonder what Neech would have to say about this. He certainly would not be pleased, that's for sure. *Would he ask me why I didn't do anything?* she wondered. Maybe.

At that moment, the seer grabbed someone's hand, then another. Facade realized that this meant a ferrying was about to take place. She had to do something. She was not sure what Neech would have wanted, but she felt fairly confident that he would criticize her for doing nothing—whether it was the smart thing or not.

Maybe I can salvage something out of this after all, she thought. She dashed out of her hiding spot and sprinted towards the group, whose hands almost all joined at this point.

Instinctively, she wanted to veer away from the big guy, but at the same time, she sensed that the man who originally held the gun could be an ally for her—whoever he was. She adjusted her direction so that she would converge with the man held by the seer's dad.

Immediately, the forms holding hands started to fizzle, and Facade's foot scraped the ground in one last push to reach them, even though she thought she missed it. The next thing she knew, she was holding the free arm of the man and everything else but the moon disappeared. Eventually, even the moon winked out.

Now, Facade watched the man sleep. "Chiclero," whatever that was, did not sound too useful. She finally found a small, angled boulder to set her back on and lightly lowered her eyelids. Her choice in coming to this world was made in a split second, but Facade at least took comfort in the fact that she had some days until the moon reciprocated. She felt determined to make back some of the gains Neech lost at that time. And it would all start in the morning, when she found the seer's group and followed them to wherever they went.

The next morning, Felipe woke with a start. "Where you goin', voodoo girl?" Felipe must have heard her walking over the mound where they slept and followed to where she currently crouched down in front of some cattails on the edge of the marshy dale where they spent the night.

"I don't answer to you, chiclero," Facade did not even turn around as her eyes scanned the small, marshy dale in front of her. "But you're welcome for saving you from that big guy who had you in a death grip."

Felipe grunted. "What is happenin' to me? Where are we, an' who are you?"

Facade still looked forward. "Don't act like you're a tough guy that deserves answers. What are you going to do, threaten me with your pistol? Oh wait, you had that ripped away from you in a matter of nanoseconds after ferrying to our world."

"Maybe I don't have my revolver, but they never did take my machete! They was too busy talkin' 'bout other stuff to check what was around my waist."

Facade heard a menacing unsheathing of something from a leather scabbard. She fingered one of the cattail plants in front of her, nonchalantly. Felipe's footsteps came within a machete-strike of her.

"Now. I'm gonna get sum answers. I'm tired o' being thrown around with some kinda magic, without any explanation a' what's been happenin'."

Facade slowly turned around. She did not even glance at the machete leveled to within inches of her chest. "There are three reasons I'm not going to listen to a word you say," she asserted. "One, the 'magic' you are talking about has to do with the moon, which is now about to set over the far horizon over there." She glanced across the marsh, and Felipe followed her gaze. "Two, the group that brought us here will be leaving any minute now that dawn has arrived."

"I still don't get number one," Felipe's glaring eyes returned from looking across the dale at the setting moon. "But what is number three?"

"Three is that your machete looks about as effective as a cattail. Now if you ever hope to get back to your own world alive, you'd better stay put until I come back and tell you what the plan is."

Shocked, Felipe looked down to see that he was, in fact, holding a cattail . . . not his machete. Before his stuttering exclamations could make it out of his mouth, Facade disappeared into the marsh, adeptly navigating through the wet landscape towards the last position she knew the group to be at.

By the time she saw the seer and her entourage making their way east next to some kind of stone channel, she secured the machete to some inside straps of her trench coat, having decided she would never see Felipe again if she could help it.

Facade kept more of a distance between her and the group than she wanted to, mainly because she noticed the seer's dad doing regular sweeps of the area all around them as they walked. When dealing with him, Facade knew that she would need to show extra caution.

That meant that when the Roman soldiers intercepted them, Facade could only witness from afar, not hearing the exchange between the two groups. Once the soldiers started escorting them down the hill, however, a lot of pressure was relieved. She knew that the soldiers would assume they caught all that would be in the group and the seer's dad would be most focused on the most immediate threat of the soldiers.

Facade watched them file into the small valley where she observed a swarm of laborers picking up and relocating large stones, working on equipment of some sort, and a dozen other things. *That's a lot of eyes that might see me,* she thought. But her consolation was that they seemed focused on their work and trusted the soldiers to keep them safe. There were also enough of them that Facade guessed that they probably did not all know each other. She looked at her clothing. The dark trench coat she wore was not normal clothing for this world, but it was far less conspicuous than the blue jeans and t-shirts that the others wore.

Facade kept an eye on the workers' camp from behind a small outcropping of rock while she tracked the escorting of the seer's group to a large, white canvassed tent somewhere in the middle, next to some dilapidated stone pillars. After a moment's reflection, she came to a realization. *I've got to listen to what they are going to talk about in that tent.*

Looking at some of the laborers nearby, Facade picked out one who stopped for a breather after fully loading his cart with large stones. He was a brute of a man, carrying a filthy tunic with a rough and light brown, hemp-looking sort of jacket covering. She slid the machete out from her trench coat and laid it to the side of one of the large stones nearby.

After a ginger approach from behind, Facade took a breath and then stepped out in front of the man, animated and rushed. She knew they would be speaking a language she did not know, so she relied heavily on her gestures. She pointed behind the man and tugged on his sleeve. Facade saw that the worker barely had time to digest that a young lady had just appeared in front of him before he found himself on his feet and following her. Once she got the man to the stone where the machete lay on the ground, he looked at the blade curiously, then at Facade and then back at the blade.

He said something that Facade would never understand. Then he started to reach for the machete and what he did after that, she never knew. Facade now found herself back at the wagon where the man originally sat. She wore his hemp-like covering over her trench coat, and she hunched over, hefting one of the smaller stones out of the wagon before making her way towards the tent where the seer's group had gone.

While walking in that direction, she was careful to act as if she were simply walking to the next gathering spot of workers, but each time she got close to them, she would then sidestep their area and make it look as if she were just leaving that group and heading for another one along the general route she wanted to take. The whole time, she hefted the stone along with her as if it were destined for a particular station and kept the hemp jacket trailing over her hunched shoulders, drooping her head so as to bring as little attention to herself as possible. No one stopped her or seemed to suspect any of her subtle movements.

In this way, she approached the tent from the same side that the seer's group had gone, hoping to get near to the entrance and see if she could hear the conversation from the outside through the canvas. However, after stepping around one of the crumbling stone pillars, she saw a large shadow sitting right at the tent entrance, beside the two soldiers guarding it. The large shadow Facade recognized as the form of the seer's dad and immediately diverted to a different path, working to the side and then towards the back end of the tent. While there was no entrance at the back end, and there were even two soldiers manning posts on either corner, she felt particularly more at ease approaching that end, especially with the knowledge that the seer's dad sat at the other side of the tent.

Carefully, Facade shuffled close by the soldiers at the back end of the tent. She went past one and noticed that he did not even give her a second glance. The heat of the day caused him to perspire underneath his helmet and he seemed lost in thought as he gazed meaninglessly out over the field of labor. Unless there was an actual invading army, Facade thought, he had seen too many workers wandering back and forth all day to give her any second thoughts. The other soldier at least glanced at her, albeit indifferently and without much scrutiny.

Facade sealed her lips and tightened her chest, throwing her voice to call out some gibberish mixed in with the din of the laborers beyond the soldier who watched her. He immediately swiveled his head over in that direction and Facade took advantage of the lapse and went low to the ground to the back flap of the tent, rolling up to it and carefully arranging the hemp jacket to look like a wad of discarded clothing.

As she hoped, her position just outside of the tent allowed her to distinguish most of the conversation happening on the inside. From her limited experience listening in on this group talking from the parking lot earlier, Facade did not recognize the voice speaking, but after a minute or so she conjectured that it was the girl that Neech had affirmed here earlier. *How did Charlotte do this? She ferried here without physically being with the girl they affirmed. Could a seer do that?*

Facade thought back on her experience with Neech. She felt that if he could have ferried without a person being with him, she would know about it. The next question was whether Neech knew it could be done. Not for the first time, Facade second-guessed her rash decision to surreptitiously ferry with the group, especially considering that she would have to accomplish a similar feat to return. She knew, if she could manage to do so, she would have plenty of questions about this seer for Neech. At the same time, she also knew that he would appreciate any of the information she gathered about the seer for him.

The discussion that she listened in on did little to address any other questions she might have about the seer. Instead the girl, who they kept calling Tina, spoke to them about her experience building an aqueduct, an attack by the Visigoths, the town council requesting her to help rebuild and gambling on sending all the available troops to guard the construction site. While it was all interesting enough, Facade had no use for this kind of talk and wondered if someone might bring up the ferrying or seer. There was a brief discussion on understanding language—basic seer stuff that even Facade knew about. How was it that Charlotte did not seem to be very familiar with it, even though she has this strange ability to ferry to someone's world without them?

Finally, after Tina left the tent, Facade knew it was time for her to go. She was lucky she had not been caught yet, and it sounded like they were not giving helpful information. As she lifted up her hemp covering to check on the status of the guards to either side of her, she suddenly heard the seer's dad mention something about being on guard for a Visigoth attack. Facade nodded internally. She had not considered it, but the man had a point. If the aqueduct workers were successfully attacked before when people were building, the Visigoths would surely attack a second time if people were rebuilding.

Charlotte's response seemed to mitigate the fear of this attack, something that Facade also agreed with. The Visigoths might attack again, but this time the soldiers seemed prepared to repel it.

Then the seer's dad responded again, this time quietly. Had Facade not possessed excellent hearing, she might have missed it, but he basically agreed with his daughter . . . but in a way that felt like he still had more concerns. *What would those concerns be? Does he know about me now? Have I given myself away?* Then she realized that, no, he was not thinking about her, but about Felipe—still loose in this world, according to them. The seer's dad did not know, like she did, that Felipe was a harmless idiot who was not worth having second thoughts about. But he did have second thoughts, because he was careful.

Facade thought for a moment. And then she smiled. Maybe this trip was not such a waste after all.

In another moment, Facade disappeared and somewhere on the edge of the laborer's camp a discarded hemp jacket lay unattended.

Chapter 4
RETALIATION

One thing that Luke liked about this whole ferrying situation was that, technically, it was all in one night—even though, between the two worlds, a couple of weeks had passed. Because of that, in the last couple of weeks (or minutes, whichever way you chose to look at it) Luke felt more purpose and worth than he had for most of his life. In his world, he was the expert and was turned to for guidance. In this one, his experience with the group led them to trust and treat him as an equal, rather than as someone who needed special attention, or worse, who was ignored because people did not know how to act around him.

That led to Charlotte's dad using Luke to make his rounds on the camp and keep an eye out for danger. Luke appreciated the skill of a natural born bodyguard because it depended a lot on body language rather than spoken communication. Mr. Reeves pointed out several assumptions just from observations of body language alone. For example, he could note the difference between laborers who had arrived recently and those who must have been with the work crew when they were attacked by the Visigoths. Those workers, he pointed out, would often unconsciously peek out to the north while working. Others, he instructed Luke, must have been recruited from the city after the attack because they kept their eyes on their work, their movements more loose and less anxious.

Then, in observing the Roman military leaders, Mr. Reeves helped Luke notice their slitted eyes and arms that either folded across chests or fingered weapons every time they crossed paths. It showed that they were unsure of how much to trust these strange foreigners—him and the others that Charlotte had ferried here—in spite of Tina's support of them.

It was that sort of careful attention to detail that led Luke to scrutinize a worker who managed to stray farther out of the way than necessary any time a Roman military detail passed by. After noticing it for the third time over the course of several hours, Luke waited until another military detail passed by and pointed out the man to Mr. Reeves. No words needed to be spoken.

Mr. Reeves put a hand approvingly on Luke's shoulder and then approached the man. The worker acted jumpy and seemed to want to look for an escape route, but something must have told him that running from Mr. Reeves would do him no good. Mr. Reeves said nothing, as it would be useless to try to communicate with him, but he did glance the worker up and down and then reached out and physically pivoted him the other direction.

Luke at first wondered what Mr. Reeves wanted the suspicious worker to see, but after a second he realized that he was not redirecting the man's gaze but inspecting his back. Luke nodded his head slowly. That was one of the things that seemed so strange about the man's actions. Any time he shuffled away from the military detail, he was always facing them, never turning his back on them.

Seconds later, Mr. Reeves lifted up the man's tunic and removed something that had been concealed there. Mr. Reeves looked it up and down, then motioned for the man to follow him and joined back up with Luke.

"Look familiar?" Mr. Reeves held the object up to Luke.

What at first glance might have looked like a normal Roman soldier weapon, was actually quite out-of-its-place in this world. "A machete," Luke muttered. "Now how did he get that?"

Mr. Reeves coaxed the agitated man towards Tina's tent. "My guess is a rogue chiclero, but we're going to find out for sure."

Luke watched the interrogation and could tell by the worker's submissive posture that he felt inclined to tell everything. As Tina passed along the information from the man, Luke and Mr. Reeves both asked her to press him again on the details. The man repeated his statement and Luke watched carefully. Nothing in his demeanor suggested that he was lying, yet his statement still did not make sense when Tina passed it along.

"You're sure you're understanding him correctly?" Mr. Reeves asked Tina.

"I don't know how this language thing works, but I'm certain I understand him. Why?"

Luke and Mr. Reeves looked at each other. "You said that it was a woman in dark clothing who took him aside to show him the machete."

Tina nodded. "That's right."

"Who is this woman, and how did she stumble across that machete?" Mr. Reeves pondered out loud.

Luke's newly heightened observations noted that Mr. Reeves's thoughtful expression indicated that this machete was only unearthing a larger suspicion growing on the bodyguard's mind.

It was a risk, but Facade needed some chaos to fix her obvious disadvantage in numbers, and if anyone could provide chaos, it would be the half-savage Visigoths themselves.

As worrisome as it was to approach the camp of the Visigoths, Facade was less perturbed by that than by the fact that she had to put up with the chiclero as they traveled together to the camp in some foothills to the north. She had no problem leaving the chiclero in that marsh until he became a permanent fixture, but her plan of chaos worked better with his participation, so she grudgingly fetched him.

Facade could tell that after being alone in a completely unfamiliar world for a day, the chiclero was relieved to see her. Still, though, he acted like he wanted to be in charge and felt as if he were at least an equal in planning out their next step in this mess.

Facade never liked to work with other people, even when she realized that it was necessary. Neech was at least good enough to give her plenty of space, but this guy constantly pestered her with questions, directions, and complaints. It was all she could do to not go back into that workers' camp, find the machete she left there, and use it to make this guy's tongue "disappear."

When they got to within view of the sentries of the camp, Facade finally turned and faced the chiclero. "Do you speak Visigoth?"

"Wha . . . ? Visigot? I doan know what is 'Visigot.' How come you—"

"Okay, so you are useless to me. Wait here while I work this out." Before the dumbfounded chiclero could protest, she stepped out into the open, arms extended as a non-threatening gesture. The sentries immediately made some sort of call and lowered some spears. Facade took a few more steps and then stopped.

"Bring your leader to me. I would like to counsel with them." She said this knowing they would not understand, but she understood that her voice would let them know her tone and attitude: she was not antagonistic, overly-aggressive, nor panicked. She was confident, open, and willing to talk.

The sentries yelled back at her something that she could not understand. She responded by repeating her first statement. This went on for a minute before one of the sentries snapped at his partner, and that one lowered his spear and ran back into camp.

Ignoring the chiclero's distant query of whether she knew what she was doing or not, Facade reached to the ground—slowly so that the sentry with his spear still extending would not feel threatened—and cleared out a space in front of her where she could use the dirt for drawing a map and explaining her purpose to the Visigoths.

A few minutes later, some noises indicated that the other sentry had some results. A small group of fierce-looking warriors, with irate looks on their faces, impatiently marched towards Facade's position.

Though this should have made her nervous, Facade immediately felt resolve. *Excellent,* she thought. *Now I just have to speak to them without speaking to them.* But Facade felt comfortable doing this. Words in the magician world were usually quite secondary. An audience does not have to hear a magician's words, they simply need to see what the magician wants them to see for greatest effect. And she wanted them to see where an attack would be most beneficial for them—which, like most magician acts, really meant that it would be most beneficial for her purposes.

While Eric, Charlotte, and Sally worked their way to the top of the hill overlooking the valley where workers below scrambled back and forth with all the urgency of ants around an ant hill, Sally made sure that the air around them did not remain empty of discussions.

" . . . but I don't think movies do enough to show just how dirty it is in the non-modern world. A little bit of actor make-up showing a bit of muck on their face doesn't really show how bad people smell and how much dust is constantly in the air or how rare bathing is for even the most sophisticated people that . . ."

Eric quickened his step so that he walked on a level with Charlotte, leaving Sally a couple steps behind him. When Eric met her eyes, Charlotte saw Eric's look of irritation caused by his sister's incessant rambling. Charlotte smiled.

"That's so true, Sally," Charlotte piped in at a rare pause where Sally must have been gathering her breath. Eric gave Charlotte a look that might have well bordered on panic as it seemed to say: *What, are you crazy?! Don't encourage her!*

"I know, right?" Sally exhaled in response, words tumbling after words as she expounded on further observations. She only stopped when they reached the lookout point at the peak of the hill where Tina stood looking through some sort of measuring instrument and discussing something with some supervisors.

They waited patiently to the side until Tina wrapped up her discussion and the supervisors individually asked questions before peeling off to their separate stations. Tina noticed her three friends and waved them closer to her.

"What are you guys up to?" she queried, good naturedly.

"Mr. Reeves and Luke were making some rounds down in the valley, so we thought we'd take some time up here and check for any movements to the north for a little bit," Eric said. "A little bit of crow's nest duty, as we'd call it on a ship."

Tina smiled. "Sounds boring to me, but you keep to your ships and I'll keep to my aqueducts."

Eric laughed. "Easier said than done! We need better access to the ocean before that could happen."

Charlotte recognized a look of contentment coming from Tina. "You seem especially pleased this morning," she said.

"I am," Tina hid nothing. "I couldn't sleep last night as I tried to consider the construction process, and I realized that I might be able to speed it up significantly."

"How's that?" Charlotte asked, even though she suspected that she may not understand the reply.

"Well, with the current gradient of the aqueduct, it's going to require a double level layer of aqueduct pillars to account for the angle of . . ." Tina must have seen the empty looks of her audience, because she adjusted. "I think I may have figured out a way to just have one set of taller arches rather than two levels, which would save months in the construction process. We'll lose some of our slope on the aqueduct channel, but I can make up for it on this end without a whole lot of time-consuming adjustments."

"That's good news," Eric said. "That will make it a lot easier to protect the work crew if they aren't going to be here as long."

"Does that mean they'll finish before we get ferried back?" Sally hopped forward. "I was really hoping to see the water running in the aqueduct before we leave."

Tina laughed good-naturedly. "It'll be faster to build, but not *that* much faster. The filling in the gaps on the arches is kind of complicated and isn't something that can really be rushed. Still, it will mean there'll be half the amount of arches to build."

Charlotte noticed Sally smile politely, though she could tell her hopes had been high. Tina must have noticed as well. "But if you're really eager to see water running in the aqueduct, then come with me. A few hundred yards down this slope, there is a small spring that they've just connected to the aqueduct. It's not much, but you will at least see how it works once water is in it."

Sally's face lit up. "That'd be great."

"Are you sure you have time?" Eric asked Tina. Charlotte could tell he suspected his sister was being a burden.

"Of course," Tina replied. "I just sent the supervisors to make initial adjustments, so it will be a while until they'll need my newer calculations. All of you can come if you want."

Eric shook his head. "I'd better keep my eye on the northern horizon."

Tina looked to Charlotte, who shrugged, "I'd better keep my eye on this guy to make sure he doesn't start any fights with any of your workers that might have eye patches and peg legs."

Tina chuckled and grabbed Sally's hand to lead her down the path of the part of the aqueduct coming from the Cordovia.

Charlotte quietly took a seat on a large rock while Eric's eyes scanned the terrain to the north. She knew that Eric had wanted to speak to her ever since they ferried to this world, and a part of her dreaded it. It was a discussion she had been purposely avoiding. So she jumped to another conversation.

"You're a natural born pirate hunter," Charlotte declared, "Not a pirate."

Eric raised his eyebrows at this out-of-the-blue statement. "Now why would you tell me that when I said I didn't need to know?"

"I want to be completely honest with you," Charlotte answered. "You deserve the truth."

Eric smiled. "It's funny that you say that, because it means that you told me the truth from the start . . . but you meant for me to doubt it."

Charlotte pushed some dirt around with her foot. "That was probably me manipulating—old seer me. I guess I just wanted to emphasize the point that the person matters more than the ability."

Eric nodded slowly. "Even if you think it was manipulative, I definitely appreciated the lesson." His foot joined hers in drawing in the dirt. "Thanks for being completely honest with me."

Charlotte waited for a bit longer. "Anything else you'd like complete honesty on?" She knew the answer but wanted to wait to hear him voice it. She did not need to wait too long.

"That talk with your dad right before we ferried here," Eric piped out all of a sudden, his eyes still on the horizon, "that means you're moving, doesn't it?"

Though Charlotte was quiet before, the silence that followed Eric's question held an ominous edge to it. Charlotte tried a couple of times to respond, but the words would not come out of her mouth. Eventually, Eric turned to look at her. Charlotte blinked hard, and then nodded.

Eric turned his face back to the north. "How far?"

Charlotte gathered herself. "Too far."

Eric nodded. Charlotte saw him pull in his lower lip. "Why?"

"My parents say that it is dangerous for me to be a young seer. They say that a lot of people who know about seeing want to take advantage of seers and use them for . . . for their own purposes, which aren't always good." Charlotte paused for a moment before continuing. "That's why, whenever I locked eyes with another seer, I was supposed to tell my parents about it and we would always move immediately—usually within a day or two."

Eric turned back to Charlotte. "That's why you moved so much growing up."

147

Charlotte nodded. "It's like I told you, though. I didn't mind. I always liked meeting new people, seeing new abilities."

"But now?"

"Now," Charlotte repeated and then fell silent. She knew Eric knew. She simply looked at him. "Now, It's different."

"But you don't have to move," Eric retorted. "You were careful. No seer saw you—you didn't look anyone in the eye."

"I know," Charlotte murmured quietly. She waited.

Eric scraped the ground with his foot. "But we are disrupting a natural bornapping. And only a seer could do that. And you've even got special seeing powers that you didn't know about, which makes you even more of a target, I guess."

Charlotte nodded.

Eric took a deep breath. "Your parents are probably right. And it's probably best for you to move." Charlotte had never disliked someone agreeing with her assessment so much.

Eric looked her in the face. "Everything you just said makes complete sense . . . but, Charlotte, I am going to fight against it anyway."

Charlotte smiled. "Thank you, friend."

Just then a boy came running up the trail on the side of the hill. Charlotte turned and saw him going straight to them. He gestured something while pointing down into the valley.

Eric looked at Charlotte and Charlotte looked back at him. "Where is body-language-reading-Luke when you need him?" Eric asked.

Charlotte reassessed the boy's face and movements. "Probably down in the valley where the boy is pointing."

Eric nodded. "Maybe they saw some hint of the Visigoths?"

The boy looked around in an effort to try to explain himself in a better way. Just then, he saw Tina and Sally, who were returning from their excursion. He went up to Tina and repeated his explanation while she nodded.

"Visigoths?" Eric asked when the boy seemed to wrap up.

"No," Tina shook her head. "Sounds like Mr. Reeves and Luke found something . . . some weapon or something . . . that they thought you might want to see."

Eric immediately stepped towards the trail leading down to the valley before stopping and turning. "You coming, Charlotte?"

"You go ahead," Charlotte waved her hand. "Maybe I'll stay up here and keep my eyes up north while you boys obsess over your little toy weapon."

Eric smiled. "I'll be back."

Sally jumped behind Eric. "I want to see it too. Wait for me!"

Charlotte could have sworn she saw Eric deliberately start to walk faster just as he heard Sally's plea.

Charlotte and Tina watched them until they disappeared around a bend. Tina took a deep breath and sat down next to Charlotte. "You and Eric seemed to be in a pretty serious discussion when Sally and I were walking back," Tina offered.

Charlotte nodded while looking to the northern horizon. "Yeah." She paused, wondering how much to share. "I'm going to be moving when we get back to our world."

"Oh," Tina replied, a little surprise in her voice. "That seems a bit sudden."

"It is," Charlotte's eyes wavered a bit. She looked over to Tina and shrugged. "Seer problems."

"That's not fun," Tina put her hand on Charlotte's back as a gesture of comfort. Then she ventured, "Did those seer problems have anything to do with those symbols you were trying to see on the temple in Luke's world but couldn't?"

"No," Charlotte said. "Though I'd love to have another look at those symbols. Maybe they could help me figure out what I'm supposed to do about all this because I feel like I could really have some direction right now."

Tina nodded. "I was actually thinking about it last night. When I couldn't sleep and I was trying to figure out how to improve the pillars for the aqueduct, I went outside to look at them and the moon came out. The moonlight on the pillars made me think of your experience looking at the wall of the temple. That's when the thought occurred to me that the reason that Eric's cell phone camera did not work was because it used the flash."

Charlotte perked up. "What do you mean?"

"When you talked about waking up and seeing the moon and being drawn over to the side of the temple, it made me wonder if there was something special about the actual *moonlight* that helped you to see the symbols."

"Right," Charlotte said. "I thought so too. That's why when the ash from the volcano eruption blocked out the moonlight, I couldn't see anything."

"So if you are using the flash on the cell phone camera to take a picture of the side of the temple," Tina submitted, "then it is no longer the moonlight but the light from the camera. The artificial light drowns out the moonlight and erases the view of the symbols."

Charlotte's eyebrows came together as she considered this idea.

Tina filled the silence with more thoughts. "Turning the flash off on the camera might have allowed you to—"

Charlotte laughed. "No flash should show the figures."

"Right," Tina affirmed.

Charlotte dug her hand into her pocket and pulled out Eric's phone, which she had held onto ever since borrowing it that night on the top of the temple. It had been turned off to conserve the battery. She turned it on now. As it turned on, Charlotte explained to Tina. "I took a photo of the temple wall without the flash because I didn't let the phone charge enough in-between snapping a photo."

"You mean . . ." Tina prompted.

"That this whole time I've had a picture of the wall without the artificial light of the flash, and I never even thought to look at it."

Tina scooted closer to look at the screen of the phone, but then a person called out some sort of title-sounding word followed by Tina's name. Charlotte and Tina both turned around, and Charlotte recognized one of the aides to the Roman military leader in charge of protecting the aqueduct workers.

The aide catapulted a flurry of words in their direction. Tina said something in return and then turned to Charlotte. "Marcus Oleas Lectorius has just captured some foreigner. I'm guessing it's the chiclero. They need my help translating because your dad is already interrogating him but the Romans don't know what they are talking about, and no one can explain to them."

Charlotte nodded. "You'd better go." She held up the phone. "I'm going to see what I can see."

Tina smiled, "Such a seer statement!" She got up to join the aide and started walking down the trail Eric and Sally had gone down several minutes earlier.

The phone was turned on by this time and Charlotte started to open the camera app, but she somehow managed to tear her eyes away from the screen for a moment. "Tina!"

Tina paused and turned around.

"Thanks for the help."

Tina waved. "I don't know how much you'll be able to see, but maybe you'll see enough to figure out a solution to all those seer problems!"

Charlotte waved back and then returned her gaze to the screen. "I don't think it can keep me from moving," she muttered to herself. Yet she could hardly focus on anything else as her finger found the most recent photo taken, the darker one that did not use the flash on the temple face. Her finger pressed on it to magnify the image into full view.

Felipe knew it was a terrible idea. The girl kept on treating him like he was some sort of annoying mongrel dog that she got stuck with and had to drag around with her, but if she would have listened to him from the start, they would never be in this mess. Who knows? he thought, he might even be back in his world and have had his revenge on the boy.

Now, however, the big man towered over him again. This time, he did not seem likely to let him escape. The fact that he was surrounded by a team of professional soldiers, and the boy—Luke—who had ruined his career, plus the other boy who knew his way around a machete and his—little sister, maybe? . . . all of them standing to the side of the large man, seemed to further solidify this point of escape being futile.

"Where have you been this whole time?" the man asked, his voice intense but bridled.

"I'm not gonna tell you. You'll have ta knock me down if you wanna get anything from me," Felipe dug in his heels. He refused to be intimidated by this large, clearly muscular, physically imposing presence with a hefty mind hidden behind those dark eyes. The thought alone caused him to try to swallow down the lump suddenly formed in his throat.

"Knocking you down is going to be the least of your worries," the man stated drily. "Now, if you want to have any hope of returning to the place where you came from, you'd better start to answer questions. Fast."

"I have no loyalties to the girl, but I'n no traitor. I'll never talk."

Luke, the boy next to him, and the man all looked at each other. The man turned back to Felipe. "What girl?"

Felipe realized his error. These guys did not yet know about the girl. He regretted mentioning her. At the same time, however, he would not be here right now if not for her stupidity.

"She's not the smartest, but she's smarter than any o' you." Felipe crossed his arms stubbornly. "She'll get me back to my world while the rest of you are either killed by the savages or taken prisoner. Either way, I'd hate to be you in the next day or so."

Just then a girl showed up that Felipe did not recognize. Whoever she was, the soldiers parted for her and the big man, Luke, the other boy, and his sister immediately turned to her. *What is with all the powerful girls in this world?* Felipe thought.

"The chiclero?" the girl asked them.

How does she know about me, but I doan know about her? Felipe thought.

Luke nodded. The big guy pointed to a soldier. "This soldier's crew found him slinking around the other side of the western hill."

The girl said something to the soldier, who then responded. She took a second longer to explain something to him. She turned back to the big guy. "They say they were patrolling in the area when they heard something slip on some rock shale and found him at the bottom of it." Felipe cringed at this retelling of his failed attempt at being furtive. The girl continued, "What else did I miss?"

"An interesting development," the big man stated. "He's here with a girl, and it sounds as if they've made some kind of deal with the Visigoths or at least know something about their movements."

Did I say anything about the Visigoths? Felipe wondered nervously. He did not remember saying anything about the Visigoths . . . maybe he said "savages" but definitely not Visigoths. Felipe felt a bit ashamed, but then anger resurged within him. This is all the girl's fault. It was her mistake to accidentally leave behind the machete at the edge of this camp, it was her idea to try to recover it in case this group found it and suspected that they were spying on them.

It could have been worse, Felipe realized. Originally the girl was going to try to recover the machete herself, but Felipe knew that she would only bungle it and get caught, so he insisted that he be the one to go retrieve it.

Granted, Felipe was now caught, but the girl would certainly have been captured quicker than he had been and undoubtedly would have not known how to keep her mouth shut as carefully as he had. That did not stop these villains from guessing a lot of information, but Felipe felt sure that the street magician (as she called herself) could not have resisted their interrogation with the fortitude that he had been showing.

"So there is going to be a Visigoth attack in the next day or two, huh?" the large man followed up.

"I didn't say that!" he cried out indignantly. How were they getting this information?!

"If this girl is so smart, then why would she convince the Visigoths to attack us after this place has clearly been fortified with an alerted troop presence?"

Felipe chuckled, in spite of himself. "I told ya she's smarter than you, and you'll believe me soon enough!"

The large man turned to Luke to see his response. Luke's eyebrows only furrowed. The other boy stepped forward at this point so that Luke could see him. "If she is that smart, then she knows that this place has been reinforced with troops. Is it possible that she found out that the troops came from the city and that the city is only guarded with a skeleton crew?"

The large man looked at Felipe, and Felipe did his best to hide his surprise.

The boy must have seen Felipe's response. He queried, "She's told the Visigoths to attack the city, hasn't she? Then, once the city is taken, they'll cut off supplies and surround this construction site and take out the workers and soldiers."

Felipe tried not to let his eyes grow wide, but he felt certain that the boy must have seen some sort of reaction because the man and Luke confirmed the boy's statement. "That's it. We need to warn the soldiers. If they hurry, they might be able to get to the city, fend off the attack, and maybe even rout the Visigoths for good."

A flurry of events set in motion. As Felipe was being moved to a place where he would be secured and tied up, he could not help but wonder if these guys were the magicians by the way they somehow guessed everything about their moves without him ever mentioning a thing.

Before the flap on the tent where he was being guarded was tied down, the large man looked in on him and said, "Next, you're going to talk to me about that girl."

Felipe knew he would never give away anything deliberately about the girl, but he also could not be sure that these guys would not be able to figure it all out anyway.

Marcus Oleas Lectorius had a hard time figuring out what was going on. First, Lady Tina shows up and feels like a gift from the gods. Then her friends show up . . . who knows from where. The next thing he knew, one of his patrols captured this pathetic-looking man who seems to have a connection to Lady Tina's friends, and after an interrogation—of which he cannot understand a single word—Lady Tina informs everyone that the Visigoths are planning an attack on Cordovia at any moment. In a whirlwind of action, Marcus managed to put together his centuria and set off on a quick march towards Cordovia, leaving only a handful of soldiers behind, and he could only hope that they would not be too late.

With only one more set of hills to cross before the slow descent into the valley where Cordovia lay, Marcus moved to the front of the column to discuss the approach to Cordovia with his subordinates. Before he could even get a word out, however, a disturbance from behind interrupted. Marcus turned to see a soldier escorting a babbling young woman toward him. The blonde hair told him that this was not Tina but one of Tina's friends, the one called Charlotte. He did not know Tina's friends well, or really interact with them much thanks to the language barrier, but he had managed to learn their names. Marcus turned around to meet the soldier and Charlotte.

"What is it?" Marcus asked.

The soldier was about to explain, but Charlotte hurriedly said something unintelligible and then gestured behind them. Marcus noticed that she was holding some kind of thin metallic-looking box. "She just keeps doing that, Sir," the soldier finally squeezed in an explanation. "I'm not sure what she's saying, but it seems like she's trying to get our attention to something behind us."

Marcus noted the gestures. "Yes, I think you're right. But why?" He caught Charlotte's eyes and saw urgency there. "What is it?" he queried, knowing full well that she could not understand him.

Charlotte made a motion of swinging a sword and pulling back a bow and arrow.

"An attack," he and the soldier said at the same time. Marcus pointed behind them. "Back at camp?"

Charlotte nodded firmly—apparently guessing their meaning.

The soldier and Marcus looked at each other. The soldier must have sensed Marcus's confusion. He stated, "I would be surprised, Sir. When we left there were no signs of any Visigoths nearby. For them to bring an attacking group out of hiding, close the distance to the construction site and attack, and then to have this girl come running to us after an attack has started . . . well, I think that puts it all too soon. It would all have to happen a half an hour later at the earliest. Plus, don't you think one of our runners left behind would have been sent and got here before she did?"

Marcus nodded. "Good points. But why is she here? I cannot believe she is trying to deceive us."

The soldier shook his head. "Maybe, maybe not. Perhaps she is confused?"

Marcus saw that Charlotte, while not following their conversation, at least caught on to their hesitation. She held up her small, metallic tablet. They both stepped back when the thing actually lit up and a strange light emitted from it. She waved her fingers above it while muttering stuff, then finally she turned it so that the light shone on them, yet she gestured into the box. Marcus, at first nervous to look into it, finally saw a sort of picture shining out of the box. In the picture were drawings showing people figures with weapons or something . . . but it was all hard to see and there were other things around it that confused him. Charlotte once again strongly gestured behind them.

"Is this some sort of witchcraft?" the soldier asked, a tremor in his voice.

"I don't know," Marcus responded. "If it is, it might explain how she might know about something in advance, like an attack."

The soldier tried to hide his trembling hand. "Then why didn't she tell us about it when we were already there with all of our soldiers? It seems suspicious that it's not until we go to stop an attack on Cordovia that she shows up and waves this mystical device hoping that we turn back." He glanced sideways at Charlotte. "Either way, Sir, witchcraft can't be good. That's the sort of thing that the Visigoths rely on."

Marcus saw Charlotte put the shining object in her pocket and then renew her insistence on something behind them. Marcus felt torn. His march to Cordovia came at the insistence of Lady Tina, after a conversation with a stranger that he understood nothing about. Next, Charlotte comes and tells them, without him understanding a single word, to turn back. He felt blind and spread out and vulnerable on all sides—without the means to have any information first hand.

"Should we just take her along with us and then check with Lady Tina afterwards?" the soldier proposed.

Marcus wavered for a moment. "No," he finally decided. "But we can't just turn our whole force around based off of this strange display either." He watched Charlotte, whose face never lost its intensity. "I can't believe she would purposely deceive us, but we need more information before we act on her appeal."

"Then that leaves us with my suggestion," the soldier reiterated.

"No," Marcus asserted. "You are going to go back to investigate. Take her with you and when you get to Lady Tina, have her interpret. Send a runner as soon as you know."

The soldier fidgeted.

"Is there a problem, soldier?" Marcus asked.

The soldier eyed Charlotte nervously. "I wouldn't want the others thinking that I was a coward and tried to get out of defending Cordovia against the Visigoths."

"Well," Marcus rejoined, "I wouldn't want to think you were a coward and were trying to get out of escorting a witch."

The soldier took a deep breath and then saluted. He tried to corral Charlotte on the path back to the construction camp. She resisted. She made one last appeal to Marcus.

Inwardly, Marcus faltered, but on the outside he shook his head firmly and motioned her to accompany the soldier. She gave him one last look of desperation, and then abruptly turned and started running back. The soldier looked at Marcus, Marcus looked at him and raised his eyebrows, and the soldier took off after his intended escort personage.

Marcus watched them go and hoped that he had not made a big mistake.

After all the troops had been gathered and set off on their march out of camp, and once the chiclero had been secured in one of the tents, Eric thought he should go to the top of the hill and give Charlotte a heads up for what was happening, since otherwise she would sit up at that post meaninglessly all day. Besides, he did not feel as if he really got to finish his conversation with her.

By the time he worked his way up the steep trail to where he had last left Charlotte, Eric was a bit out of breath. He became even more so when he saw the spot where he left Charlotte vacated.

"Charlotte?" Eric called out, tentatively, wondering if she was just around a corner or something. After no response, he decided he should just take up the spot where he left her. *She'll probably be back any minute*, he told himself.

As he sat on the promontory, looking out over the northern landscape, his mind settled into the quandary of Charlotte's imminent move. Instead of figuring out how to stop it, however, he grappled with an even more difficult realization: why did he care so much?

On the surface, Eric told himself that Charlotte was the one who brought him out of his funk, who showed him his potential when even he had given up on himself. How could he just say farewell to such a person?

But underneath, Eric knew it was more than that. In the pirate hunting world, he also had friends who brought out his excellence: Samuel, Mr. Gary, Lieutenant Curtis, and even Captain Bellview. Didn't they help him reach the confidence and inner satisfaction that he had now? Yet, when it came time to leave, though it was difficult, Eric did not have any regrets. This thing with Charlotte, though, this felt much different.

Eric could hardly get Charlotte's image out of his mind. Her voice still guided the way he saw himself and the choices he made. He always felt that vague sense of something missing any time they were apart. It was not obvious, but it loomed in the periphery of everything he did. *I don't just need her*, he considered, *it's something different than that.* It was a feeling unlike any other that he ever experienced and he struggled to voice what it might be even to just himself.

A strong wind whipped up the northern edge of the hill, drawing Eric out of his thoughts, if only momentarily. His sailor instincts pushed him to find the origin of the blast, as if he were about to give orders for setting the sails. His eyes traced the dust trail caused by the wind. *That's an awful lot of dust for a wind burst to cause*, he thought to himself.

Eric secured the origin of the dispersing dust clouds to a small bluff to the northwest. His eyes narrowed. If that bluff were a large ocean swell, it might disguise a few small ships behind it. This made him think back to the dust. If there were a significant force of people marching behind that bluff coming in from the north, it would kick up enough dust to justify the amount Eric had just seen.

But who would have a force there? They just figured out that the Visigoths were attacking Cordovia miles to the east, and all of the Roman soldiers had already left in that direction.

Unless, Eric reasoned, *unless the Visigoths were not attacking Cordovia.* Eric shook his head. That chiclero was easier to read than a treasure map—there was no way that he would have been able to fake his way into accidentally revealing the Visigoth plan of attack.

Something felt wrong, though, and it did not take long for Eric to realize why. Whenever he felt confident about something in the world of pirates, Eric realized, that is when he got outwitted by his enemies. While he still felt sure that the chiclero did not have the capacity to deceive on this level, Eric remembered him mentioning a "smart girl." *How smart was this girl?* Eric wondered. *Smart enough to trick the chiclero into believing the wrong story about the Visigoth attacks, and then smart enough to put him in the position to get caught by us, knowing that he would not be able to hold back spilling the beans about the fake attack plans?*

It seemed like a stretch, Eric admitted, and maybe he was being paranoid due to his past experience. But when in new worlds with other natural born abilities, it did not do to underestimate an opponent. Resolved, Eric suddenly stood up to race down to the camp and put out a warning, hoping he was wrong.

And if he was not wrong, hoping that he would not be too late.

Had Eric taken one more glance to the bluff in the northwest, he would have seen small black dots spilling out the southern end of it, racing to close the gap to the construction site. Had he turned around and looked down the gradual slope to the east, he would have seen two figures running in their direction. The shorter of the figures was in front and the other, dressed in a soldier's uniform, trying to catch up.

Sally stayed close to Tina, since Eric had gone wandering off somewhere. If Tina minded, she was at least good at hiding it. Still, Sally could not help but feel as if she were mostly a tag-a-long, shifting from Eric to whichever of the English-speaking group members found her least annoying.

The last thing Sally would want to do about this is complain, first of all because they really were going out of their way to be nice to her. Second of all, because she sort of forced her way into this adventure when she insisted to Mr. Reeves that she would be fine and no trouble at all. Sally wanted to find some way to be a contributor to this experience and not just a tourist.

She decided to ask Tina some questions about the situation here to see if there was anything she might be able to help figure out. After a couple of rounds of her venturing some solutions for the water problem, Sally realized she was completely out of her depth, even though she could tell that Tina was trying to validate her questions when in reality she was really dumbing it down for her.

Sally left Tina alone for a minute while the natural born aqueduct engineer took some sort of instrument and used it to gauge the progress of each pillar that was nearly ready to spread out into the arch section. Sally's gaze dropped onto the tents set up below the pillar and noticed one with four soldiers standing guard around it.

That reminded her of the conversation that she listened to between the chiclero and Mr. Reeves, Eric, and Luke. Once they learned about the attack on Cordovia, they cut the questioning with the chiclero short. But, Sally recalled, Mr. Reeves had said something about how he was going to talk to the guy about the girl next. *Well, I may not know much about aqueduct engineering,* Sally thought, *but even Eric would admit that I know how to talk! Everyone else is busy, this may be my chance to help.*

Sally mumbled something to Tina and then strolled over to the tent with the soldiers. She explained what she was doing to the soldiers, who looked at each other and then her and collectively gave up on understanding anything she said, but they did allow her to go into the tent—Sally guessed it was because they knew that she was with Mr. Reeves, who had ordered the chiclero bound and placed under guard in the tent in the first place.

After replacing the tent flap, Sally saw the chiclero tied to a chair and staring at a corner of the tent with a grumpy look on his face. He seemed to have noticed that someone had walked in, but he kept his head still.

As Sally approached his chair, she tried to think about how to go about an interrogation. She had seen plenty of movies with them, and she knew that the kind of interrogations that did not involve threats of violence usually did not just ask the questions they wanted out and out. *Okay*, Sally considered, *I'll just get him talking and see if the information slips out.*

"What is your name?" Sally ventured.

The chiclero finally looked over, probably surprised to hear the voice of a young girl. "Who are you?" he immediately queried, his inflection showing that he was genuinely curious but also not pleased by the visit.

"I'm Sally. Sally Francis. Eric is my brother . . . I don't know if you remember him, but he is one of the boys in our group, the one that—" Sally paused. Whoops. She was supposed to get him talking. This would maybe be harder than she thought. "But what about your group?"

"My group?" the chiclero responded. "You took me from my land after ruining my future. I have no group. But if you take me back to the magician girl, she promised to take me back. If all goes well, I'll bring the boy who ruined me. I'll save room for you too, girl."

His gravelly, irritated threat caused Sally to remember how this was the guy that jumped out of nowhere to hold Luke at gunpoint, and she now started to second-guess her idea of coming to interrogate him.

"Magician girl?" she followed up, trying to sound firm, like a tough cop in the movies, but her shaky voice betrayed her.

Sally never caught the chiclero's response since they both heard a commotion burst out from beyond the tent. Someone was yelling from a distance and Sally could hear the scraping of feet moving rapidly across the ground. If she was nervous before, she bordered on panicky now.

"What's that?" the chiclero spat out. "Go find out what's wrong. Maybe your soldier friends going to town got beat back already."

Sally began to edge towards the tent flap, but then she stopped. Why was he trying to get rid of her? When there was a distraction during interrogations in TV shows or movies, it usually led to the prisoner's escape because someone went to investigate. She tried to suppress this idea because she felt super uncomfortable and wanted to leave. She moved another step towards the tent flap. She reached her hand out towards the flap and then stopped.

Something in the back of Sally's mind saw Eric sighing and saying she should have just stayed home like he had said from the beginning. She turned around. "Don't change the subject," she asserted, her voice still shaking. "We were talking about the magician girl."

"You really not gonna check outside, girl?" The chiclero looked confused.

He's putting on an act, Sally told herself. *Don't fall for it*. "How do you know she is a magician?"

The chiclero went quiet for a long moment, staring intently at the closed tent flap. The commotion outside seemed to abruptly die off and an eerie silence settled over the immediate surrounding. Finally, he turned his attention back to Sally. "Girl, you are in way over your head."

With the noises gone, Sally wondered if the danger had passed, in spite of the eeriness of the silence. She gained some new, albeit unstable, confidence and locked her gaze back with the chiclero's. "If I'm in way over my head, then how come you're the one tied to a chair?"

It was a great line, and Sally wished someone had been there to appreciate it, but suddenly she felt a literal rumbling pounding the ground and penetrating into her chest. Too shocked to move, she instead sensed the sound overwhelm the tent in a mass of frenetic, barbaric cries and unnatural screams that bore a pit deep into her stomach. The noises seemed to come from everywhere all at once, so it was hard to tell how imminent the danger was, but then suddenly some noises separated themselves from the tide of general tumult, and Sally noted specific stamping feet sounds gathering around the tent they were in. Then she saw the shadows of a pair of feet working their way around the tent to the entrance.

Sally did not know what was happening, but she did know one thing. She should have listened to the blasted chiclero.

Chapter 5

NEGOTIATING
ROCKY TERRAIN

Sally's Scribblings

Well, Eric, I've been wanting you to read my Scribblings Diary forever, and now I guess I finally figured out how to do it. In hindsight, though, I really should've just bugged you to read it until you finally did, instead of getting kidnapped and being forced to write the ransom note in my diary!

So, yeah, that's my way of saying that I'm with the chiclero and the girl he was talking about. The girl is in charge and she's making me write this so that you know that I'm okay. I am. I'd be lying if I didn't say I freaked out a couple of times since they took me away from the work site back to the Visigoth camp. But now that a day has passed, I've been able to calm down a bit. The girl is not too talkative, but she definitely is not like a crazy-bad-guy-villain person. She does creep me out a little bit, but I'm not sure how much she'll let me write so I'll just stop there. Anyway, they are not hurting me at all or anything. I guess they wouldn't let me write about it if they were, but I would find a way to leave a secret message in my writing to tell you the truth, but I haven't done that so that's how you know that I really am okay.

The girl is giving me a look like, "I just told you to write a simple message, how could you possibly be writing so much?" I think she has no appreciation for setting the tone when you are writing about something. But I'd better get to the point. The girl is holding me to make sure that she and the chiclero will get back to our world when it is time to ferry. She says that she will release me back to you guys only if Charlotte includes both of them in the ferrying, and only if we leave Tina here, and only after you take Luke and the chiclero back to their worlds, since that was the original purpose of her boss, who must be the natural bornapper that Eric met and that originally sent Tina and Luke to their worlds. Yeah, she has a lot of demands. I don't know why she's surprised that it is taking so long to write them all down!

Oh yeah, and she also doesn't want you to share this with Charlotte's dad because she doesn't want him to ferry back either. So she wants you to sneak off when the moon reciprocates so Charlotte's dad doesn't come with. She's pretty insistent about that one. I think she is kind of nervous about him. I have my opinions about what you guys should do about all of this, but I don't think she wants me to write them, so I'll just let you guess.

Okay, I'd better end here. I know I should be brave, and I'm trying to write like I am, but I'm starting to panic a little bit. I just want everything to be okay and back the way it was. I'm so sorry that I left Tina to go to that blasted tent with that blasted chiclero. I'm sure you'll figure out how to fix this all. See you soon . . . I hope!

Facade did not want to be the one to deliver the diary. The less these guys knew about her, the better. But after the last fiasco with the chiclero, she did not want to risk having this messed up. This was her only ticket out of here, and possibly her way into fixing this whole situation. She could not afford an incompetent chiclero bumbling his way into another screw up.

Perhaps the most disconcerting thing was that she did not know exactly how the chiclero screwed it up. She was careful to keep all the vital information away from him, and clearly her plan worked to some degree because the Roman troops had momentarily cleared out of the aqueduct construction area. Yet, somehow, someone figured out the plan because those left at the construction site had received a last-minute warning and retreated before the Visigoths arrived, and the soldiers ended up coming back a lot quicker than she would have expected. Though Facade's original intent was to nab the seer in the confusion, she figured she was lucky to find the girl, who apparently was not supposed to be where she was.

Now, nearing noon on the next day, as Facade watched the expression of Sally's brother, Eric, and Charlotte as they read the diary together, she wondered if she had somehow stumbled across an even better alternative. If Facade had just managed to grab Charlotte, as she first hoped, the seer may not have been willing to cooperate with the plan of just ferrying her and the chiclero back. Now, with Eric's sister as leverage, Facade wondered if she just might be able to get everything she needed.

Facade kept an eye on the trail down to the workers camp. She waited all morning to find Charlotte or Eric alone. The last thing she wanted was for Charlotte's dad to be anywhere near when she delivered the diary. "If you can agree to those terms," she said when it was clear that they finally finished reading the note, "then we will meet at the swamp on the day of reciprocation."

"We're not leaving anyone behind—not my dad, not Eric's sister, not Tina. Not even the chiclero or you for that matter," Charlotte stated firmly.

Facade could tell that Charlotte was determined. That hardened Facade's resolve. "Look, I'm not here to threaten—I don't even have anything personally against you—but I will tell you this: I will do whatever is necessary," Facade made sure to harden her gaze with Charlotte, "—whatever is necessary—to complete my task. If you want Sally to go home safely, then you will meet these demands."

Eric stepped forward and put his hand out, as if to assure Charlotte that he had this. "She looks pretty serious, Charlotte. I can't let anything happen to Sally. Let's just agree to her terms. The rest of them will be fine here in this world."

Facade saw Charlotte look at Eric curiously. If Eric returned any message in his glance back at her, Facade did not see it.

Eric turned back towards Facade. "You just go and tell my little sister that we're going to take her home."

Eyeing Eric carefully, Facade took a couple of steps backward. Then, she stopped. "Eric, I don't know what your natural born ability is, but if you think that you are going to be able to follow me back to where your sister is, then you do not understand the extent of *my* natural born ability."

Then Facade disappeared.

At least, that is what she hoped it looked like. Illusions are a lot more complicated and a lot more work than people might think. For instance, the three seconds that it took for her to disappear included no less than six individual steps, each of which had been meticulously thought out and practiced beforehand.

Step one. Facade took the handkerchief of chalky dust out of her trench coat pocket and tossed it forcefully to the ground, creating an explosion of dust. That seemingly simple maneuver was the hardest one in the whole illusion. She had a difficult time finding the right kind of dust that would shoot upward after tossing it to the ground and linger long enough to give her a smokescreen for her next steps. Eventually, she found she had to take some fine sediment from a nearly dry creek bed and grind it to an even finer batch of dust with a hefty, round rock. Once she had it ground to the proper consistency, she found that she still had to mix it with some gravelly material so that it would have better heft when she threw it. Finally, she had to practice the throw dozens of times, even though it meant more and more grinding to replace the used up dust. She knew if she could not get this right, someone could easily see through the illusion, and nothing could be worse for a street magician than to not have the confidence that their audience is being deceived. So she practiced time and time again until she figured out just how hard to throw the cloth-shelled dust bomb and how to hold the handkerchief so that it would come apart just right upon impact with the ground. That was all step one.

Step Two. While in the cloud of dust, reverse the trench coat. Her dark trench coat makes for a great cover at night, but during the middle of the day, it made her fairly easy to spot in this bright and dusty landscape. So she took the inside of her trench coat and smeared it with a mixture of water, clay, and dust from the same creek bed where she made the dust bomb. When the compound dried, it gave the inside of her trench coat a very earthy look that matched the surrounding terrain impeccably. Then, by perfecting the move where she ducked under her trench coat and then gripped the ends of her sleeves while she flipped the coat inside out, it managed to convert her from being the conspicuous person in the dark coat to being able to blend in with any place on the ground.

Step Three. Take two steps in the wrong direction. As Facade had said, she was unsure of what Eric's natural born ability was, but he certainly did not seem like an amateur. Illusions often have strong initial effects but a smart person can deconstruct them using clues afterwards. Facade would be hiding within plain sight and she did not need two curious people snooping around by her hiding spot. So, she took two steps in the wrong direction. She made sure that her two steps in the wrong direction went back towards the path she used to get up the hill. That would make her old tracks easier to confuse as new tracks and keep the two occupied along that path, giving her time to make a retreat along an entirely new route and complete the deception.

Step Four. Catapult herself backwards to a new hiding spot. When she practiced this, she did not know what the lay of the land would be when she met with Charlotte and Eric, so she prepared herself for multiple possibilities. When she did find Charlotte and Eric, Facade made sure to position herself in a place that would give her the greatest maneuverability for her deception. The rock where the two sat before she approached them was ideal for her purpose, so she made sure to stay close to it after they stood up to accept Sally's Diary as she handed it over to them. Being that close to the rock made her backwards leap within the cloud of dust simple and difficult to detect.

Step Five. Cover herself with the reversed trench coat. Once she burrowed tightly in-between the ground and the rock, she allowed the reversed trench coat to settle down on top of her. Even this simple step was not without careful thought. She knew that she should make her body form as bumpy and irregular as the rock she hid by, so she used her hands and legs to have angular protrusions to match as close as possible the surface of the rock. Facade knew that the human eye could catch any small shape that seemed to not fit naturally within the landscape, and she wanted to eliminate as many possibilities as she could.

Step Six. Wait. This is perhaps the most mentally difficult, but the most important step in any illusion. Having patience when you are afraid someone has or will have discovered your deception is supremely difficult, but it is essential for ultimately consummating the deception. The audience needs to settle into the new reality you have created, since they will be warily expecting another shoe to drop at any moment. Facade had to trust that her efforts were not in vain and hold her breath while Charlotte and Eric, two very savvy observers, tried to figure out what had just happened.

Her efforts were not in vain.

"Where'd she go!" Facade heard Eric jump down from where he stood and scrape around.

"She's a street magician, Eric," Charlotte piped out. "She's naturally born to disappear."

"Great," Eric mumbled. "But even still, it's an act, right? She didn't disappear for real." Facade knew that this would probably be the most crucial moment. A second later, Eric followed up by saying, "It looks like she might've gone back down the trail where she came from."

Facade could hear scraping and movement, but they emanated from below her on the hill. She hoped that they would continue to look in that direction. She kept her breathing shallow and held as still as possible.

"Do you think Luke has skills as a tracker?" Eric asked. "I could follow a boat through shoal-infested waters, but all this tracks-on-the-ground stuff is pointless to me."

"Maybe," Charlotte responded, but her voice failed to denote a lot of confidence. "Probably he's mainly trained for finding chicle trees, which I doubt make a lot of tracks."

"What about your dad?" Eric followed up. It sounded as if he had stopped searching the ground. Facade hoped they would go ask Charlotte's dad, giving her the space she needed to complete her retreat.

"Basic observational skills," Charlotte said, "but he's more about protecting than hunting."

Protector, Facade thought, *that explains something about him. But what kind of protector? The guy feels more dangerous than a simple night watchman or something like that.*

Silence settled in as Eric and Charlotte thought through their predicament. Facade wanted to shift her uncomfortable position, but she knew that stillness at this point was essential.

"Was Facade right? Were you just hoping to follow her back to Sally?" Charlotte asked.

"Yes. To recover you when you got captured by the Willard Pirate Twins, I had to come up with a complicated plan, but I could do it because I knew where you were. I figured I would just find out where Sally was and then come up with a plan from there." Eric paused. "It may not be that easy if Facade is expecting it, however."

"We know where she will be in nine days. And we know that she can't get back without me," Charlotte observed. "We don't know how desperate she is to get her way. Who is she? How dangerous is she?"

Facade wanted to assure them that she could be as dangerous as she needed to be. She held her tongue.

"She's dangerous enough to not think twice about using someone's innocent little sister as leverage to get what she wants," Eric replied bitterly. "Which means that you're right. I shouldn't try finding her and spooking her into doing something rash when we'll see her in nine days anyway." A pause. "Still, I don't care what we do, but I *will* get Sally back. I never should have let her come in the first place."

"There is a real simple way to get Sally back," Charlotte ventured.

"How?"

"Submit to the girl's demands."

Facade somehow kept herself from nodding in agreement, but she liked where this conversation headed.

"Impossible!" Eric said. "I don't care how dangerous she is, we are not natural bornappers. Leaving Tina and Luke in their worlds—and your dad especially—might as well be murder in our world."

Murder? Ridiculous, Facade thought. *They will be alive and well.* It was difficult for her to hold still while someone made silly comments like that one. Then, she

"I don't know how we're going to get Sally back, but we will, and submitting to the girl's demands is not going to be how we do," Eric asserted after another moment's pause.

171

"I'm not so sure," Charlotte said quietly after a moment. "Come on, we've got to think this through and figure out exactly what our options are."

Then Facade heard the shuffling of steps retreating past the rock and over the crest of the hill towards the path that would take them down to the worker's camp.

Facade knew better than to remove herself from her hiding spot earlier than necessary. She worked too hard to be caught by stepping out from underneath her trench coat just as one of them came running back because they forgot something. She would wait long enough to make sure that they were a good distance away but also before they could bring someone like Charlotte's dad back to investigate.

That gave Facade more time to think than she was comfortable with. The seer girl, Charlotte, seemed to have a practical head on her shoulders, and it was promising that she seemed willing to consider caving to all of Facade's demands. However, there was something about her final statement that made Facade unsure of Charlotte's compliance.

As someone well-versed in deception, Facade felt that Charlotte was up to something. She wanted to be prepared for whatever that was. On her walk back to camp, she would have a lot to think about.

After sending out his scouting patrols and getting messages back from Cordovia, Marcus Oleas Lectorius took some time to really survey the damage done to the aqueduct construction site yesterday by the Visigoths before he was able to arrive with the troops to scatter them. The destruction was complete and utter. No two stones stood one upon the other. The scaffolding lay in complete disarray. Tools not taken in flight were bent, disfigured, wrung apart. The first attack was crippling. This one? This one was strangling.

Still, he had to recognize the positive: as far as they knew, not one person was killed, something that surely must have frustrated the Visigoths, who delighted in gruesome and violent deaths. The little girl had been taken, so it was possible the Visigoths took her to torture and then kill her, but Marcus found it unlikely that they would show that kind of restraint in the midst of a raid. More likely, they kept her alive for some purpose such as a ransom, bargaining chip, or for information (which, seeing as how she did not speak any language they would recognize, would be fairly useless).

But what was the next step? Rebuilding what they lost, for the second time in just a span of a few days, seemed too heavy a burden for any of the laborers to conceive. Marcus mulled on the gloomy possibilities as he scanned the scene before him. Suddenly, he spotted Lady Tina sitting on one of the strewn stones and staring despondently out into nothing. She had avoided him most of the day after the soldiers had driven off the Visigoths, and all this morning she was nowhere to be seen.

Marcus took some determined steps towards her. Whatever their next step would be, Marcus knew that it should involve her.

"Lady Tina," Marcus voiced once he was within range. Tina's head barely moved. "Lady Tina, I know it must be difficult to see your hard work undone, but I hope that you are not despairing." No response. Marcus shifted uncomfortably. "Projects like these often run into multiple setbacks and—"

"Rome wasn't built in a day," Tina threw out, still not looking back at Marcus.

" . . . Well, yes, that's true. Rome wasn't built in a day." Marcus confirmed, caught a little off guard by its cleverness but also wary by the bitter tone he detected in her voice.

After another pause, Marcus decided to charge forward. "Perhaps we can leave Cordovia and move south for the time being. I will take you with me. When Rome sends reinforcements, we can come back and finish this job without having to worry about attacks on either the aqueduct site or

Cordovia." Still no response. "Or perhaps I can take you to some other sites that could use your expertise. We were maybe too ambitious with the Cordovian Aqueduct."

"Rome wasn't built in a day," Tina finally announced with her face still looking outward, "but by some chance was it built in eight days?"

"Well . . . no," Marcus had to admit, bemused.

"Then that doesn't do me much good."

Marcus thought he saw Tina take her hands to her cheeks and wipe.

The centurion shook his head sadly. He just about followed up when one of the leaders of a patrol he sent out hailed him as they returned back to the main camp. He gave Tina another look and decided that she just needed some time before she would be able to think clearly.

He went to discuss the patrol leader's findings and gave some follow up orders before there were a dozen other tasks brought to him by other soldiers reporting on the situation and needing guidance with some issue or other. All afternoon, he kept an eye on Tina. She never moved from her spot.

By the time evening came, Marcus had finally arranged their main camp so that the laborers were all accounted for, guards were set, and the area felt secure. He entered his tent. *Tomorrow,* he thought as he reviewed all of the day's events, *we're going to have to go tell Cordovia that they will need to evacuate as we will not be able to complete their aqueduct.* He thought of Tina sitting alone outside all day. *Tomorrow, I'll tell Tina the plan and convince her to join us.*

Decided, Marcus turned around to pull down his tent flap just as twilight creeped across the sky, but he halted. There in the doorway to his tent stood the boy named Eric. Seeing him reminded Marcus of another loose end. The girl Charlotte. Hopefully tomorrow Tina would feel up to translating a discussion with Charlotte about how she knew what she did and what that magical object was that she held . . . but, one thing at a time. The more Marcus thought about that strange occurrence, the more confusing everything else became.

174

So instead he watched as Eric made signs that seemed to be inquiring as to the direction of the Visigoth camp. Marcus had a fairly good idea of where they were, and one of his returning patrols seemed to confirm it to him, so he pointed out directions as best he could, including some landmarks and distance as best and gestures could convey. Eric seemed to comprehend and then left.

Marcus watched his shadow dissolve into the night. Just one more mystery that Marcus felt unsure he would ever uncover.

Charlotte awoke with a start. The moon was out. She could tell by the slight luminescence seeping through the tent canvas. Also, she could just tell when the moon was out because of who she was.

She distinguished the sounds of movement outside, making its way towards the tent. Something felt wrong. She looked across the tent to the other cots. Quite a few of them lay empty. She knew that Tina had been sitting outside inconsolably for most of the day and had never come into the tent to sleep. Charlotte's dad was probably making the rounds as he often did throughout the night. But Luke's cot held no one. So did Eric's. What was happening?

The noises outside came nearer. Charlotte stood up just in time to see her father open the tent flap and come inside, someone trailing behind him. Her father saw her awake, gave the look of a concerned parent, and then he put his large hand on her shoulder. "He slipped away while I was making my perimeter. He knew my routine and waited for the right moment."

"Luke or Eric?" Charlotte asked.

"Not Luke. He's been sitting with Tina for the past little while."

Charlotte thought things through while speaking out loud. "But Eric told me that he didn't think it would be helpful to try to find out where—"

Charlotte's dad stepped aside and revealed a delicate Sally standing behind him. Though Sally seemed unsure of what kind of reception to expect, Charlotte immediately embraced her so fiercely that Sally had to catch her breath.

Had Charlotte been asked to explain her emotions at that moment, she would have been speechless. Her hug was definitely one of relief at finding Sally safe, but also all the emotions of Eric being missing left other untapped, worrisome details yet to be revealed. The hug delayed them only for a moment.

"Is he . . . okay?" Charlotte finally asked Sally while constructing in her mind what must have happened.

Sally, strangely quiet, nodded. She pulled out her diary, something Eric and Charlotte had been holding and reading just that afternoon. Sally opened it to the page following the one with her message to them, and Charlotte noticed that it had new writing on it.

Dreading the message, but knowing she had to read it, Charlotte scoured the words found there.

Dear Charlotte,

Maybe if we'd talked more, we could've figured something better out, but every moment I did nothing was a moment Sally was left alone and scared, and I just couldn't take the thought of it for another minute, let alone nine days. I'm not that bad of a brother! I just had to do something, and I couldn't let you talk me out of it, so I went for it. Luckily, the street magician girl agreed to let me write a note to explain to you (and to repeat her previous terms . . . but I'm guessing you didn't forget about those), and since I brought Sally's diary with me, I felt like this would work as well as anything for writing to you.

Basically, I figured you were right about not doing anything immediately to try and rescue Sally with some complicated plan since it *more than likely would just put her (or our friends) in harm's way. But then I wondered if I could do something simple, like just offer myself up in exchange for Sally. If I went alone and managed to get myself captured by the Visigoths, they would find a way to get me to the street magician and Sally. If the exchange worked, great. If not, well then, at least Sally wouldn't be alone anymore.*

And . . . it worked. The magician, who calls herself "Facade" agreed to my exchange and even said she would take Sally to within sight of our camp and release her as a sign of how she can be true to her word. If you got this note from Sally, that is exactly what happened.

I'll see you in nine days . . . maybe eight by the time you get this. Thanks for taking care of Sally, and I'm sorry I left a bit early. Partially because of the circumstances, but mainly because if you're moving when I get back, I want to cherish every moment I get with you. But at the same time, if you're moving either way, maybe this is better than a drawn out goodbye and if something goes wrong—well, it wouldn't change much anyway. Just know that no matter what, I will be okay. I've thought about and accepted the worst that could happen.

Charlotte looked up and saw Sally crying. Then she realized that she was crying. She hugged Sally again, then she felt the large arms of her father envelop the two of them and hold them both.

Tina was not sure how long Luke had been sitting near her. Because he sat down just behind and to the side of her and made no noise, he could have been there for hours or minutes. All she knew was that the sun had set a while back and at one point when she wiped a tear off her cheek she turned her head enough to see him patiently waiting, respectfully looking in the opposite direction, but clearly demonstrating his support by his mere presence. She wiped her other cheek and then turned around to face him. Luke detected her movement and turned in her direction as well.

Though she had not been prepared to discuss her predicament earlier with Marcus or even Charlotte and Eric who had both briefly come to comfort her earlier in the day, she suddenly felt the need to talk.

"Whenever I run into a problem at school, I usually get out the syllabus, reread the course objective and grading parts of it, and then ask myself how to use that to work around my problem. You know?"

Luke did not answer. He did not even respond. He simply sat and watched her, his face covered in the shadows of night, but his glinting eyes clearly fixed on her and paying attention. Tina realized that she must feel comfortable talking to Luke because the lack of daylight made it so that he probably could not understand anything she said. She would get to unload herself to another person face-to-face, but not have to be worried about being ashamed of her feelings.

Encouraged, Tina continued. "But there is no syllabus in this course. There is no teacher for me to talk to and say, 'Hey, it's not fair that the Visigoths ruined the aqueduct. I'm a natural born aqueduct engineer not war strategist.' Before, I always had control over getting my 4.0 one way or another, but now it's like my 4.0 has been busted—unfairly—and all my work was for nothing. It's like I just lost my dream job as an international lawyer because of this one stupid little mistake. And what's the point in anything anymore if my dream has fallen apart so easily when it seemed so invincible?"

Luke shifted, but said nothing.

Tina found that she had involuntarily caught her voice a couple of times at the end of the last monologue, so she got ahold of herself. "I don't even know what I'm talking about any more. Am I talking about scholarships and grades or aqueducts? I just feel like a failure for the first time in my life . . . I mean, a complete failure. And it scares me. I've been scared of failing . . . well, not even failing . . . I've been scared to death of getting an A minus since I've been getting grades, but I was so good at controlling my grades that I insulated myself against any thoughts of failure. Until now."

Tina shook her head. "And the worst part is, I mean the part that really hits me while I'm down, is that my failure led to Sally being lost and Eric being hurt and—" she momentarily faltered, "—and I not only have to suffer this failure myself, but my friends are punished by it too." Tina's voice lowered. "I couldn't even tell Eric I was sorry when he came to make me feel better. *He* came to help *me* feel better. And I was so ashamed by my failure that I couldn't express how horrified I was that his sister got taken. I couldn't find the words to tell him that I knew it was my fault, that I knew I screwed up."

More tears fell. "I just need to read the syllabus again or talk to the teacher or principal or someone. I just need . . . I don't know. I don't know what I need anymore." Then Tina sobbed.

And finally Luke scooted to the stone next to her and put his arm around her. He said nothing, but Tina turned into him and cried for a long time. Finally, exhausted, she fell asleep, and he carried her into the tent and onto her cot.

Chapter 6
UNDER PRESSURE

Do you want to know the real reason that I agreed to your exchange?"

Eric had to admit that he felt baffled by the move, but he managed to keep quiet about it. Interested in better hearing Facade's explanation, Eric shifted uncomfortably on the rock floor of the hollow within a butte where Facade had secreted him. He found that, with his feet bound together by some Visigoth cords, the move only made him more uncomfortable, and he regretted the extra effort.

"I was suspicious of your offer," Facade continued, "but after thinking it over, I realized that you were one of the wildcards that I could not account for. And now, all of a sudden, the Visigoths bring you to me."

Eric swallowed the last of the bitter-tasting bread-like substance Facade had brought him to eat.

"Do I trust your explanation that you just wanted your sister safe, regardless of what Charlotte chooses to do?" Facade's eyes narrowed. "No. Absolutely not."

Eric thought about protesting, but he realized that he would feel the same in her position.

"But, if I can take one of the wildcards against me and tuck it up my own sleeve," Facade motioned towards the sleeve of her trench coat, "then I don't have to worry about it being hidden in the deck or someone else's hand to come against me when I least expect it."

"Then why return my sister?" Eric asked, not sure why Facade initiated this conversation. From the very little he knew about her, he could already sense how dangerous her mind was—clearly an astute person who had already used deception and misinformation to throw them off and nearly get them all captured or killed by the raiding Visigoths. Still, if she was going to talk, Eric thought, he could at least make sure she was not in complete control of the conversation. "I had no leverage when the Visigoths brought me to you. You easily could have kept both of us."

"True," Facade noted. "And I instinctively wanted to hang on to both of you." She looked away momentarily. "But Charlotte's incentive to follow my demands would not be any stronger with me holding both of you. And I am not the type that likes to babysit a large group of people. It's hard to keep them from communicating and plotting. It's so much easier to control your audience when there is only one perspective to account for."

Eric could tell that Facade was doing more than just talking. She was reading him as she spoke. He tried his best to make his face as unreadable as possible. "So, I knew it wouldn't hurt for me to take Sally back with your note in order to show that I can follow through with promises," Facade concluded.

"To at least *give the impression* that you can follow through with promises," Eric corrected.

Facade shrugged. "Maybe she believes it, maybe she doesn't. I've dropped off Sally and removed you to a location that nobody knows—not Sally, not even the Visigoths. Through this exchange, I've minimized excess baggage, and I think I've come out ahead of where I was with the possibility of even bigger advantages later on."

Now that Eric had finished eating, Facade made him put his hands behind his back and she lithely secured his hands behind him with a complicated series of knots that only a magician would know to make inescapable.

"Speaking of wildcards," Facade said while working her way back around to face him. "Tell me about the quiet boy in your group."

"Luke?" Eric asked, then immediately regretted using his name.

"I guess so. Is that what he's called?"

Eric thought about it for a moment. "But you already knew that, didn't you? If you work for this natural bornapper, then you were aware of who Luke was before we even got here."

Facade eyed Eric carefully. "My associate does not share information very freely. I just do as I'm told. But now that I'm in this situation, I would like to learn a little more about this Luke person."

"I can tell you that you don't want to cross him. Ask your chiclero friend."

"He's not my friend," Facade dryly noted. "I left him with the Visigoths. He still thinks I'll be back for him when the moon reciprocates."

"He was friend enough to you when you convinced him to get in a position to be caught and relay bad information without his even being aware of it," Eric tested out his previous theory.

Facade smiled. "Even some of the best tricks can't be hidden from some of the most skeptical audience members." Facade paused. "What about my other wildcard?

Eric could tell she was hoping to see who *he* thought the wildcards were. That would let her know how much he knew that she knew. His mind started to twist. Maybe he should not continue this conversation, but instead he simply averted. "Which one?"

"The seer's dad," Facade clarified.

"I think you might not want to cross him even more than Luke," Eric stated.

"He doesn't seem that dangerous," Facade coolly flicked at a fly meandering between them. "Mostly muscles without a lot of thinking power behind them. Must be in the genes, too, because his daughter seems pretty ignorant of how to be a seer."

"Ignorant?" Eric smoldered indignantly, "Charlotte is so 'ignorant' of a seer that she saw your plan with the fake Visigoth attack and foiled it."

Facade's eyebrows rose. "'Saw' it? Are you telling me that not only can this airhead girlfriend of yours ferry to a world without having the person with her, but she can also see into the future?"

Eric went quiet and immediately felt ashamed. Facade had managed to make him angry and let down his guard. "I never said she could see into the future or ferry without the person with her." Even Eric had to admit that his own defense sounded weak.

Facade rolled her eyes. "You're a lot better at playing the would-be boyfriend than the dumb tag-a-long."

Eric tightened. "Anything else you want to ask that I'll refuse to answer?"

"Oh, you've answered perfectly," Facade's eyes locked on his. "But now that you're asking, I'll put one more question to you. Is your natural born ability to be useless? Because that is what you are to your group right now."

"I'm not—" Eric started and then stopped. How did she manage to tap into his old fears so capably? He wanted to deny it and prove to her otherwise, but he knew that would mean she was getting more information, which was exactly what she wanted. Eric felt rattled, a feeling that reminded him of the sound of the blocks and tackle when a ship stood "in irons," stuck in the wind.

This thought immediately helped Eric reframe his situation. Right now, Facade had the weather gage on him in this conversation. It was time to bring the ship about and try resetting the sails from a new angle. He realized that might mean disengaging until a change in the wind direction.

"I'm tired," Eric finally announced. "I'm going to sleep." He awkwardly slid onto his side and closed his eyes until hearing Facade quietly stand up and leave.

HOW TO BECOME A **SEER**

Tina found Luke outside the tent early the next morning. She walked around so that she could face him. "Couldn't sleep?"

He shook his head.

"Am I the reason?" she ventured.

"Yes," he replied. "That and the fact that Eric's bed is empty but Sally is back."

"What?!" Tina said. She made as if to walk back to the tent.

"I'm guessing they will tell us when they wake up," Luke held his hand up to make her pause. "They look like they could use the rest."

Tina's eyebrows lifted. "How can you be so patient with such big news just waiting to be told?"

Luke shrugged. "I guess I'm used to being left out of most big news updates. Usually, if it is important enough, I find out eventually."

Tina turned her back on the tent once more. "Speaking of being left out. How much of my talking could you even pick up last night?"

"Not much of the talking."

Tina caught the implication that Luke did not need to hear what she said to understand the general takeaway of her emotional state. "I don't think I would have told my parents, my best friends—anyone really—what I told you last night."

Luke nodded. "I don't know exactly what you're going through, Tina, but I get the feeling that we've both experienced a lot of the same emotions recently."

Recalling the circumstances recounted of the world of chicleros, Tina began to make some previously unnoticed connections. "How low were you before you got ferried to the world of chicleros?" she asked.

Gazing outwards for a moment before looking at Tina, Luke said, "Low."

"When you decided to face the jaguar without a machete . . . ?"

"I was prepared for either result," Luke confirmed.

Tina trembled. "I got low most of yesterday. Really low."

"I know."

"What got you out of it?" Tina asked, "Defeating the jaguar?" She waited, nervous for the answer, but desperate to hear it.

"No," Luke said after a moment's hesitation. Then he clarified: "When I was under pressure from the jaguar and felt alone, I realized that I never really was alone. My parents were there, Eric and Charlotte were there. In that moment of pressure, I realized that no matter how many times I failed, I still had people who believed in me. That got me out of my low. And that is what helped me beat the jaguar—not the other way around."

Tina looked at the scattered stones all around her, the markings of her defeat. She noticed the stone she sat on all of yesterday, where she had wallowed in her failure and questioned her life's direction . . . but right next to it she recognized the stone where Luke sat quietly next to her for who knows how long without her realizing it. She felt so alone and lost late into the night yesterday, but she was not. She then recalled Marcus, Charlotte, and Eric all trying to lift her up and care for her since the attack, even if she did not want to hear it.

Tina found Luke's eyes once more. "Thanks for not letting me be alone."

Luke lifted his pointer finger on one hand and twirled it in several circles. "Always," he translated.

Using her arm to sweep across the landscape, she glibly noted, "Unfortunately, my jaguar left undefeated, and I'm no longer under any pressure like you were in your fight. This means that I won't get a chance to fix anything."

Luke chuckled. "Would you like me to invite the Visigoths back so that we can put you under pressure again?"

Though she knew he was joking, Tina felt it necessary to clarify, "I guess the Visigoths weren't causing the pressure—it was the need to finish the aqueduct in time that was the real pressure. But now that I know that the aqueduct can't be finished before the moon reciprocates, there's no more expectation to complete the job . . . and without being under pressure—" Tina stopped. "Under pressure," she softly repeated.

Tina noticed Luke watching her for the next minute. She was tempted to explain her sudden silence, but something in her mind clicked and she had to consider her thoughts carefully before committing to anything. She already knew that Luke could be patient when it came to getting information.

As Tina finished assessing her thoughts, Marcus Oleas Lectorius cautiously approached.

"Lady Tina," he announced, "we will be packing up camp and escorting the laborers back to Cordovia so as to then prepare them to abandon the city." He shuffled awkwardly. "Could I have the honor to presume that you will join us so that I can engage you in the construction of other aqueducts within the Roman Empire?"

Tina looked at Luke and smiled. "No."

"No?" Marcus followed. "My lady, if I may be so bold, you must not let this setback ruin the rest of your truly remarkable future career."

"Nothing will be ruined," Tina declared. "It will be built."

"This aqueduct?" Marcus asked. "Why not move on to another project? With this one, within a month Cordovia will be abandoned, and all our resources have been lost or destroyed."

"All the resources we need are here already, and as for time . . . well, maybe we'll see if we can't build Rome in eight days after all."

Marcus's eyes bugged open. "How?" he finally managed.

Tina knew that Luke could not understand the words of this discussion with Marcus, which was in Latin, but she suspected that he got the general idea from her body language. And she was fairly certain he would catch enough meaning out of the final words to appreciate, at least in part, what she said.

"How?" she repeated the question, then answered: "Under pressure."

Luke's smile proved her right.

"Facade won't hurt him," Sally said quietly. She still felt uncharacteristically shy and timid with Charlotte and her dad in front of her. The whole incident of her capture blasted Sally with guilt for overstepping her bounds and causing so much trouble for everyone—especially Eric.

One look at Charlotte and Mr. Reeves, however, confirmed that they passed no judgment on her. They were simply searching for as much information as possible. This gave Sally more incentive to elaborate so that she could help instead of being a hindrance. "I mean, she's definitely a shady character, but she was never mean to me, and she even talked to me to keep me from being lonely."

"Or to get more information from you," Mr. Reeves observed.

"No, it was more just about . . ." Sally started, then she stopped and thought. "Whoops. Yeah, I think you're right."

"That's okay," Mr. Reeves comforted. "We just need to know what you talked about."

Sally considered this for a moment. "Hmmm. Well, I talked a lot about myself, I told her the entire plot of the *Shadow Creatures* TV series, but I'm not sure she was paying attention to any of that . . . but she did ask questions about you guys."

"Did she ask about natural born abilities?" Charlotte jumped in.

Sally's face fell. "Yes. I guess. Well, she didn't out-and-out ask, but it did come up. I pretty much told her everyone's natural born ability." Sally paused. "Well, except mine because I don't know what that one is, but she didn't seem to care about that anyway so—"

"That's fine, Sally," Mr. Reeves spoke. "What about Charlotte? What did you discuss that dealt with Charlotte and her ability?"

"I don't think I said anything that Facade didn't already know," Sally decided. "I mean, she knew that Charlotte was a seer already. She was curious about the whole ferrying thing, but since I'm new at it, I told her I didn't understand it. I think not knowing my natural born ability, made it easy for her to believe that I didn't understand what's been going on with—"

"Right," Mr. Reeves interrupted softly, "Was there any discussion about the hieroglyphics or Charlotte seeing images about things that had not yet happened?"

Sally scrunched her face trying to recall the conversations she had with Facade. "No. I told her that Luke wrestled a jaguar, because that was pretty epic. I don't think I'd know what to tell her about the hieroglyphics. I'm not sure I still understand what that's about."

"Did she wonder how we knew the Visigoths were coming?" Charlotte pressed.

"Yes," Sally nodded. "That was the first thing she brought up. She asked how we knew to warn everyone about the Visigoth attack, but I had no idea." Sally looked back and forth at them both. "Did we know?"

"We did," Mr. Reeves affirmed, "but not in time to save the aqueduct or keep you from getting caught."

"Oh," Sally said. "I'm so sorry about that again."

"That's okay, Sally," Charlotte assured her. "You're safe now."

"Only because Eric is caught," Sally mumbled.

Sally thought she noticed a brief look of pain in Charlotte's eyes. Whatever it was, it was gone in an instant. "Eric is just fine. He knew what he was doing."

They kept telling Sally that same thing, and she even told them Facade was someone who could be trusted to keep her end of the bargain, but that did not change that a part of Sally panicked at the thought that she would never see her brother again. "I know," Sally whispered. "I just wish we were together."

"Me too," Charlotte whispered back. She hugged Sally again.

Luke burst into the tent and immediately addressed Mr. Reeves. "If you have a moment, Tina could use your help."

Mr. Reeves looked at Charlotte and gave a thumbs up which she returned. He turned back to Luke. "What is it?"

"She needs us to bind together some quarry spikes into a circular pattern. Do you have any idea how to do that?"

Mr. Reeves lifted his eyebrows. "No. I've never had a request like that before, but show me what materials we have and what that even means and maybe we can figure something out."

"That'd be nice. She says we only have eight days for this plan to work."

Mr. Reeves gazed at Luke questioningly, Luke shrugged, and the two exited the tent.

Three days into their newest phase of building the aqueduct "under pressure" and they were making incredible progress. With the path of the aqueduct already set, measurements long since made, it really was just a matter of redirecting resources. Marcus Oleas Lectorius provided the cover, and the laborers threw themselves into the challenge with a vigor that surpassed even Tina's high expectations.

This led her to think ahead and brought her back to the marsh where she first ferried into this world. In one of the shallow, clear pools of water Tina dipped her hand, digging her fist past the first layer of sediment and into a slick substance below. After a slight sucking, she removed a heap of oozing clay and switched it from one hand to another to check its consistency. *This will do perfectly*, she thought.

She had plans to use the clay with the aqueduct, but the feel of it in her hands suddenly caused her to consider a time about a year earlier when she held clay in her hand, but did not have nearly the same feeling of appreciation for its benefits.

"This is dumb," Tina had said back then. "Why should a class like ceramics ruin my GPA—no, not just my GPA, but my future?"

"That seems pretty extreme," Ms. Judley handed the clay over to Tina. "I don't think a B+ is going to 'ruin' your GPA, certainly not your future . . ."

Tina plopped the clay to the potter's wheel. "Wow, you just don't get

189

it. That B+ will snap my 4.0, break my valedictorian status, kill my chances at the highest schools . . . you are literally costing me tens of thousands of dollars because I can't make this icky brown stuff look perfect."

Ms. Judley went quiet. "I think you put too much pressure on yourself," she eventually said. "And me."

Tina stared at the blob in front of her; she could not believe she was spending time here at the end of her semester. "I made the dumb figurines and other stuff like I was supposed to. Can't you just give me an A?"

Ms. Judley clearly felt uncomfortable by Tina's prodding. "Completing your projects is great, and I feel good about you getting a B or B+ for doing everything you were supposed to." The ceramics teacher swallowed, "But ceramics is more than just being able to make something. It's about symmetry and balance, form and thickness, contrast and texture, and purpose. It is an art, and I'm not just giving credit for doing a checklist but for showing that you actually learned something useful and applied it."

The mechanical potter's wheel started to whir as Tina shook her head with impatience looking at the slimy, misshapen pile of clay wobble in front of her. "Sure. Because we all know how crucial a life skill making a pot is," she mumbled.

If Ms. Judley heard Tina's criticism, she at least made a good show of ignoring it. And as the wheel swiveled round and round, she gave tips, applied more water, pointed out potential problems—all to no avail. Though Tina went through the motions, she simply did not have her heart or mind in the work. She kept thinking how stupid and unfair this was. She kept thinking about her next college entrance exam. She kept thinking what her letter to the school board would look like if this pointless elective killed her GPA. In the midst of this lack of focus, the pot started to rise from the wheel and her hand drifted too far outward. Before she could hear or respond to Ms. Judley's warnings, the clay spat apart in inglorious heaps all over the wheel, her apron, and the floor.

Ms. Judley tried to tell her that this happened all the time, and that she could help her get started again but Tina had enough. She threw off her apron, grabbed her backpack, and stormed out of the room. On her way out, she informed Ms. Judley that she would be talking to an administrator about this.

Now, somewhere in ancient Rome, Tina handled the slimy clay with an appreciation for its simple yet practical ability to complement the stones that were being repurposed in the valley below. Tina thought of the lettering that Ms. Judley had put above the classroom door as students exited: "For dust thou art, and unto dust thou shalt return." At the time it seemed like a silly pun for a ceramics class that dealt with clay everyday. Now, it seemed prophetic.

Tina never entered that classroom again. The semester ended the next day, and at some point after her long conversation with the vice-principal, where she used her best argumentative rhetoric, he must have walked under that class motto and explained to Ms. Judley how she must not keep a student of the caliber of Tina Ortiz from getting her well-earned A grade.

The report card came out, and it was with some relief, satisfaction, and only a slight tinge of guilt, that Tina noted the A in ceramics. She justified it as the right thing and that it was really just Ms. Judley being overly picky in the first place. As she fingered the clay before her, however, the regret seeped into her like the slime oozing between her fingers. Tina switched the clay from one hand to the other, thoughtfully.

Finally she stood up and went to the Roman supervisor who accompanied her and stood a respectful distance off. "There," she pointed back to the pool where she removed the clay. "When your workers are finished with the trench, have them come here and extract as much clay from there as they can."

The supervisor nodded. "You have something special in mind for it, Lady Tina?"

Tina nodded. "We won't be able to maintain the proper pressure without it."

As she walked back towards the camp, she held the clay purposefully in her hands. *Plus, it'll give me a chance to actually earn the A I got in ceramics.*

HOW TO BECOME A SEER

Charlotte took a break to wipe some limestone dust off of her moistened forehead. Sally scraped across the block with her own granite brick a couple more times before setting it down and tightening and loosening her fingers.

"How is this supposed to work again?" Sally asked. The limestone block, one of the hundreds that had been knocked down by the Visigoths, just had a perfect circle a couple feet across pounded out of it by the team directed by Luke and Charlotte's dad. Once they figured out they could drive eight quarry bars through a skinny slab of limestone and keep them in it with the spikes sticking out of the other side, then they suddenly had what essentially worked as a cookie cutter that—with a team of four men and some mallets—just needed to be set on top of a block and driven through the block, extracted, pivoted, and repeated until there were enough holes in a diameter to make it easy to knock a cylinder out of the middle part of the block. This left a hole that could be the exact same size and placement for all of the hundreds of blocks gathered from the deposed aqueduct. The gouged blocks would then need to be smoothed over by another team, which Sally and Charlotte joined, by taking granite bricks and essentially "sanding" down the sides of the block with the hole in it so that each side was completely flat and devoid of uneven ridges. If any bumps were too large to sand, chiselers would come by and lop them off.

Charlotte's arms felt like jelly. They had been doing this for hours. "Let's see . . . how it's supposed to work? I think you're asking the wrong person," Charlotte admitted, picking up her block and resuming to scrape it back and forth on the block in front of her. "This is definitely not my area of expertise."

"That's fair," Sally replied. "Okay, then I have a question that is more your area of expertise. I've been thinking about this since I came back." Sally paused before venturing, "How did you know about the attack? I remember

192

your dad saying that you knew there would be an attack. Was it really the hieroglyphics on the temple wall in Luke's world?" Sally massaged her cramped fingers. "I mean, how is it even possible that something from Luke's world could show you something from this world . . . or really, well, something about you? You aren't from either of those two worlds."

Charlotte shook her head. "I guess I should be more of an expert on that, but the truth is that I don't know. It means that there was a foreseer long ago that saw us . . . saw me . . . and the things that are happening to us right now."

"That's kinda . . . creepy," Sally said. "I mean, it's kinda cool too, but mainly kinda creepy."

"I agree," Charlotte replied. "I don't understand how foreseeing works in general, but I especially wonder how a foreseer from such a remote time, place, and—well—world can have a connection to . . . me . . ."

After a short pause Sally continued, "So are there more hieroglyphics or is that it?"

Charlotte took a short breath. "There's more."

"Can I ask what . . . well . . . what happens next? Or is that too spoilery?"

Charlotte smiled. "It's not too 'spoilery.' In fact, I wish it were because I've been thinking over the next hieroglyphic and I can't figure out what it means. It has some figures facing some other figures under a waxing moon, then in the next space, one side of the figures has disappeared."

"Is that what will happen when we ferry again?" Sally asked after a moment's reflection.

Charlotte shrugged. "That's what has me confused. It seems like a ferrying, but if it is, the numbers don't add up."

"What do you mean?"

"I mean that there are five figures on one side, the five that disappear. And on the other side there are six. Right now," she held up her fingers to count, "there is you, me, Tina, Luke, my dad, Eric, Facade, and Felipe. That's eight. In the hieroglyphic, there's eleven. That means even if we count everyone who has ferried to this world, it falls three short of what the future shows."

"Are we going to take some Romans with us? Marcus and a couple soldiers?" Sally asked.

"Maybe," Charlotte considered. "I'm not sure."

"Do the other hieroglyphics that are after that one help it make more sense?"

"Possibly," Charlotte responded, "but I won't know because last night when I was studying that hieroglyphic we're talking about, the power finally went out on Eric's phone. If there are answers in the other hieroglyphics, there is no way for me to know right now."

"Oh," Sally sighed. "That's too bad."

Charlotte nodded, but said nothing.

It was not true. While the battery on Eric's phone was very low, there was still some power left in it—certainly enough to check the rest of the hieroglyphics.

Charlotte was not used to lying, but she felt very little choice in the matter. How could she explain the truth? How could she explain that as she studied the hieroglyphic, that she suddenly felt manipulated, like this person who created these pictures was using it to mess with her emotions or affect her actions in some way? How could she explain that by relying on the pictures, she was acknowledging in some way that seers *should* meddle with other people's lives?

That night, Charlotte turned the phone off and put it away, an action that she felt stuck to her principle of avoiding people's eyes and not telling Sally her natural born ability. If she was truly going to claim a new way forward for her as a non-seer, then she had to start walking the walk.

"I guess I asked because I still feel terrible about Eric being captured, and it would be nice to know if he is going to be okay or not. I mean, I'm sure he is, but just to know for sure, you know?"

Charlotte nodded again. "I'm going to go wash up and get something to eat. You?"

She stood up quickly and Sally had to put a hop in her step to catch up. At that moment, Charlotte reflected on one more reason—perhaps the real reason—she had a difficult time looking at the hieroglyphic. In looking at the previous glyphs, it was pretty easy to identify at least two figures: hers and Eric's. And one thing that disconcerted her was that in the last hieroglyphic she looked at before turning off the phone, Eric was one of the figures that disappeared and hers did not.

One part of her ached to know what would happen next. The other part feared it. What if this time there was no Eric in the subsequent hieroglyphics? Or, worse, what if he was but it was something horrible that happened to him? Could she even bear to take in that information?

Charlotte's fears won over, and she shut off the phone.

While there were many unknowns with the hieroglyphics, there was one thing Charlotte was starting to realize. All of her concerns stemmed from the time she almost lost Eric as a pirate hunter. It made her question her role as a seer, it made her fear what could happen if she and her parents moved again, it made her afraid to face the fact that—instead of being the one to always help someone else—she depended on someone else just as much if not more as that person did on her.

It was a shattering realization for someone with Charlotte's confidence: recognizing that she was afraid.

"This is not the most effective way to fix a cart," Luke noted.

Tina sat in front of one of the carts that the Visigoths had savagely dismantled. It sprawled sideways on the ground, missing the forward half and one of the wheels with its remaining wheel facing upwards. Tina had been spinning the wheel with one hand and trying to shift the cart under it with her other hand when Luke found her.

"I'm not really trying to fix it," Tina replied. She knew that Luke had been joking, but Tina always felt it necessary to correct mistakes—even purposeful ones. She hated the idea of a loose error just sticking out there . . . even though she also hated how it made her seem humorless sometimes. She hurried and continued the conversation so that she did not have to focus on yet another thing about herself that she was discovering that she did not like. "I'm actually trying to get this so that it's level with the ground."

"That sounds like something that an aqueduct engineer would have a definite eye for," Luke said as he bent down and started to load some rocks under one corner of the cart.

"Right there," Tina held her hand out so that Luke could see it as he slid a thin piece of sandstone underneath. "That's it. Thanks for the help."

"Anything else I can do?"

Tina shook her head. "This is something I need to do alone."

Luke nodded. He turned and strolled away. Tina watched him go before bending over and picking up a large lump of clay that she had put in a canvas bag. She then dipped one hand in a pot of water she had set to the side and lopped the clay onto the middle of the wheel with her other hand. She took a big breath and focused on the clay for a moment. Then she spun the wheel with her hand, increasing the speed until it got a decent revolution under way.

Here goes nothing, she thought. Then she attempted to take her fingers to the spinning blob and shape it. She made a bit of progress before she had to pause and spin the wheel again. The lump of clay started to take actual shape until the slowing wheel caused the clay to wobble and fall apart.

Tina stopped for a moment to sigh before gathering the scattered pieces into a single mass again. She moistened it with the water from the pot, placed it in the middle, and then spun the wheel again. Her efforts got a little bit farther this time before the pot-in-embryo dissipated in front of her again. Determined, she re-gathered and gave it another effort. The results were the same, even if the methods differed.

Hours later, Tina tried to hide her frustration as she admitted that something needed to change before she could hope to succeed. She decided to take a break and get something to eat.

"Can I ask you something?" Luke asked Tina when she came back to the camp and they both were being served a meal in the shade outside her tent.

"Sure," Tina said, though her mind still lay back on the clay in the canvas bag next to the turned-over cart.

"You are in a time crunch to complete an ambitious, experimental aqueduct project, but you take a morning to adjust a cart's wheel for something you need to do alone?"

Tina's lip lifted in acknowledgment. "Sounds dumb, doesn't it?"

"Knowing how careful you are with your time at school, it sounds like nothing could be more important," Luke shrugged. "I'm just not sure why."

Tina nodded. "I've laid out the plans for the aqueduct project and the teams are working on the trench, the block pieces, and the clay. So really, there's nothing for me to do until it's all in place—hopefully in the next couple of days."

Luke's eyebrows rose when she said, "nothing," so she clarified. "Well, I mean, I could be going around and directing some things and overseeing the teams, I suppose. It's just that . . . well . . . when I found the clay that we're going to use, it made me regret that I never did quite finish making a pot on the wheel for Ms. Judley's class the way I would've liked. I guess . . . I guess I just want to try to get it right."

Luke chewed his food thoughtfully. "Your 4.0 is no secret. I'm pretty sure you got an A in the class. What about the pot was not right?"

"That's the thing," Tina looked down. "I don't know that I deserved an A."

Her mouth was down, so it must have been difficult for Luke to see, but he seemed to have read her body language enough to understand.

"Can I ask one more question?" Luke replied.

Tina nodded, and Luke continued. "Why do you think you have to do it alone?"

It was a fair question, so Tina considered it a moment before lifting her face and replying, "The same reason you tossed aside the machete when you wrestled the jaguar."

"I did not use a machete," Luke agreed, "but I definitely wasn't alone." He let that sink in before he finished by saying, "And I couldn't have done what I did alone either . . . not by a long shot."

Tina took a long draught of water. "What's your afternoon like?"

The soldier managed to find Marcus Oleas Lectorius in a moment where the centurion had actually found a rare few minutes to himself.

"Sorry to disturb, Sir," the soldier apologized, though it was clear to Marcus that he was not sorry at all, "but I wondered if you had a moment."

I thought I did, Marcus thought to himself. "What is it?" he asked.

"Aren't you just a bit curious what Lady Tina is up to?" the soldier asked, watching Marcus carefully.

Marcus gave a discerning look back to the soldier. "Tarquis, isn't it?"

"Yes, Sir," Tarquis could hardly disguise his pleasure at being recognized by the leader of the troops.

"Weren't you the soldier who questioned Lady Charlotte when she accurately warned us about the Visigoth attack?"

Tarquis's smug face fell. "Well, er . . . I did . . . uh—"

"And now you are questioning Lady Tina's actions after it seems as if she's been sent to us by the gods themselves?"

Tarquis mumbled, "I had not meant to question . . ." His words died for a moment, but he seemed to gather new gumption. "I just do not understand how we can be making such an obvious waste of our time and resources." Marcus lowered his brow, so Tarquis brought his hands up and explained further. "I mean, she has been a wondrous help, without question. I'm just not sure if this task is within her considerable skills. First of all, how can she hope to make an upside-down aqueduct that will actually work? Perhaps her friend, the witch you call Lady Charlotte, is planning to help with that, but making a light come out of a metal case for an instant is one thing—making water run up a hill for, well, for years and years on end? I don't know magic very well (praise be to the gods), but I feel like that is asking a bit much."

"Soldier," Marcus snapped, "have you really not heard of such an aqueduct being built before? I have not seen one myself, but there are such aqueducts within the Roman empire. I have spoken with several who have seen them with their own eyes and discussed the science behind them with aqueduct engineers." Marcus paused and then added thoughtfully, "The most remarkable part is that, when Lady Tina proposed her plan, she had not known that such a design actually existed before. It was as if she thought through the whole process independently and was surprised, even encouraged, when I told her that such things had been done before."

Tarquis clearly still felt skeptical. "I've heard of many marvelous things, but most of them seem to be connected to the dark fringes of black magic and the realm of the warring gods. Does it not make you wonder that she expects to complete this job in eight days time?"

"It is one of the most ambitious things I've ever heard proposed. Yet, we are on a timeline to accomplish it . . . without the use of any dark arts or other suspect powers," Marcus noted. "The fact that all the blocks needed were already here on site, her two friends were able to figure out a way to pound holes in all the blocks in a condensed time frame, and the location needed only to mirror where she and others had already surveyed for the above-ground aqueduct—all these things, plus the manpower of all the laborers and even our soldiers digging the trench and joining finished blocks (which should include yourself right now!) make what should have been an impossible task quite within reach."

Tarquis reluctantly nodded his agreement. "Yes, but we still don't know if any of this will work."

"I am tiring of this discussion, Tarquis," Marcus's eyes narrowed. "A soldier's duty is to do as asked without question, and I humored your criticisms disguised as questions for long enough."

Tarquis grimaced, almost saluted and left, but then must have decided to venture one more comment. "I apologize that I don't have the wisdom to be as trusting in Lady Tina as you are, but if she were so confident of our ability to complete this project, then why has she been spending all day sitting at an upturned cart and treating the wheel like a potter's wheel with one of the strangers she's with spinning it around? Doesn't seem like someone as interested in our well-being as we'd hope for . . ."

Marcus brought his eyebrows together. He had not seen Lady Tina all day, so as duplicitous as Tarquis had been up until now, it was likely he was telling the truth in this regard. "Follow me," Marcus ordered.

Their march to where Lady Tina sat with the boy Luke spinning the wheel was only interrupted by a stop that Marcus took in the workyard where the final holes were still being punctured into the last of the limestone blocks. There, he grabbed the head mason, Claudius, before approaching Lady Tina, who seemed intent on the lump of clay forming in front of her.

"As I was saying, Sir," Tarquis mumbled as soon as they approached.

"Yes," Marcus affirmed, "you were quite right, Tarquis. That is why I brought you along." Marcus could see Tarquis beaming at his side. "You see, there is no reason that Luke should be doing the hard work of spinning when you've apparently been resting up for quite some time rather than doing work you're supposed to while you've spied on others."

Tarquis's face fell. Marcus motioned to Luke, "Be so kind as to move over, Luke." Luke understood the motion and moved. Marcus shoved Tarquis into Luke's spot. "Start spinning."

The commotion was enough to cause Lady Tina to look up from what appeared to be a fairly decent, small pot forming on the wheel. "Marcus," she said, then she saw his company. "And Claudius. I'm sorry I've been out all day. I'm not really sure how to explain it, but I really need to make a pot right now."

Marcus smiled. "Lady Tina, you will never need to explain anything to me. Or anyone," he gave a hard look to Tarquis, whose spinning of the wheel increased with the glare. "I am not here for explanations, but for help. This soldier Tarquis will spin this wheel for you as long as you need it, be it hours, days, or months. I only ask that you do not take breaks or slow down on his part."

Marcus next clapped a hand on Claudius's back. "And you know Claudius as our chief mason, but I also happen to know that his father was a potter. The holes are almost all finished in the blocks, and I feel that he can be as helpful to you as you might need."

Lady Tina took a moment to absorb Marcus's statement. "Thank you, Marcus." She snuck a look over to Luke before concluding. "I am definitely open to any help I can get."

Marcus looked at the small, forming pot. "It looks like you are doing fairly well on your own."

Lady Tina smiled. "Well, I'd say I'm at least at a 'B' right now. I'm hoping that I can manage an 'A' before we're done."

Marcus had no idea what she was talking about, but he smiled back all the same.

Sally's Scribblings

Two more days before resippro— . . . Uh . . . I don't really know how to spell that word, but you know what I mean. One more day until we get up early in the morning, go back to the ferrying spot, and ferry back home. Hopefully with Eric and, well, everyone.

There's a lot happening here, which in some ways is nice. If we weren't sanding huge blocks of limestone or slapping clay all over the cracks between the blocks set down in the trenches then all I'd think about is if Eric is going to be okay or not—or if any of us is going to be okay for that matter.

Pretty soon, though, we'll stop. Almost all the blocks are in place, with nearly all the clay jammed between them. After six days of night and day work from every single person here—soldiers, workers, us . . . everyone—Tina thinks we can finish a day and a half ahead of schedule, which will give her time to check it and make any little fixes that she needs to before we have to go.

While we've been doing this Marcus Oleeus Lekt-blast, I can't spell his name either. Anyway, it works out well for Marcus because he said that they can now start making signs of retreat to see if the Visigoths fall for it. I mean, fall for believing that we gave up on the aqueduct. The idea is that by burying the aqueduct underground, they'll think we carried the limestone blocks to another Roman settlement south of this one (Marcus was going to make tracks that make it look like that), just so it seems like we've decided that this one isn't worth it. (How surprised will they be when they see Cordovia flourishing with plenty of water somehow in the next weeks, months, and years! Marcus says the Visigoths might try to investigate, but he has enough men to fight off any scouting party or something like that—he seemed to know what he was talking about when he told Tina and she told us.)

So, like I said, there's a lot going on and plenty to think about. But even if it's keeping me from going crazy thinking about Eric, I can't say the same for poor Charlotte. She's super distracted and not herself lately. She keeps on holding onto Eric's phone and looking at the turned off screen. I wonder if she knows more than she's telling, but I'm not asking her because I think she's told me everything she's comfortable talking about. (Believe me, it's not very easy to keep from asking Charlotte like a hundred questions a day!)

I get all the reasons why she's trying not to meddle, but . . . I don't know . . . I can't think of any good movie where someone tried not to meddle or use their talents, you know? And a hundred years of movies can't all be wrong, can they?

Charlotte, if you are picking this up to read it (wishful thinking . . . it took me getting captured for Eric to read it), then I want you to know that I'm sorry you're struggling. You told me that ability shouldn't matter, that we should just get to know each other for who we are and not obsess about abilities so much. But the way you help other people feel good about their abilities . . . that's who you are. Hiding from that has changed the Charlotte that I know.

Okay. Enough drama. The next time I write, it'll be from the comfort of my home with Eric and

Charlotte spending way too much time whispering to each other in the kitchen while my mom and dad give each other knowing smiles as if I can't figure out exactly what's going on.

Charlotte set Sally's diary down. Clever Sally. Charlotte had not picked it up to read Sally's entry, just to reread Eric's note, but seeing the new entry with her name mixed in made it hard to keep herself from reading it.

"How much longer until the water should come up?"

Charlotte never knew exactly where her dad was at all times, but she was never surprised to find him close by. That was the reality of being the daughter to a natural born bodyguard. The moon had not yet risen, and would not until early morning, so she could only see the dark outline of her father while he worked silently up the hill to sit next to Charlotte.

"Any minute now," Charlotte said. She volunteered to monitor the eastern basin of the aqueduct to see if Tina's experiment worked. "They are going to light a lantern as soon as they send water down the pipe and Tina said it'll take five to twenty minutes for me to see any result on this side."

Charlotte's dad fingered the lantern sitting next to her. "And then you light this if it works?"

"Yep."

The two fell quiet. Usually, Charlotte would not feel pressure to talk around her dad, but she knew that both of them had a lot to say. She just did not know how much to say or how to say it.

"Going over Eric's note again?" her dad looked down at Sally's journal.

"Actually a note left by Sally for me . . . kind of," Charlotte replied.

"Still thinking about the terms that Facade demanded?" he asked. Charlotte had not even hesitated to share with her father the conversation she and Eric had with Facade, even though Facade had expressly forbidden it.

"A little. I just know that I can't leave anyone behind. I'm just not sure how to do that and protect Eric."

Her dad nodded thoughtfully. "You leave the protecting to me. I'll make sure everyone is okay, and you just worry about getting us home."

"Stick to our natural born talents, I guess," Charlotte said. Suddenly a light flickered across the small valley. "Speaking of talents, it looks like Tina has opened her side. We'll see if her aqueduct building skills can handle an upside down track or not."

Her dad sat down next to her and the two stayed quiet for a few minutes. Charlotte looked into the empty basin where the water was supposed to emerge. She felt a similar hole in herself.

"What is it?" her dad perceived. He waited, then said, "Is it the move?"

Charlotte's eyes stayed riveted on the vacant basin. "Can I at least know why we move when I'm discovered as a seer? I mean, I know that it's because people can take advantage of a seer, but in a worst-case scenario, I can let you know if someone is trying to use me for some harmful purpose and you can tell them to back off or, well, or maybe then we can move if it seems to get really bad."

"That's not a worst-case scenario," her dad gruffly replied. His voice then softened, "Charlotte, I'm sorry that you've had such a transient life. I know that you deserve to live a quiet, normal life with the same friends and home." He put his hand on her shoulder. "But that's just not possible. Your mom and I take your safety very seriously. Very seriously. And what's happened makes it clear that staying in Nibleton would be very dangerous, not only to you but possibly the friends that you care for."

Charlotte's face hardened. "I never cared when we did all those moves before, Dad. I never complained. Not once. But all of a sudden, I make a real connection with someone—a non-seer connection—and it's time to move again? Don't you see that I was willing to drop everything seer about myself."

She turned to face her dad and caused his hand on her shoulder to slide to the side. "Dad, I was so careful. I was so so careful to not get identified by another seer. For heaven's sake, I stopped looking people in the eye! Do you realize how awkward I've been while meeting other people for the last couple of months? I mean, no one can one hundred percent say that I am a seer. I could just stay real low for a while, or we could go on an extended vacation before quietly slipping back into town."

Charlotte knew as she said it that her dad would not be convinced, so she reassessed and then offered her next proposals with a bit more submission. "Can't I just stay in contact in some way? We'll be really careful. You could monitor everything just to make sure that no one would be able to trace it back to me and we could find a way to . . . I mean, I'm not ready to give up on . . . I just—" Charlotte kept waiting for him to interrupt, but he just let her talk. "Daddy . . ." she suddenly fell into a hug with him.

The worst part was that Charlotte knew that her parents understood. They appreciated her willingness to move each time and on such short notice. They noticed and did not suppress her recent closeness with Eric—even letting her ferry him to the world of pirates and back (though the agreement had been that she would simply send him alone and not go with him, which led to an unpleasant discussion and halfhearted punishment when she and Eric ferried back).

As Charlotte held her father and released her frustrations into him, she could not help but marvel that he was the cause of her pain but also the reliever for it. *What a strange thing it is to have loving parents!* she thought.

After a long moment Charlotte's dad lifted her tear-streaked face away from his shoulder. "All of your life, your mother and I have watched over you. We have protected you in the best way we knew how. When we get home, I promise that we will sit down with you and explain why your case is not so simple—you are getting old enough that you deserve to understand it. I hope, then, that you will understand why we have done what we have done, and why it will be necessary for us to move again and—for your sake and your friends' sakes—cut all ties of contact with them."

Charlotte sniffed. "I'll do my best to understand, Dad," she said, "but what if I still think that it's not worth moving?"

"Then," he sighed, "then we did not properly explain to you the reasons why."

All went quiet, and Charlotte despaired at her father's firm insistence on closing out all hope of future connections to Eric.

Out of nowhere, her dad ventured, "Have you looked at the other hieroglyphics?"

Charlotte was not sure what made him think of asking that. Perhaps, she thought, he hoped that seeing an inevitable separation from Eric in the hieroglyphics would bring her more likely into submission. "Battery is dead," Charlotte muttered.

Before the lie could sit in the air for too long, a series of crescendoing gurgles bounced out of the basin. A peculiar whooshing of air slurped in, or out, of the pipe—she could not be sure which. And then a thick flow of water emerged into the basin from the hole at the base. Fascinated, Charlotte and her father observed the basin fill up with clear spring water until reaching the lip that took it to the section of the aqueduct leading down the hill towards Cordovia.

As prearranged, Charlotte tried to light the lamp. She struggled with it until her dad helped—something she was both grateful for and embarrassed by. Once lit, he put his hand back on her shoulder. "I'm sorry, Charlotte. I truly am. Please know that even though, as a father, I have always protected you first, I promise to do everything I can to protect Eric while we are here."

Charlotte nodded, but she could not face her father. After waiting for a minute or so for a verbal response from her and getting none, he disappeared. But Charlotte knew that he was somewhere nearby, watching her—he always was.

Tina resigned herself to not seeing a light come from the other side of the small valley of the aqueduct. In a weird way, she was prepared for it. She wondered if that feeling had something to do with the expert-looking clay pot sitting next to her where the aqueduct first started heading into the ground. Watching a lump of clay disintegrate countless times over seemed to help desensitize one to absolute failure.

For some reason she could not help but keep her eyes more on the pot than the place where Charlotte would light the lamp if the aqueduct succeeded. The pot was exquisite. Not in the sense that it was a masterpiece and that she was going to drop everything and become a potter for the rest of her days. But considering where she was a few days ago (or even a year ago) and what she looked at now . . . this was a perfectly gorgeous and functional piece of work—worthy of an "A" . . . if that sort of thing even mattered anymore. In fact the reality was—she heaved a sigh of relief—that ultimately it did not.

The functionality of the aqueduct, however, was something Tina felt quite unsure about. That it was an engineering marvel in principle, she would modestly acknowledge—though she would try to offer credit for the idea to Luke. Their discussion on being "under pressure" caused her to realize that the Visigoths would continue to harass and vandalize the aqueduct as long as there was a visible aspect to it to attack. If it were somehow under the ground, however, then the Visigoths might assume that the project had been abandoned.

Once Tina considered the idea of being "under pressure," she at first despaired at the lack of machinery that would not allow her to pump water up a hill. Then she thought more, and her natural born aqueduct designer mind took in all of the observations she ever had about water flow. Perhaps, she toyed with an idea, she did not need machinery after all. Plumbing in homes do not use a pump to get water from under a sink to the faucet above. Water flows there because of pressure, because gravity is pushing it from a remote source somewhere higher up, a reservoir above the town or a water tower above or on top of the tallest buildings. As long as the water is in enclosed pipes, she thought it through, then the water will travel "up" hill on its own only because its source is still higher than the point it is traveling up—no pumps or machinery necessary.

When Tina made this realization, she got excited, until she checked herself. For it to work, she needed piping. She felt relatively certain that the Roman Empire had the means of making pipes, but not in the eight day time frame that she was working with. All she found at her disposal was a field of ruined scaffolding and more limestone blocks than she could ever figure out what to do with.

At the time, Tina scrutinized a couple of nearby blocks. They were the exact same size and dimensions. She knew that the head mason had been meticulous about that. She considered the amount of water that needed to be transported and then looked at the size of the limestone block. She fingered its surface. If it were possible to knock a circle out of this block, and then another out of the next, and then place the two blocks perfectly next to each other ...

Her eyes suddenly swept the field of hundreds of similar-sized blocks. She calculated the distance between the two points of the hill where the aqueduct was supposed to span and then looked back to the blocks. More than enough. If only she could find a way to pound out a hole the exact same size in each of these blocks, then she could create a pipe out of limestone blocks by laying them perfectly end on end in a trench leading from a basin on the higher point to a basin on the opposite side. The pressure from the upper basin would be sufficient, in an enclosed pipe system, to push the water down the valley and back up again to the lower basin, where it could then spill out into the ground-level aqueduct leading from that hill down to Cordovia.

When Tina made the proposal to Marcus and the head mason, she expected immediate skepticism. Instead, she was surprised to find out that just such a design had been employed in several aqueducts in the near east of the Roman Empire. The complicated engineering of the feat had kept either of them from ever even considering it an option in their situation. Tina changed their mind quickly.

With no further need for persuasion, Tina put the crew to work, which made vast jumps when Mr. Reeves and Luke helped figure out how to make a hole-creating template of driving rods to apply to the blocks. Then they employed Henry Ford's idea of an assembly line in order to speed up the process of preparing the limestone blocks, and the work crew put their whole hearts and all of their physical efforts to the task. Marcus assigned his soldiers the task of digging the trench while a few patrols kept on the lookout for scouting Visigoths and gave the impression that they were slowly retreating by breaking down some of their reconnoitering outposts.

It was then that Tina thought that, no matter how careful they were to cut the limestone blocks, there were sure to be small gaps and crevices where air could sneak in or water could sneak out and ruin the pressure of her system. She needed some kind of paste or something to slap between the blocks and in cracks. She remembered the pliable mud on her shoes from the marshy area where she first ferried here, and she took a patrol up with her to investigate.

Tina looked at her pot. That is where she found the clay and discovered a dual purpose for it: to seal off her limestone block pipes, and to help her refocus her education to one of learning rather than tabulating.

The silhouette of the opposite hill remained dark, without any sign of light from Charlotte's lantern. Tina began to resign herself to failure again. She picked up the perfectly cylindrical pot, with nearly indistinguishable horizontal lines where her fingers had carefully prodded and coaxed the clay into submission. And Tina suddenly felt at peace—all the pressure within her equalized. Whether the buried aqueduct worked or not, she definitely learned something. And she realized that to fail and learn is far better than to succeed without improvement.

As soon as she had that epiphany, though she did not see it at first since her eyes were glued to the smooth circling of her pot, a light peaked out from the hill across the valley.

Chapter 7
FERRY, MYSTERIOUS

*I*t must have been sometime in the early morning when Facade woke Eric up. Eric rubbed his eyes and noted the very earliest glimmer of light on the horizon extending out from the hollow he had spent the last eight days in.

"Get up, Pirate Hunter," Facade prodded him. "Drink some water and get ready for a hike."

"Reciprocation time?" Eric asked. It was the first moment he spoke to Facade after she had goaded him into revealing information about Charlotte days ago. Not that Facade had not made further attempts at conversation, but Eric kept disengaged, like a ship staying just out of cannon range.

"Finally talking again? Figured you've done all the damage you could?" Eric did not respond. Facade shrugged. "Well, it may comfort you to know that you are right: it's reciprocation time. I've been watching the moonrise carefully over the last couple of days and it looks like it'll be coming up in the next couple of hours. For your sake you'd better hope that it's just Charlotte, Luke, and your sister at the meeting spot. I guess we'll see soon enough. Now let's get moving, this isn't a date with your girlfriend you'll want to be late for."

The casual reference to Charlotte as his girlfriend would have angered Eric into saying something he regretted a few days before. But Eric had plenty of time to think about his next move when the winds would be in his favor, and now the response was quite different. "No," he stated. The winds, he felt, had definitely shifted.

Facade had turned to gather materials but now she stopped and pivoted carefully. She looked at Eric, and he could sense her reading him. "Explain," she demanded.

"I've got nothing to go back for," Eric said. "And you can't physically force me to go with you. You're not going to be able to drag me for a couple of hours on your own. You'd need to go get help from Felipe or the Visigoths, and by that time Charlotte will have ferried with the others and be gone."

Facade did not even flinch. She kept her eyes hard on Eric. "She's not going anywhere without you."

Eric raised his eyebrows. "Charlotte is moving when we get back, moving far away from me. There's nothing left for me back home. I hinted that much to her in the note I wrote to her, which I'm sure you read. She'll know what I am proposing by not being present at the ferrying point, and she will be willing to grant my wish."

"Your wish is to be stuck in this world? I don't buy it."

"Here's a history lesson: I know there were pirates back in the Roman days. Did you know that pirates once kidnapped and held for ransom Julius Caesar himself? This isn't my perfect world of pirate hunting, but it's certainly better than Nibleton and worlds better than anything without Charlotte."

"You're bluffing," Facade determined. She sat down and crossed her arms, looking out towards the horizon. "I don't know what you're hoping to get out of me, but it won't work. I will sit here all day if I have to, and if you ever want to see Charlotte again, you will have to stand up and walk with me to the point of ferrying."

Eric could afford to smile since she was not looking in his direction. "Fine by me. I'm going to take a nap. Let me know when you're tired of watching over me so that I can make my way to the coast and go hunt some pirates." He lay back down, completely and entirely calm.

He heard her shift uncomfortably, even though he could tell she was trying to hide it. He had the weather gauge once more.

Twenty long minutes passed, but Eric felt enough confidence in his position that he actually fell asleep for a few of those minutes. When he woke, it was not under pleasant circumstances. "If you don't come, I will kill you." Facade's voice was a whisper directly into his ear, intense and bordering on angry.

Eric waited again, long enough to let Facade see that he was still in control. "I don't think you are the killing type," Eric finally responded. "Maybe, just maybe, if you were desperate enough you could try to kill me," Eric's eyes fluttered open enough to look at her, but he did not move. "But I'm not sure you would succeed, and I can assure you that it would be a battle, even with me tied up. I've faced death before, and I am willing to do it again. Besides, it would not help your situation at all and certainly could make it far worse."

Facade slammed her hand on the ground next to Eric's head. "Then I'll leave you and go to the reciprocation point on my own. If Charlotte is going to ferry anyway, I will find a way to join her. Maybe I can disguise Felipe and put a bag over his head claiming he's you or . . . well, there's plenty of other options for a street magician like myself."

Eric almost started at this. He had not expected a retaliation along those lines. But he calmed himself. No. She's certainly capable of tricks and deception, but not something that complicated at such short notice. Almost, she had forced Eric into bringing his ship about too early and handing the weather gage back to her.

"Go for it," Eric closed his eyes again. "I find it hard to believe that Charlotte would fall for something like that, but go ahead and try. It's got nothing to do with me. Whatever you're planning, you'd better do it soon because you are wasting precious time talking to me."

Facade went quiet. It was a silence full of intense implications, and it lasted for two minutes though it felt like hours. Finally, in a whisper so silent that it was almost impossible to discern, Facade said, "What do you want?"

Eric's eyes came open. He had thought for a long time about this as well. "We're all ferrying back. You, me, Sally, Luke, Tina, Charlotte's dad . . . even that blasted chiclero, Felipe."

"I can't do that," Facade murmured stubbornly.

"Then don't. And you and I can go our separate ways. I'm sure there are plenty of streets in Rome that would be fascinated by your street magic. Whatever you choose, choose quickly because the reciprocation time keeps approaching, and I'd like to go back to sleep."

Another moment of silence. Another voice through gritted teeth. "Even if I could do what you ask, there wouldn't be time to get Felipe from the Visigoths and get to the reciprocation point before Charlotte ferries."

"Charlotte does not have to ferry right when the moon comes up," Eric deliberately shifted so that he was now sitting up. "If I go to the reciprocation point and you go to get Felipe, then I will tell Charlotte to wait for you two before ferrying. That will give her time to send back for her dad and Tina and it will give you time to gather Felipe and return." He held his breath.

"How stupid do you think I am?" Facade looked at him intently. "What would stop you guys from ferrying and leaving me here with—"

"Because," Eric interrupted, "because that's something we've been clear about from the start. We're not natural bornappers. We don't leave people in worlds that aren't their own or without their permission. I'll give you my word that we'd wait for you."

Eric waited and then made one final point. "You're not stupid. In fact, you are scary smart as far as I've seen. That's why you know I would not waste your time with a move like this unless you knew I meant it."

Facade's jaw set. She looked Eric in the eyes for a long moment. "Your honesty is your weakness . . . but it's also your strength." She paused one moment longer before untying Eric's knots in an insultingly short amount of time given how tightly they had bound him for so long. Then she walked around to face him. "Walk out of the hollow, turn left, and the aqueduct camp will be a couple hours to the southwest of here. You'll find it." She nodded in the designated direction. "Now, give me your word, Pirate Hunter, that you will wait for me and the chiclero." Facade put out her hand.

Eric's eyes remained locked on Facade's. He reached his hand out. "You have my word."

After they shook hands, Eric walked out of the hollow a free man—Facade, and the wind, fairly at his back.

The marshy area clung to patches of mist with as much tenacity as Sally clutched at Charlotte's hand. Luke stood to the side, his eyes scanning the area carefully. Charlotte glanced back at the small mound where her father and Tina had secreted themselves. The silence caused Charlotte to want to speak, but she also felt so nervous that she was not sure if she could stand a meaningless conversation for the sake of conversing. And she was especially afraid of a meaningful conversation about Eric.

Left to her thoughts, however, she kept on imagining that the worst had happened to him. She kept on thinking of his note and shuddered at the finality in his closing sentences. *He wouldn't really consider staying here, would he?*

Charlotte thought she knew Eric. That he cared for her was no secret, but the gesture of marooning himself in someone else's world because she was moving when they got back seemed extreme. Plus, Charlotte personally witnessed Eric give up the world of pirates so that he could return to his family. It seemed unlikely that the instinct to stay with his family would have changed between now and then. At the same time, if he felt that his sacrifice would clear the path for Sally and Charlotte and the others . . . well, that *did* seem a lot like Eric.

How did we end up here? she thought. Once again, the answer that mocked her was that it was all because of the actions of a meddling a seer.

Once again, she told herself that she just wanted to disappear into the unassuming solitude of Nibleton and avoid looking into people's eyes for the rest of her life. And if she could just manage to get Eric to join her, then they could go together.

"I think the moon is out," Sally remarked, pointing to the bright haze on the horizon that rose out of the mist. "Almost time to go home."

Luke nodded after following Sally's finger. "Just waiting for one more thing to show up."

With the added light came added urgency, and all three of them scanned the mists in front of them with the pit of uncertainty in their stomachs.

"Who is that?" Sally piped out, her voice holding a quiet intensity.

Charlotte saw Sally pointing into the fog banks some distance in front of them. Luke tensed. Charlotte focused more and saw the mist swirling unnaturally. A form materialized, dark and unrecognizable. It walked forward purposefully, stepping around puddles and matted spots of ground.

"Eric," Charlotte breathed without thinking, her body recognized him and unconsciously said his name. Then she and Sally both jumped forward to grab him.

Eric put his hands up and stopped them in their tracks. "Wait," he insisted softly.

"Eric!" Sally exclaimed. "You're okay!" She paused. "Right? You are okay?"

"Yes," he said in a low voice. "Is everyone here okay?"

Charlotte nodded and looked back at Luke. "Yes," she just about pointed out the hill where her dad and Tina hid, but she stopped. "Where is Facade? And the chiclero?"

"They won't be here for another hour or so," Eric answered.

"You escaped?!" Sally said. "How?"

Eric shook his head. "Facade let me go."

Charlotte looked at Eric carefully. "No she didn't. She wouldn't."

Eric shrugged. "She did."

Charlotte's dad suddenly emerged from seemingly out of nowhere. "How did you convince her? Or did you escape?" he asked. Charlotte guessed that he must have overheard that Facade was not there and that was enough to bring him out of hiding with Tina joining him.

"No escape. She was too careful for that. I simply told her I wasn't going to go back to our world and that she would have to drag me by force. I told her that Charlotte would see I wasn't there and would leave without me . . . and Facade." Eric looked at Charlotte meaningfully.

"But I wouldn't have," Charlotte said firmly. His statement brought up an image of the hieroglyphic that had so bothered Charlotte, the one where they were separated by a ferrying.

"You would have been forced to ferry without me," Eric followed up just as quickly, "for everyone else's sake. Even my own."

"No." Charlotte asserted. The image of her and Eric separated continued to stare her down. "No," she repeated stiffly.

"Luckily the bluff worked," Charlotte's dad filled the awkward void that followed her statement, "so we don't have to find out what anybody *would* have done."

Charlotte felt tired of being pushed and pulled by "what ifs" and "would haves" or "would not haves." This is not who she was, and—she determined—she was going to do something about it.

"When did you say Facade would be here?" Charlotte's dad queried, "an hour?" Charlotte could see by his stance that he had yet to let down his guard.

"It doesn't matter," Charlotte moved towards Eric once more, realizing that as long as she touched him, they could not be separated. "We have everyone here. Let's ferry."

Eric backed away. "I gave her my word. I made her go get the chiclero and gave her my word that we would wait for them."

Inside, Charlotte wilted. She was afraid of this. That is why Eric kept backing away from her. He did not want to ferry prematurely. "Who cares? Facade tried to bornap. She deserves this. Let's get out of here."

Eric shook his head.

"Remember chopping down the white flag of truce when the pirates came to talk terms?" Charlotte tried again, another step. "We're doing the same thing right now. Let's chop the white flag and get out of here"

Eric stepped back once more. "That was with pirates who were not playing by the rules of war. Facade showed more than once that she can keep her word. And I will keep mine. I must."

Certainly it was noteworthy, and any other time Charlotte would have been proud of Eric for his integrity. Now, however, she felt the hieroglyphic obstinately return to the forefront of the moment. She refused to relent.

"Dad," Charlotte called out, watching Eric carefully the whole time, "you said you would do anything you could to protect Eric. Grab him. Then we'll all link hands and ferry out of here right now."

Eric lifted his eyebrows, staring at Charlotte quixotically. Charlotte's dad hesitated. Charlotte looked towards him now. "Dad," her voice broke, betraying the emotion she hoped to hide, "you promised. You are taking me away from him forever. The least you can do is guarantee that we leave each other on our own terms."

"Charlotte," he mumbled, "you know I love you . . . but . . ." his voice faltered.

Eric looked at her. "What's wrong, Charlotte. What is going on?"

Charlotte ignored him. "Luke!" She turned towards him, not sure if he could see her face well enough to understand her or not, but not caring. "Wrestle him to the ground. We're leaving right now."

Luke seemed to understand, but he too paused.

"Won't anyone help me?" Charlotte despaired. She went from face to face, seeing that none of them moved. All of them watched her, puzzled.

Suddenly, Sally's face opened up. "Eric was in the other group, wasn't he? In the picture that showed the future, he was separated from you."

Charlotte collapsed, her face buried in her hands. "I can't . . ." she wept, "I can't lose you, Eric."

Charlotte's dad started towards her, but Eric held his hand up. "Everyone stand back," Eric said. Then he approached Charlotte, knelt down and embraced her. "I'm right here."

She cried for a while. The last time Charlotte could even remember crying, let alone so much, was when she almost lost Eric to Jedediah Willard. This was far worse because that was after she *almost* lost him. This . . . this was before she still would lose him. In spite of that, it felt comforting if not good. She had Eric. For that moment, for that long—seemingly eternal moment—she knew that they could not be separated.

After a while she whispered. "I could take you right now, you know."

Eric smiled. "But you wouldn't leave everyone else here."

"I don't trust anything about myself anymore," she said. And within her, she could feel the tug of the reciprocated moon. She could feel the possibility of ferrying. It would be as simple as just allowing it to happen in her mind and they would be gone.

"I trust you. Even if you can't trust yourself," Eric said.

And then the magic urge left. Charlotte let go of the sensation of being someone else. She knew that she would wait for Facade.

That did not stop her from holding on to Eric indefinitely.

Facade paced herself well ahead of Felipe, disgusted with the fact that she had to deal with him after she assumed that she was done with him for good. Even with the deal she made with Eric, it was all she could do to not abandon Felipe again completely to the black night.

The disgust could only account for a small portion of her feelings, however, because the main portion assigned to her was fear—something she rarely felt or acknowledged—yet in this moment it dominated her to the point of near panic. *What if Eric had bluffed his way through the whole thing and they were all long gone now?* she questioned, her eyes constantly peeling off the path to check on the status of the risen moon. Within just a few minutes, that moon would either be a symbol of her return or her marooning in this world for good.

While Facade knew that she had little choice in agreeing with Eric's terms, she still regretted the way things played out. She had underestimated him because she knew of his attachment to the seer and his sister and friends. What she did not realize was that his attachment was strong enough that he was willing to sacrifice himself for their well-being. She shook her head. It is hard to account for someone with nothing to lose. Harder to account for someone with everything to lose.

Facade examined her own situation. In some strange way, she felt that it mirrored Eric's. Yet she had never considered an action such as the one that Eric proposed. She was not sure that she could.

Upon reaching the lip of the rise before descending into the marshy area, Facade paused long enough to take a hard look into the mists below. It gave Felipe enough time to catch up to her. She was grateful that his heavy breathing from being pushed to walk so far and fast kept him from talking to her, because she could not trust how much she would be able to resist knocking him out at the slightest irritation. She would hate to have to drag him through the marsh to the reciprocation point.

She could see nothing through the mists below, but Facade knew which way to go. She just did not know if there would be a way to go home once she got there. As she started down the slope towards the reciprocation point, the panic welled up once more. If they were gone, if they had ferried without her as she most certainly would have done to them had she been able to, she would be trapped in a completely alien world—alone (she quickly dismissed Felipe) and abandoned for the rest of her miserable life—all because she capriciously chose to hop into the chain of a ferrying group and then assume she had control over one of its members.

This can't be happening to me, Facade lamented while quickening her already rapid pace, *I can't be stuck here. This can't be how it ends for me!* Yet the more she thought about it, the more her mind could not conceive of any other possible outcome. Of course they had left without her. Of course they would not hesitate to give her, a bornapper's assistant, a dose of her own medicine. Of course—

Her foot splashed into a shallow depression of water, displaying an uncharacteristic lack of focus. Felipe managed to get both feet in the same depression, displaying a perfectly characteristic lack of focus. Yet, Facade did not even need to try to ignore him, because her eyes found the shaded forms of six people in front of her.

Hope immediately welled up inside of her, but she did not dare to feel relieved yet. She stumbled forward, her wet foot squishing awkwardly. The forms materialized, all of them looking in her direction since the splashes she and the chiclero had made.

There was Tina and Sally. Luke stood on the fringe. The seer's father caused her to shudder involuntarily, in spite of her relief at seeing him still in this world. The final two forms were before her, kneeling on the ground, held in a comfortable embrace. Charlotte and Eric, she knew. And while she could not be exactly sure what brought them into this position besides their obvious companionship, it was all Facade could do from not rushing forward and embracing them herself.

Instead she stopped. She took a breath, and she slid carefully towards the group, angling for Luke. She could hear the chiclero behind her, but she could sense his reluctance to come closer to Luke. He hovered between the edge of the mist and her.

"You kept your word, pirate hunter," Facade announced, "and I brought Felipe, as agreed."

Charlotte stood up, though she left one hand fiercely clinging to Eric. "The moon is up, and I am ready. Let's all hold hands and return, then I will send Felipe back to Luke's world."

"And then . . . ?" Facade murmured.

"And then you and I are going to have a chat," Mr. Reeves intoned.

Facade had just gotten over the panic of not having a way to ferry back, but hearing the seer's father matter-of-factly allude to an interrogation led her to feel resurging dread.

Time for some magic, she thought.

Strategically, she reached for Luke's hand. The last thing she wanted was to be holding hands with Mr. Reeves. As she took in the layout, she knew that her instinctive move towards Luke before this conversation was the right one.

Luke, for his part, eyed her suspiciously for a moment but seemed to realize that someone would need to hold her hand and it might as well be him. He grasped her right hand. On the other side of her, she felt Felipe—eager to not be left out—grab her left hand. Tina linked hands with Luke, Sally with Tina, Eric with Sally, obviously Charlotte with Eric (she had not let go of him since Facade had arrived), and Mr. Reeves, protectively, with Charlotte.

Facade felt satisfied with this arrangement, this put her at nearly the opposite end of the line from the bodyguard. That would provide her with plenty of opportunity for disappearing as soon as they had ferried. She took an inventory of her illusionist possibilities and recalled the layout of the parking lot where they would be landing. She started to nod to herself as she formulated a quick plan for–

"Let's create a circle," Mr. Reeves insisted. "I'd rather not be so spread out." He walked towards Felipe, who—not having any option—closed out the circle by allowing Mr. Reeves to grip his left hand. "There, now we're much more cozy." The deliberate look he gave to Facade, with only one person between them, was chilling.

"Okay, Charlotte," Eric said, and Facade felt as if she could detect some emotion under the surface, even if the exact kind eluded her, "this is everyone. I guess it's time to go home." There was something about the way Eric said home that caught Facade's attention, but before she could pick it apart, she was interrupted.

"But the numbers." It was Sally, who was looking around the circle and bobbing her head as she counted. "The numbers don't add up."

"What do you mean they don't add up?" Tina asked. "Do we have to have a certain amount of people to ferry?"

Sally turned to Charlotte. "There are only eight of us. Where are the other three?"

"Exactly," Charlotte said with quiet intensity. Suddenly, Facade noticed the ground underneath them disappear, the scene of mists around them swirled into nothingness.

They were ferrying, Facade knew immediately, and what would happen at the other end was anybody's guess. But before they even landed in that split moment of transition, she was already planning her next move.

PART FOUR

RIVER PIG

Chapter 1
FERRY, FORETOLD

D ude, how did you know where I was?" Dave Gardner's hard breathing created small puffs of steam as he squinted into the soft lamplight just a street or two removed from the modest bustle of a weekday evening in downtown Nibleton.

"My name is Mr. Neech," the man said in a low voice, apparently not appreciating being labeled as "dude." His eyes narrowed. "I just didn't want you missing out on the great opportunity that my scholarship can offer you."

Dave's relaxed face seemed to always hold a half grin on it. "Right. But that doesn't answer my question. How did you find me? Nobody is at my house right now 'cause my dad is working late and my mom's teaching a night class."

Mr. Neech tried to shuffle closer, "I . . . uh . . . talked to . . . one of your friends."

Dave, half-grin still on his face, slid effortlessly back, mulling over Mr. Neech's claim. "Eric?" Then he laughed. "Are you telling me that instead of coming to do parkour with me, Eric betrayed me to some college recruiter dude?" Dave chuckled in a way that showed more amusement than annoyance. "I'm gonna get him for this!"

"Excellent idea," Mr. Neech hissed with an awkward smile, his slicked-back blond hair reflecting a soft sheen of lamplight. "I can give you a ride to where he is . . ."

"I don't take rides from strangers," Dave waved off the suggestion, benignly preparing to walk away.

Mr. Neech's forced smile disappeared. "Then I insist on no longer being a stranger." He stepped forcefully forward.

Dave scrutinized Mr. Neech. "Dude, you're serious, aren't you?"

"I can explain when we get there," Mr. Neech voiced with an edge, "but let me assure you, *Dude*, that I am very, very serious."

Dave nodded. "Fair enough." The words were placating, but his body tensed. "To be equally fair, I should tell you that I'm never serious—life's too short!" With a burst, Dave swiveled around, hurdled a garbage can as if taking a stroll in the park, and sprang lightly, though athletically, into an alleyway. "Catch you on the flip side, Crazy-Serious-and-Apparently-Desperate-College-Recruiter-Dude-named-Neech!" echoed out of the black passage.

Before running up the side of a brick wall to handle a sharp turn, Dave saw Mr. Neech running after him using startling agility. He shortcut all of Dave's side jumps and freestyle diversions, which helped him close the gap between them as he pumped his arms intensely with brows furrowed and breathing in quick, regulated, bursts.

Dave ran up a wall and onto an escarpment around the building's power transformer. "Whoa! Dude, you weren't kidding about being serious. Keep this up and you really won't be a stranger. We'll be parkour buddies for life!"

Mr. Neech did not seem as conversant as Dave. Instead, he leapt up the escarpment wall, gripping the top with his fingers and edging his feet upwards. Though not nearly as adept or quick as Dave, Mr. Neech's dogged pursuit gained a nod of respect from the parkour aficionado. "Sloppy but effective. You've got the drive and that's something that can't be taught."

He waited until the hard-breathing Neech crested the top of the wall before recklessly running along the edge and flipping head forward off the end and landing neatly on his feet near the exit of the alleyway. Dave turned back to Mr. Neech, who took a second to catch his breath after watching Dave's effortless retreat. "I'm concerned about what's driving you, though,

Dude. 'Cause you don't look like you're enjoying it—and pure enjoyment is the real magic of parkour."

Mr. Neech looked up from his bent over position. "I can't say that I enjoy this part," he said, his voice still strong in spite of his physical efforts to capture Dave, "but I will enjoy five minutes from now when I ferry you out of this world for good."

Dave Gardner laughed. "Whoa. I don't know what substance you're abusing, but there's probably some support group out there that can—"

Something grabbed Dave's wrist from behind with such speed and firmness that before he could even think to jerk his hand reactively away, he found it painfully paralyzed. "What the—" he turned around.

A large man with an even larger mustache, stared back at Dave under eyebrows as black as his near shoulder-length hair. Troubling gray eyes were the only thing that betrayed any emotion as he held Dave with an impossible grip. A couple of resistant tugs from Dave told him that if he was hoping to get back to parkour, it was not going to be while this man anchored him.

"Dude," Dave tried, "you wanna hold hands with me, you're gonna have to take me out to eat first."

The man barely even acknowledged that Dave existed. He simply looked to where Mr. Neech scrambled deliberately down from the escarpment and onto the alleyway ground while calmly keeping his hand melded to Dave's wrist.

"Well done, Mr. Haley," Mr. Neech said once his feet touched the ground, "now let's wrap up this business."

The man dubbed "Mr. Haley" walked behind Mr. Neech without considering whether or not Dave Gardner cooperated. He did not need to—his lock on Dave's wrist and intimidating stature assured that Dave followed him whether it was willingly or simply being dragged.

A minute later, Dave found himself sitting in the backseat of Mr. Neech's car, Mr. Haley still as much a part of him as if he had always been an awkward extension of Dave's wrist.

The silence in the drive led Dave to start to take in what was really happening in this situation. "Is this a kidnapping?" Dave eventually ventured.

"I don't mean to be critical if it is, but my parents aren't exactly rich. If you want me to point you out to some really well off houses up Nibleton's luxury neighborhoods, we could get you a lot bigger bang for your buck . . ."

Dave might as well have been alone for the response he got. He looked from the backseat to Mr. Neech at the steering wheel then back to Mr. Haley. Both simply gazed forward.

Dave shrugged. Vaguely, he recognized that he should be feeling panicked, but worrying about things out of his control had never been his habit. For one thing, getting worked up about a test he never studied for or being late to class never helped him to do better on the test or get to the class faster. For another thing, Dave felt sure that Mr. Haley was going to have to release his wrist at some point. And that was all Dave would need to make his escape. Unless the dude happened to be a secretly awesome traceur—Dave doubted if old stone face would even know that traceur was someone who practiced parkour—then Dave would be long gone before Mr. Haley and this super relentless college recruiter would be able to take a single step.

Before Dave could voice his next one-liner about whether there was a special scholarship for kidnapped students, they pulled into an empty parking lot, the one on the top of a hill in Nibleton that Dave dimly remembered as being a hospital years ago until they built a new and bigger one on the outskirts of town. Innately, open parking lots bored Dave—nothing to parkour on.

Mr. Neech parked, leaving Dave and Mr. Haley to exit out the same door. "A bit more over there," Mr. Neech joined them, and they walked smoothly across a few parking spots.

When they stopped, Dave noticed how Mr. Neech deliberately avoided eye contact with him and spoke to Mr. Haley. "We'll have to make this quick because he's going to want to take off as soon as you let go of him. At the same time I don't want to ferry you with him."

"Got it," Mr. Haley finally spoke, his voice gravelly, as if upset that it was being required to be part of this exchange.

Dave's half-smile twitched upwards a tic. *Dudes, I'm totally gonna take off as soon as you let go of me!*

"Okay," Mr. Neech announced, "on my signal."

Dave Gardner's body tensed, preparing for the release. His mind also considered what parting shot he would say while looking into the eyes of Mr. Neech just before he cleared the parking lot and worked into streets, backyards, roofs and any other obstacle that would lead to his inevitable escape.

The release never came.

Just a dozen feet in front of Dave and his captors emerged some sort of shimmering mass of particles from out of nowhere. One second, they had been in an empty parking lot, the next thing Dave knew a crowd of people gripping hands in a circle appeared.

If it was any consolation, he was not the only person confused by this scene as he noticed Mr. Neech and Mr. Haley furrowing their eyebrows.

As Dave scanned the crowd in front of him, he saw them taking in their surroundings. On the far side of the circle, he noticed the faces of Luke and Tina, students he knew from school. On the near side of the circle, facing away from Dave, he recognized the back head of someone who he sat behind for most of the school year in Mrs. Weston's math class: Eric Francis.

Quickly, his attention was brought to someone he did not recognize—a young woman in a long dark coat holding onto Luke's hand. As soon as the shimmering that accompanied their mystical appearance in the parking lot ceased, the young woman made a move. She slipped her hands free of the circle and pushed the guy standing next to her into a larger person already gripping that same guy's hand. As far as Dave knew he could not recognize either of the men involved, though the larger one had his back to Dave.

With a swift movement that large person stopped the guy shoved into him, but while this happened the young woman had already zipped across the middle of the group and started wresting a girl out of the circle.

While Dave might have struggled to keep up with each new development, Eric did not hesitate. He immediately freed both of his hands from the circle and jumped onto the attacking woman. The next thing Dave knew, Eric and the young woman in the dark coat disappeared. Dave blinked a couple of times while everyone in the circle looked back and forth, confused.

"Where is he?!" Dave heard someone voice his own thoughts. It was a voice he recognized, coming from a girl facing away from him. He did not need to see her face to realize that it was Charlotte.

The large person stepped forward. "They can't be far."

"Dad, you promised me!" Charlotte pressed. "You promised me you would protect Eric! Did she ferry him?! Are they gone?!"

"Facade is a street magician," Charlotte's dad said calmly, "not a seer. She was wearing a black trench coat. She must have used it to cover them both and roll to the ground."

"She's not strong enough to hold Eric," Charlotte replied. "Where are they? What did she do to him? Eric! Eric!"

It was at that moment that Dave noticed his wrist was suddenly free. Mr. Haley, his silent sentry, was gone. Then he detected a muffled noise to his right, followed by some shuffling and scraping.

Back in the circle, Charlotte's dad retraced the young woman's path of assault and swept his feet in small arcs over the dark parking lot where they disappeared. "Stay right where you are, Facade!" he voiced into the darkness, "Don't make this harder on yourself."

Before Dave could even process Mr. Haley leaving him, Mr. Neech had grabbed his other wrist, "What's going on, Facade?!" Neech hissed.

"I'm about to get you out of a big mess," Facade whispered intently. Then Dave saw the young woman in the dark coat emerge out of the darkness. Mr. Haley crouched near to the ground just behind her, one of his large arms clasping someone with his other hand wrapped around that person's mouth. Eric, Dave realized. *How did they get here? They were fifteen feet away only seconds ago . . .*

Neech growled, "It looks like you've made more of a mess than I—"

"Shut up, and listen. We've only got seconds until we lose our chance," Facade interrupted. "Take the river pig and have him holding onto the boy Haley's got. I'm going to try to draw that big guy into grabbing one of the two of them. As soon as he does, you ferry the river pig out of here. Once the big guy and the other two are ferried with him, we'll clean up the rest of them easily enough."

Mr. Neech's face may have snarled, but he did as told and yanked Dave over to Eric, placing his hand on Eric's head. Dave still felt as if he needed several minutes to put together even the most simple actions and comments that had happened over the last several seconds. He would not even get a moment.

Next to him, he heard Facade clear her throat. "Here goes," she muttered, apparently to herself. Then, out loud, she called out, "I've got Eric. The safest thing for everyone is to stay away while I get out of here!"

"Eric!" Charlotte's voice rose as she turned her head to face them. Charlotte's dad started to pivot their direction, his body tensed.

"Get ready," Facade said in a low murmur. Mr. Haley used the warning to remove his hand from Eric's mouth. "He will want to protect Eric, so as soon as he . . ."

Dave tried to listen in, but instead he heard his name and saw that Eric was looking up at him. "Dave," Eric's jaw barely moved. "They're going to try to let go of you in a second. Don't let them."

Dave's head swirled. *I thought we were trying to get away from these guys!* But he mentally shrugged. *I guess I gotta trust the dude that's not as confused as me!*

The speed with which Charlotte's dad closed the gap between the two groups was breathtaking. In a moment, he had one hand on Eric and the other had reached past to grab Facade, who clearly had not expected such a quick response.

"Not yet, Neech!" Facade's eyes widened. "Wait 'till I'm free."

Dave saw Mr. Neech nod, but his hand was now removing itself from Dave's arm. Following Eric's instructions, Dave reached across with his free hand and snatched Neech.

"Let go of me, boy!" Neech snarled. A similar command echoed out of Mr. Haley's mouth. Eric must have grabbed Haley as he was trying to let go.

Facade started to squirm with surprising agility, but she remained stuck to the implacable hand of Charlotte's dad. "You think I'll let you slip away once I've finally got a hand on you?" he stated.

Dave did not know this Facade girl, but she did not seem the type to scare easily. She was clearly scared now.

In the other direction, Dave noticed that the circle had suddenly disintegrated. "Eric," Charlotte stated while striding their direction, "are you okay?" As she came, she scanned the group with a bemused look. "And who are these people that—"

"Charlotte!" the voice of a young girl cried out, "there's three strangers with them. Three!"

Shouting at the same time, Eric warned: "Don't look!"

The warnings landed, but not before Charlotte could withdraw the current sweeping of her gaze as it slid across Dave's eyes. The last thing he saw was eyes that widened.

And I accused the college recruiter dude from using a substance, he thought as the world he knew swirled out of existence.

Chapter 2

THIS LITTLE PIGGIE ...
AND TWO SEERS

Immediately the night air resounded with some hard slaps, bonks, and splashes accompanied by a string of curses.

"I did *not* look at the river pig! How did we end up ferrying?" Dave recognized the voice of Mr. Neech from somewhere beneath him. In fact, all of the sounds were beneath him. Dave was the only person still standing on his own two feet.

In the moonlight, he tried to gather his surroundings. The ground wobbled, and Dave noticed that he stood on two different logs bobbing in the black waters of what must have been a river or lake of some sort. A river, his mind assured him as he detected a trickling sound emanating from several points all around—though it was difficult to see the water's surface, since it was dotted with downed tree trunks all over the immediate area.

Facade answered Neech's irritated query. "The girl. She's a seer too. She must have looked at the river pig, and since we were all touching at the time, we all ferried."

Dave knew that moments before they—what did they call it? ferried?—Charlotte's dad had been holding onto her and Eric, but since they were now on logs on a river, the two had been separated while falling in and Dave could hear Facade slinking away from the group.

Mr. Neech must have found some footing because he suddenly stopped wading and rose a little bit out of the river. "Then we need to all be holding onto the river pig. She might ferry him back at any moment."

"Maybe," Facade replied, "but more likely, she'll join us once she's figured out what she's done." Facade looked around and called out, "Haley, do you still have that boy?"

Mr. Haley grunted in the affirmative.

Mr. Neech acted exasperated. "What do you mean, she'll join us? She missed her chance when she ferried us without touching any of us."

"This is no ordinary seer, Neech," Facade warned. "That's why I'm telling you that our best bet is to get ourselves out of here and find some place to hunker down until the moon reciprocates."

"What are you talking about?" Mr. Neech complained. "What in the world is going on here?"

"I'm telling you," Facade spat impatiently, "that this girl is unlike any seer I've heard of before, and unless you want this big guy and pirate pro to get reinforcements, I advise that we grab them and get out of here now."

Charlotte's father had found his footing and stood in the river as well. "We're not going anywhere," he stated.

Facade sneered, though at a safe distance, "I think you will. Mr. Haley is not one known to let go of a captive until he's told to. And I know that you promised your sweet seer daughter that you would protect Eric. That means you're going to come with us so that you can assure nothing bad happens to Eric. And if you do as you're told, nothing bad will happen to him. Otherwise, Mr. Haley has a knack for disposing of property that is no longer useful to him."

Dave noticed that Mr. Haley, still gripping Eric, now gravitated towards Facade. Both of them held the discussion while navigating around floating tree logs and working towards the opposite river bank.

"I can take care of myself," Eric spoke out towards Charlotte's dad. "I got away from them before, and I can do it again. You wait for Charlotte. Protect your daughter."

Dave could see Charlotte's dad hesitate. "You know that your daughter's boyfriend is in greater danger than she is right now," Facade hissed. "You promised her. Or are you one of those dads that makes empty promises all the time?"

Charlotte's dad took a breath before deftly wading towards Facade, Mr. Haley, and Eric, who were now climbing out of the river. "Not too close," Facade warned as he came.

Dave squinted. It seemed like he was forgetting something.

Suddenly Eric called out, "Dave, watch out!"

All of a sudden, someone grabbed his foot. He looked down. During the conversation going back and forth, Mr. Neech had been able to slink back to where Dave stood. Now his hand held tight onto Dave's foot. "Let's go, river pig. It's time to clear out this place."

Though too late to warn him about Neech, Eric did not give in. "Get away, Dave, and then make sure you tell Charlotte what happened when she comes!"

Mr. Neech shook his head. "If you think I'm letting go of you for anything, then you're quite mistaken."

Dave felt the log underneath him bob as Neech adjusted his grip on the foot to make it stronger. Yet, Eric's instruction gave Dave purpose, and for some reason he felt strangely confident in this situation. He gazed down at Mr. Neech for a moment before his other foot left the log it stood on and slammed down behind his captive foot. This caused the log he stood on to see-saw upwards and thwack Neech in the side of the head. Neech instantly released his hold on Dave's ankle and screamed while grabbing his head.

"Dude," Dave quipped, "I must be mistaken, 'cause I thought you weren't letting go of me."

Dave looked to the river bank and saw Mr. Haley tense, as if he wanted to correct the mistake, but Facade put her hand on his shoulder. "We'll never catch him. He's in his element. Hang on to Eric."

Neech either did not hear Facade's statement towards Mr. Haley or he did not put much stock into it, because after Dave's taunt, he squinted upwards. "The next time I won't let go until you stop moving from me holding your head under the water!" he growled and lunged.

It was useless. In an exhilarating way that Dave could not even begin to understand, he leapt from the log he stood on to another as Neech's hands snapped at air. The other log's surface was wet and smooth, without bark, and it bobbed and spun unpredictably upon his landing. Yet Dave's foot made some subtle adjustments as he slid into another leap that took him to another nearby log. His movement repeated and repeated and wind filled his face in a way more satisfying than even parkour could ever accomplish as he danced on the logs. It felt so natural that he decided he would never be able to walk on solid ground again without it feeling coarse and beneath him.

It took considerable restraint, but somehow Sally managed not to say the obvious: this was the scene predicted in the picture that Charlotte saw—six ferried while five stayed.

The question in Sally's mind was, what was the next step? She looked towards Charlotte. There she saw the same semblance of recognition that Sally just went through flitting across her face. Except as soon as Charlotte hit the "what's the next step" phase of the thought process it became clear through Charlotte's strong eyes and set jaw that she knew exactly what her next step would be.

While Luke, Tina, and even the chiclero started to mumble concerning the startling disappearance of the others, Charlotte looked straight up in the sky, immediately locating the moon. She was going to ferry after them.

A small part of Sally wanted to stay silent and thus be left out of the ensuing action. She had been eager, even stubborn, about joining before. She did not want to be left out. How come Eric always got to do things while she didn't? It wouldn't be fair! All these were thoughts she harbored before, but now? After being part of a sliver of a night's adventures which really translated to nearly a month's worth of trudging, waiting, stressing, fearing, and not knowing if they would ever get back to the boring life that she now longed for, Sally finally stood on the cold, real, ground of her hometown of dull—gloriously dull—Nibleton.

She saw Charlotte's eyes fix on the moon above. All it would take to avoid the uncertainty of what lay beyond the next ferry would be to say nothing. Certainly Sally had contributed nothing to their earlier ventures. Her heart fell as she realized that—if anything—her presence had made things worse, leading to the capture of Eric.

Eric. Eric, who refused to abandon her. Who, even though he was annoyed with her, did not hesitate to offer up himself to free her. Remembering that caused Sally to realize that, scared or not, helpful or not, she would not just watch Charlotte disappear and then turn her back on her brother.

Charlotte's eyes started their mystical focus on the moon. Now or never. "Charlotte, wait!" Charlotte's eyes reluctantly ripped from the night sky. "I'm coming with you," Sally asserted, walking over and grabbing Charlotte's hand.

Charlotte seemed about to contradict her, but then—as if recognizing how much effort and time it would take to talk Sally out of it—she instead squeezed Sally's hand to confirm her approval.

Without speaking, Tina and Luke realized what had just about happened. They jumped forward—Tina grabbing Sally's free hand and Luke gripping Charlotte's.

The seer nodded and began to track her sight upward once more. She was interrupted one final time.

"There's no way I'm staying here. I don't know if you'll be coming back! If I'm gonna get back to my home, I'm coming with the witch!" Felipe ran to join the group. At first he almost snatched Luke's hand, but a quick look changed his mind and he awkwardly scrambled over to Tina.

Charlotte shook her head, then shrugged. Finally—eager to avoid further interruption—she gazed up, focused . . . and the world disappeared.

I will never get used to this, Sally thought, then followed with, I hope!

Charlotte was prepared to step straight out of the ferry and throw herself headlong into Facade, Neech, and whoever else might be in the way of her freeing Eric.

Instead she found herself wobbling and unable to move either one of her feet. On either side of her, she lost her grip and heard two gasps followed by splashes. I'm next, she thought as she finally lost equilibrium. But the tumble downward never came. Arms wrapped under her armpits and over her shoulders, cinching down tight and keeping her impressively steady.

"Wish I coulda grabbed you all," a voice directly behind her stated, "but Eric specifically told me to watch over you, Charlotte, so that's why you're dry and the rest are wet!"

"Dave!" Charlotte announced without turning around. "Where is he? How did you get away?"

Some sputtering below her told that the others were now standing up and taking in the new surroundings of what must be a river littered with dozens of floating logs.

"Eric," Dave announced, "was taken by Dr. Loco and company in the direction of that far bank with your dad." Dave's hold loosened as he helped turn her around. "And I'll show you how I got away if you follow me with your best impression of slow motion parkour."

Charlotte was not sure what her impression was, but she felt certain it did not resemble parkour of any speed and probably most nearly mirrored some type of intermittent seizure. Fortunately for her, she recognized that Dave was in his element, and he danced neatly around her, leading her delicately from one log to another while supporting her each time she nearly fell and pushing or pulling her into a leap where needed. Behind her she heard the others following, trudging through water waist deep to chest deep while taking in sharp breaths from what must be brisk water.

Once Charlotte stood firmly on some rocks that constituted the bank for what she now realized was a sizable river, and they were joined by soaked companions, Dave looked at Charlotte. "Is it cool if I take a turn at some questions now?"

As much as Charlotte chafed to avoid lengthy explanations and immediately set after Eric, she realized that she at least owed Dave that much. For the next several minutes Charlotte did her best to convey the fantastical details of their situation to Dave while Tina and Sally intervened with clarifiers and Luke placed a comforting hand on his shoulder.

"So I'm a natural born river pig?" Dave concluded.

Charlotte nodded.

"Not exactly exotic sounding," Dave noted, " . . . I love it!"

Luke waved his hands to grab attention. "Where is the chiclero?"

Everyone looked around, seeing no other person in the dark night. Tina finally sounded out. "He was next to me after we dropped in the river. It seems like he scooted off shortly after . . ." she seemed to make a connection mid-sentence, " . . . after Dave told Charlotte the direction the others had gone."

Charlotte immediately attempted to step from the rocks onto logs and make a hopeless break for the other side. Luke held her back.

"What will you do?" his slight tonal deficiency contributed to dampening her fervor. She still tried to push forward. Luke insisted on having her hear him out: "Facade now has Eric and a way to control your dad because of it. She also has two guys that look like they mean business. Plus, Felipe probably figures that Facade is still an ally. That's a pretty tough group."

Charlotte paused. She turned so that the moon reflected off of her face, allowing Luke to read her lips. "I won't let anyone take Eric away from me!"

She meant Facade or Neech, but she could not help but think of her dad as she said it.

Tina reached out, took Charlotte's hand, and led her to more firm ground. "Of course not. We'll get Eric back. First, we need to come up with a plan."

Charlotte instinctively shook her head. No more waiting! Her fists clenched.

Sally stepped forward, "A wise person once told me that instead of machetes and fists, sometimes all you need is a bag of chicle."

Charlotte put her hand on Sally's shoulder and nodded. The point was a good one. If she wanted Eric back, recklessly charging across a river and into an awaiting group of enemies would not get her very far.

Their problem, she thought, was that they did not even have a bag of chicle this time around.

After Facade explained everything, Neech sat speechless. "I've never heard of a seer who could alter the phase, and without the natural borner with her, no less," he finally spoke out. After a pause, he said, "But I know someone who probably does . . ."

Eric noticed Facade's eyes narrow, but she did not say anything. Neech continued, "It can't be a coincidence that I follow him to this backward town in the middle of nowhere, and we happen to stumble across a seer with extraordinary abilities." Neech refocused on Facade. "He was looking for her. In fact, I think she must be the one he's been looking for all these years."

They had taken rest in a clearing cut through the woods that obviously had been harvested by loggers, since freshly cut stumps scattered all around. The one called Mr. Haley deposited them in the far side of the clearing, then pulled out some zip ties from his jacket and used them to secure Eric and Mr. Reeves. Eric noticed that he took particular care in ensuring that Mr. Reeves was properly bound before alerting Neech and Facade that he was going to take up watch. He disappeared into the shadows in the direction they came.

As he left, Eric wondered who this person was that Neech followed to Nibleton. Second, he wondered how the person could know about Charlotte and what he knew about her abilities.

"You'd better get some rest while you can," Neech flung at Eric and Mr. Reeves. "We might be on the move again real soon, and I am not going to listen to any whining about how tired you are at that point."

Needing no further motivation, Eric and Mr. Reeves plopped to the ground. Eric shifted uncomfortably as he felt a sort of rock or something on the ground beneath the dead pine needles he sat down on. With his hands latched behind his back, it took some awkward movements to be able to dig through the ground cover to reach the rock.

Except, it wasn't a rock. The object he felt was smooth, hard, and manmade. As his fingers slid along the shape, he found that one far edge converged into a sharp line. The same fingers soon discovered a perfect hole about the size of two of his thumbs that went from one end completely through to the other. A vision of the object now clarified in his mind. He looked around at all the stumps with new purpose.

Eric had just plopped down on some logger's discarded axehead. Considering how sharp the edge was, it must not have been something that had been purposely discarded but must have slid off the haft of the axe and landed where the logger could not have seen it. Possibly while up in a tree taking the top off or dozens of yards away swinging as hard as possible. Either way, Eric knew that this discovery gave him and Mr. Reeves an instant advantage.

While Neech continued to press Facade on details of Charlotte and their previous ferrying, Eric managed to catch Mr. Reeves's attention. He rolled slightly to the side so that he could manage to reveal the axehead in his tightly bound hands while using his body to screen Neech or Facade from seeing anything.

Mr. Reeves's eyes widened immediately. He looked over to Neech and Facade carefully, then motioned Eric to slide closer to his back, where his own bound hands reached out. "Hand it to me, and then hold still," he managed to mutter without moving his lips.

"What's the plan?" Eric asked, likewise holding his lips as still as possible as he shifted the axehead carefully into Mr. Reeves's hands.

Mr. Reeves kept his face down, but spoke quickly as Eric felt the axehead sliding back and forth against his zip ties. "If you get away then they'll lose any leverage against us they hoped to use. The first chance you get, escape. I'll do my best to keep them from coming after you as long as possible. If I have a chance, I'll even get away myself. But if not, you guys ferry back without me. They won't leave me here, and even if they did, once the coast was clear, Charlotte could come back for me."

Eric had some objections, but he would not get to voice them. In one instance, his hands were released, in the next he heard a warning hiss from Mr. Reeves. Eric snapped his eyes closed, as if resting, while rolling onto his back and keeping his hands hidden there to maintain the illusion that he was still bound.

"Pirate hero," Neech kicked him. "I know you're not asleep. Tell me what you know about your seer friend . . ."

Eric remained silent, eyes closed.

"He stopped being talkative after a productive chat he and I had," Facade stated drily.

"I'd wager the seer's daddy knows a lot more than the quiet boyfriend here," Neech observed, "But natural born bodyguards tend to guard information almost as efficiently as they do bodies."

Through the slits in his eyes Eric saw Mr. Reeves open his own in order to look Neech straight in the face, yet he still managed to not betray any emotion—an act that appeared to unsettle Neech.

The bornapper broke the gaze to presumably resume his discussion with Facade. "I can't imagine that this is another coincidence. A seer with unheard of capabilities that would attract all sorts of interested parties just *happens* to have a father who is a natural born bodyguard. Seems pretty convenient, don't you think?"

Facade did not seem interested in having a staged conversation, but she did eye Mr. Reeves curiously.

"There's no question that daddy seer knows all about her abilities. The question is who is Mr. Reeves working for? Who assigned him to this duty sixteen years ago? Was it her real parents? Or did someone—forgive the harsh usage—*kidnap* her and put her under this bodyguard's care until she started to develop her skills . . . ?"

Neech knelt down next to Mr. Reeves, reconnecting his gaze to finish his monologue: "That would be rich. Eric condemns me as a natural bornapper and in reality the father of his friend turns out to be the stooge of a *real* kidnapper!"

Mr. Reeves's next move came at lightning speed. Before Eric realized what happened, Mr. Reeves crouched his legs up, jerked his zip-tied arms underneath his feet, which allowed them to come forward and slam over Neech's head while tightening around the back of his neck. Neech tried to squirm free, but every movement caused Mr. Reeves to clench tighter until Neech, his face now shoved into Mr. Reeves's chest, caved into pitiful submission.

"I can imagine someone like you would have no understanding of a parent's love for their child. Clearly, you had no such advantage," Mr. Reeves's statement slid out of his mouth quietly yet firmly. "So in consideration of your ignorance, I'll only request this one time that you keep your speculations to yourself. If that simple feat is asking too much, then I might have to snap this pathetic little neck without so much as a—"

"I think he got the message," Facade appeared, wielding a dagger inches from Mr. Reeves's side.

Mr. Reeves acted as though he expected this interruption. Calmly, he widened his arms and released Neech from his hold. Neech crawled piteously away, hands checking his neck as if to assure that it remained connected to his body.

Everyone sat speechless for a while, and Eric realized that if he had wanted to, Mr. Reeves could have used the axehead to do permanent damage to Neech. Yet, the axehead was nowhere to be seen, and Eric realized what Mr. Reeves must have: that killing or holding Neech hostage would maybe work momentarily, but could have been damaging in the long run.

After some deep breaths, Neech shot a contemptuous look towards Mr. Reeves. "It doesn't matter. Not only will we leave you in this world—a shame since it will be a perfect waste of your truly exceptional natural born talents—but I don't care what you're hiding about this girl Charlotte, because once we're back, I'm going to recruit her to the affirming cause."

Mr. Reeves's eyes glazed over at this point, but Neech continued. "Whatever you were saving her for, she'll never find out. Instead, she'll be able to help me affirm in unprecedented ways. Imagine! If she can alter the placement of the moon in a single night, what is to stop her from altering it over days at a time . . . full phases of the moon accessed at a given moment! We would not have to wait for someone's phase of the moon in order to affirm them, we would only need to have their place of birth. It would change everything . . . the breakthrough I've been waiting for!"

Eric could not help but jump in at this point. "Breakthrough? Breakthrough in essentially murdering a person by taking away the only life they've ever known and separating them permanently from their friends and family?"

Neech narrowed his eyes and swiveled to Eric. "I shouldn't even waste my time speaking to someone so weak that he actually had a choice to reach his fullest potential and deliberately passed it up. No wonder you use such vulgar terms like 'murder' when referring to the only thing that will actually give someone meaning in their life. In my view an unaffirmed life is simply a slower and more definitive murder than any action I might take."

"Against their wishes? Don't you think they should have a say about whether they say goodbye to their family forever or not?" Eric countered.

"Pathetic." Neech shook his head. "If left alone to be ruled by their emotions, mankind will never reach the apex of their evolution. Ask the baby bird if it wants to be pushed out of its nest and I'm sure it'd choose to use two legs for the rest of its pointless life. Push it out and it will soar to heights greater than it could have ever imagined."

"Seems like the pusher never expected to get pushed out of the nest himself," Eric pointed out.

"This isn't my world!" Neech retorted, irritated. "Nor is it yours. But if you want to talk choices, your poor choice of meddling where you don't belong is going to leave you stuck in a world that has neither the benefits of your natural born ability nor even the shallow comfort that your weak nature has for family and friends."

"We've heard enough of your threats and proselyting," Mr. Reeves spoke out. "Your whole premise is that Charlotte will willingly work for you, yet you think she'll do anything of the sort once you've abandoned her friend and family in a world they don't belong to?"

Neech chuckled. "Facade, they believe that I can't convince someone to do something they would normally be adamantly opposed to doing. What is your take on that fascinating concept?"

Facade returned Neech's look coolly for some hard moments. Neech sported an irksome grin. "I think we're wasting time talking to them," she finally stated. "Let them get back to pretending like they are asleep while we talk strategy."

Neech's grin slowly melted away. "Fine," he said, "since you're in no mood for fun."

Facade ignored the retort, "We've got two of their number right now—two of their most formidable—but no one in their group is a pushover besides maybe the little sister. And they've got the natural-borner in that river pig. That's always been a strong home turf advantage. Plus, they know the place and time we will meet to ferry back. It's always tricky to pull off a deception when the onlookers know exactly where and when to watch."

Neech nodded slowly, grimacing.

A sudden muffled sound surprised them. They looked into the darkness from where it emanated. Out of obscurity strode Haley, forcefully dragging someone with him, one hand covering the captive's mouth the other wrapped around his waist. Eric did not take long to identify Felipe, wide-eyed and panicky.

"Found him lurking this way," Haley declared, dropping him thoughtlessly before the others.

His mouth freed, Felipe immediately began jabbering nonsense until Facade interrupted. "This is the chiclero I spoke of. That's another added to our numbers, though, it's hard to say if he'll be a help or a hindrance."

"There's something else you might be interested in, Neech," Haley proposed, his voice neither harsh nor urgent yet still insistent. The two disappeared for a few minutes while Felipe whimpered and shivered.

When Neech returned, Eric saw that his grin had come with him. "Things are about to swing in our direction again, Facade. And if we play this just right, we might even get that seer started on the path towards affirmation."

Eric shifted his freed wrists thoughtfully. *We'll see about that.*

Chapter 3
LOGJAM

Sally's Scribblings

You'll notice that I soaked the Scribblings Diary . . . not my fault! I'd blame Charlotte, since she's the one that ferried us into the middle of a river, but I doubt that she has much control over where the ferry landing takes place.

Still, she—and Eric's cell phone—are dry while the rest of us got wet. Maybe I'll blame Eric, since he is the one who told Dave to take special care of Charlotte. I mean, I know that they have a crush on each other that Eric is too shy to talk about, but I am family after all.

Oh well, at least we found an empty lodge in the forest where Dave and Luke could build a fire so we could dry off and not freeze (and where I could leave the diary all night so it would dry off as much as possible). The lodge was empty, but it looks like it usually has people because there is a lot of equipment and packs and . . . well . . . some smells. There isn't anything that you could plug into though, so whenever this is, it must be pre-cell phone/internet. Why couldn't Dave's natural born ability be a Tropical Resort Manager or something?

Whatever a river pig is, he must be testing it out right now because Charlotte left early this morning while we were all asleep and she was supposed to be on watch. When Luke woke up and found her missing, he immediately set out to make sure she was okay. Dave said, "There's no way you're leaving without me, bro." I guess river pigs think everyone is their brother. Anyway, Tina said she would stay at the lodge with me until they get back. She went outside while I tried to sleep more, but I haven't been able to, and since the diary is relatively dry at this point, I figured I might as well jot down some . . . hang on. Tina's talking to someone. Maybe they found Eric? I'm going to investigate.

"Nibleton?" the man said. "Never heard of it. Also, never seen someone wearing such a strange outfit, let alone a young woman, and I've been everywhere from the Great Lakes to the Columbia River Gorge."

The man speaking did so through sporadic whiskers with a high eyebrow and eyes that dominated his face, regardless of a diminutive though sharp nose. His cheeks must have sunk in beneath the whiskers because of how narrow his face looked. As for his garb, Sally noticed suspenders topping a checkered, long-sleeved shirt gripping into pants cut off just past the knee. His boots swallowed large feet wrapped in thick, woolen socks.

Sally had difficulty determining the man's age, but she did observe some scattered gray hairs on his head and face.

"And there's another Little Miss!" he declared, noticing Sally. "Now, I ain't got no problem with a couple visitors, but if you're hiding a platoon's worth of pants-wearing women suffragettes in our crew's lodge, then I may have to formally petition for re*dress*!" The man acted like the emphasis on "dress" proved him the most clever man between the Great Lakes and the Columbia River Gorge.

Seeing no response from Sally or Tina, who looked at each other, confused, he charged forward. "I'm suspecting you came to watch us break up the logjam, seeing as how the logjam of Grand Falls brought quite the crowd. Well, I hate to disappoint, but it won't be happening for probably another week or so. Had to send some boys down to Lakota Junction to get more dynamite, since we used all ours up. Now, that ain't cause I didn't know what I was doing, seein' as how I doubt you'll find a river pig with more logjam explosive experience from the Great Lakes to the—"

"Columbia River Gorge . . ." Sally could not help but append.

The man eyed Sally critically. "That's right. But them logs were being infernally stubborn, and now they're packed in so tight that you couldn't fit a greased roundshot in the wall."

Sally and Tina looked at each other again, still clueless. "So I don't know if you're here jes yourselves or if you got family or a crew, but I'm thinking you might've just wasted your time. I mean, I could take ya by the logjam to give you a tour—so to speak—and yer group is invited if'n you has one, but otherwise, you'll be camping out for sometime while we wait for the dynamite to arrive. I mean, I just seen them off downriver heading toward Salmon Point Landing. That's why I's gone all night, but now I'm here there's not much to—"

Sally felt absolutely confident that the man would have explained them through the week had they not been interrupted by the arrival of Luke, Dave, and a surly Charlotte.

"Dude!" Dave jumped in, "Did I hear you offer a tour of the logjam? 'Cause I'm more interested in that than an indie documentary on parkour!"

The man's lower lip shoved his upper lip back and forth in intense concentration. "Nibleton, you say?" he finally muttered to Tina. "Might as well be China for as much sense as that jes made." His widened eyes swiveled to take in the full crew.

"Still, I'm at least piecing together that yer interested in a tour. I'll be honest: I ain't got nothin' to do 'cept thumb-twiddlin' fer the next little while, so I 'spose we can hike that way and take a gander."

Amidst the flurry of words that escaped his mouth they found out that their tour guide's name was Jimmy Sellers. They also learned that he was the best river pig from the Great Lakes to . . . well . . . you get the drift.

What was a river pig? According to how Sally could best piece together the Jimmy Sellers's meandering tour guide chatter, river pigs were part of a logging operation. Lumberjacks would select and chop down trees far up river, they'd strip the trunks of branches and bark. Instead of loading them on trucks and transporting them to industries by roads, since there weren't that many big trucks or nice roads back in this time, they found a more cost effective way to move the lumber: roll it into the nearest river.

That is where the river pigs came in. Logs will generally move downriver just like any other old thing that floats, but Sally gathered that river pigs were kind of like log herders. They would follow the logs downriver and keep them from getting bunched up too much or from losing too many strays. They would do this using some kind of spear-like pole with a hook at the end . . . and a lot of balance, running out on logs floating in the river helping to coax logs in the right direction while following the current downriver to where the big companies would fish the logs out and use them from there.

After Sally picked up on these main details, she found Jimmy Sellers repeating himself enough during the mile-long trek upstream to the logjam that her attention started to slide elsewhere. She managed to slip back to a stewing Charlotte. Forgoing her instincts, she said nothing at first. Her hard-fought patience paid off.

"I couldn't even find the river," Charlotte spat out. "I thought it was to the left of the lodge, and I heard running water, but I guess it was actually just a creek that connects to—" Charlotte threw her hands in the air.

The two walked in silence for a while. "The boys said they would find out where Eric is and promised we would get him, but I . . ." Charlotte stopped walking and took a deep breath.

Sally looked at her. She was used to seeing Charlotte as a self-assured, assertive role model—someone who could give a pep talk to even Eric on his worst days. Now, though, Charlotte seemed confused and frazzled.

"It's too bad Eric's cell battery died. It might be nice to know what's going to happen," Sally mused.

Charlotte's hand immediately went to her pocket where Eric's phone sat, inert. She gave Sally a funny look, then she lifted her hand away from the pocket. "Yes, too bad," she mumbled.

Charlotte started walking again, and Sally tried to stay in lockstep with her. Out of the blue she said, "I'm moving, Sally. Far away. And I won't be back. I won't even write or communicate at all."

"What?" Sally blurted. "Why?"

Charlotte's fists clenched. "Because I'm a seer and my parents think I need to be protected. They act like being a seer is some sort of powerful, coveted ability. All it's ever done for me, though, is keep me uprooted and alone." Charlotte's eyes hardened. "And now, even though I got us here, I can't even save my best friend for maybe the last time I'll ever see him. I am useless."

"Tell me about it," Sally responded, and then, before she could stop herself, "But at least you know what your ability is and why you feel so useless."

Charlotte looked Sally in the eye. "You're right. But that's the whole problem, isn't it? If I didn't know I was a seer—if no one knew—then my parents wouldn't be so careful and I could stay in one spot and—"

"—and never meet Eric, never help Eric," Sally interrupted.

Charlotte shook her head. "And if I never see Eric after this is over, isn't that the same thing?"

Sally could tell that Charlotte was stuck and any prodding Sally might try would get her nowhere at this point. The rest of the walk to the logjam occurred in silence and even though she had tired quickly of Jimmy's talking earlier, Sally found it a relief when they made it to the logjam, grouped up, and Jimmy opened the floodgates.

"As you can see, she's loaded higher than two grizzly bear standin' one atop the other'un," Jimmy pointed ahead. They gasped. The river had disappeared. Piled exactly where it should be was a wall of the most hopeless mess of timber Sally could have thought possible.

"How did they get there?" Tina voiced their thoughts.

Jimmy sucked in a large batch of air, preparing to expand, "Well," he let slide out, "we—"

"You were moving cut logs down the river, and they must've bunched up on a snag, then the ones behind it got sucked in, which caused the next batch to pile up wider and higher. I mean, it's just like a bottleneck on a highway causing a chain reaction of one car after another car!"

The voice of enthusiasm came from Dave, whose eyes devoured the scene in front of them. Spouts of water escaped from crevices in the logjam and from underneath the bottom, but otherwise Sally saw no hint that a river formed any part of this picture. The forest and boulders framing either side seemed to mute every noise save an eerie trickling of water, which suggested something ominous to this otherwise peaceful location.

Jimmy Sellers eyed Dave with a look that hinted he did not know what to make of him. "That's right, young feller. Well, mostly right. I ain't so sure 'bout that fool-headed nonsense dealin' with highways n'—whaddid ya call 'em, 'cars'?—but you've managed to sum it up well enough fer . . ."

"That's the ferry point," Charlotte whispered loud enough for all but Jimmy to hear.

"We ferried into the river right in front of that huge wall of dead trees that looks like it could crumple at any moment?" Sally's eyes widened. She saw some stray logs lazily swirling just in front of the logjam as if they fell over top of the wall but were not quite ready to leave it yet. She recognized them as

252

the ones where Dave had nimbly snatched Charlotte, then Sally saw the bank they congregated at in the dark when Charlotte threatened to chase after Eric on her own.

Sally frowned. "Looks like unless we're Dave or someone Dave is holding onto, we're going to have to get wet if we want to ferry back home."

"Some of us could use the bath," Luke winked at Sally, and in spite of her taking pride in her hygiene habits, she could not help but snicker, thinking, "I'm going to have to put that in my Scribblings Diary. That was a good line."

Jimmy must have noticed that they had stopped paying attention because he paused in the middle of some elaborate informational gem and asked what they were talking about.

"Oh," Tina quickly replied. "We were just wondering if this is where you planned to use the dynamite?"

"Dynamite?" Dave's voice slipped in before Jimmy Sellers could complete his inhaling, "Dude, as much as I love a big bang, you're gonna lose quite a bit of timber that way. I'm betting the logging company will take a pretty steep loss from all that lumber being blown into mini-toothpicks."

"True, it's no small price," Jimmy Sellers admitted, "but it's a might less than they're losing everyday that these logs is stuck up river. We ain't talking breaking even by the time the boys come back with the TNT—we're just trying to keep from losing so much that the companies don't sink and we lose our jobs."

Dave nodded. "Well then, I'd say it's worth a second look, wouldn't you?"

Before Jimmy Sellers could contradict Dave, the traceur lightly trotted over to where the wall of logs touched the river bank. Without pausing, Dave scaled the steep confluence of protruding trunks without even using his hands. Then, like a spider weaving a web, he zigzagged up and down the wall eyeing the pattern of chaos as he swept across towards the opposite bank.

Sally and the others stood in awe. It would have taken Sally a half an hour just to make it to the top of the logjam—assuming she did not slip and tumble into serious injury. For Dave, however, he might as well have been going on a morning stroll, albeit one where he made impressive leaps over daunting gaps, danced capably on logs that shifted with his every movement, and glided with a quickness of thought that made it seem as if he operated under the guise of thinking twelve steps ahead. In a matter of minutes, Dave had traversed the entire span of the logjam and made it back. Jimmy Sellers was more out of breath after one of his long explanations than Dave appeared to be.

"That's a pretty tight group of logs—no doubt about it!" Dave peered back at the wall. "But I think I've pinpointed the breaking point, right over towards the middle there."

Jimmy looked at him incredulously. "How did you . . . ?"

"Well, I mean, it'd take some doing," Dave clarified. "Right now, that sucker's not going anywhere. But is there a way we could add more water to the back end? Raise the water level by two feet, or even a foot and a half would do the trick, and it'd be in the perfect situation. A flick of the foot on the right log, and I could clear the whole thing out for you in a matter of minutes, and you wouldn't have to wait for your bros to come with dynamite."

"There's Summit Creek 'bout half a mile over that ridge. It's got enough water to raise things up enough in a couple of days, but we got no way to git the water ta this side without taking weeks to dig a canal er something that . . ." Jimmy caught himself, "But enough of that! I don't even know who you are. Now tell me what crew you workin' fer, son? I ain't never seen you 'round these parts."

Dave grinned. "Work? That's the first time someone's accused me of working." Dave winked at Sally, "Wait 'till my mom hears about this!"

Jimmy Sellers scruffed his beard as he thought. "Now, hang on. Are you one of the new ones from ole' Dickey's crew in the camp downriver on the opposite bank? I know they got yanked to another river jes before the logjam, but I seen smoke over yonder this morning as I's hoofin' it fer our—"

Dave, Luke, Tina, and Charlotte all looked at each other. "Eric," Charlotte voiced intently.

"Dude, how far downriver?"

"It's 'Jimmy' not 'Dude,' and more or less same distance as our lodge, but across the other side of the river, over a dell and into a clearing. Are you tellin' me you ain't part of Dickey's crew?" Jimmy's hand now transferred to rub the back part of his neck in consternation.

"I'm going," Charlotte determined. She looked at the group, defying them to contradict her. No one did.

Neech looked over the group of a dozen men that Haley had intercepted. Recruiting them had proven simple. Neech always carried with him gold trinkets and coins. He never knew when his work might carry him to other worlds, and gold happened to be common currency in most of them. An offer of a handful of gold bought their services for the foreseeable future—and a formidable crew they seemed to be. They were all river pigs, the same profession as the natural born ability of Dave Gardner. Because of their all day work on the river, hefting logs, removing snags, agilely moving from one spot to another, just a few of them would have been a physical match for their ferried counterparts.

"Gentlemen," Neech said, "this is Mr. Haley. He is going to clarify the specific services we have in mind for you. Remember, if you perform as instructed, you'll get double what I've paid you just to listen."

Haley stepped forward. Though the sun just passed its zenith, Haley still managed to find just the slightest amount of shade to cover his face from a nearby pine tree. The quiet man always seemed attracted to the shadows. Haley spoke, giving out instructions for an ambush and capture of the seer's crew, which he expected to be heading this way sometime this afternoon or evening.

Neech carefully watched the faces of the men to see if any appeared to have reservations against Haley's blunt directives, but their eyes only reflected their greed, and he felt confident that he could count on them for anything now that he set the price just right.

Feeling a bit more at ease, Neech began to lose himself in some ruminations while Haley worked out the specific details. Seeing the men cow to a handful of gold reminded Neech that there was a cold, hard predictability in human nature. Some people despaired at the negative manifestations of it, but Neech had long learned to embrace it—whether that meant paying off a morally ambiguous group of men or using collateral to manipulate a situation to his advantage.

Neech thought back to the boy and bodyguard back in camp. Facade seemed to suggest that the boy could not be used to extort the seer. No doubt Facade was a clever manipulator, but leveraging someone by threatening a loved one was probably not her strong suit. Besides, she only had one person to use as leverage. It is hard to call someone's bluff when eliminating your bargaining chip kills the bargain. But now, they had more than one chip. It would be quick and effective to have the seer witness the death of one of the two to convince her that there was no bluffing involved in this situation.

What a weakness to have connections with family and loved ones, he resolved. They have nothing to do with natural born talent, except that they so often get in the way of it. Neech could not help but be grateful that his ties with family had been cut when he was just a youth of no more than eight. At the time it was painful, sure. Pain is a human weakness, something Neech acknowledged, but when his single mother ran into a male seer and discovered that she had a natural born ability that could remove her from the trappings of her current world—a day-to-day job, financial instability, him—she jumped at it.

He still remembered it viscerally. It no longer made him sad as it used to. He mastered those emotions long ago, but the picture of the moment still remained and he could dispassionately recall it. She told Neech that she was going to pursue the life that she deserved, so that she could finally be happy. She gave him a peck on the forehead and told him, with a distracted look in her eyes, that there was no reason he nor anyone else could not do the same.

"Find out what you are born to do, son. And don't let anyone stop you from doing it."

Then she left forever.

Neech never got to meet the seer that ferried her, but he knew that it was a seer. As he grew and discovered his own seer abilities—the whole event began to make so much more sense. And the more he grew, the more determined he became to make sure that his mom's actions made the most sense.

Some of the other seers he came in contact with tried to explain that a seer's calling was to open eyes to other life possibilities. Neech knew better—his mom had not left him for a possibility but a personal destiny. Neech's ability, he determined dogmatically, was not to *show* people but to *place* people, to affirm their natural born existence by sending them to live out their best lives.

In time, Neech met with other seers who saw things his way, seers who refused to be satisfied with people choosing the mundane over the ultimate life experience. They began affirming. Yet, with only a handful of them, and only being able to affirm in single locations for no more than a couple of days before the affirming-caused-disappearances start to arouse suspicion, Neech despaired at creating a perfect world order where all people eventually found themselves in the world where they truly belong.

However, if they were not restricted to the phase of the moon, Neech once again pondered, then that one night or two would only be limited by the amount of people they could track down who had been born in a single area. Perhaps they would make enough of a dent at that point to attract and recruit more seers, to cause a chain reaction that would go worldwide. Who knew, he dared imagine, what if they were able to create a world of seers, with the rest of the population being ferried to their natural born worlds, perhaps even the minute they were born?

If they were ever able to achieve that, then the natural world order will have been achieved and this silly connection to someone you were arbitrarily born to will be irrelevant. Instead, you will find yourself raised by your own passions and natural born talents in the world destined to be yours. Neech no longer felt the pain that ensued after his mom left him as a youth, he respected her devotion to becoming her best self. And with Charlotte's help, he would become his best self by providing the same experience for countless others.

Neech smiled. Not that he cared, but he could not help but feel as if his mother would be proud.

A stirring among the group brought Neech out of his thoughts. Facade had appeared from one side of the clearing, looking for Neech. Their eyes locked, and he knew that she had bad news. She glided to his side with a quickness and silence that constantly defied his expectations—someday he would need to affirm Facade to the world she belonged in . . . but not yet. She was far too useful now.

"The boy got away," she whispered, causing Neech to flinch more visibly than he preferred. "Got a hold of something sharp, cut the zip ties, and must have taken off when you came to see this group with Haley and I turned my back for a second to get the chiclero to shut up. Couldn't be far."

Neech and Facade both looked at Haley who was just wrapping up some final instructions to the group. "Sounds like a job for a natural born fugitive slave catcher," Neech glowered.

When your job as an affirmer requires you to track down and forcefully snatch reluctant natural borners, Haley's specific skill set was also far too useful for affirming him for the immediate future either.

"Haley," he ordered as soon as the fugitive slave catcher wrapped up. "We've got another job for you."

Chapter 4
NATURAL BORN
FUGITIVE SLAVE CATCHER

Eric did not dare look back as he sprinted through the thick forest undergrowth, but he hoped no one followed him.

The circumstances of his escape were not ideal. Neech and Haley had left, but Facade and Felipe were still in the vicinity. Facade could not have seemed less interested in the job and sat at the far edge of the camp musing or meditating or sleeping with her eyes open . . . Eric could hardly tell, especially not with the enigmatic Facade. Felipe sat at the opposite side of camp and appeared to be muttering to himself. Both were watching them, however, so any immediate plans for escape would have to wait.

"Mr. Reeves," Eric whispered, eyeing Facade.

Mr. Reeves kept his eyes closed. "Yes, Eric."

"There is a lot I don't know about you and Mrs. Reeves, but I know that both of you care for Charlotte as deeply as if you were her parents. I've seen that in every interaction you've ever had with her."

Mr. Reeves opened his eyes and nodded. "Thank you, Eric." He looked at him for a long moment before adding. "And we are her parents."

"I believe you," Eric replied. "That's why you promised Charlotte that you would protect me and why you cut my zip ties before you had me cut yours." Eric's voice, already low, somehow descended. "But I'm going to make sure we both get out of here so you can get back to protecting Charlotte instead of me. If you slip me that axehead, I'll shuffle in front of you so that they can't see what I'm doing and cut your ties. Then, it'll be two against two, we can subdue them and get out of here, then find Charlotte. I'm sure she is here by now. Then we'll ferry back with her."

Eric thought he almost saw Mr. Reeves smile. "If you think that Facade won't suspect any movement that we make, especially one that will have your hand doing a sawing motion near my zip ties, then you underestimate her. We'd be discovered in a matter of seconds and then the fact that I've freed you will have been negated and we'd be out of luck again. No, Eric, we're stuck together for now."

"Just for now, though," Eric noted quietly. "Once we get back, then you're moving and taking Charlotte away forever." Eric took a breath, "That's why I'm more willing to take some risks, because even if I get stuck here, as long as you and Charlotte get back, then it wouldn't matter because—"

Suddenly, Felipe went over to Facade to whimper about something to eat. He stood in front of her for only a moment but it was enough to cause Mr. Reeves to urge Eric to make a break for it.

There were so many other possibilities in that moment, but Eric knew that the chances of failure for both of them escaping far exceeded that of him making a break for it alone. He knew it, and Mr. Reeves knew it.

So Eric simply squirmed behind a log, stayed low to the ground while keeping Felipe's body blocking the view of his movement before reaching the cover of the surrounding forest. Then, he charged recklessly forward through the woods to get as much distance between himself and the makeshift camp as possible, the whole time hoping that he was doing the right thing. It wasn't until five solid minutes passed of leaping and whipping through trees and bushes that Eric took a second to pause and angle his head to listen for any sounds of pursuit. None came. He was far from at ease, but he at least felt he had a moment to think.

They would obviously expect him to try to find Charlotte, and Eric's sense of direction—though not quite as keen as it would have been on the open ocean—managed to lay out the area as a map in his mind. Eric thought it through as if it were a region of the sea.

He had just sprinted for five minutes in a westerly direction—the opposite direction of his ultimate destination, which Neech and his crew knew to be directly to the east of their camp. The river, in Eric's mind, served as a sort of wind or current moving southwards in the middle of his path. How to get to Charlotte then?

If he were sailing, Eric would want to take the long way around to avoid incidental run-ins or traps set by the patrolling ships of the enemies. That meant heading north or south for a ways before making his way east, past the river and then back to where he could find Charlotte. So which way, north or south? Sticking to his ocean analogy, going to the north seemed to make the most sense as being upriver would give him the weather gage on any pursuers. Obviously he knew that he was not really on the ocean, but he determined that he should stick to his instincts and take the route upstream rather than down.

While Eric felt good about that plan, he still sensed that an extra layer of caution might be appropriate. He did not know Neech too well, but he had seen the dangerous cunning of Facade and cold determination of the man called Mr. Haley. They were not the types to be underestimated. With that in mind, Eric decided to not only take the northern route, but to make that route as far out of the way as possible, which meant heading farther north than might be deemed necessary before turning to the east. Even more, he decided to work farther eastwards than necessary past the river for a couple of miles before finally coming down and then approaching Charlotte and the others from the completely opposite direction that anyone would expect.

Not enough? Eric further decided that he would do all this while packing on every extra piece of canvas his ship could manage. Or, to put it in landlubber terms, he was going to race as fast as he could so as to try to cover all that extra distance in the same time it might take for him to reach his destination without going the long way around.

Eric took a deep breath. It was a good plan, perhaps a bit overly cautious, but one that he felt good about. Once there, they could plan how to get Mr.

Reeves back. Maybe, he allowed himself to think, they might be tipping this towards bringing things back to normal.

The back of his mind told him that "normal" did not account for the whole "moving Charlotte" situation, but he quickly turned off that manner of thinking. He had some running to do.

Mr. Haley was not one to show emotion, but put him on the chase and it took all the self-restraint he possessed to not howl like a hounddog on the scent.

It only took a moment for him to find the axehead once they rolled Mr. Reeves over. Neech wanted to talk about it and make some plans, but Haley ignored him, already meandering to the west edge of camp. "Wait," Neech said, "give me a few minutes and we can have a whole posse coming with you."

Haley answered Neech's suggestion with a glower. "I'll be back in one hour." Haley pushed through the undergrowth for a dozen yards before stopping. The tracks he followed were headlong and impetuous. The boy would have reassessed after a quarter mile, Haley estimated. And then he'd turn back.

Next Haley looked north and then south. The boy would not come straight back as that would lead directly through their camp. He would go north or south before returning eastwards. Haley could not quite put a finger to it, but something about the boy and the area told him that the kid would choose the northern route. *They always run north*, he told himself.

By not following Eric's westward flight, Haley could cut out a large portion of the pursuit. *I'll head north until there is an obvious eastward path where I can wait him out . . . or until I run into his trail if he has managed to*

*outrun me to that point, then I'll close the gap and have him back in camp a
half an hour before I told Neech to expect me.*

Haley's stout body did not seem like it was made for running, and when
he moved it could not really be described as running, but the rate he moved,
with his body low to the ground and legs sure-footedly skimming across the
terrain, seemed almost surreal. In no time at all, he coasted to a stop at an
established logger path that seemed as if it would be the obvious route of the
boy heading back towards his group.

In an instant, Haley dropped near the ground and searched for signs of a
recent passing. After a minute or so of fruitless scanning he stood up and
waited. Perhaps his short cut was enough to beat the boy to this eastward
path. If that were the case, he simply needed to wait for the prey to come to
him. He found a shady spot, well-hidden from the path and waited. A minute
passed. Two. Three. Haley left his spot and checked the ground once more.
Had he missed something? He knew that he had not, but he checked again
anyway. Five minutes. To the west there was not even the faintest sound of
someone bolting in this direction.

Knowing his quarry, Haley felt confident that the boy would not be
wasting time. He would be running, whatever direction he was heading, and
if that were the case, he should have passed this way by now.

This left two uncomfortable possibilities: one, there was a strong
likelihood that the boy went south instead of north in his endeavor to return
to the others. Haley grimaced at this idea. If true then it would mean that
Haley had chosen wrong, and he despised being wrong, especially when it
involved his natural born ability. His grimace deepened. It would also mean
that he turned down help from Neech when he probably should have
accepted it because he could have sent a group south and a group north. His
hands converted to fists at the thought and his teeth ground against each
other.

After a moment of consideration, Haley dug in his heels. No. He would
just ignore the possibility of being wrong. That brought him to the second
possibility. That alternative posited that the boy was deliberately avoiding
capture by going farther north than anyone might anticipate. Haley nodded,

convincing himself of this option. The boy knew he was up against formidable foes, and he was bright enough to be cautious. That is exactly what he did.

With this theory lodged, Haley decided that he did not need to move any more north to meet Eric. Instead, he would make up the time he lost in waiting by rushing eastwards to the river. While he could not say how far north the boy would have gone, it did not matter, because Haley knew that at some point he would have to come back south again. Haley would cross the river and then simply wait at a spot on the far bank for the boy's path to lead southwards where he could be easily intercepted.

With a plan formulated, the thrill of the chase returned and Haley's sturdy form traversed the path with deceptive ease until reaching the river. While keeping an eye north, he made the crossing without hardly slowing down. Then his dripping form settled into a perfect hideout within a shaded copse just a stone's throw away from the river and adjacent to an obvious southward path.

Once more, a minute passed. Two. Three.

Irritated, he extricated himself and found a point where he had a wide view of the path northward. Nothing. Five minutes passed.

The doubts came nagging back at him. The boy went south and by now he is reunited with his group. He should not have assumed that Eric went north, he should not have—

Haley stopped. No. He could not be wrong. He refused to allow the possibility that he was wrong. His pursuer mind whirred. Then, it clicked. What if . . . what if the boy had been even more cautious than he originally supposed? What if he purposely overshot the connecting path so as to double round and come back to his friends from the opposite direction, a direction no one would ever suspect him to take?

While the back of his mind continued to nudge at him the clearest likelihood that Eric had simply gone south rather than north, Haley ignored this. If the boy did, indeed, overshoot the river path, then Haley could once again cut out a portion of the route and place himself to the east of Eric's final destination and intercept him.

Taking this desperate gamble as fact, Haley once again scurried to a new spot, one along what must be the now most obvious route. He settled in and waited.

One minute. Two. Three. Haley reluctantly started to entertain the idea that he had failed—truly this time.

And then it happened. Snapping branches, the pounding of feet, ragged breathing.

Even though he had convinced himself this was possible, deep down, he logically expected it to fail. Yet these sounds seemed to indicate that he had somehow, in spite of the odds stacked up against him, figured it out. Then the boy stumbled into view and Haley knew he had done it.

Clearly Eric had been running at top speed for the past hour or so and he was exhausted, breathing raggedly, sweating, losing dexterity. Five more minutes, and the boy's distance running gambit would have paid off. Now, it just made Haley's job easier. From his hidden spot, he slid a branch into the path at the last second. The boy's feet, already dragging, got hopelessly tangled and he crashed to the ground in a clump.

Within a matter of seconds, Haley pounced, zip tied Eric's arms and legs, placed a gag over his mouth, and then hefted him on his shoulders. Though Eric was no light burden, Haley seemed to move the same whether carrying something or not. In a matter of no time, Haley swiftly plowed along, making his way back to the river. He deliberately worked to the south of the logjam, since that would have more shallow water and make it easier to lug his trophy across.

By the time he could hear the stifled current of the river, Haley could tell that Eric managed to catch his breath enough to make an attempt at wriggling free, or at the very least make Haley's job carrying him more uncomfortable. Haley smiled at the pathetic efforts. He had so effectively tied the bonds, there was not much anyone could have done regardless of how much energy they had.

Suddenly, just before he stepped out of the cover of the trees, he heard voices. He paused. They had to belong to the other members of Eric's party, Haley reasoned. Sure enough he heard teenage voices responding to the backwoods dialect of a logger. One of them he clearly recognized as the irksome, laid back, voice of Dave Gardner.

From the snippets of conversation he heard, he could tell they were talking about the technicalities of the logjam, nothing of interest to him. He decided to quietly go south past a bend in the river where he could cross undetected.

Before he took a step, however, he heard the logger mention something about seeing smoke from a campfire, and Haley knew that the man must have seen the smoke from the campfire of the men they recruited—very close to the clearing where they camped out. Would the teenagers catch on to that?

Then he heard the girl, the seer, make a follow up question about the campfire's location. Haley knew immediately that she was correctly guessing it would lead to them. Hearing this and adjusting his grip on the boy who had almost outsmarted him—him! A natural born fugitive slave catcher—Haley recognized that this was a sharp group tailing them. One not to be underestimated.

As the logger gave some vague directions to the location of the camp Haley thought, *I don't have much time. Now that they're figuring out where we are, they'll plan out how to best come at us so that they can free their–*

"I'm going."

Haley distinctly heard the words from the seer girl, Charlotte, carry across the air. He immediately knew two things: one, this seer had impressive mettle. And two, he now had even less time than he thought.

Without wasting another second, Haley took his planned route to the bend in the river. By the time he got to the other side, he went upstream just enough to see that the girl and two of her partners were already across, while the river pig had just about finished helping the final one to reach the other side.

If he hurried, Haley realized, he just might be able to set up an ambush for their daring move. He had started to feel the edges of fatigue nibble at him, but he pushed it down. One capture of a clever quarry was stimulating, the possibility of netting the whole group? That rejuvenated him to the point that he had to keep himself from sprinting back to camp just so that he did not prematurely wear himself out considering the burden he shouldered.

In an impressive amount of time, Haley jogged into camp and dumped Eric to the ground next to the bodyguard. Neech looked relieved to see him, but he managed to quip, "You said an hour, not an hour and a half. I hope you enjoyed sniffing the flowers because we've got a whole crew here that—"

Haley ignored his comment. "The rest of the group is on their way, and if we hurry, we can ambush them. Where are the men?"

Chapter 5
FERRY, CLOSE CALL

Dave glided around the perimeter of the group, bouncing around trees and eyeing possible leaping points from one fallen log to another. Yet he held back. Even Dave could sense when frivolity was going a bit too far, and while he never knew Charlotte as an overly exuberant person, he—or perhaps anyone—had never seen her have such a serious, determined look on her face. He considered this for a moment and appended: Well, the look on Mr. Heugly's face when Dave would manage to come in tardy to chemistry one more time . . . or Tina Ortiz, well, at any time *maybe* could offer a comparison, but that was about it.

Not only was Dave holding back some of his urges to engage in forest parkour, but he almost felt sympathy for the dudes that were holding her dad and Eric. Obviously, Dave had seen that they were a pretty daunting group, but he could not be certain that Attila the Hun and his whole army could withstand Charlotte's gumption at this point.

They were about to head up a hill, probably the one Jimmy Sellers had mentioned came just before the river pig camp, when Luke called out, "Hang on. My shoe just came untied." Luke dropped to his knee and brought his hands to his laces.

The thing was, Dave noticed, Luke's shoelaces were already tied. He actually untied them before slowly starting to tie them up again. "We're surrounded," Luke said, still looking down at his feet.

"What do you mean?" Charlotte snapped, but Luke could not see her.

He continued, unaware. "For the past two hundred yards, those little birds that had been in the trees have disappeared. I should have thought of it before, but it didn't occur to me until I saw a few shadows dodge behind some trees in front of us. We must have just walked past the points where someone is setting up an ambush."

Luke finally looked up as he tightened the shoelaces of his second shoe.

"How many?" Tina asked him.

Luke shook his head slowly. "If there's three or four in front, then there would be at least that many behind us. Possibly more in-between."

Sally's eyes grew big. "They got more people to help them? What do we do?" She tried to look around to see the figures Luke referred to, but Tina motioned for her to keep her eyes in one spot.

An awkward silence ensued. Dave hopped closer to the group and bent down. "I need to tie my shoes too!" he announced, before quietly adding, "to give us more time to figure out what to do."

"Your shoes don't have shoelaces," Tina noted.

Dave grinned. "I guess that means it'll just take extra time to tie them."

"If we all start running back the way we came and then spread out once they start to close in on us, we might give them enough of a surprise that a couple of us can get away," Luke suggested.

"But Eric . . ." Charlotte said.

"We won't free Eric by all getting captured," Luke reasoned.

Suddenly, someone stepped around some trees. "Done tying your shoes yet?" It was the guy that caught Dave just outside the alleyway, Mr. Haley. Dave's wrist still tingled just looking at him. "Or are you just realizing that we've trapped you."

"Watch out for this dude," Dave told the others, "once he's got you, he doesn't like to let go."

"Charlotte," Luke intoned, "you and Sally take the middle path back to the river. Tina, you veer left, I'll veer right. Dave, you—"

"I cause chaos," Dave jumped out and immediately ran straight at Haley. "With pleasure!"

Dave could not say why he went straight at Haley rather than away, but something in him simply did not like the idea that Haley expected people to run away from him. Dave's instincts must have paid off in some way, because Haley seemed unsure of how to respond to someone sprinting right at him.

Smiling, Dave took an effortless leap off his leading leg so that it looked like he would slam head first into the increasingly surprised Haley, who shot his hands up to his face in a desperate attempt to soften the blow. It never came.

Dave sailed over Haley's head and then crouched into a rolling dive-landing, but kept on moving once he touched ground. He could not resist a glance back to see Haley turning to take in the maneuver with a scowl sprouting beneath his protective hands. "Rear guard, I need all hands moving west after this boy!" he called out in a low voice.

Dave noticed that behind Haley, Luke and Tina had started running towards the river, as Luke had directed. He could not even see Charlotte and Sally, so they might have even got a head start. *They'll still need to get past the front guard dudes*, Dave thought. *I better make my way back around to pitch in.*

Circling around did not prove as easy as he thought it would. He was able to move north or south readily enough, but any time he tried to swerve east back towards the river, the Haley guy seemed to have one of his men just in the right position to cut him off.

Dave took some consolation in the fact that at least they could not catch him. Any time they got close, he simply needed to take a sudden sharp turn by jumping off a tree or pogo-jumping off a rock.

After a couple of minutes, Dave determined that he would need to try something else. He scurried around until he got sight of Haley, who directed his crew from the middle, doggedly eyeing Dave as if he were Vice Principal Olsen looking for kids skipping class.

Dave stopped, squared up towards Haley, and charged again. Haley could not be taken by surprise twice. He faced Dave, planted his feet shoulder-width apart, and held his arms in front of him with elbows bent and hands open as if he were a linebacker ready to tackle. In this way, Haley's stocky form would be prepared for either a direct blow from Dave or be able to wrangle an airborne Dave from the space immediately above his head.

But he was not prepared for a third alternative.

Dave used a protruding stump to power leap through the final gap between Haley and himself. By all appearances, Dave's nearly horizontal form seemed to be slicing straight for Haley's face. Yet, earlier than anticipated, Dave tucked his head, which brought his legs rotating forward and his body down. Because of this, before Haley could adjust his stance, Dave landed on the soft, pine-needle-studded forest floor and power slid directly underneath Haley's open legs.

Haley immediately swiveled, but Dave was already up and moving east. "Catch ya later!" Dave quipped, "'Cause you know you're not gonna catch me!"

Dave disappeared behind a small slope, hearing Haley call his men, "Regroup! We won't engage with him yet. We're just going to cut off any retreat west and make sure he gets flushed towards the river where we can recruit the help of the others. They'll have captured everyone else by now."

Dave slowed down and wondered if that was the case. He took in his bearings and quickly adjusted his route so that it would take him to the spot where they first split up. He figured that he could start there and then follow the same direction the others would have fled in to see where they might have ended up.

A minute or two later, he glided into the place where Luke had stopped to "tie" his shoes. He took a second to capture in his mind the last place he saw Luke and Tina speeding off.

Dave tried to gauge which direction Charlotte could have taken off from and instead was surprised to see Charlotte and Sally standing in the clearing, apparently all alone and seemingly in a moment of indecision, which was super odd to Dave after seeing Charlotte so recklessly set on her course just moments ago.

"Charlotte!" Dave called out, startling her and Sally. "I thought you two would be at the river by now . . ."

271

"Dave," Charlotte caught her voice at his unexpected presence. She gathered herself. "No we . . . I couldn't head back. Now that we're so close to Eric, I—" Dave could see that she realized that she did not want to give a long explanation. "Well, anyway, I started running for the river like Luke said but then just ducked into a bunch of bushes. Sally was the only one who saw and she stopped with me."

"I love your pluck," Dave nodded with admiration, "but I'm not sure you'll get to Eric. Those dudes are pretty set on capturing us, and the main dude leading them is pretty pro at it. Even if we get back to the river, we'll have to be genius smart to avoid them completely."

"That's what we just heard," Sally piped in.

Dave looked around. Who did she "hear" that from? Before he got a chance to find out a voice interrupted them.

"Mr. Haley," a voice announced, "I think I see someone. Or a few someones."

Dave realized that the crew chasing him had finally caught up. They were out of time.

Charlotte and Sally looked at each other, then Dave.

"It's the girl!" the voice followed up. "The one you said to keep an eye out for. And there's the slippery feller and another little girl."

"Charlotte?" Dave prompted.

Charlotte seemed to take ages to look at Dave, then her face went crestfallen and she nodded. "Back to the ferry point at the logjam. Let's go."

"Alright!" Dave announced, excited to have a plan. "You two start running that way," Dave pointed toward the river, "and I'll make sure to keep them from getting too close."

Before he finished his sentence, Charlotte had grabbed Sally's hand and took off. The approaching men were caught off guard before yelping that girls were running east. Dave lowered his voice and called out, "I think they turned south!"

"Shift to the south!" someone barked.

272

Dave smiled as the men slid near his position and then stopped. "They ain't moved south—this scallywag is trying to throw us off!"

"'Scallywag'? Dude, I haven't been called something so cool since Mr. Olsen called me a 'dunderhead.'"

That was when three men lunged at him. Though they were fast, Dave was faster. In a whirl of leaves and after a ricochet off a low stump, Dave evaded the grasping hands of his pursuers. He occupied them for a moment before Mr. Haley's voice charged their direction. "Forget him! After the girl."

Dave had bought Charlotte some precious minutes, but Mr. Haley seemed determined now to ignore him. Dave swiftly slipped past some men who had now redirected themselves eastward towards the river and then he sprinted that direction himself. Dave knew he was no slouch, but those river pigs were managing to move pretty quickly. He hoped Charlotte had made some progress.

In too short of a time, he saw Charlotte and Sally sprinting in the direction they thought was the river, but Dave saw that they had drifted a bit north. "This way!" he chimed and swerved them more directly to the river. "And if you got any energy left, now's the time to burn it!"

Charlotte and Sally were breathing heavily, but Dave was impressed by the way that both of them managed to pump their arms somehow even faster. Behind them, he saw the shadowy forms of men fanning out to block off any slipping back past them once they reached the river.

Dave started strategizing some desperate maneuver to fend off their pursuers for another couple of minutes, when they crested a hill with a clearing and he saw the river with the logjam just to the south of them. They just might make it after all.

The sight did more than boost Dave's confidence, because the girls seemed to rush forward with the effort that can only come when you know you'll be done soon. The fanned forms behind and to the side of them also seemed to quicken their pace and tighten the semi-circle around them.

This is gonna be a close one! Dave thought to himself, too fascinated by the exciting circumstances to consider the gloomy prospects of being caught.

The girls stumbled up to the first logs of the wall of the logjam and Dave hopped in front of them to help them work their way onto the chaotic mess of timber. While doing so, he saw Mr. Haley materialize out of a dark stand of pine not twenty yards away from them. He had to have been running hard to stay up with them, but if he was tired, he did not show it.

Haley paused to take in the scene before him as a general entering a battlefield might. Mr. Haley and Dave's eyes locked momentarily. Dave saluted and winked, something that usually managed to put Mr. Olsen into a fit. Oddly, Mr. Haley seemed largely unaffected. His persistent yet low voice took command as he addressed the moving river pigs speeding towards Dave and the girls.

"Half of you get on the river and circle around to cut off their path across the edge of the logjam wall so they can't get to the other side of the river. The girls will slow him down so you'll have time to get in front of them before they're even halfway across." Mr. Haley looked at Dave while he spoke, perhaps hoping to see his despair as he realized the inevitability of their capture. Haley continued. "The other half of you will take them from this side. Don't come back without the girl."

A handful of men adeptly took straight to the river and began performing the delicate dance of river pigs traversing logs as they hurried to flank Dave and the girls. The others plunged straight onto the logjam in an effort to pluck Dave and the girl up before the others even had a chance.

Dave knew that Mr. Haley was right. The girls, though exhausted, were trying their best to crawl across the jutting maze of the logjam, but there was no way that they could make significant progress compared to the group of river pigs behind who could basically jog along the logjam edge as if they were strolling through Nibleton's lone alleyway.

They needed more time. "Dudes," Dave called out after some quick words of direction for Charlotte and Sally, "if you're so interested in this girl, why don't you try flowers or something less aggressive. I just don't think this is working for you. Besides," he added with a bit more edge, "if you keep chasing her down, I might have to convince you to leave her alone."

It was a super fair warning, but the river pigs did not seem interested in his heads-up. Dave sighed. The nice thing about parkour is that it made him good at running away, something that did not really hurt other people. Yet, he knew that he could just as easily use his skills to hurt others if he wanted . . . he just never wanted to. Now, though, he had little choice.

"Fine, dudes," Dave muttered, "but don't give me that look where you're shocked when something happens that you don't like!" Dave stomped on a log just to his right, which caused a chain reaction leading one of the river pigs to misplace his foot on a log that no longer sat underneath him. He plunged unceremoniously onto some loose, floating logs before sliding into the river.

Within moments, Dave reached out to a log sticking up about chest height and shoved it towards another approaching river pig, the log pivoted as if on a fulcrum and slammed into the guy, knocking him awkwardly backward before wedging him into a tight space of logs.

The other men behind Dave's first two victims had seen enough to pause at this point. That gave Dave a minute to look back where he saw that Charlotte and Sally had made some progress. While encouraging to see, less encouraging was the sight of the second wave of river pigs now working their way from the other end of the logjam and closing in on Charlotte and Sally fast.

"Charlotte! Sally! You're getting close to the ferry point. Start climbing down the jam and I'll help you get there in a second." Dave lightly hopped in their direction, passed them as they worked down the wall of logs, and then met up with the other river pigs.

"Unless you like headaches or baths, I suggest you leave the girls alone, dudes," Dave advised. "Don't believe me? Ask your buddies on the other side."

"The ones that are about to catch the girl?" one of the river pigs noted.

Dave swiveled and saw that as soon as he had run after these guys, the others recommenced their pursuit. He even saw the two he had incapacitated recovering.

"Not cool," he muttered. Behind him, he heard the river pig he just spoke to pushing forward. "Don't push your luck, dude," he said without looking behind him. Instead, he jounced the log underneath him and heard a grunt as the unsuspecting river pig behind him slipped to his knees. Dave then rocketed back towards the first group now closing in on Charlotte and Sally.

The two girls were nearing the bottom of the monstrous wall of logs, a mere couple of log lengths away from the open water where everyone had ferried into this world. But they would never get there in time, Dave saw. The first group of river pigs had taken enough advantage of his brief absence to make up a lot of ground. Within seconds, two of the closest would have their large, log-herding hands firmly gripping Charlotte.

"Hate to see a waste of good running effort," Dave mused. "Hey little piggies!" Dave took three leaps from jutting log to jutting log before launching himself recklessly in the air. A lot of the thrill of parkour came from the improvised nature of each venture. When he first started leaping in that direction, he was not sure what would happen next. By the time he sailed off his launching log, he noticed that his airborne route was converging on the two river pigs.

Dave took advantage by tucking his head and allowing his feet to come forward into a delayed flip, which he completed just in time for one foot to land neatly on the shoulder of one shocked river pig while the other foot planted firmly on the burly head of the river pig just behind. As a result, all three of them tumbled off of logs and rattled into the semi-open river just below the logjam.

Popping out of the water first, Dave whooped, "Whoa! Didn't quite stick the landing, but it was still pretty smooth." He was not sure exactly who he was talking to, but he noticed Charlotte and Sally sliding onto a log that Dave had just knocked loose with his acrobatic version of human bowling. Shadows above them scrambled down the logjam wall. The second group of river pigs was making their move, and Dave sat in the river without the ability to interfere, since there was nothing he could use to jump from.

Charlotte and Sally launched the log into the open river water, but Dave knew that they would never get far enough away to be out of reach of the approaching river pigs. "Watch your back, Charlotte!" Dave spurted, while trying to splash towards the logjam wall again in order to help, even if it would be too late.

Charlotte, with her legs straddling the log, found Dave's eyes at the same time that she found Sally's hands. "I'm coming back soon. Tell Eric that I'm coming back for him," she urged.

You got to leave before you can come back, Dave thought but never had time to voice. Two of the river pigs had launched on a log of their own and one of them prepared to leap at Charlotte before Dave could do anything else.

The pig made his jump. Dave blinked as he saw the river pig arc into the air and then land awkwardly on . . . what was suddenly an empty log. In a whirl of shimmering particles, Charlotte and Sally had disappeared just in time.

The breath of relief came just before Dave felt a sturdy hand grab his shoulder from in the water behind him. "You ain't going nowhere!"

Dave smiled. "That's what my school counselor told me too, but now look at me!" The humor was somehow lost on his captor.

PART FIVE

SCRIPT DOCTOR

Chapter 1
CHARLOTTE AND
SALLY'S CHOICES

As soon as Charlotte and Sally found themselves gripping hands and kneeling on the cold asphalt of the empty parking lot in Nibleton—after so much running, scrambling, close calls and the mental exertion of focusing on the moon at the ferry point while in the midst of hard pursuit—Charlotte simply leaned forward to collapse face forward onto the ground.

Sally quickly shifted next to her, probably hoping to see if there was something physically wrong with her. Physically, however, Charlotte was just fine. Emotionally, on the other hand, she felt stretched to a breaking point.

Even with her firm resolve to retrieve Eric after the ferrying that separated them, circumstances forced her to retreat. And not just regroup to a different spot in Dave Gardner's world, but things turned out so dire that she retreated all the way back to their world. If that weren't enough, she managed to bring just one person back with her. Everyone else by now, she bitterly recognized, would have been captured by Neech.

"She'll get Eric," Sally comfortingly patted Charlotte on the back of her head, somehow guessing what she was thinking. "She promised. She'll get him."

Sally's remark referenced a remarkable scene that occurred in the midst of the chaos of the ambush back in the river pig world. With her face plastered to the cold hard pavement of the parking lot, Charlotte reviewed the fascinating incident just before their escape.

279

It all happened after Luke and Tina sprinted back towards the river when the ambush fell down on them. In that moment, Charlotte made a couple of steps as if heading behind them before dodging behind a large jumble of shrubs.

Sally was the only one to notice, and she inconspicuously joined her while the world around them turned into a whirl of the noise of retreat and pursuit, both in Luke and Tina's direction and Dave's, who went the opposite way. This meant that after a long pause, their position remained undiscovered.

"Okay, it's been quiet long enough," Charlotte announced. "Let's get Eric while they're chasing after the others."

"No," a voice disagreed with Charlotte, "you need to ferry out of here, right now."

Charlotte and Sally both knew that the voice did not come from either of them. They turned a complete circle, but it was not until they started a second turn that they noticed someone materialize out of the shadows of the trees around them. It was someone Charlotte did not need another second to recognize.

"Where is he!" Charlotte demanded. "Where is Eric, Facade?"

"We don't have a lot of time," Facade stated, "so listen very carefully. I will make sure nothing bad happens to Eric and your father, but under no circumstances can we let Neech get you. You need to go back and ferry to your world. Do not return under any circumstances." She looked at Sally and added as an afterthought, "You might as well take Sally as well."

Charlotte and Sally looked at Facade with wide open eyes and dangling jaws. Charlotte snapped out of it first, "I don't know what kind of game you're playing right now, Facade, but there is no way that I'm ferrying anywhere without Eric holding my hand."

Facade had been looking around them guardedly as Charlotte responded. When Charlotte finished, Facade stepped even closer and took her by the shoulders. "Neech has recruited a dozen river pigs with the sole purpose of capturing you, Charlotte. We can arrange the escape or release of anyone in your group, but once Neech has you, Charlotte, he will never let you go."

"I don't care," Charlotte started, "I still—"

"But *I* care!" Facade hissed. "*You* are my freedom."

As determined as Charlotte had been, this unexpected statement managed to throw her off guard. Facade pressed her advantage, "But once you're taken, that's gone. For all of us," Facade removed a hand from Charlotte's shoulder in order to sweep her hand in a way that included Sally.

Charlotte felt troubled, but she recovered. "I'll have to risk it. I came here to get Eric and I'm not ferrying back without him."

Facade took a deep breath. "Haley is very good at what he does—he's a natural born fugitive slave catcher. He's got the other two by now, which means that in a matter of no time at all, he is going to figure out where you are and start to close in. You will not escape him in this world, so you will need to go where he cannot."

Charlotte was ready to doggedly interrupt, but Facade overpowered her, "Neech will not be able to ferry back until the moon reciprocates, so he will not be able to immediately follow, and you'll be safe."

Charlotte was shaking her head.

Facade continued. "With you gone, that will give me time to work out a way to free your friends without causing suspicion to myself."

"Sorry to interrupt," Sally said, clearly not sorry at all, "but maybe you forgot that you're with the bad guys. Why should we trust you?"

Facade seemed exasperated. "I don't have time to explain. In fact, we've possibly taken too much time already." She looked intensely over to Sally. "Let's just say that I need Charlotte, but if Neech gets her then she'll be useless to me."

Facade turned back to Charlotte, "Eric gave me his word that you wouldn't ferry without me back in that other world, and he held true to his word. I took a big risk in trusting him, but it paid off. Now, I'm asking you to take a big risk and trust in me."

Charlotte's head continued to shake, but the resolution was not as firm. Facade's eyes melded deep into Charlotte's. "Charlotte, I give you my word that I will get Eric to you. All you need to do is stay in the parking lot and wait until I send him to the ferrying point."

The snapping of branches behind them told of someone approaching. "I can't be seen with you or my chances of helping Eric will be gone," Facade announced.

Charlotte's face held tears streaming down her cheeks. Facade looked past the tears, "They're coming. Maybe two river pigs are taking Luke and Tina back to camp. Dave has got a few of them distracted for the moment. The rest will be coming to capture you right now, Charlotte."

Charlotte felt the pressure to respond but resisted still.

"Whoever it is, they're almost here!" Sally urged.

Facade squeezed Charlotte's shoulder. "I give you my word."

A moment later there was a whooshing sound as Facade's trench coat flew up and then she disappeared. Charlotte thought she might have seen a hint of the street magician hidden nearby, or maybe that was her slithering off under an earth-colored trench coat or maybe it was just a breeze picking up some random forest detritus.

Either way, out of the trees sprinted Dave. "Charlotte!" Dave called out, startling her and Sally. "I thought you two would be at the river by now . . ."

Seconds later, pressured and indecisive, Charlotte chose to have Dave help them get back to the logjam. In the moment, Charlotte felt as if she had no choice but to accept Facade's offer. Now she looked back with regret.

Now that she had rerun the situation back over in her mind, Charlotte had to readjust to being sprawled on the parking lot surface back in their original world. She breathed deeply for a moment but kept her face down. "Sally, we were probably only minutes away from Eric. Now we're worlds away and I don't feel anything waiting at the ferry point on the other side." She shook her head. "This is a mess—a hopeless mess. We're the only two left, Sally."

"I don't know if Facade is playing a trick on us or not," Sally said, "but she did seem, like, for real scared of Neech. And I don't know what she gets out of this if she keeps you from being captured."

Charlotte was unmoved by Sally's logic. "She kept me away from Eric by promising to bring him to me. And I fell for it. Now we're alone, in another world, and they're all captured."

"We don't know that for sure," Sally offered. "And now you have some time to figure out what to do. We could even get Eric's phone charger so that you can check the pictures."

Charlotte took another deep breath. "It doesn't need to charge," she said so softly that she could not be sure if Sally heard.

"It doesn't? I thought the battery ran out," Sally said, confused.

After a pause, Charlotte replied, "No. The battery is low, but it never ran out completely. I just . . . I just . . ." she lifted herself off the ground and onto her knees so that she could look eye to eye with Sally. "I can't bring myself to see how things end up."

"But what if it helps?" Sally pressed.

"Did it keep you from being captured by the Visigoths? Did it keep Eric and me from being ferried separately?" Sally had no answer for this so Charlotte continued, "That's why I feel like this is all being dictated for me in spite of anything I do. Either my parents, or the hieroglyphics, or fate, or . . . I don't know . . . something has taken it out of my hands. It's all stacked against me and there doesn't seem to be a point in even trying anymore."

Sally nodded and stayed quiet for a while. "You could be right that you and I can't do anything about it," she concluded. "And we can go ahead and do nothing—then you'll be right for sure. If you can do something, though, the only way we'll know is if we try. I don't know about you, but I'd rather not let fate be right just because I didn't try."

There was nothing to say against that, but Charlotte could point out, "Okay, but I don't even know what I could *try* to do."

"Didn't you say that Eric was once too proud to get help from other people?" Sally offered, "What if we got help?!"

Charlotte felt too overwhelmed to ask Sally how that could possibly work, so she listened.

"You're a seer. You know people's abilities. Why not round up a whole bunch of natural born fighters. Haven't you met any here in Nibleton?

Natural born soldiers, or warriors, or . . . uh . . . boxers, or samurais, or . . . I don't know—fighters?"

A half dozen names flitted through Charlotte's mind of people with abilities that could be helpful in a pinch. For a second, she almost had hope. But she looked at the moon's position advancing in the sky, and then back to Sally. "I can think of some, sure, but we don't have a ton of time. Besides, I'm not sure how to go to someone's house at night and—first of all—get them to listen to me, then—second of all—somehow convince them to help in a dangerous rescue mission to another world."

While Sally took this in, Charlotte expanded her point. "I mean, what do I tell them? I could tell the truth, but then they'd be more likely to commit me to a mental facility than to help. Besides, it would mean leaving this spot, and what if by the craziest chance, Facade did manage to bring Eric to the ferrying point and I was gone . . . ?"

Sally nodded slowly, acknowledging Charlotte's reasoning.

Charlotte sighed. A part of her wanted it to work but another part was relieved that it could not work. Thinking there were no other options was debilitating, even despairing, but at least it meant that she was done meddling and trying to make decisions—however well-intentioned—that could hurt people. There was a deceptive solace in failure. She sank back down to the ground cradling her face on her arms, not sure how to cry but feeling like she should.

All of a sudden, Charlotte felt something give her a hard shove. She lifted her head up and saw Sally kneeling next to her shoulder, still trying to budge Charlotte from her supine position. "What are you doing?" Charlotte queried.

Sally stopped for a moment. "You told me that you had to push Eric to get him out of his funk. I know you probably didn't really push him, but I'm not sure how else to get you out of your funk . . . 'cause this isn't the Charlotte I know . . . and it's totally not helpful."

Charlotte sat up a bit more but remained speechless. Sally continued, "Now, it's true that getting a bunch of people right now would be tricky, and

284

that you probably shouldn't leave here. So maybe that's a bad idea, but unlike someone else in this parking lot, I'm not ready to give up on my friends, whether or not someone is moving once this is all settled."

The accusation stung just as much for its truth as for its reminder that she, of all people, should know better seeing as how she was the one to make this same type of observation to Eric when he found himself at his low point.

Charlotte fingered the phone in her pocket. She was so afraid of what was going to happen in the future that she was losing her perspective in the present. Charlotte could not account for what the hieroglyphics suggest will happen to her or her friends. She also knew that her parents' decision to move was something she could not control.

Yet as Charlotte considered Sally sitting before her, still trying to figure things out, she recognized Sally's earlier point: giving up now was a guarantee that things would not work out. Trying, even in the face of what might seem like certain failure, at least gave her some semblance of hope for success, however slight.

With these thoughts running through her mind, Charlotte faced their problem . . . and then ran into a wall. *Was* there something she could do? Anything she could think of led to another dead end. They were literally in a different world and she felt anchored to one spot. Maybe she was being too morose and cynical before, but that did not mean that there was an easy solution.

Sally, oblivious to Charlotte's thoughts, tapped her lips with her finger. "So getting a lot of help and leaving here might be hard to do, but what if it was just one person, and I went to find them and bring them here for you so that you don't have to leave?"

Charlotte thought about it. "Not to keep shooting down ideas, but one person that could take on Neech and his small army of mercenaries?"

"No," Sally shook her head, still thinking, "someone who could be the . . . you know . . . the strategist. Someone who could figure out how we got into this problem and, well, fix up the mess somehow."

Charlotte gave Sally a hard look, but Sally missed it. "Can you think of anyone like that? Maybe your mom? What is her ability?" Charlotte kept looking at Sally but did not respond, so Sally continued, "Maybe a . . . I don't know . . . a con artist? In the movies they're always good about coming up with elaborate plans to pull off impossible heists with the odds stacked against them."

Sally finally noticed Charlotte staring at her and went quiet. Charlotte let the silence sit, leaving Sally to interpret it on her own. "You think I should go home," she finally determined.

Charlotte had not been thinking that. Now, though, she found it strikingly relevant. "Do *you* think you should go home?"

"Maybe I should," Sally answered honestly, frowning, "because I've not really helped much . . . I've even caused some of our problems." She perked up suddenly, "That doesn't mean I want to, though. When I figured out that you were set on ferrying to Dave's world alone, I almost let you. Then I thought about Eric, and I knew that I didn't want to be left behind while there was a chance that I could help him like he helped me."

Charlotte nodded. Sally's voice lowered. "But . . . I really don't want to get in the way, you know. Especially if it's gonna hurt Eric's chances. So, if you were thinking about how it'd be easier if I went home, then . . . then, I guess I can understand that."

Silence settled between them again, and Charlotte sensed this was a watershed moment. If she truly wanted to stop meddling in other people's lives as a seer, then with one word she could remove Sally from the whole mess. The very possibility of taking that step towards releasing herself from the seer role promised a relief unlike any she had ever anticipated.

By looking at Sally's face, though, Charlotte came to another sobering realization. By deliberately not including Sally in whatever happened next, she was just as much meddling. Like it or not, Sally was part of this story. Denying opportunities was perhaps just as problematic as bornapping: both were done without the other person's choice.

What about my choice? Charlotte pushed back against her own thoughts. *Where do I get my own say in all of this?*

One more look at Sally had a transformative effect as she realized that some of Sally's features suddenly stuck out as ones shared with her brother Eric. It gave her a glimpse of the Eric she first met: lacking confidence, despondent, lost. Charlotte had helped change that, and it made her supremely satisfied. *What about my choice?* she asked herself again, this time without as much resentment. *What do I really want?* She looked at the Eric within Sally. *I want to have that same kind of effect I had on Eric with other people for the rest of my life.*

During Charlotte's prolonged reflection, Sally reached her own conclusion. "I'm sure you're trying to figure out how to tell me that you'd rather have me go home. That's okay. I get it. I'll just go back and come up with a story that will calm my parents down until—"

"The strategist you suggested," Charlotte interjected, "the one that could fix all our problems . . ."

"You thought of someone?" Sally noted, "That's great! Are they close? Do you think they'd be willing to listen to a wild story and then jump in and help?"

Charlotte took a deep breath. "They are close, and they will listen . . . but the choice still needs to be theirs."

"Sure it does," Sally agreed, seemingly confused by the obvious nature of the statement.

Here goes, Charlotte thought. "Sally, it's you. *You* are the strategist I need."

Sally's mouth hung open. She looked ready to spill out a whole river's worth of queries, but a thought-logjam kept her from saying anything more than, "What?"

At this point, Charlotte knew there was no going back. "Sally," she said deliberately, "*you* are the strategist I need."

Sally could not have acted more shocked if Charlotte told her Eric had requested to read her diary, so Charlotte just went ahead with the explanation. "When you mentioned that we could use someone with an ability to figure ways out of problems, I tried to think of the abilities I've met in Nibleton that have that sort of skill set. Nothing came to mind . . . until I realized that I was looking right at one."

"Me?"

"But you can't accept this assignment because *I* need you," Charlotte clarified. "You can only accept it if it's what *you want* to do, what you're *willing* to do—it's got to be your choice."

While Sally digested this, something occurred to Charlotte and she voiced her thoughts. "Maybe it's not fair of me to put this choice on you. You're still pretty young to be making big decisions like this."

Sally gripped her diary tightly, "Maybe I am too young for this. I hate not being included, but over the last couple of ferries everything has been a lot less fun-adventurous and way more scary than I was thinking it would." She reflected a moment before continuing, "But I guess I still want to try. And if you think I might be helpful at all even though I can't imagine how, then—"

"I need you," Charlotte affirmed, "and your answer convinces me that you aren't too young after all."

Sally allowed a crooked smile creep across her face. "Does this mean that I get to know my natural born ability?"

Charlotte smiled back. She still could not feel confident that she was making the right decision, but at this point she just had to trust her choice and move forward. She was done feeling bad for herself and ready to act. "Sally, you are a natural born script doctor."

"Script doctor?"

"Yes. I think it's someone who will take—"

"They fix up movie scripts that have problems!" Sally jumped in. "Any time movie studios have issues with a film or the screenwriters are at a dead end, they bring in a script doctor to figure out how to get the movie back on track by—"

"I see you're already familiar with what a script doctor is," Charlotte observed wryly. "I guess I'm not too surprised."

"I mean, I knew that I loved movies, but I guess I kind of thought I might go into acting or directing . . . maybe even screenwriting—but a script doctor . . . that feels, well, it just feels right!"

Immediately Charlotte began to feel the satisfaction that comes from watching someone realize their full potential. She smiled as Sally began to list off some of the obscure info in the behind-the-scenes of several movies she had watched dealing with how they used script doctors. " . . . in fact, that one princess character from the space movies—well, not really the princess character but the actress who plays the princess—she was actually a really talented script doctor that studios would—"

"Hey, script doctor," Charlotte waved her hand at Sally. "Can we focus on the current movie at hand?"

Sally's eyes settled back on Charlotte. "Um, yeah . . . I mean, yes! Let's see. How do I do this?"

"I'd start by treating our situation as if it is a movie script where the screenwriters have written the good guys into a corner," Charlotte suggested.

Sally nodded. "Okay," she said. "Okay. That's good. A movie script . . . let me think." Sally tapped her fingers thoughtfully on her diary. "First, we need to get all of our loose ends tied up. Can't leave anything dangling at the end, right?"

Charlotte nodded while another grin burst onto Sally's face. "Script doctor! I can't believe that I'm doing this right now, it feels so cool and . . ." Sally noticed Charlotte's facial expression, " . . . and, well . . . I should focus. I've got to focus on this problem."

"That would be great," Charlotte encouraged patiently.

"If we're going to tie up loose ends, then," Sally noted after another second of thought, "then I guess we need to know which characters are, you know, free to use and which ones aren't because they're captured." Sally gave a meaningful look to Charlotte.

Neither of them needed to look at the phone to know what Sally was referring to. Charlotte's hand hovered by her pocket but did not grab the phone yet. While she had already made the choice to move forward, that did not remove all her reluctance to look at the foreseer's signs.

"Once I know if Eric will be with us, then I'll start putting together a list of characters, resources, dangling plot threads, possible threats, and timing . . . then, I'll get us to a happily ever after." Sally smiled. "That's the kind of movie we're going for, right?"

One more second of hesitation. "Yes. Happily ever after," Charlotte agreed, though in the back of her mind she knew that Sally was not accounting for her inevitable move if they ever managed to get everyone back in one piece.

Still, Sally's eagerness was infectious, and Charlotte removed Eric's phone and turned it on. She ignored the low battery warning and navigated to the phone's photo files. She pulled up the picture and zoomed into the most recent hieroglyphic she had studied: the ferry with Eric on one side and her on the other.

She scrolled sideways past the next few hieroglyphics, skipping the foreseer's mysterious knowledge of her ferrying with Sally, Tina, and Luke. Then, painfully sliding past the hieroglyphic that showed her meeting with Facade and having to make her difficult decision to retreat. Next, she saw the depiction of her and Sally's near escape as they ferried back again. *All caught up*, she thought. She took another large breath. *Do I want to do this?* she asked herself.

She decided that she was not ready yet. Before she could stop herself, however, her finger slid to the next frame. She squinted her eyes, recognizing the logjam and . . .

"What do you see?" Sally asked.

It took only a moment longer for Charlotte to recognize Sally. "You!" she responded. "I see you. And not only that, but I'm supposed to ferry you, like, right now."

Chapter 2
VERSUS ... AGAIN

"Sorry I ruined any future chance at escape," Eric mumbled after things quieted down in the camp.

"It was our best chance," Mr. Reeves replied. "We had to do it then or never."

They now found themselves within a twenty foot radius of a zip tied Dave, Luke, and Tina. Shuffling around them were Neech, Haley, Facade, Felipe, and dozens or so river pigs.

"'Never' is right," Eric suggested. "It's only a matter of time before they catch the rest of us."

"Don't be too sure of that, dudes!"

Mr. Reeves and Eric did not realize that Dave could hear them, but he rolled over so that he was facing them. "They might be strutting around like they're pretty hot stuff, but what they're not telling you is that Charlotte and Sally ferried out of here!"

Mr. Reeves and Eric both felt untold relief at this news. Eric looked over at the enemy crew and now he started seeing things in a new light. The faces of the river pigs seemed dissatisfied, and he noticed them in small groups, mumbling to each other.

Neech, Haley, and Facade found themselves in a diminutive cabal. Facade faced away from them, but Haley appeared particularly disgruntled. As for Neech, he clearly showed an aggravation that Eric found strangely satisfying.

"He really wanted to get his hands on all of us, didn't he?" Eric mused.

"On Charlotte," Mr. Reeves clarified.

"True," Dave threw in. "I mean, that Haley dude was pretty interested in grabbing me, Luke, and Tina . . . for sure. And—I'll tell ya—he's hard to shake. The dude's no tracer, but he's still pretty strategic-minded." Dave appeared to rethink that statement, "Course, on the other hand, when I ran straight at him, it was like he froze; you know, like he was a computer forced to do something he wasn't programmed for."

Mr. Reeves and Eric both looked at each other, then back to Dave. "What are you saying?" Eric asked.

Dave squinted. "Oh, yeah, sorry. Sometimes I talk like I do parkour, just kind of let it happen naturally and see where it leads. But I guess the point I was trying to make at first was to agree with Mr. Reeves. As much as the Haley dude wanted to catch me, he mostly seemed dead set—I suppose you could say, 'computer programmed'—to nab Charlotte as priority numero uno."

At that moment, one among the small groups of river pigs consulting with each other wrapped up his discussion then turned towards Haley. He approached with an equal sense of trepidation and affrontery.

Neech held up his conversation with Haley and Facade. The river pig spoke loud enough so that all of his fellow river pigs could hear his speech. "Mr. Haley, Mr. Neech. Me and the boys, well, we'd like to have a moment to speak with you."

"Not now," Neech waved his hand, annoyed.

"Asking yer pardon, sir, but we insist," the river pig clarified.

"What is it?" Neech demanded.

Facade stepped between them. "Do you really think we should be having this discussion in front of the captives?"

"Who cares what they hear?" Neech snapped.

After considering Facade's statement Haley piped in, "She's right. I've noticed that they're a sharp group. The less they know about what's happening the better." Haley turned to the river pig. "Gather up your boys, and we'll make this quick."

Neech shrugged. "Fine, Haley. But that means you'll be the one talking to the pigs. I'll stay here with the chiclero and Facade. We'll keep an eye on the captives. When you're done speaking to them, then you, Facade, and I will finish our discussion on what to do about having too many captives." Neech's statement came as a deliberate threat that he made loud enough for Eric and the others to hear.

Haley grunted and immediately left with the river pigs out of the clearing towards a secluded spot only several dozen yards away.

"Neech," Facade said once they had the area back to themselves, "I want to go find that other river pig that Haley said Charlotte and the others were with. I'm curious how much he was involved in this whole thing and I don't like the idea that he's still out there."

Neech nodded, "Makes sense. Don't need too many loose ends out there. I guess that leaves me and the chiclero to watch over these leftovers. Don't be surprised if there's quite a few less of them by the time you come back."

Facade shrugged. "Less for me to worry about, but as someone who has a flair for theatrics and manipulating an audience, I've gotta say that I'd be pretty hesitant about knocking off the seer's friends or family just cause they're inconvenient."

"That was your problem before, Facade," Neech frowned. "They didn't take your threats in the aqueduct world seriously enough because you weren't willing to show them you were committed to killing if you had to."

Facade nodded. "Fine. We can both agree that you're the expert at extorting people, so do what you think is best. I will say this, though: I didn't have more than one person captive to make my threat real in that other world. Killing my captive might have shown I was serious," she clarified, "but it also would've left me completely without leverage. What good does it do you to take out friends or family without her even in this world to witness it? Leaves you with quite a bit less clout when she actually does show up."

Neech waved his hand in impatient recognition of Facade's point. Yet, as Eric listened to this cold take by Facade, he inwardly recognized that Facade *did* have the chance to have more than one captive when he went to exchange himself for Sally—yet she deliberately did not.

"We're wasting time. Go find that other river pig and then we can discuss this with Haley when you get back," Neech noted as an apparent concession.

"Chiclero!" Facade turned away from Neech. Felipe, who had been rummaging through the river pig food stores, quickly dropped a couple pieces of dried meat and some nuts while sulkily shuffling over to Neech and Facade.

"I'm giving you back your machete," Facade told him while pulling out the weapon that had somehow been concealed inside her trench coat. "Any of these prisoners makes a move, you kill them. You screw up this one simple task and that's all the reason we'll need to leave you behind when we ferry out of here."

Felipe grabbed the machete and looked it over with satisfaction. "You can count on me, girl!" He slid the machete into the leather sheath hanging from his belt.

In disgust, Facade picked up some of the dried meat he had just dropped to the ground. "And stop being a slob," she said, thrusting the meat into his belly while he fumbled to grab it and threw out some groveling apologies.

"And while you're at it," she continued, "Give some of that meat to the captives. If they've had something to eat, they're more likely to sleep tonight, which will make it easier to watch them."

Felipe seemed a bit wistful to lose the meat that he had just scrounged up, but one look from Neech caused him to mumble his obeisance. Eric was not particularly hungry, so he did not appreciate Felipe's awkward visit where he had to rip off chunks of meat and feed each prisoner by hand since their own were zip tied behind their backs.

By the time Felipe had finished, Facade had disappeared and Neech found himself moodily perched on the edge of camp keeping the captives in the corner of his eye. "Get some rest," he chirped at them. "There's going to be some exciting developments soon."

Neech could have left things at that, but since he had been convinced to wait before doing anything, he seemed to feel the need to reestablish his authority over the captives. He glanced over at Eric and Mr. Reeves in particular. "Sadly, most of you won't be here for the conversation that I'm going to have with Charlotte when we bring her in—I'm tempted to keep daddy around so that he can see the sense of betrayal in her face once we talk about her real heritage, but I don't always get my way, so no promises!"

If the comment had any effect on Mr. Reeves, he hid it well. He simply closed his eyes and turned towards the log he lay next to as if to sleep. Since Neech got no reaction from Mr. Reeves, he simply forced a chuckle and turned his head towards where Haley had taken the river pigs.

"Do you think he'll really get rid of some of us?" Eric asked in a small whisper. More and more he felt the frustration of nearly escaping but getting caught at the last moment.

"Facade is right. They'd be dumb to get rid of collateral without Charlotte around to have her hand forced by it," Mr. Reeves noted. "Still, Neech seems unpredictable right now and he might do something rash . . . I mean, at this point, he does have several people to take his anger out on and still leave a few for manipulating Charlotte."

Eric considered this before taking the conversation on a different tack. "I do worry about him having a conversation with Charlotte," Eric stated. "I mean, what happens if Neech gets a chance to ask Charlotte the same questions he asked me earlier about you and Mrs. Reeves as her parents? I feel as if she would not take it as well as I did—she's a lot closer to it than I am."

Mr. Reeves mulled over this statement for a moment, but before he could say anything, a voice interrupted. "If Neech gets a chance to ask Charlotte anything, then it will have been too late for her. We have to keep her as far away from him as possible."

Eric could not be sure what surprised them more, that the voice came from Facade—who had somehow managed to slide underneath her trench coat along the side of the log by Mr. Reeves, just out of sight of a distracted Neech—or that she seemed to want to protect Charlotte from Neech.

He would not get time to decide. Before either of them could express their thoughts, Eric felt his zip ties drop to the ground. He turned his head and saw, to his surprise, Facade extending the handle of the machete she just used to free him. So many things had happened that needed explaining: this was the same machete he just saw her hand over to Felipe right before telling him to feed the captives.

"Magicians don't explain their tricks, and I need you to hurry, pirate hunter," Facade pushed the machete even closer to Eric. Eric took a glance towards Mr. Reeves, who seemed to be just as lost as Eric, before tentatively taking the weapon comfortably in his grip.

"Listen carefully," Facade now urged. "You are not to free Charlotte's dad or the others."

"I think you're forgetting who has the machete here," Eric pushed back, though his mind still raced for an explanation to this inexplicable event. "If you really are trying to help, why not just release all of us?"

Facade seemed agitated, carefully eyeing the oblivious Neech while her whispered voice gained more urgency. "Before I got half of you released, Neech would discover us and call over Haley and the river pigs." Eric about made a point, but Facade cut him off. "If I just freed a couple of you, then . . . well, Haley is a practical guy. If he needs to capture two or three people, he's going to use as many of the river pigs as he needs to do it. But he's also proud. You nearly got away once, Eric, and it took him longer than he said it would to catch you. If you are the only one to slip away again, he would see it as a personal challenge to capture you by himself as a way to redeem himself."

Eric nodded. As someone who understood egotistical maniacs thanks to his pirate hunting skills, this made sense to him.

"Come or don't. Release the others or don't. I have a plan that could save you all, but I'm risking everything in even offering . . . and I can't stay here any longer or I'm endangering all of us. I'll be waiting by the two pines just above the boulder directly west of camp."

With an envious dexterity, Facade disappeared as quickly as she had come. Mr. Reeves and Eric looked at each other. "What are the odds she's tricking us somehow?" Eric asked.

"Not nothing," Mr. Reeves decided. "But we're one set of hands freed more than we were a couple of minutes ago."

"We had that before and it didn't amount to much," Eric pointed out. "I'm not sure I'm the right person for—"

"Executive decision," Neech suddenly spoke from his watch point. Eric froze, worried that in spite of their caution he had somehow overheard them or could tell that Eric's zip ties had been cut, even though his body should have blocked that from Neech's view.

Neech continued, "I've decided that you captives have nothing worthwhile to talk about and that you should stay absolutely silent until I say otherwise."

Eric risked a glance in Neech's direction. Neech returned the look with one of cold mastery. "The next person to speak gets ferried to a different world at my hand—the kind of world-ferrying that does not require a moon."

Satisfied that his message had been delivered effectively, Neech broke off his gaze, impatiently looking back towards where Haley was meeting with the river pigs.

Eric knew that his second chance for escape would be in this moment or never. After Haley was done with his meeting, there would be multiple people watching over their group rather than just one. It would not take long before someone would notice the machete or his hands loose.

Eric craned his neck over to look at Mr. Reeves. Charlotte's dad gave him a strong look of confidence, nodding his head and locking his eyes in a way that let Eric know that he believed in him. Eric thought of how that was a trait he must have passed on to his daughter because he had seen it before when Charlotte helped him in the world of pirates although no one else could.

At this point Neech had bent over to retrieve a piece of meat that Felipe had failed to recover, wiping it clean and apparently debating its sanitary state. Eric lightly rolled over, gave one last look to Mr. Reeves then crawled stealthily away. As he did so, he pondered how after the look of confidence from Mr. Reeves it seemed as if, had he been able to do so without inciting the ire of Neech, the bodyguard wanted to give some parting advice.

What was Eric missing? What was Mr. Reeves wanting him to know? Before he could think too much on this question, Eric found himself in the first line of trees and trekking right up to the two pines sitting on a rise in the ground caused by a halfway submerged boulder.

Facade appeared out of nowhere, as usual. Also as usual, she wasted no time on formalities. "Haley will hunt you down again. He is a natural born fugitive slave catcher and that means he's impossible to run away from."

"Then why are you releasing me?" Eric asked, exasperated. He had just risked a lot by leaving his friends and making this second escape.

"Because, before I can arrange for the rest of you to escape, I need to neutralize Haley," Facade patiently explained.

Eric remembered his careful attempts to throw off any pursuit in his first escape—all of them pointless. "But I got caught!" he hissed. "I'm no match for a fugitive slave catcher. I tried and failed to keep him off my trail."

"Exactly," Facade agreed, "impossible. He's sure to catch you again if you just try to run."

Before Eric could voice his increased chagrin, Facade clarified. "I'm telling you to not play into his natural born ability and to play to yours. You were born to hunt, not to be hunted."

"Wait. So instead of running, you want me to just . . . take him out?" Eric asked. At first it seemed ridiculous to contemplate such a move. Haley had overpowered Eric in a single blow and then used his incredible strength to carry him a couple of miles back to camp like it was nothing. No small feat.

Still, Eric mulled it over some more, she had a point. Eric's experience with Haley came when he was running. He was caught completely off guard doing something that came unnaturally to him. What if he weren't running? What if he were *hunting*? Could he take down someone as formidable as Haley? Suddenly his adrenaline started to pump. The old excitement of hunting down a pirate on the high seas began to trickle through his veins.

"You'll need to get some distance from camp first so that reinforcements won't be nearby," Facade explained while Eric thought, "but then take him out. I can't work out anyone else's escape until you remove Haley from the equation."

Facade added, "Now, just to make sure we're clear. If Haley captures you, just as he was born to do, this time he's going to make sure you can never escape again—either by severely maiming you, or, if you're lucky, killing you. Haley takes great satisfaction in the misery of his captives, and he's been forced to pull back on that lately, but after something like this, I'm thinking Neech would give the go ahead."

"Nice pep talk," Eric mumbled.

Facade seemed unamused. "It's the best I've got, but if I'm being honest, I don't really know what to expect when you pit two hunters against each other."

Eric immediately recalled the thrill of going against Jedediah Willard, a pirate against a pirate hunter. Before he could hold himself back, he said, "I do."

Facade nodded. "After you take out Haley, go to the ferrying point. I promised Charlotte I would free you, and she needs to see that I can keep my word as well as you can. Tell her that now that Haley is gone, I'll be able to work out a way to free everyone else and to be ready to ferry them back."

Eric was so caught up with his hunger to hunt down Haley that he had to check himself. "Wait . . . why are you doing this?"

"We don't have time for this, pirate hunter," Facade glanced back towards the camp where the silhouette of a fidgeting Neech could barely be seen through the line of trees. "Trust me when I tell you that it is entirely in my best self-interest to keep Charlotte away from Neech. I need your help to do that. Now, there's one last thing that you need to know."

"Only one?" Eric quipped, "Because I'm starting to feel like—"

"Felipe, you impossible idiot!" Neech's voice sounded as if it was right behind Eric. He swung around, ready to strike, but instead only saw the shadowed outline of Neech storming around the edge of camp.

Eric pivoted back around in time to see that Facade had made her exit. He still had so many questions left unanswered, not the least of which was the last thing she felt he needed to know. But time was up. Haley was about to be alerted and would be on his trail within minutes if not sooner—precisely why Facade had disappeared so quickly. If Eric hoped to attack Haley, he recognized the importance of getting some more distance from the camp to make sure that it would just be Haley and him.

Eric's hand gripped the handle of the machete, and his pumping adrenaline pushed all other thoughts and doubts into the background. "It's time to capture a bad guy." Then he tore off through the undergrowth.

Haley found the darkest spot in the clearing and waited for the group of river pigs to all arrive and settle in. Once all were there, it was obvious they were waiting for Haley to ask them what they wanted, but he was not about to give them that pleasure. He waited in silence. Eventually, the awkwardness forced the river pig who had called the meeting to clear his throat.

"Mr. Haley, we've been talking and we decided that we ain't gettin' involved in no witchcraft hocus pocus. I don't care how much gold your greasy pal offers," the river pig voiced. The other river pigs—especially those who had witnessed that disappearance of the two girls on the log—grumbled their agreement.

Mr. Haley's eyes narrowed, but he chose a diplomatic route. "Why do you think we're trying to catch them? The use of those kinds of dark arts must be punished." The men seemed to process this statement for a minute before Haley continued, "I know that may make you nervous, but I can assure you that their witchcraft at this point is harmless. That is why we must capture them now, before their dealings get more dangerous."

A look at the group of river pigs, which showed several bruises and a few missing teeth after encounters with Dave and Luke, proved them skeptical.

Mr. Haley clarified. "Any damage that's happened up until this point has come because you couldn't cleanly grab a few kids that don't even have magical powers."

"Either way," the river pig responded, "we're through helping you. We captured a few of the kids and we took more welts than a whole season of logging in the process, so we'll just collect our second payment and be heading out."

Mr. Haley nodded, taking in the information. "I see. Then it looks like you've got two problems with your position." The authority that Mr. Haley used in his quiet but firm statement kept the river pigs in suspense for a moment before he continued, "One, you never captured the girl, which was the only reason we hired you . . . the others were just bonus. And two, not a single one of you is leaving this area until we decide we're through with you."

Silence lingered for a moment. The spokesperson river pig looked around at his companions and then snorted nervously. "Oh? And who's going to stop me?"

"I've no plans to stop anyone," Mr. Haley clarified. And then his blood started to pump. "But if you leave, I can promise you that I will catch you before you can get more than three miles away."

Haley eyed everyone intensely. "And if I have to do that, you'll forfeit the second half of your payment and be joining those other hogtied individuals—'pig-tied' should I say?—or, if I'm annoyed enough with you, meet a far worse fate."

Silence settled in for a while. Haley watched the river pig spokesperson carefully. Clearly, the man felt intimidated by Haley's assertions, but Haley could also tell that he did not want to show himself cowed in front of his fellow companions. "Did you ferget that there's a dozen of us compared to the few of—"

Before the river spokesperson could even finish his sentence, Mr. Haley lashed out with his foot and knocked the river pig over at his knees. Seconds later, before the river pig could even take in his surroundings, he found his

301

hands zip-tied behind his back with his legs joining before he could let loose the first expletive. Even then he never got a chance.

"You had warning enough," Mr. Haley spat down at him before standing up. "Anyone else want to forfeit your pay and join your comrade?" Silence. A few shaking heads.

"Then it's time to get back to business," he growled. "I want two of you standing guard on the captives we've already got and we'll set up a rotating guard of four of you at the logjam wall where the girl disappeared. She might come back at some point, and I want her captured as soon as she does."

Haley started to arrange the guard assignments and shifts when suddenly he heard Neech yelling. It took a second to realize it was at Felipe, which did not surprise Haley much considering Felipe's clear lack of competence and Neech's horrible mood. It was a recipe for an outburst. Yet, this yelling seemed a bit more pointed and in the harangue Haley heard the word "escape." He immediately charged the river pigs with figuring out the rest of their assignments, and marched towards the captives.

By the time Haley arrived at the small circle, Neech had leaned all the way into his tirade. "What do you mean, you can't find the machete?! Facade barely gave it to you five minutes ago, you idiot! He must've snatched it from you when you were clumsily going around and feeding them." Neech already had Felipe tightly gripped by the front shirt, seething with an anger that trembled through his body. "Thanks to you, that's how the kid got away. Again!" He wrapped up his rant with a couple choice expletives.

Haley wisely refrained from pointing out to Neech that regardless of how the zip ties were cut, Neech was supposed to be helping keep guard on the captives. He could not have been more than thirty feet away and in plain sight of all the captives during the incident.

More importantly, Haley quickly picked up from their conversation which captive had escaped. The pirate hunter. Somehow Haley held back the smile he felt, the one that always threatens with the thrill of a chase at hand. The pirate hunter had been clever in his escape last time, Haley thought, but now it was time to show the bothersome boy just how much out of Haley's league he really was.

Haley calmly went over to grab a swig of water. He had done a lot of running in one day, and he wanted to make sure he was topped off with plenty of water before embarking on this next chase.

"Where are the river pigs?" Neech suddenly turned to Haley. "I'll send you with half of them."

After swallowing the last gulps of his canteen, Haley deliberately wiped his chin and meticulously replaced the lid. "Just me again, Neech," Haley said.

Neech was still worked up from his encounter with Felipe. "I've had it with captures and escapes, Haley! It's time we started winding down this operation," he seethed. "I'm not going to let you waste our time with another prolonged chase when we've got plenty of manpower right here."

"Don't worry," Haley stated as he tranquilly set down the canteen, "I'll be significantly faster." He reached around his back and pulled out a gun from his waistline, checking the magazine for bullets. "You see, I won't be needing to carry him back this time."

This had a soothing effect on Neech. "Good," he nodded, "but you should still take some men, just to make sure."

Haley's relationship with Neech was a good one. It was a pleasure to work with a man who could always find meaningful jobs for him to do, so they rarely disagreed and Haley usually found it easier to just go with what Neech asked. But here, Haley found himself nearing an edge in their partnership. "I go alone," he stated, simply, resolutely.

Neech seemed thrown off by Haley's response. He took a step back and just nodded.

As Haley started on Eric's trail westward out of camp, he noticed the worry in the wide eyes of a few of the captives, who clearly saw Haley's determination to capture and kill. Strangely, the adult captive—the bodyguard—his eyes did not reflect the concern of the others. If anything, they were emboldened. It momentarily discomfited Haley.

What does he think he knows? Haley thought. For a split second, he wanted to go back and interrogate the man.

A second later, the idea passed. Now that Haley was on the trail, his blood began to pump. All that mattered in this moment was the chase. While there was always a reward, dead or alive, for a capture, this time the greater reward would be for the dead kind.

Eric made sure to mimic the panicked flight of his first escape westward through the woods. Although he felt calm, he wanted Haley to assume this escape to have started just as reckless as his last one.

Then, he stopped. He tried to imagine Haley as a pirate zeroing in on his prize. Eric did not want him to have any reason to suspect anything other than his own skill at capture. *I can't tip him off by making my escape too textbook*, Eric thought. *Last time, I went north. I'll make it look like I stopped to think of doing something different by heading south.* He almost turned south, but then he thought, *No. First I will make it* look *like I decided to follow the same route I took north before backtracking south.*

Eric sloppily stomped northward before backtracking and then lightly working his way south. He tried to play the delicate balance of making it look like he was trying to hide his tracks but also not being so thorough that his ruse worked too well.

After a few dozen yards, Eric began to move normally. Next he needed to find the right place to make the confrontation. As he trekked through the trees, he tried to imagine how to set this up as a pirate hunter.

He would want the weather gage on Haley, the advantage of wind. In reality, there was not a lot of wind, nor would it matter on land, but Eric figured the best comparison is to having the higher ground. He started to veer towards a rising knoll in the terrain.

Next, he would want an open sea. The maneuvers of the enemy ship are a lot easier to anticipate without a lot of obstacles to throw things off. As Eric worked his way up the rising ground, he located a clearing and zeroed in on it.

Once there, Eric made sure to hike to the top of the clearing, giving him a strong vantage point. He turned, found a stump, sat down, and waited. At this point, it would have been tempting to relax. He will have led Haley into a one-on-one confrontation. He had the weather gage and an open space on which to charge directly into the attack, taking Haley off guard.

Relaxing, however, even in the world of pirate hunting, had not served Eric well in the past. So he determined to dig deeper. *Is it possible I'm missing something?* he queried. Eric expertly twirled the machete while he thought. Then he stopped.

Weapons. I would know how many and what kind of cannons the enemy ship would have, Eric realized. He knew that he had a machete, but Eric suddenly recognized that he would be a fool to assume that Haley was coming after him with his bare hands and some zip ties. He tried to think. He had not noticed Haley ever handling a knife. As far as he had discerned, Haley did not even have anything—like a sheath or a bag—that could hold a weapon.

He had to have one, though, Eric reasoned. He tried to imagine what kind of weapon a fugitive slave hunter might carry. Just thinking of the natural born ability made him shudder. The man was naturally born to chase after people looking to find freedom and to bring them back into unjust captivity. Despicable. Yet, he was good at it, Eric realized, thinking about how he had so capably found his way around all of Eric's careful, strategic precautions when trying to escape the first time around.

A fugitive slave catcher might have a dog, something Eric knew Haley did not have, but then his mind reluctantly came to the obvious: a gun. An older kind, yes, but a gun none-the-less. A modern fugitive slave catcher like Haley would not need an old gun.

Only in that moment could Eric focus on a snapshot of Haley dropping him on the ground back at camp after being captured the first time. His eyes replayed the scene of Haley standing up and his shirt going down to cover something slightly sticking out from his back waistline.

That was it. The gun. Eric looked at his machete and knew that his skills with a blade would be useless if he could not get close enough to make it matter. As a pirate hunter, he would also feel comfortable with a gun, but there was none to be had.

At that moment he realized that was precisely what Mr. Reeves and Facade wanted to tell him. Mr. Reeves, a natural born bodyguard, would have been well aware of the gun after only spending a few moments near Haley. Facade, as his associate, would have known from the start.

This changes everything, Eric thought. And then a sudden movement at the bottom of the clearing interrupted him.

It was Mr. Haley, already arrived, with his gun out and ready.

With more time, Eric would have certainly panicked, but because Haley had a gun, time could only help the slave catcher more. For some reason, probably related to Dave's innocuous statement earlier about running straight for Haley, Eric simply made a snap decision and sprinted toward his foe.

This choice evoked a strange sequence of events with quite a bit happening in a very short time.

First of all, Eric's position above Haley and the downhill slope allowed him to succeed in gaining three tremendous steps before Mr. Haley's eyes, still searching the ground for tracks, were able to lock in on the noise above him and actually see Eric.

Then, another few steps were amassed thanks to the effect of Dave's rambling mention of Haley freezing when he ran towards him. Eric could see it in the eyes of the fugitive slave catcher, a sort of crazed thrill at seeing his quarry mingled with a flurry of bemusement trying to process Eric charging straight for him rather than away from him.

After that is when the advantage wore off. Although Haley was clearly uncomfortable with Eric coming straight at him, basic human instinct eventually got his hand with the gun to start raising towards Eric.

Perhaps because the whole situation was prompted by Dave's observation, his friend's instructions from seemingly ages ago about parkour somehow surfaced to Eric's mind: "You've just got to move first and trust your body will figure out the rest!" Eric let go of his thinking and let his body take over.

The next thing he knew, Eric's foot found the mound of an ant colony and used it as a springboard to dive headfirst towards Haley and his raising gun. Because this action off the mound required his arms to fling forward, Eric allowed himself one strategic thought and used the forward momentum of his left arm to suddenly propel the machete ahead of himself, spiraling towards Haley like a disconnected helicopter blade.

Eric watched the result as if in slow motion. The approaching machete made Haley cringe just enough that the ensuing pistol shot came earlier than he meant it to, staying low and beneath Eric's flying form. The machete zoomed over Haley's dodging head and—adhering strictly to the creed of Dave zen—Eric found himself trusting his body, which tucked his head, allowing his body to flip and his legs come forward just in time to land awkwardly on Haley's chest. They both went tumbling violently to the ground and rolling down the slope until crashing into some tree trunks at the bottom of the glade.

Before taking stock of anything else, Eric looked at Haley's hands and found that the crash landing had ejected the gun at some point. Relieved, he now scrambled to extricate his limbs from Haley's and stand up. Within a few moments, they both found themselves on their feet and facing each other.

Haley, who still seemed stupefied by the whole order of events, also scowled his hatred. He scanned the ground, as if searching for his gun. While the gun did not appear, he did quickly bend down and pick up Eric's machete, which had landed ahead of them on the ground, not too far from Haley's feet.

"Thought you would've learned your lesson," Mr. Haley growled. "But that's fine, because when I bring a piece of your corpse back to camp, you'll teach the other captives the lesson you should have learned."

Rather than feeling despair at the situation, a sword—or in this case a machete—leveled at his chest only caused the pirate hunter blood within him to surge. Eric saw the white gleam of a dead pine tree branch on the tree they had rolled into. Without taking his eyes off Haley, he reached out and snapped the branch off the trunk, then swiveled it around so that he held it something like a sword.

"Ever considered that *you* would have a lesson to learn?" Eric asked.

Haley looked at the branch. He did not have the kind of face conducive to a smile, but Eric could tell that amusement tugged at the corners of his mouth when his mustache trembled ever-so-slightly. "For me to learn a lesson, I'd have to be wrong." He hovered the machete menacingly. "I wasn't wrong when I chased you down the first time, and I won't be wrong when I kill you this time. I'm never wrong."

Haley immediately jabbed the machete straight for Eric's chest. It was the easiest move for Eric to parry, since it allowed his branch to avoid the sharp edge of the machete while knocking it sideways. This caused an opening that allowed Eric to complete the movement with a crack to Haley's face. "Well, there's a first for everything, I guess," Eric noted.

Within seconds, the blow revealed itself with an open wound to Haley's forehead, blood trickling down his face. Eric resumed his defensive position, holding the branch in front of him while watching Haley ponderously. "I remember accepting that I made a mistake when hunting a pirate. It made me a better pirate hunter."

Haley spitefully wiped the small stream of blood away from his eye. "If you think I'm wrong, then you're wrong . . . again."

Haley took deliberate swing, not at Eric but at the branch this time—clearly expecting to chop it in half and leave Eric weaponless. That was the disadvantage to having a piece of wood as a sword, Eric knew, it could only parry thrusts but not cuts.

Still, even though he stood on uneven ground rather than the deck of a ship and wielded a piece of wood rather than a sword, Eric was in his element. He raised his branch out of the way of the cutting machete while pulling his body back, causing the attack to miss. Then immediately after the machete passed untouched, Eric's raised branch came down as he leaned forward and smacked Haley on the top of his head.

Haley nearly dropped the machete in pain, reaching one hand up and cradling the crown of his head where the blow landed. He cursed vehemently and his brow cemented a look of venom towards Eric while his mustache bristled.

Eric took in the look of passionate hatred with the calmness of an outside observer. "This must be a new experience for you in a couple of ways," he noted. "You are not used to being wrong, and you're not used to your victims having an advantage over you." Eric lowered his branch slightly, "But you can save yourself more pain if you learn that lesson now and give up."

Haley's teeth ground together. "I was going to make your death quick because I'm in a hurry, but it's going to be worth slowing this down." Eric knew that Haley meant it. From the bottom of his blackened soul, Haley truly revelled in the very notion of Eric's tortured demise. That kind of sadistic resolve was nothing to toy with. Eric had seen it before with Jedediah Willard, and he was not about to make the same mistake of the overconfidence that Haley was demonstrating even in this moment of weakness.

Before the slave catcher could coalesce his hatred into motion, Eric struck. His wooden branch came down so hard on Haley's machete-wielding wrist that he could literally hear the pop of it fracturing on impact. In a subdued snarl of pain, Haley dropped the machete.

"I told you," Eric said as he deftly used the branch to slide the machete across the ground back to himself, "as a slave catcher you've only ever known how to attack, not to defend against an attack. Recognizing your weaknesses and mistakes is not wrong . . . in fact, it may be the best thing you can do."

Haley's sniveling almost disguised the desperate spring towards Eric, but the pirate hunter had been careful to never let his guard down. He capably sidestepped the attack and used the butt end of the machete to strike Haley on the back in a way that knocked the wind out of him.

This immobilized the slave catcher long enough for Eric to reach inside the man's jacket and grab a zip tie. He yanked Haley's wrists behind his back and secured his arms, to the anguished moans of someone whose broken wrist was already swelling. Then, following the pattern that Haley had taught Eric from his own captive experience, Eric brought Haley's legs up behind his back and zip tied them to the secured hands.

Haley's breathing was ragged and laced with the agony of his physical state. His inner rage, however, had not subsided, and Eric saw him eyeing his every movement with an acrimony that had all the intent of murder in it.

Eric ignored it as best he could as he searched the area. He found the gun a little ways up the slope and looked it over, noticing some buttons and other fascinating features that did not exist during the era of piracy. "What happened to the good old days of powder and shot?" he pondered out loud before pocketing it. Then he sheathed the machete in his belt and took his bearings before turning his back to the setting sun and stepping eastward.

"Pirate hunter!" Mr. Haley growled. Eric stopped but did not turn back. A part of him expected some calls for mercy, but the tone in Haley's voice, while clearly hurting, still burned of defiance. "You talk about making mistakes." He had to pause because a spasm of shooting pain interrupted him. "But you are the one making the biggest mistake by leaving me alive." More gurgling followed.

Eric stopped for a moment, still facing forward. "The biggest difference between the two of us is that I can admit that you might be absolutely right."

Then Eric strode toward the river.

Chapter 3
FERRY, DISTRACTED

Although Sally was prepared to get wet with this ferrying, it still did not make the water any less cold. She caught her breath as soon as the splash into the river occurred. The next thing she heard was a collective gasp from four figures surrounding her.

"There she is!"

"Grab her!"

Within seconds, she had been subdued by no less than four burly river pig arms—not that she was struggling. "Easy!" Sally called out. "Don't get my diary wet . . . then my brother will never get to read it!"

One of the river pigs grabbed Sally's Scribblings Diary out of her raised hand. "Take her to shore!" she heard one grumble. "Stewart, go on ahead and tell the boss that we got the witch."

Sally heard someone push ahead in the river and splash out onto the bank. By the time they got halfway across it was clear Sally was neither capable nor interested in putting up much resistance, so she got transferred to just one river pig's care. The other two spread out—one in front and the other behind—and the pigs fell silent.

The front guard helped the man holding Sally to get her onto the bank and then they waited for the rear guard to join them. After a dozen seconds of fruitless anticipation, Sally saw them looking at each other.

"Eddie," the front guard called out tentatively, "you find something? Where are ya?" The next couple of minutes passed by in strained silence with the two river pigs glancing at each other nervously.

The river pig holding Sally seemed to have to subdue a slight tremble in his grip. "You ain't casting no spells now, are ya?" he finally ventured.

It took Sally a second to realize he was talking to her. "How could I?" she asked. "You're holding my spellbook."

Though she was being sarcastic, the river pig's eyes grew while he glared at her diary with a mixture of awe and fear. Just in that moment, out of the darkness up river from them, a guttural wailing managed to rumble across the black void and penetrate their senses.

Immediately the river pigs glanced at each other, then Sally, who shrugged. *What is that?*

"Eddie?" one of the river pigs voiced.

"That ain't human," the other responded.

As if to confirm his conjecture, the noise gained traction, rising in decibels and ferocity until it managed to sound like a dull knife sawing through cardboard with a megaphone amplifying it by a thousand.

Just when Sally felt confident the river pigs would not be able to take another second of its grating arrhythmic bursts, it stopped and the night went as silent as it was black.

"You think it's a cougar?" one of them hesitantly broke the stillness. "You think..." he gulped, "... you think that's what got Eddie?"

"Never heard a cougar sound like that," his crew mate responded with wonder in his voice, "but I don't rightly know what else could make that sound... or take out Eddie."

Before either could follow up, the noise returned, starting low and escalating to a shouting, spine-tingling growl. Finally, when it reached its zenith and stopped, the river pig holding Sally shoved his partner upriver. "I ain't walking back to camp with that thing at our backs. Go find out what it is and make a ruckus to git it outta here."

"Why me?" The river pig stayed rooted. "Why don't you go?"

"'Cause I'm watching the witch!" he snarled. "Don't worry. If it did get Eddie, it won't be hungry no more. Now go see!"

The river pig took a deep breath, grabbed two branches from the ground that wielded before him like clubs, disappearing into the dark. The noise began again. This time it felt as if it echoed all around them and somehow seemed stronger without another person with them.

Suddenly it stopped, mid-bellowing.

The river pig, whose grip had been tightening with each ear-splitting howl, suddenly loosened his hold. "Took 'im long enough. That should take care of that problem." After a couple of deep breaths, he called out. "Alright, you got 'im, now come on back!"

But there was no response. At least, not until Sally inadvertently laughed. She had not meant to, but when she suddenly realized what the mystery behind the noise was, she could not hold back the inevitable guffaw.

The river pig, who already stood on edge, looked at Sally hard. "What did you do?"

"Me?" she asked, surprised that he thought she would be up to something. Then she saw the way he gripped her Scribblings Diary and that his eyes tried to hide a building fear. *He thinks I did this using some sort of magic!*

As she faced the river pig, she suddenly saw past his shoulder and recognized Eric striding calmly out of the darkness, wielding a machete. Sally smiled but shook her head to hold him off. *He shouldn't get all of the fun!*

"Course you!" the river pig answered her query while loosening his grip on her and taking a hesitant step backwards. "You're laughing 'cause you made this happen. You've become powerful enough to cast spells without yer book. Maybe you changed Eddie into some kind of beast and he devoured Will and . . ."

The more the river pig spoke, the more he seemed to convince himself of these dark schemes. Sally did nothing to stop him. In fact, his wild conjectures only made it more difficult for her to keep a straight face, which—in turn—seemed to confirm his suppositions even more.

"What've ya done to Stewart?!" his eyes grew wide. "I don't want to be no wild beast! And I ain't lookin' to be eaten by one neither!" He suddenly seemed to see her diary with new eyes and tossed it to the ground as if it seared his fingers. "I'd rather take my chance being hunted by the Haley fellow," he babbled, then faced Sally with wild eyes. "I've given ya back yer spellbook, now just leave me be and I promise ta never return to these parts again!" A few more steps back and Sally saw that the river pig was about to bump into her brother. Though tempted to see how that might play out, she mercifully decided to release her "captor."

"Because you returned my book of spells," Sally said in her most imperious tone, "I will allow you freedom, but you must never return and can only do good things from here on out. If you don't I'll know because I can see you when you're sleeping and I know when you're awake, and I know if you've been bad or good, so be good for goodness sake!"

Before Sally had to figure out what the second verse in the song was, the river pig sprinted chaotically southward into the darkness with a speed and recklessness that suggested he may not stop until dawn or until collapsing from fatigue.

"Wow," Eric watched the river pig disappear with raised eyebrows. "I mean, I knew your singing of Christmas songs annoyed me, but never *that* much!"

Sally ran up and gave Eric a hug, in spite of his brotherly tease. "You should talk," she replied eventually, "that was the most pathetic impression of a howler monkey that I've ever heard." Eric about protested, but she cut him off, "But I will admit that it was a pretty good way to separate those two river pigs."

Eric nodded and he released Sally from their embrace. "Fair enough. And I'll admit that was a pretty good way to get rid of a guy without having to fight him."

"I've got some questions for you," Sally picked up her diary and sat Eric down. "Was it Facade that released you like she said she would? What is she up to? And how did you get rid of that first river pig behind us? And did you know that Haley is a natural born fugitive slave catcher? How did you escape him or do we need to be on guard for him? How did you—"

"Easy," Eric motioned for Sally to slow down. "I've got questions for you too. So, I'll give you the short version, then you can get as much as you want after you've answered mine." Sally nodded in agreement, and Eric said, "Facade released me, but I'm not sure why. She warned me that Haley was a natural born fugitive slave catcher, so I . . ." he paused for a second, " . . . I was able to outmaneuver him and left him trussed up in the woods."

Sally would have taken a lot more time to explain all of that, but she was left satisfied with the thought that she would get a chance to have follow up questions later—Eric knew her well!

"As for the river pig, I was climbing along the logjam to reach the ferry point when you popped in from out of nowhere. It was pretty lucky for me that you did because I was about to stumble unprepared into four hefty and on guard river pigs. When you showed up, they nabbed you and as soon as they spread out, I was able to take the rear river pig pretty quickly since I got him from the side and before he could really settle into his surroundings. After that, I figured that I'd better come up with a way to separate the other two . . . you know the rest."

Sally nodded. "Okay, that all makes sense. I will say this: it wasn't luck that I showed up when I did."

Eric squinted his eyes. "I wondered about that. Okay, then, your turn to start answering questions."

Excited that she actually had something to say that Eric wanted to listen to, Sally needed no second prompting. She explained in the kind of detail that Eric neglected, how she and Charlotte hid during the ambush and how Facade found them and convinced Charlotte to ferry back. She knew that Eric had more questions about their encounter with Facade, but with baffling restraint, he managed to not interrupt her with them. She sighed inwardly and moved on to explain their retreat and timely ferrying and then their discussion in the parking lot.

"That's when she finally came to her senses," Sally said, her excitement culminating. "Because it was at that point that she decided to reveal to me my natural born ability." She paused at this point, waiting for him to ask what it was. Vexingly, he said nothing. "Well," she followed up, "don't you want to know what it is?"

"You're a script doctor," Eric said flatly, "whatever that is."

Sally sat perplexed. "Wait, how did you . . . ?"

"She told me a long time ago," Eric stated. "After she first met you, I think."

"And you never thought to tell me?!" Sally replied.

"None of my business," Eric shrugged. "Anyway, you were talking about you and Charlotte trying to figure out how to get us out of this mess . . . ?"

Sally still could say nothing. Her mouth gaped at the audacity of her brother's indifference for several long moments. "Ugh," she finally muttered. "If we weren't busy rescuing people from some natural bornappers right now, I'd spend the next couple of hours giving you a serious talking to about learning to respect your siblings!"

Maddeningly, Eric appeared mystified by Sally's outburst. She put her hands up in the air. "Fine. But this is far from over!" The threat fell on impassive ears. "Anyway, we figured out my natural born ability, and decided that I would be the one to fix up this whole mess, but I wasn't sure who we would need to free, so I convinced her to check the hieroglyphics on your phone, and she saw that she needed to ferry me back right away."

"How did she know the timing?" Eric asked, finally interested.

"She didn't for sure," Sally answered, "but then she did a crazy thing where she did this sort of half-ferrying thing."

"What do you mean?"

Sally still could not get over the fact that Eric asked questions about this but not earlier. Grudgingly, she held back her criticisms and responded, "Well, you could kind of see the shimmering all around her, as if she were about to ferry, but she never disappeared. Instead, she just kind of sat between the two worlds. I mean, I could see her, but she couldn't see me, she was looking at this world."

"How did she know she could do that?" Eric mused.

"She didn't," Sally answered, "at least, it didn't seem like she knew. She just kind of had the idea and tried it. I was nervous because I knew that Facade said not to ferry back, so I warned Charlotte about that. She couldn't see me, but she could hear me and told me not to worry, that she was just peeking."

Eric shook his head in awe. "What else does she not know about her ability?"

"Well, we also didn't know if she could ferry a person to someone else's natural born ability world without going herself, but she said that she felt she could half-way ferry to that sort of limbo, in-between spot holding my hand and then let go of me as a way of dropping me into Dave's world. And it worked!"

"Wait, but you didn't tell me what she saw when she peeked," Eric backtracked.

"Don't worry," Sally assured him, "I was definitely going to explain that. You see, that's when she saw you climbing along the logjam about to run into the river pigs and she figured that the hieroglyphic showed me ferrying so that it would distract them from catching you because they would think that I was her."

"So that's when she ferried you?" Eric asked.

"Not at first. She was going to check the next hieroglyphic to see if I turned out okay. She didn't want to ferry me straight into getting captured."

"The next hieroglyphic said it would be okay?" Eric said.

"Don't know," Sally shook her head. "I told her to just ferry me, because you were going to be caught at any second, and I didn't need a hieroglyphic to tell me that you'd free me pretty quickly after I got captured. So then she ferried me immediately after that . . . you know the rest."

Eric stared at Sally. "You put a lot of faith in me."

Sally rolled her eyes. "We were in a time crunch, and I was right." Sally saw that Eric was not about to accept this flippant remark. She tried again, "Your lack of communication skills can be pretty annoying most of the time, but I'm one-hundred percent sure about your protecting-your-sister skills."

Eric blinked a couple of times before finally taking a hand and placing it on Sally's shoulder. "I . . . I'm . . . floored by your trust in me. I know I'm not always the best brother so, I—"

"That's quite enough of that," Sally patted his hand on her shoulder. "I finally have you communicating your feelings, and now I find I don't even want to hear it."

Eric smiled and removed his hand. "You're right. We should go back to pretending I don't care about you."

Sally raised an eyebrow. "I don't know if I would go that far, but right now we've got work to do."

"Okay," Eric slapped his hands on his thighs and looked around. "Maybe we'll set up some sort of camp so we can see if Facade manages to free anyone else and—"

"Did you not listen to anything I said?" Sally interrupted. Eric paused with a bewildered look. "I'm here because I'm a script doctor and my job is to fix everything." Eric nodded slowly, and Sally continued, "So save yourself the trouble of thinking of solutions and leave the strategizing to me."

Eric seemed to be holding back a smile. "Okay, Sis, er . . . I mean, script doctor. You've got a better idea?"

Sally smiled. Eric may have taken away the thunder of knowing her natural born ability before she told him, but she knew that he would not be expecting this next statement, so she delivered it with all of the confidence that an award-winning actress would expect on her script: "Of course I do. I need you to take me to Neech so that I can talk him into giving us back one of our friends."

Because they did not have a lot of time, Charlotte was unable to ask Sally how she knew that her depiction in the hieroglyph showed her raising one hand above her head as Sally did in this moment. Yet, as soon as Charlotte took Sally into ferry limbo with her and then let go of Sally's hand, the mystery revealed itself. Sally must have remembered that she was going to plop in the river and wanted to keep her diary dry this time by holding it above her head. Charlotte was both awed and amused at the precise realization of the foreseer's sign.

Though she wanted to stick around in-between worlds to watch the ensuing scene unfold, Charlotte found that balancing between two worlds was tricky enough. She could not be sure that she would not incidentally—or purposefully—will herself into Dave's world once she got too invested in or distracted by what she saw, and Facade's warning not to ferry back into Dave's world hovered at the back of her mind with vague foreboding.

So instead Charlotte decided that she could study the hieroglyphics to determine what to expect next. That way she would remain out of Dave's world but also might stumble across information that could be useful.

In the blink of an eye, she found herself firmly back in the parking lot. Just as she lifted Eric's phone up to her gaze, a voice interrupted her. "Well, young lady, I've been looking for an opportunity to speak with you for a while."

She inadvertently lifted up her eyes. There, staring straight back into her eyes, stood Mr. Pickney's hero, Dr. Corinth. "Ah . . ." he said with a knowing glint, "just as I suspected. A seer."

Chapter 4
ACCORDING TO SCRIPT

Facade heard the pop of the gunshot in the distance and winced. She thought it might not get to the gun, but that sound did not bode well for the pirate hunter. She should have given Eric a heads up, but they were seconds away from being discovered together, and that would have been the end for her. Neech was in a bad enough mood as it was, suspecting his own right hand gal of betraying him would not have ended well for her.

Facade had hoped, perhaps naively, that the pirate hunter would have been able to surprise Haley before he could use the gun, but in hindsight she was probably overestimating Eric or underestimating Haley. Either way, she would soon lose the trust of the captives once they heard the news, and she could only hope that Neech would never discover her attempted treachery.

Irked, she continued on her made up errand of finding the rogue river pig. She had no desire to find him, but sometimes a magician has to keep their smile on well after a trick is over or else the mirage of magic might lose its luster on the audience.

A couple of hours later, she slid back into her camp. She had managed to find the river pig—a burly, talkative, but not exceptionally bright fellow—holed up in a cabin on the other side of the river. She conversed with him long enough to find out that the guy had no knowledge of any of the happenings. It took all her evasiveness to avoid his queries about who she was and how she was connected to the other young people he had seen earlier.

That was difficult, but the thing that felt impossible was finding a pause long enough in his chatting for her to break off their discussion and leave—something she barely managed to do without having to pull off an actual magic trick.

At this point she had enjoyed at least an hour of silence as she worked her way back across the river, into the outskirts of her camp, and stepped around sleeping river pigs, stumps, and captives. She noted Felipe had found himself bound with zip ties and tossed into the group of captives. Had Felipe been a more sympathetic character, Facade might have felt a tinge of guilt for pinning Eric's escape on him. As it was, she simply glided past him without a second thought.

Her thoughts instead rested on the other captives. She could possibly release some of them in the dark of night right now and urge them to make their way back to the logjam and Charlotte. Facade had promised Charlotte she would get Eric to her, but that chance came and went now—would Charlotte still accept an offering of the other captives as consolation?

Just past the captives, Facade saw the silhouetted form of Neech sitting thoughtfully in front of a subdued fire. For what must have been the hundredth time, she felt a strong urge to take advantage of his turned back, pull out her slender dagger, and plunge it into his unsuspecting form.

For the hundredth time, she quelled the thought. Neech held too strong of a hold over her, and they both knew it. She looked around for Haley. Her safety right now depended on how much Haley learned from the pirate hunter before he killed him. She could not see the fugitive slave catcher.

Facade figured that the pirate hunter probably set up an ambush for Haley, successfully surprised him, but had not prepared for the gun. The likelihood that Haley shot Eric before having a chance to interrogate him was high, she reasoned. She watched Neech for a moment longer.

Like some of her more difficult magic tricks, she was just going to have to rely on the strength of her bluffing. She stuffed any doubts down into the deepest folds of her trenchcoat and softly appeared on the stump to the side of the fire.

Neech jumped and cursed. "Facade, I need to attach a cowbell to you!"

She ignored his statement. "Found the river pig. He's harmless, just waiting for his crew to return from gathering supplies—probably be a week or more before they get back."

"You didn't see Haley did you?" Neech asked.

Facade paused. Haley had not yet returned. "No," she breathed. "He's not in camp?"

Neech cursed again. "Right after you left, that idiot chiclero managed to get his machete swiped when he was clumsily going around and feeding the captives. The pirate kid escaped." Neech spat on the ground contemptuously. Facade hung on the next words. "That self-absorbed imbecile Haley insisted on going after the boy alone, as if it were a personal insult to him that he escaped again."

So far it was what Facade anticipated, but not the result she expected. "He went after him but hasn't returned yet?"

"A couple hours ago, I heard a gunshot from pretty far away—at least I'm pretty sure it was a gunshot, had to be. I figured that Haley got his man . . . as usual." Neech snapped a nearby branch with subdued wrath and tossed it into the fire. "But he hasn't come back. The longer he's gone, the more obvious it is that somehow Haley has been bested at his own natural born ability."

Facade did not even come close to smiling on the outside—she was far too well trained than to show that kind of emotion. But on the inside? She felt an immense dosage of relief at this news. It seems as if Eric might have figured this out after all. If that were the case, he had probably found his way back to the logjam and Charlotte.

Facade allowed her eyes to slide back to the pile of captives. With Haley gone, it was a fairly simple matter of providing the captives a way to get loose from their zip ties, waiting until some dull-headed river pig was guarding them, distracting or deceiving him, and then the captives could simply stroll out of camp with no fear of Haley coming after them.

"Good thing you didn't kill off the other captives," Facade finally responded. "We still have back up collateral."

Neech did not seem to appreciate this silver lining too much, but he did nod grudgingly. "The pirate hunter'll be back now," Neech growled. "There's no way he leaves his friends behind without trying to free them."

He won't need to. I'll be the one releasing them, Facade thought. But to Neech she simply nodded and quipped, "Seems likely."

Neech suddenly settled a hard glare on Facade. "That's why you'll be solely responsible for watching the captives from here on out."

Facade could not tell if the look was accusatory or just intense. "You want me in charge of the captives? That's not my thing, Neech," she tried, "you know that."

Neech's clenched jaw showed his earnestness. "You're the only one I can trust now." He took some deep breaths. "We can't afford to lose any more captives if Haley isn't coming back."

While this statement was relieving in the sense that Neech still clearly did not suspect her, it single-handedly killed any ambitions she had of freeing the others as she told Charlotte she would. It was simple enough when Felipe or someone else was in charge, but if Neech put her in charge it would be far too obvious if someone escaped after that. It'd be like trying to pull off a complicated magic trick on the spot without your own materials.

"I don't know if I would be much of an improvement—I'm better at making things disappear than at getting them to stay put. Besides, that'd make it hard for me to go on info-gathering trips or see if I can figure out a way to trick Charlotte into coming back," Facade made a feeble pitch.

Neech had made up his mind. "This is more important. Believe me, you may not be a natural born prison guard, but you at least have brains, something we can't say about that chicle gatherer. And these river pigs are only as good as the money I pay them and the threats that Haley made to them." Neech shook his head. "It's you or no one."

Facade knew that pushing too much would be suspicious. The edge she traversed right now was far too dangerous to take reckless chances. The possibility of Charlotte had momentarily given Facade hope to not be dependent on Neech, but ultimately she knew that she was indelibly connected to this loathsome figure sitting at the fire with her.

323

"Whatever you want, Neech," Facade looked into the fire hard enough that she felt as if it burned through her pupils and seared the inside of her mind. She knew that by agreeing to be responsible for the captives, Facade was committing to ensure that not a single one escaped again—no matter what the price. *You're on your own now, Charlotte.*

"Absolutely not, Sally!" it was obvious that Eric had decided to take a stand.

"Very well," Sally responded. "You look pretty set, so I'll agree with you."

"Well, for one," Eric charged forward, "even though I don't exactly know what a script doctor does, I'm sure that it *doesn't* make you invincible!"

Sally smiled. "Eric, I just agreed with you. I won't go see Neech."

Eric had been digging in for a prolonged debate, so pulling the rug out from under him really threw him off. "Wait, what?"

"It's too dark right now. I'm going to need better lighting for this meeting . . . it'll make for a better effect," Sally said. Eric looked ready to respond, but Sally beat him to it. "And besides, you are going to need a little bit more time to get everything ready."

"Ready?" Eric remarked. "Sally, you're going to need to turn your ship into the wind and wait for me to catch up because I have no idea what is going on here."

Sally rolled her eyes. "Let's just say that I've done a character breakdown, and we are way too outnumbered—even for a good underdog story. It's time we balanced things out a bit by shifting a character or two in our favor."

"And what is your plan for me to make that happen?" Eric did not try to hide his skepticism.

"Haley is not doing us any good being tied up somewhere to eventually free himself and then come after you for revenge. I mean, that's Movie Plot Basics 101. So you're going to go find him before he sets himself free and keep an eye on him until tomorrow morning. At my signal, you will release him."

Eric looked at Sally as if he had never met her before. "Find and release Haley? Why would I release that dangerous predator, and what signal are you thinking of giving? And how in the world are you even acting like this is all a set thing when one world ago I had to rescue you from being held captive?"

"I didn't know my ability then," Sally answered. "Now I do, and so you can mark this down as me returning the favor, because I promised Charlotte a happy ending, which I should be able to do if you would just listen to—"

"Well if it ain't one of my little friends! Yer the one named Sally, ain't ya?" Sally and Eric both jumped at the sudden appearance of a person materializing out of the darkness. "And who you got here? He looks enough like you to be family."

"Jimmy Sellers!" Sally recognized the river pig. "Boy am I glad to see you. I thought I was going to need to hunt you down."

"You've been looking fer me? You young'uns were the ones to disappear earlier! The only reason I'm finding you now is because some girl that I thought mighta been looking fer your group dropped by my cabin at dusk. She didn't stay long, but sounded like she'd run across some other river pigs, an' I just wanted to investigate and make sure it weren't my crew lollygagging on their way to git the dynamite."

"I think this is a different group of river pigs than yours," Sally said. "There's one named Eddie and another named Will and—"

"Dickey's crew!" Jimmy Sellers jumped in. "They musta finished their other job and made their way back here so's to not miss the clearing out of the logjam."

Sally smiled. "Sounds like you know them! They've fallen in with some rough people, but I was actually hoping that we might get at least Eddie and Will recruited to help us."

"Eddie and Will?" Jimmy followed up. "They're persuadable enough. But you said to recruit them to help us. Help us do what?"

325

"We're going to break up that logjam of yours, without waiting for a week for your crew to come back with dynamite."

Jimmy looked at Sally confused but prepared to laugh. Then he looked at Eric. Sally saw Eric shrug at him. "I'm in the same boat as you," Eric told the river pig. "But I'm used to hearing orders from her, and even though I usually ignore her, she sounds like she knows enough of what she's doing that I might even give her ideas a chance if she'll ever let me in on them."

Sally's grin widened. It was not reading her diary . . . but it was a step in the right direction.

Neech woke up to the smell of some sort of tasteless grub that the river pigs regularly used for meals. He sighed. Usually, his passion had him moving from town to town affirming as many people as possible without arousing suspicion before moving on to the next. It was not glamorous, but at least it did not require him to regularly sleep on the ground and eat the most bland combination of food imaginable.

On the rare occasion that his mission took him to other worlds, however, most of those worlds did not provide the comforts of modern civilization. Neech shook his head. Somehow, he still got labeled as a natural bornapper, a criminal, a bad guy. The sacrifices he made to realize his passion for a new worldview were lost on short-sighted moralists with no appreciation for the grandeur of his scheme.

Neech eyed the captives and saw, with relief, the silent form of Facade asserting her skills of observation in keeping them from escape. Yet even Facade—as talented as she was in helping his cause—did not seem to share his vision. Neech knew he could rely on her allegiance, but her stoic distance and cold efficiency revealed nothing of his same devotion.

Haley on the other hand at least seemed to enjoy his job, something Facade never exhibited in all the time he worked with her. Neech would not go so far as to say that Haley cared all that much for the bigger picture of their work, but the fact that he appreciated the opportunities that affirming provided him to exercise his immense talent . . . well, that made the loss of Haley sting anew.

Facade and Haley were one thing, Neech reasoned. How important, now more than ever, would it be to attain the services of the uniquely gifted Charlotte? Once he could increase the amount of affirmations, he felt confident that he would be able to attract the assistance of more seers who would suddenly catch sight of what affirming can do to elevate mankind past the plateau evolution had brought it to.

But everything hinged on Charlotte. She was the difference between him being just another rogue natural born affirmer—one of maybe a dozen or so working independently around the world—and the leader of the movement that would change forever the trajectory of human development.

"Neech." Facade's voice had the edge to it that made him realize that she had probably been saying his name multiple times while he had been lost in his strategizing. Neech looked over at her.

Rather than saying anything, she simply nodded towards the edge of camp.

"Hi! Good morning. Sorry to barge in on breakfast," Neech saw the young girl named Sally waving to them from the edge of camp, "but if we're being honest, it doesn't look that appetizing anyway!"

Having just been removed from a daze of deep thinking, Neech was already confused. This did not improve his state. He looked over to Facade, quizzically. He had never seen the street magician baffled, but he felt this was as close as he would get. She, too, stared at Sally as if suspecting some sort of wild deception.

The river pigs were at first as startled as anyone, but when they saw it was just a little girl and that she was here to speak to Neech, they seemed less interested and went back to getting their meal.

"Where's Charlotte?" Though he had an abundance of questions, Neech decided that he might as well get straight to the one that mattered most.

"Oh, she's safely ferried away," Sally responded, as if surprised by the question and eager to get down to the business that mattered. "But the better question is what I'm doing here. In fact, I'd have you say something like, 'Why if it isn't Sally. To what do we owe the honor of your visit?' or something campy like that."

Neech felt tempted to look at Facade again, but he knew she would have no answers for him. "What do you want?"

He could tell that she felt disappointed that he refused to employ the line she gave him, but she went ahead anyway. "I want to offer you a trade."

"Besides a worthless notebook," Neech said, "what could you possibly have of value to trade with me? I could tell you that I'd exchange every one of your friends except for the bodyguard for Charlotte, but I already know that you won't do that."

Sally's face scrunched. "You know, I'm going to tell my brother that you and he share the same bad taste in the quality of my diary. Maybe that will get him to appreciate it more. Of course, I'd have to do that after he releases Haley for you."

Neech felt annoyed by Sally's tendency to draw out a simple conversation into something far more showy, something he vaguely attributed to Sally's natural born ability as a script . . . something or other. Yet, he had to admit, the last line caught his attention. He tried not to show surprise, but he knew that his mouth dropped. He glanced once more over at Facade who seemed to be staring even more intently at Sally.

"What good is Haley to me if he can't even catch a silly pirate hunter?" Neech waved his hand dismissively, hoping that the statement would make up for him obviously revealing too much surprise at her statement.

"Oh," Sally mumbled. "Well, I thought that . . . I thought that he was, like, a friend of yours or . . ."

"He's a worthless waste of space," Neech stated.

Although he had been thrown off guard at first, Neech could see that he was now asserting more dominance in the conversation. Sally had come in with a pretty big trump card, but she played her whole hand far too early.

"So . . ." Sally ventured, "so you wouldn't think of trading him for all of my friends?"

Neech stood up and took a couple of steps towards Sally, who now appeared to be more and more out of her element. "Little girl," he said, "bring me Charlotte and then we'll have something to discuss. Until then, we're just wasting each other's time."

"I guess this is why Eric told me that this was a bad idea," Sally fingered her diary nervously. "I can't bring Charlotte because she doesn't even know I'm here."

Things were starting to make more sense for Neech now. Somehow, Sally convinces Charlotte to send her back in order to get Eric. She finds out that Eric has Haley and figures she can just talk Neech into making an exchange.

Good idea, in theory, Neech thought. But now that she was doing it, it was clear she was way over her head. Sally's nervous fingering of her diary had now led to her dropping it to the ground. She bent over to pick it up, but then she seemed to realize that she should not keep her eyes off her enemies. This meant that she looked up before grabbing it, which left her fingers fumbling all over the ground amongst the downed branches from the lumberjacks before she found her diary. Neech wanted to laugh at her to further unsettle her, but she was not even looking at him, she was looking at Facade with a weird intense look on her face.

While amusing, it was also tiring. Neech felt sick of exchanges and negotiations. He wanted to get straight to the ending, which resulted in him with Charlotte. But one does not become a natural born affirmer, walking around hundreds of people everyday who are in the wrong world for their ability but who cannot be affirmed for days or weeks at a time, without learning some patience.

As frustrated as Neech was with Haley getting captured, being down to just one core team member left him feeling vulnerable. It would be useful to have Haley back. Unlike Sally, though, he would need to play his cards more subtly. He waited until Sally stood back up and faced him.

"Charlotte doesn't know you're here," Neech repeated, "I see. Well, I can tell that this didn't exactly go like you expected." He took another step towards Sally. "Tell you what. It took some guts for you to walk in here with a plan, even if it wasn't very well thought out. How about I give you . . . how about I give you the man from the chiclero world, Felipe? And then I can take Haley off your brother's hands."

"But Felipe tried to kill one of my friends. He's the last person I care about right now . . ." Sally complained.

"True, but if Charlotte is so worried about people not being removed from their worlds against their will, then she might feel good about sending him back. It'll give her a little consolation to losing her father and friends."

Sally fidgeted. "Maybe Eric was right. Maybe I should've let him kill Haley," she said this almost to herself. "I . . . maybe I should just be going. I thought that you'd, well, you know what I thought . . ." She shuffled backwards a few steps.

Facade had warned Neech that Eric was capable of killing, and Neech did not doubt that someone as dangerous and brutal as Haley—the very reasons Neech wanted him back—would make Eric feel justified in such an action. He did not want that to happen. At the same time, he loathed the idea of actually allowing Sally to walk away from here with even the slightest success in negotiating. Neech decided to try a different approach.

"Now where are you in such a hurry to go?" Neech asked. Sally stopped her backwards shuffling. "What makes you think you can just show up, chat with me, and then go your way as if I'm the type of person that you sit down to have tea with?"

Sally's eyes widened and she looked around. The river pigs were still only vaguely interested in this conversation, but Neech knew that they were ready to hop up and grab Sally as soon as he gave the word. He could tell that Sally was putting that together as well.

330

"Now, what if I just explain to you that your friends won't be hurt if you can just tell me where Eric and Haley are right this minute?" Neech smiled menacingly. "Then we'll gather everyone up. I give you my word that we'll treat everyone civilly until the moon reciprocates and we can all go back to get Charlotte."

Neech felt satisfied with how he led Sally into this complete flip of the situation from the moment she had walked so confidently into his camp. Yet, as he looked at Sally, he saw her hesitation switch to a small but fragile pillar of resolve.

"I actually have no idea where Eric and Haley are," she blurted out. "I told him not to tell me. I couldn't even point in the general direction since I barely made it here myself without getting lost."

Neech wondered if this were true, but on the surface it made sense. Sally continued, "Maybe you think I'm lying, and you'll hurt my friends to get me to talk. I'll want to tell you at that point, I might even lie to you and say that I did know all along, but I promise you that any information I give you when that happens would be worthless because I truly don't know."

Neech frowned, but Sally was not done. "This much I do know, though. If you dare hurt any of my friends, or if you take me captive so that Eric doesn't get my signal in the next hour, then you are choosing to kill Haley. Not only that but Eric will then join Charlotte and warn her what you've done, and you'll never see either of them again."

Neech ground his teeth. His show of force did not have the desired effect. Sally may be naive and simple, but he should not have pushed her into a corner like he did. At the very least, she prepared for the worst case scenario, and it effectively made him nervous that anything too rash he did at this point would not just jeopardize Haley—a loss he did not desire but could recover from—but could possibly instigate the complete inability to nab Charlotte once they reciprocated back.

Neech hesitated before deciding to shift this conversation back to its previous track, where he held the advantage but appeared less threatening. "Of course I was only asking hypothetical questions. No reason to get defensive."

In a show of his deescalation of the situation, Neech took a few steps backward and even sat down comfortably on a stump. "You've come a long way and I'd hate for it to be nothing. I still don't care much for Haley, but I've got an awful lot of captives here that I don't need. I suppose I could entertain a swap of one of them for Haley."

He eyed Sally carefully after his proposition and saw her brighten immediately. Then he watched her collect herself and try to maintain the same firmness from her last statement. "You can keep Charlotte's dad, he can take care of himself, but I want the rest of my friends back."

Neech smiled. "Why, little girl, this is simple mathematics. You can't have one person and ask for three. Believe me, I'm doing you the favor by offering even one. I don't need to, but I'm inclined to show you how reasonable I can be by agreeing for an exchange of one."

He saw the discomfort in Sally's eyes. "Haley is kind of a big strong guy, though," she ventured as if not even convinced by her own reasoning, "maybe he would be equal to Dave and Luke together."

Neech now had the names of the ones that she wanted, a significant blunder on her part. The talented one and the strong one. She was trying to build a team that could go up against his and possibly aim to overcome them to get everything back the way it was before. This told him exactly who he could *not* give to her.

"Now that's some clever math, changing people into parts and then trying to weigh their equality that way. If we're doing that, then you'll understand why I can't release Dave or Luke at all, unless it is for Charlotte herself. You see, they were far too much work for us to catch once. Ask any of the guys over here with bruises and cuts," Neech waved his hand towards the river pigs, who seemed annoyed at having their injuries pointed out publicly. "If things were to get out of hand, I would regret having let Dave and Luke loose."

"Oh," Sally responded, a little deflated. "Well, I . . . maybe just Dave then?"

Neech had her right where he wanted her now. "Tell you what. How about I offer you this other girl, the aqueduct engineer, and then why don't you two and Eric ferry back to Charlotte—I assume she'll ferry you back if you go to the logjam—and tell her that I just want to talk with her. That's all. If she just agrees to talk with me, then I can release her other friends and even her dad." Neech leaned back casually on the stump as if he had just made the most innocent proposition in the world. He waited to see if Sally would take the bait.

"Haley for Tina?" she asked.

"And a meeting with Charlotte," Neech prodded.

Sally hesitated. "We'd need a few days to figure things out with Charlotte."

Neech could tell she was already prepared to accept his terms. "Of course."

"And you would have to make sure that you brought every captive to the logjam to meet with Charlotte so that you could release them to her before she will speak to you," Sally pressed.

Neech nodded soothingly. "That seems only fair. I'll have all the captives with me."

"And no river pigs," Sally added, "except Dave."

Neech folded his arms. "It might be hard to transport all these captives if it's just Facade, Haley, and myself," Neech allowed. "I might use one or two river pigs to help get them to the logjam, but then I'll dismiss them." This was a needless compromise, since Neech had no plans whatsoever of not having the whole crew of river pigs join him, but he had to make Sally feel as if she were working for her deal or else she might think that it came too easily and be suspicious.

Sally considered his proposal and then nodded slowly. "Okay. But the minute you get to the logjam, they have to be sent back to this camp."

Neech nodded earnestly. "Very well. So you've already determined that we will meet at the logjam and that you will need a few days. So, three days from now at the same time?"

He saw Sally nearly agree but then noticed that she thought better of it. "Noon. Let's meet at noon."

"High noon it is," Neech agreed as if she had driven a hard bargain . . . what did it matter to him what time it was? "I guess all that's left is for you to give me Haley so that I can give you Tina."

"Nope," Sally determined. "You release Tina and then I'll give the signal for Eric to release Haley."

Neech shook his head, "You're the one that came to me with the proposal, you should be the one to carry it through first."

Sally shook her head right back. "You're the one that took captives first. That means you release first."

Neech held back his smile. Again, he already got what he wanted from this, even if he did not get Haley—he had negotiated a meeting with Charlotte. Still, it would not hurt to let Sally think that she had some control in this arrangement. "Very well," he sighed, trying not to make it overly dramatic. "Facade, cut loose the girl."

Neech did not look at Facade, simply expecting her to follow through with his orders, but he heard no movement. He turned his head to Facade. "Release the girl," he repeated.

Facade stared at him a moment. "You wanted me to make sure we didn't lose another captive."

What a strange thing to say, Neech wondered, annoyed. Facade could be so mystifying sometimes. "This is not losing one, it's exchanging one." He tried to speak softly enough that Sally could not hear, but it was difficult to do since Facade was not right next to him.

"If this works out, then Haley will take back the responsibility of watching over captives, something you never wanted to do in the first place," he reminded her. "Besides, if it doesn't work, this is exactly why we have multiple captives, like you were saying before. We're giving up the one that is least harmful to us when freed, and we're getting back Haley."

Facade looked at Neech for another long moment, then looked curiously towards Sally. Finally, she slid over to Tina, cut her zip ties, and helped her to stand up.

Tina took a moment to rub out her soreness and to look at her friends on the ground. Neech noticed Mr. Reeves nod to her, encouraging her to join Sally. Tina eventually picked her way over the log strewn ground to Sally. They gave each other a strong hug.

Neech waited for what he felt was ample time for them to enjoy their reunion, but inevitably he cut it off. "Now Haley. I've done my part."

Sally and Tina ended their embrace and Sally nodded. "Fair enough. Just fire your gun once in the air and Eric will free Haley. Haley will make his way back to camp within the hour."

Neech furrowed his eyebrows. "Your signal is for me to fire a gun?" Neech asked.

"Do you not have a gun?" Sally followed up. "Oh, I just assumed you did because I . . . well . . . I thought that . . . oh dear. How are we going to alert Eric now?"

Neech felt irritated. He did not like others to know that he carried a gun. It is a secret best revealed when the other person is least expecting it. Now, though, she was calling on him to reveal that he had a gun. He tensed up. The negotiations were done, and they had gone over extremely well for him. He just wanted things to wrap up so he could have Haley around and they could plan out the meeting at the logjam.

"Maybe I could go back to the river pig lodge and see if there is a gun there that we could use," Sally tapped her finger to her mouth. "Oh, but that would take longer than an hour and by then Eric would kill Haley and ruin the whole thing. Does anyone know how to make a really loud sound that might be mistaken for a gun, like hitting one ax against another?"

Neech shook his head and then pulled the revolver out from his back. Annoyed, he pointed it in the direction of Sally. "What if I fire once, but I do it at you?" Neech said coldly. "Then Haley gets released and I get rid of a menace."

Sally should have been quaking at seeing Neech directing his gun at her. Instead, she smiled. "If you fire at me then Tina gets away and Eric finds out before Haley makes his way back to you."

Neech shook his head, his patience now running very thin. "Then I shoot her too. I'm tired of trying to keep track of captives and having all these amateur kids tell me what to do!"

Sally almost laughed, making Neech's irritation grow. "Why, Neech, it's simple mathematics. You shoot twice and Eric knows that something went wrong at the negotiations. Goodbye Haley, goodbye your chance at talking to Charlotte."

Neech held the gun for a prolonged moment, his hand tense, his eyebrows tightened in frustration. Finally, he raised the gun in the air and fired. The sound of the shot ricocheted through the clearing and into the surrounding woods for a long distance. Wherever Eric was, he would hear the gunshot.

"We'll see you at the logjam at noon in three days," Neech grumbled. He got the best of Sally in the negotiations, and yet somehow her handling of the signal and her demeanor as she left with Tina in tow left him aggravated.

The culminating insult came with her pithy departing line as if taken straight from a cheesy movie: "It's been a pleasure doing business with you!"

He did not want to play into her silly witticisms, but he could not refrain from replying with a statement that left her smile somehow widening as she left. "Believe me, the pleasure was all yours."

"I'm sorry that I'm the best you could get out of all of that," Tina said after they had made their way far enough from the camp to feel safe.

Sally turned to Tina, almost as if she were surprised. "The best I could get?"

"Well, I know that it would've been much more helpful to have Dave or Luke or Mr. Reeves. I don't think this has really changed so much for us except that they have that creep Mr. Haley back. I mean, I appreciate it, but part of me feels that maybe it would've been better for me to just have stayed with the others."

Instead of saying anything, Sally stopped in her tracks, forcing Tina to stop as well. She fingered the pages of her Scribblings Diary before opening to a specific spot and pointing to what she had written there. At first all Tina saw were a bunch of words scribbled, but as she looked closer, she saw a heading and then a list:

Negotiation with the bad guy:

- Set up a meeting in three days at the logjam with all the captives
- Make him think he won the negotiation
- Find out if he has a gun
- Get Tina!

Tina looked at the list, then at Sally, then at the list again. If she had not known that Sally had written nothing in it since her release, she would have thought Sally just wrote this to make her feel better.

"This is what you wanted going into the negotiation?" Tina asked both impressed and perplexed.

"Four for four. Not bad, right?" Sally grabbed the diary and continued walking, as if determined not to be late for an appointment. Tina had to pick up her step in order to catch up.

"I mean, I did get him worked up at the end, but I still think he believes he won the negotiation," Sally continued.

"But what if he didn't have a gun?" Tina asked.

"I told Eric to release Haley half an hour after I was supposed to meet with Neech either way. The signal was really about confirming whether Neech had a gun."

Tina stopped, amazed, causing Sally to stop as well. "That's incredibly clever, Sally."

"Sure," Sally replied, "but I don't know if it is super comforting to know that our main villain can shoot any of us dead at any time. Still, it is helpful to know."

Tina nodded, concerned. Sally nearly turned to continue her brisk walk when Tina grabbed her by the shoulder. "But the thing that is most confusing is why you were set on getting me rather than the others?"

Sally put a hand back on Tina's shoulder. "I need that aqueduct mind of yours. You've got a logjam to prepare to release."

Chapter 5
RISING ACTION

Tina knew very little about logjams and how to break them up, but Dave had once mentioned that the river level needed to rise a foot and a half to two feet for the river to be in the perfect position for releasing the logjam. And Jimmy Sellers, that talkative river pig, had mentioned that Summit Creek was over a ridge from the river. Once you put those facts together, all of a sudden Tina did know something, because who better than Tina knew more about getting water from one place to another?

Sally had connected those dots for Tina, and now she found herself once again in her element, even though they were literally worlds away from the place and time of Roman aqueducts. In the background, the continuous noise of axes chopping and whacking gave her the calming sense of her plans being put to action.

Jimmy Sellers and Sally had convinced the other river pigs, Eddie and Will, to help in this project. One, because it would help clear the logjam, which would lead to a big bonus for anyone on Jimmy's crew who helped to break it up. Since Jimmy's crew had left, Eddie and Will stood to gain a lot of money by dividing up the bonus between just the two of them plus Jimmy. Two, according to Sally, because they needed some way to redeem themselves for their despicable actions in helping those Neech and Haley fellows. Eddie and Will admitted that they did not feel good about joining, but most of

Dickey's crew were pretty rough guys, and they were nervous about voicing any opposition to the new, freelance job.

Tina saw that whatever their reservations were before, the two river pigs were willing workers now. It took her and Sally a couple of hours to make their way back to the logjam (Sally may have incredible strategizing abilities, but neither of them had a particularly finely tuned sense of direction, which meant that they got off track a couple of times). Once there, however, they found that Jimmy had found and settled down Eddie and Will about the whole magic, superstition thing. From there, after Sally proposed the plan to clear the logjam, it did not take too much more to get everyone in on the project.

It was now just past noon, and Tina was excited to see that the crew had already started placing the first of her improvised aqueduct. Jimmy took them across the logjam and over the ridge to Summit Creek. From there, it only took a short time for Tina to do some rough calculations on water flow, scout out the terrain, figure out the ideal spot for intake from the creek, and then the best route for getting the water to the other side of the ridge and into the river above the logjam.

The whole thing would be very crude, but by this time Tina was used to doing her aqueducts on a crunched time frame and in unorthodox ways. All she had to do was get as much water as possible into the river across the ridge in as little time possible. So the river pigs had taken down some trees in a line from a spot higher up in the creek towards a low point in the ridge, which was downstream and west from her chosen intake spot.

While two of them followed Tina, downing trees at her designated spots, one stayed behind and started chopping out large channels in the logs. The channels would be very inefficient, she knew. There would be significant water loss at each junction of these makeshift troughs, but she did not have time for quality. If she wanted the logjam water to rise by a foot and half to two feet in three days, she needed water entering the river by nightfall.

Sally had offered Tina her diary to do calculations, but for this job, Tina felt that the eye test would work just as well as quick calculations. That left

Sally following behind the river pigs as they chopped down trees, using a small saw to take off larger branches so that there would be one less thing to worry about once they needed to put the channeled logs in the proper position.

That meant Sally was nearby when Eric showed up.

"Tina!" Eric went and gave her a hug.

Tina felt equally happy to see Eric. "How did you find us?"

"Went to the logjam and then heard quite the racket across the ridge." Tina saw him notice Sally who decided to finish sawing off the branch she was working on before joining. "I don't know what to be more surprised at," Eric said, "that Sally is okay and somehow wrangled you away from Neech . . . or that I come back to find her actually doing physical labor. At home, she had the most clever ways of getting out of chores and then sneaking off to watch something on TV."

By this time, Sally had sawn off her branch and headed over to join them. She did not hear everything Eric said, but she caught the basic idea. "Some of us have to get stuff done around here," she said and fell into a strong embrace with her brother, something that told of her concern for him even if her words did not. "I figured you would be okay, but I worried about what would happen when you freed that creepy Haley guy."

Eric nodded. "You weren't wrong to be worried. When I went back to find him, he had found a way to scramble over to a rock slide at the bottom of the clearing where we fought. He managed to find a rock with a sharp edge and was slowly sawing away at his zip tie."

"Told you," Sally could not hold back from saying. "I knew the guy would figure a way out of it. That's how it is with any worthwhile bad guy."

Eric had to subdue his smile. "Well, I'm not sure what you mean by 'worthwhile bad guy,' but I'll admit that a couple of hours later, he would've been on the loose."

"I'm betting he wasn't too pleased to see you," Tina offered.

"Disgusted," Eric answered. "I knelt down to tell him that it was his lucky day, that we negotiated his release. I'm pretty sure that if he had his arms free, he would've strangled me without a second thought."

341

"Pure evil," Sally pointed out, but Tina could not tell if she was repulsed or excited by the thought.

"Anyway, I cut the zip ties that connected his feet to his hands and the ones that bound his feet together, but I kept the third zip tie that held his hands together behind his back. No reason to give him that strangling option. He looked ready to charge me anyway, but I told him to save his energy for the hike back to his camp and that I promised him I'd see him later."

"Did he go back to his camp?" Sally asked.

"Gave me a couple of sidelong glances, but he knew I had the machete and his gun, so finally he started to head back towards camp," Eric confirmed. "He's there by now and his hands are probably free at this point." Eric looked at Sally questioningly. "What's to keep him from coming and hunting us down now? That is his natural born talent, after all. It's why Neech keeps him around in the first place."

"Because," Sally stated, not a hint of doubt in her voice, "Neech won't allow it. He's got an appointment with Charlotte in three days. He's not going to mess up that golden opportunity."

"What makes you think Haley will listen to Neech on this?" Tina asked. She had been in camp when Haley defied Neech's order to take river pigs with him when chasing Eric.

"Haley screwed up, and he knows it," Sally answered. "Neech had to negotiate for his release. Haley wants revenge, but he'll do it on Neech's terms since he owes Neech for his release. Plus, he knows that Neech is good for it. The guy has given Haley plenty of opportunities for catching people before. I can imagine that he is telling Haley that as soon as Charlotte is under their power, Haley can do whatever he wants to Eric or any of the rest of us."

Tina was amazed by how coolly Sally spoke about their hypothetical demises. "That doesn't sound too good for us," Tina reminded Sally.

Sally nodded. "That's why we need to get this aqueduct finished as fast as possible. This will be our climactic explosion that will throw off the bad guys' plans."

Eric laughed. "Okay, Sis. You've talked me into it. How can I help?"

"Tina," Sally said, "put him to work!"

Tina smiled at Sally's seeming pleasure to get Eric under his authority. "Okay, sailor. You know knots, right?"

Eric saluted. "You tell me what needs tying, I'll make sure it's as secure as an anchor to a ship!"

"Jimmy Sellers brought a huge spool of rope from his storage at his crew's cabin. I need some of these smaller logs and larger branches tied together with that rope in order to make tripods that will hold the channeling logs in the air at set heights," Tina explained.

"You got it, Captain," Eric released his salute and then went down the line of fallen logs in order to get to the start of the aqueduct.

"Well," Tina said to Sally after he disappeared around a bend, "they're not Roman laborers, but it's still a pretty decent crew."

"The movie poster might say they are a misfit crew in the fight for their lives," Sally said.

Tina nodded. "Not exactly the way I thought of it, but I guess it's accurate!"

Haley tramped into camp with a mixed look of hatred and humiliation. Neech quickly had the zip ties binding his arms sliced. Before he could say anything, Haley burst out, "Give me a weapon. Gun, knife, machete, I don't care. And this time I'll take as many river pigs as you want me to."

Neech pushed Haley's outstretched hand down. "You don't get to make demands of me, Haley."

"I'm going to kill him," Facade saw Haley's eyes burning with an intensity she had never seen before. "I'm going to make him suffer. I'll fix this, Neech."

"Sit down!" Neech yelled. For a moment, Facade watched wide-eyed as the two stared each other down. Haley did not move.

"Haley," Neech growled, "I had to negotiate with a girl, a little girl, to have you released. I gave up one of our captives to get you. Do you understand what I'm telling you right now?! Do you have any idea how degrading it is to have to treat some little girl as if we are equals, just so I can rescue someone who never should've been captured in the first place? Someone who should've listened to my instructions so we wouldn't be in this situation? So that we would actually have the upper hand? And then to have you stumble in this camp and act as if you are going to tell me how you're going to fix this problem . . ."

Neech's hands balled into fists. " . . . I should kill you right now," he muttered. "I would've left you for dead, but I need you still, Haley. So I'll tell you one more time to sit down, or I may change my mind."

Facade knew that Haley was as strong-willed a person as she had ever met, but after this tirade from Neech, she saw him concede. Haley sat down. "Now, I'm going to tell you what to do, and you're going to do it," Neech continued. "You are going to make sure not a single captive so much as thinks about getting freed or escaping for the next three days. They are your responsibility. Do not mess this up."

Haley seemed disgusted. Facade could not be sure it was about the situation or at Neech, but either way he took a long moment before nodding.

"Good," Neech said. "Now, while you're doing that, I'm going to be planning out the meeting at the logjam with Facade. I'll need you to help capture the seer. Once we've done that, you do whatever you want to Eric."

This seemed to relieve some of the tension on Haley's clenched eyebrows. "I won't let you down."

Neech appeared unimpressed by Haley's conviction, but he nodded all the same. He then turned towards Facade. "You are released from your duties of guarding the captives. Now, it's your job to figure out how we make Charlotte fall into a trap. I've given you a time, Haley, a dozen river pigs, and

344

a location—I trust you'll be able to pull something out of a hat with that kind of setup?"

Facade nodded slowly. "I'll mull something over today, and then we'll make plans for tomorrow."

Neech felt satisfied. He toyed with the campfire while Haley refreshed himself with water and some food before making the rounds with the captives and ensuring their complete discomfort.

Facade, on the other hand, sat on the edge of camp and stewed. Did she help Neech? Did she risk everything and try to help Charlotte? Facade did not like the idea of taking risks that might end up making her situation worse, and things seemed to have swung back towards Neech after Sally's clumsy—but not altogether disastrous—negotiations.

The thought about Sally's clumsy negotiations reminded her about the way that Sally dropped her diary to the ground and then fumbled in trying to pick it up again. Not that Facade felt surprised by the awkward maneuver—Sally never gave off the impression of being supremely coordinated to begin with—but the long look that Sally gave Facade as she reached down to grab the diary seemed a bit out of place.

An impression burrowed into Facade's mind. She looked around the camp. Neech had taken aside the river pig, Dickey, to talk through something. Haley had his back turned as he brooded while watching over the captives. Nonchalantly, Facade stood up and started to gather some branches nearby then dropping them off by the campfire. No one seemed to think anything of it, so she continued the menial task. She circled around camp gathering branches, acting as if the activity helped her to think.

Eventually, almost innocuously, she happened upon the spot where Sally dropped her diary. According to her expectations, she spotted a paper there on the ground, tucked underneath some branches. Without hesitating, Facade reached down to pile the branches in her arms and with a movement so fast her own eyes failed to register it, she secreted the note inside the labyrinthian folds of her trench coat.

Facade made sure to continue the gathering of kindling for another fifteen minutes before she resumed her place on the fringe of camp. There, she rested her head on her knees, with her trench coat wrapped around the legs, as if she were taking a light nap while sitting up. Really, she had placed the paper on the ground beneath her, cracked open the trench coat so that it caught some outside light and now had perfect privacy, while still out in the open, for seeing what was on the paper.

Facade immediately confirmed what she suspected. The paper came from Sally's ever present diary. The handwriting was Sally's too, something Facade recognized from the aqueduct world when Sally wrote her note to Eric. Facade read:

Mr. Reeves,

I'm going to try my best to negotiate to get you and the others free, but if you're reading this, it means that I failed. I mean, it's a pretty big ask in the first place, because I don't think Naach would release anyone, not even that one demon-devourer from season two of Shadow Creatures, let alone any of you guys! At least Charlotte and Eric are safe, though. Hopefully, we'll see you really soon. In the negotiations, I'm going to try to set up a meeting at the logjam in a few days. If I do, I'm sure Naach will prepare for it. So will we. It'd be super awesome, if you could somehow come to the meeting without zip ties on and ready to move at a moment's notice. Do whatever you can to make that happen.

Sincerely,
Sally

Facade read the note, intrigued. It brimmed with naivety, but also cunning—much like, she realized, the negotiations themselves. Facade thought about this and an age-old magician mantra came to mind: the wise man can play the fool, but the fool can never play the wise man. Was Sally actually more clever than anyone had given her credit for?

She looked back at the note. There was something curious about it. She found it: "*I don't think Neech would release anyone, not even that one demon-devourer from season two of Shadow Creatures.*" Facade felt that comparison to be a pretty random one to bring into an important note. Granted, Sally by her nature was talkative and easily distracted, but this seemed to resonate with Facade for some reason. Then she remembered. When Sally was a captive to Facade in the aqueduct world, she spent plenty of time talking about a lot of things, and one of them was telling her the plot of some TV series called *Shadow Creatures.*

This note, Facade suddenly realized, was not for Mr. Reeves. This note was for Facade. That is why Sally looked at her so intently after dropping the diary. That is why she referenced the TV series that only Facade would know connected her to Sally.

Why address the letter to Mr. Reeves, then? Now that she could consider Sally as a schemer, the answer to that came easily. Sally did not want to endanger Facade by addressing the letter to her. If this note were to somehow get into the wrong hands, if Neech were to have seen her drop it or someone else came across it before Facade could have grabbed it, they would suspect nothing but a pathetic attempt to communicate with a captive, not Facade.

With this in mind, Facade reread the note and realized that Sally was asking her to get the captives free of zip ties for the meeting at the logjam. Seemingly simple, but with Haley as the newly installed guard, it could be more difficult than it might appear.

Still, though, the note and the circumstances of it getting into Facade's hands oozed with competence and layered deceptions. Facade smiled. *Very clever indeed, Sally,* Facade thought, *We have underestimated you.*

Maybe this shifts things back towards Charlotte again.

"What do you want?" Charlotte asked. "And how did you find me?"

The tension in her voice immediately caused Dr. Corinth to step back. She saw his silver hair reflecting the shine of the moon in almost a surreal fashion. His glasses, too, mirrored the moonbeams. The man seemed made for being cast in the moonlight. *Makes sense for a seer*, she thought. A second more of scrutiny showed her that his face held no malice as he contemplated Charlotte with a benign curiosity.

"Those are some loaded questions," Dr. Corinth stated. "As for the first, I wanted to extend an invitation to you."

"For what?" Charlotte kept her voice as cold as the air surrounding them, but Dr. Corinth either did not notice or remained unaffected by it.

"You are a seer. As you've probably experienced, seers are rare in this world. How many seers have you met in your short life after looking into thousands of eyes? A dozen? Maybe less?"

"Less," Charlotte said, intrigued by the question.

"And yet there is so much good that seers can do. Perhaps you've experienced that already," he adjusted his glasses while watching her reaction. "My purpose is to recruit natural born abilities of all sorts, but seers especially, to receive training and education at the GIA research institute and find ways to extend that sphere of influence to maximize your ability. I feel as if you would make for a great candidate."

As she digested this invitation, a part of Charlotte felt a surge of validation, but that immediately made her skeptical. "You don't even know me. What makes you think I'd be a great candidate?"

Dr. Corinth chuckled. "It's not too often that I am outsmarted by a high school kid. You avoided my eyes that whole time during that testing session. You knew who I was, and I could only guess who you were. I figured I'd confirm it before you left, but then you made that brilliant distraction and—"

"That wasn't me. My friend thought of that," Charlotte interrupted.

"That's the point," Dr. Corinth followed up. "That is the great potential in seers. They know how to get the most out of the natural born abilities around them."

Charlotte paused. Dr. Corinth, either through luck or experience, was touching on just the sort of debate that she struggled with up until her last discussion with Sally. It gave her hope. "So what would it entail to go to the . . . the . . . GI . . . uh . . . the—"

"The GIA institute," Dr. Corinth finished for her. "GIA stands for 'Guild of Inherent Abilities.' It's an old and fancy way to say 'place where seers train and network with each other along with some of the world's most influential natural born abilities.'"

"I see why you guys go by 'GIA' instead," Charlotte observed with the beginnings of a smile almost cracking her face.

Dr. Corinth nodded. "The name is short, but the legacy is long. The GIA has been around—in one form or another—for not just hundreds but thousands of years. In spite of that, the basic framework is the same. It is staffed primarily by seers and then divided into a cabinet, or departments, of different areas of impact where we recruit some of the world's best natural born abilities relevant to those departments. For example, the Department of Agriculture is headed by, obviously, a natural born farmer—soybean farmer is our current representative. The Department of Astrophysics is headed by a natural born astronaut. Within the GIA main headquarters, there are a couple dozen main departments, plus all sorts of divisions under those. We're not just limited to the main headquarters, however; for we have extension branches all over the globe. You name it, we probably have an expert on it somewhere within the vicinity of where they are most relevant."

"Wow. I don't know if I would belong among a group as elite as that," Charlotte wondered out loud.

Dr. Corinth shook his head. "We sound far more high and mighty than we really are. When you come to meet us, you'll find that we're just regular people. Sure, you'd be among experts, but the people we recruit are the type of experts that are more passionate about what they are doing than about making a name for themselves or comparing themselves to others. Trust me, give us four weeks, and you'd feel right at home."

Because of Dr. Corinth's open description, Charlotte could almost see herself walking among these people. She could sense a place where experts shared camaraderie and purpose. *Wait, what was their purpose?* "And what, exactly, do you do?"

"Anything we can to make the world a better place. These are the people most invested into protecting and improving their areas of expertise. We use our influence and abilities to make this world more meaningful and better for as many people as we can," Dr. Corinth noted. "It's subtle, of course, but because of the nature of our recruits our influence is vast and oftentimes effective."

"Oftentimes?" Charlotte clarified.

"There are limits to what we can do," Dr. Corinth answered. "Wars, famines, diseases . . . they still happen, even with our best efforts. Or, frequently, our best efforts cannot work through the red tape of bureaucracy or government officials eager to cling to their localized powers."

Charlotte thought about the amount of paperwork and forms she had to go through just to get into a new school every time her family moved. Even on a small scale, government could snuff out some of the most simple processes. "I didn't think about that," she noted. "Can you even make any discernible changes?"

"Like I said, this group has been around for a long time. The GIA has been directly or indirectly involved in numerous advances and movements throughout history: Asian philosophical movements on transcending suffering that changed the outlook of human living, Greek notions of democracy, the Roman Republic (not Empire!), the Renaissance, the Reformation, the Age of Exploration, the Enlightenment, the rise of Constitutional Republicanism, the Industrial Revolution, the Space Age, the

Information Age. All of these have contributed to improving the daily lives and purposes of humanity."

Dr. Corinth raised his hands in anticipation of a thought Charlotte had. "True, there have been tragic missteps and misfortunes coming about from these very same things: the mercantile slave trade, world wars, rapid natural resource destruction—evils that match and measure each step forward. But, overall, the Guild has helped improve quality of living for the whole world. In fact, our seer researchers suggest that our actions have single-handedly changed the course of the future of civilization. The range and advanced nature of future natural born abilities has changed exponentially over the past half a century, something we attribute—at least in part—to the GIA's seemingly insignificant but persistent prodding of human civilization towards improvement."

"And you need me to help you change the future of civilization for the better?" Charlotte asked. "I'm just a sixteen-year-old kid."

Dr. Corinth smiled. "We don't change the world by finding people already developed into leaders of change. We do it by the little things that seers have always been good at: seeing potential and giving it opportunity to grow."

It was a great pitch, because it was something that Charlotte personally connected to. And she felt the possibility of it swell within her. Time after time, she had given other people the opportunity to see their own potential, but she had never had a chance herself. A part of her yearned for it in the same way, she imagined, that Eric yearned for the deck of a ship under his feet or Luke yearned for a tree ripe with chicle standing before him while he wielded a machete in his hand.

"And what if I said yes," she ventured, almost a whisper.

"Simple," Dr. Corinth answered, "I meet with your parents, we arrange for your entrance into our trainee program, and within six months you join us and get to work."

The last part might as well have been spoken by one of Tina's Roman soldiers. As soon as Dr. Corinth mentioned meeting with her parents, she knew that this exciting new world of seeing . . . was gone. There would be no meeting with her parents. The minute she even mentioned Dr. Corinth as a seer, they would be putting the finishing touches on packing and leave Nibleton as if they had never been there before. They were already planning on moving, they were already paranoid about every time she ever met another seer, this would only confirm and speed up the process.

Dr. Corinth must have seen her crestfallen expression. "If you prefer to wait a year rather than six months, that could be arranged as well. I know that expecting you to change an entire life trajectory in a short amount of time is asking a lot."

"What if . . ." Charlotte ventured without even thinking about it, "What if we didn't wait a year or even six months. What if I joined sooner? A week. No. Tomorrow morning?"

Dr. Corinth's eyes grew. "Well, I . . . would we be able to see your parents by then?"

"They won't give me permission," Charlotte countered.

After nodding thoughtfully, Dr. Corinth stated, "That is certainly understandable. Perhaps, if I were to reason with them and we worked out a timeline and visiting options amenable to their preference then they would—"

"You'd never see me again," Charlotte said.

Dr. Corinth paused. "I see," he finally said. "Well that is most unfortunate." An uncomfortable silence came between them. "You are clearly skilled and have enormous potential," he spoke again, "but I am not in the habit of enabling runaways. Are you being held captive? Are they hurting you?"

"No," Charlotte quickly answered. "Nothing like that. They are firm about what they would call 'protecting me,' but they love me . . . and I love them."

Another pause. "Perhaps you underestimate them." Dr. Corinth took a card out of his jacket. "Talk to them. Reason with them. When they are ready to speak to me, I would be happy to put them at ease."

Charlotte took the card and saw his contact information. It sounded nice, but Dr. Corinth did not know of her father and mother's determination.

He must have seen her hesitation. "It might take six months or the year that I mentioned before. Worst case scenario, you wait until you are out of the house in a couple of years, but I can promise you that my invitation will remain open for as long as it takes for you to join us."

Charlotte put the card in her pocket. Had there been a trash can nearby, she would have felt like tossing it there instead of having it as a constant reminder of what she was missing out on. She drew a deep breath and decided to change the subject. "You never answered my second question."

"I'm sorry," Dr. Corinth said, "we did get sidetracked didn't we? What was your second question?"

"How did you find me?" Charlotte asked again. "A parking lot in an old part of Nibleton is not a place most people think to look for someone they've never officially met."

"Well," Dr. Corinth explained, "as I was leaving the school this afternoon, I saw a discarded flier about a meeting dealing with scholarship opportunities. When I asked Pickney about it, he knew nothing. That made me suspicious . . . who would be offering this without coordinating with school counselors? Then, when looking at the address, Pickney observed that it was up the hill by where the old hospital had once been."

Dr. Corinth adjusted his glasses, "I'm sure you can appreciate how hospitals are meaningful to seers. Since most people are born in hospitals—"

"That's where ferrying happens the most," Charlotte finished for him.

"Precisely. I got tangled up with some business in the earlier part of the evening, but as soon as I was free, I made sure to come inspect the premises," he motioned to the surrounding area.

"I didn't make the flier," Charlotte clarified.

"I didn't think so," Dr. Corinth nodded. "Natural bornapper?"

Charlotte swallowed, the developing tragedy of the evening's events still fresh on her mind. "Yes."

Dr. Corinth took a step closer and then put a hand on Charlotte's shoulder. "I'm sorry. You must be here waiting to see if the victim or victims will wander back to the ferry point once the moon reciprocates on their end."

Charlotte nodded. There was more to tell him—so much more—and she wanted to tell him, but her mind was bursting with so many new thoughts mixed with the fact that all her friends were in the river pig world without her. Her hand tightened around the phone she held, and it reminded her of what she had intended to do right before Dr. Corinth showed up.

She looked down at the phone. A warning notification told her that the phone was about to die because of the low battery. She should have turned it off while talking to Dr. Corinth, but he had caught her so much off guard that she completely forgot. In a panic, she closed the warning and pulled up the picture of the foreseer's hieroglyphics.

I may not have time to look at every single hieroglyph, she thought to herself. Her fingers paused for a moment. She decided that if she was only going to have time to decipher one last hieroglyph, she wanted to skip to the very last one. *I need to see how this ends.*

She zoomed to the bottom right corner of the picture. She recognized the characters depicted. She looked closely. *What is it showing?* she wondered. Then her eyes widened. *No.* Then they squinted, disbelieving. *No, please no!* She frantically took it all in again, as if it might show her something different. It did not. It only further confirmed what she saw.

Then the screen went blank. The phone had died.

"Is everything okay?" Dr. Corinth had watched her distractedly staring at the phone screen for that whole sequence.

Charlotte was shaking. She tried to turn the phone back on, but it was completely dead. And, what's more, she did not need to. She knew that even if the battery were to be fully charged, it would still show the same thing.

With her voice trembling, Charlotte held the tears back from her eyes while she asked without looking up, "What can you tell me about foreseers?"

Dr. Corinth removed his hand from her shoulder. Out of the corner of her eyes, she saw him look at her curiously. She could tell he wanted to ask her why, but she could also tell that he suspected she would not like the prodding. "I can tell you that they are extremely rare. Over GIA's long history, there have been only a handful that have been a part of our guild."

"If they predict something, is there no way to avoid the outcome?" Charlotte followed up.

Dr. Corinth sighed. "That is a complicated question. We have a full course on foreseers at the educational program of the GIA, and that question alone takes up a long discussion."

"I just need to know," Charlotte's lip trembled.

"The short answer is that foreseer predictions are, well, generally unavoidable," Dr. Corinth answered.

Charlotte did not want to hear it, she could not accept it. "Even if you know about it? Even if you find a way to keep it from happening?"

"The predictions, it seems, take into account any actions that might be intended to reverse them," Dr. Corinth said in a low voice. "Unfortunately—or fortunately, depending on the prediction—it's best to simply accept the prediction and move on with its outcomes in mind."

Charlotte shook her head and her eyes fluttered uneasily. Dr. Corinth watched her response carefully. "I can see that this is making you upset. Have you been in contact with a foreseer? The GIA has not been aware of a foreseer for several years now," Dr. Corinth queried.

"If you can't avoid it, then what is the point of a foreseer even sharing what they see? Why not just keep it to themselves because no one can change anything!" Charlotte was not frantic, but she still fought against the idea of helplessness.

"Well," Dr. Corinth answered, "not only do predictions seem to anticipate any attempts to reverse them, but they also can serve to guide people for achieving a set purpose."

Charlotte thought about throwing the machete up to Luke during the fight with the jaguar. They may not have thought about doing that without the hieroglyphic. What if they had not heeded the hieroglyphic? Would it have changed the outcome? But they did throw it. And the scene played out exactly as the hieroglyph predicted. Even when Charlotte wanted to change an outcome, by ferrying with Eric but without the others, the prediction did not change. Eric refused to go without the others. They ferried together then, but later ferried separately, in spite of all of Charlotte's efforts to avoid such an outcome.

"So," she observed bitterly, "so the predictions are either unavoidable or, basically, control us?" When she said it out loud, she pushed back against the thought. She and Sally had just decided that they would not let the hieroglyphics control them. Then, the thought of the attack of the Visigoths came to mind. She had seen the attack coming, because of the hieroglyphics, and she was able to save lives and the capture of all of them but Sally. Maybe that did not, exactly, change the outcome of the prediction, which never said that they would all be captured or killed, but Charlotte's actions *did* avoid the worst thing that could have happened.

"I don't believe it," she suddenly decided. "I don't believe that predictions are all unpreventable."

A long pause ensued. "I wish we could take some more time to talk about this, because it is a complex issue on which our knowledge is still very incomplete . . ." Dr. Corinth paused again but still saw Charlotte not giving in to the simple explanations. "However, it seems as if you are in need of some deeper insights right now."

Charlotte nodded, gratefully, if not desperately.

"Very well. I'll do the best I can in a condensed time frame. Perhaps sharing an example would be most instructive."

Dr. Corinth sat down on the pavement of the parking lot and took a deep breath. "Long ago in American history, a U.S. General attacked the Shawnee Indian village of Chief Tecumseh and his brother Tenskwatawa. The devastation was complete and the two brothers barely escaped with their lives. After the attack, Tenskwatawa was said to have put a curse on the American nation for its atrocity. Well, history calls it a 'curse,' but we seers call it a prophecy."

"Tenskwatawa was a foreseer?" Charlotte asked.

"That's what has been passed down in the Guild, and the actions seem to prove it. You see, the 'curse' stated that every President elected in a 'zero year'—according to the white man reckoning of time—would die during their presidency. In other words, every twenty years, a U.S. President would die in office," Dr. Corinth stated.

Charlotte looked up, "Well that can't have been true. We would've heard about it. I mean, that's a pretty big deal to have so many presidents die in office."

"Time passes, history moves on, and we forget. The first one to die as predicted? The president elected in 1840. He died one month into office of pneumonia. The crazy part is that it was William Henry Harrison, the same general that originally attacked Tenskwatawa's village."

"That is creepy," Charlotte said. "But 1840 is a long time ago. I don't think we've had that many presidents die in office."

"I'm betting you know the next president to die who was voted into office twenty years later. He was the first president to be assassinated," Dr. Corinth offered.

"Abraham Lincoln!" Charlotte exclaimed.

"Then the assassinations of Garfield and McKinley. Then Harding got sick and died in office. Twenty years later Franklin Roosevelt died in office. Then Kennedy—"

"Assassinated," Charlotte finished. "Wow." She paused. "So the prophecy came true."

"Not only that," Dr. Corinth continued, "but it was publicized and known—Tenskwatawa obviously did not try to keep it a secret. The government knew about it. The general public knew about it. Of course the Guild of Inherent Abilities knew about it. All of them tried to end 'the curse,' but they failed. Lincoln survived a few assassination attempts, some known and some only passed down through the Guild to today. In spite of those efforts, John Wilkes Booth still managed to murder Lincoln. Garfield and McKinley actually survived their assassination attempts, thanks to the alert efforts from people in the know about the prophecy, but apparently those same protectors did not expect the real death to come from incompetent doctors afterwards. It's a good example of how knowing a prediction seems like it could be avoidable, but the end result was the same."

Charlotte thought about this for a moment. "Same thing with the others?"

"Protection improved, but there was nothing to be done for Harding, who got sick, and Roosevelt, who was old and already into his 4th term. With the Guild's help, Kennedy avoided some un-publicized assassination attempts, but still could not completely escape." Dr. Corinth shook his head. "Basically, foreseer predictions simply happen as foreseen."

Thinking back to her history class, Charlotte observed, "But we haven't had assassinations since then. We haven't had deaths in office, have we?"

Dr. Corinth nodded slowly. "Yes. That's true. Ronald Reagan was elected in 1980, a zero year. Once again, there was an assassination attempt: he was shot at and hit in the back. But he survived. He also had surgery for cancer, but he came out of it healthy and well."

"So the prophecy broke!" Charlotte pointed out. "What was it? How come he made it when the others didn't?"

"The GIA finally had something to counter the curse," Dr. Corinth said simply. "At the time, we had a foreseer. The world knew her as an 'astrologer,' but she was a foreseer. People thought she was consulted after Reagan's assassination attempt, but she actually foresaw it. She could not keep it from happening, but she mitigated it—the shot that hit him was actually a ricochet rather than a direct hit. Also, she helped us know when and where to have competent medical care this time around using our own natural born surgeons and doctors for treating the assassination attempt and the cancer surgery."

"So the outcome can be changed . . ." Charlotte focused on this kernel of hope.

"Well, kind of," Dr. Corinth conceded. "I think there are two things we can learn from this. First, knowing about the prophecy did not keep the *possibilities* of the prediction from coming true. Those opportunities still came, because Reagan still got shot at and he still had cancer. Secondly, a foreseer's prediction is always strongest the closer it is to the time of events being foreseen. After Tenskawata made the prophecy, Harrison died less than a month into office. In spite of knowledgeable protection, Lincoln was shot and died within twenty-four hours. The others were farther removed from the prophecy, and it took them months to die after their assassination attempts, but they still died—as did, obviously, the others on up until after Kennedy. But Reagan was over one hundred years removed from the first predicted death. The future is a tricky thing that is malleable, constantly shifting, and vague. The farther you get from a prophecy, the less weight it holds as inevitable."

Charlotte felt a pit in her stomach. The predictions she had seen were very specific, very present, and it was still the same night as the first prediction she had seen on the hieroglyphics. Yet, she refused to give in to despair. She thought through the information Dr. Corinth had just given her. "So even if you can't stop a prediction, delaying it as much as possible might give me the chance to change it."

Dr. Corinth seemed as if he wanted to comfort Charlotte, but also did not want to give false hope. "I doubt you would be around for a delay of the magnitude of one hundred and forty years. It would be foolhardy to underestimate the strength of a freshly unraveling prediction."

In her mind, the prediction remained as fresh as if she were still looking at it on the phone. To her, however, it did not matter. In this moment, Charlotte suddenly found her old, brazen self. The whole world could be against her, but she refused to accept the final hieroglyph from the foreseer's prophecy.

"You've asked me a lot of questions," Dr. Corinth looked at the resolve forming in Charlotte's eyes. "When do I get a turn? Because I'm sensing you've got quite a story to tell behind those questions."

Charlotte nodded. "I do. And I'll be happy to tell you the whole story. But first, I've got a job to do."

"Well, we can both wait here to see if those who were natural bornapped are able to get to their ferry points. While we wait, you can tell me your story," Dr. Corinth pointed out.

"Thanks for your offer," Charlotte said, "and thank you for answering my questions without any context. However, this is a one-person job, and I . . . I just need to wait it out by myself." Dr. Corinth seemed about to protest, but Charlotte interrupted him, "I have your card. As soon as I'm done here, I'll speak to my parents and convince them that the GIA will be the best thing for all of us. I should be getting a hold of you shortly so that you can help me figure out the next step. Then, once we're on our way to the GIA, I promise to tell you my story."

Dr. Corinth paused. He seemed reluctant to leave her, but Charlotte sensed that Dr. Corinth would be resistant to trying to change predictions. This left Charlotte to do it herself. He watched her for a moment longer, then he smiled congenially. "Well, you seem quite capable, Miss . . . I don't think I ever caught your name . . ."

"Reeves. Charlotte Reeves," she answered.

His eyes glittered. "Of course." He paused thoughtfully again before breaking out of his silence. "As I was saying, you seem quite capable, so I will leave you to this task tonight and look forward to our future correspondence very soon." He gazed for a second longer and then finally turned and walked away until the darkness swallowed him up.

Charlotte watched him go, intensely intrigued. Depending on how this night ended up, she might never see Dr. Corinth again . . . or she might see him soon—sooner, perhaps, than even he expected.

Tina watched the water level at the logjam carefully. Finding the small creekbed on the river side of the ridge really saved them a lot of time on that first day. Instead of needing to continue to build their log channel system past the ridge, she only needed to get Summit Creek waters into that creekbed close to the other side. From there the displaced water naturally flowed into the river and by the end of the first day, Summit Creek had been filling up the river with a strong flow of water.

Now, on the night before the third day, Tina smiled. By noon the next day, the water level will have raised a full two feet. Off the cuff, Dave had mentioned one and a half to two feet—an unforgivable range of measurement for someone who likes to be as precise as Tina, so she had to assume that the two feet was the more preferable amount and went for that exactly. It meant that she was slowing the flow a little bit overnight by shifting the logs that picked up the water from Summit Creek—she could not be sure if going over two feet would be detrimental or not, so she decided to play it safe.

Sally watched from the bank. Tina turned and nodded, giving a thumbs up.

"I think we're ready for an explosion," Sally's grin reflected a strange confidence or excitement, Tina could not tell which.

All of a sudden, Sally's hands motioned animatedly for Tina to hurry to join her. Tina was not sure what this was about, but she needed no second bidding, quickly stepping over some of the logs, hopping across some standing puddles near the edge of the river, and then following Sally as they ducked behind a couple bushes just where the forest met the bank of the river.

From there, Tina saw some silhouettes expertly traversing the logjam. They were large and skilled. It had to be river pigs, and since Tina had sent Jimmy Sellers, Will and Eddie back to the lodge for some well-deserved rest, the assumption that it was Neech's hired river pigs could not have been too wild of a guess.

"All clear," one of them brusquely stated as he got to the edge of the logjam.

"Great," a voice came from out of nowhere just to the side of them, "that simplifies things considerably. They must be at the lodge downriver."

Tina and Sally both shrunk closer to the ground at the sound of the voice. Tina tried to peer into the black edge of the forest to see if she could identify the figure, but the very fact that she could not identify it told her everything. It had to be Facade.

"Who brought the camouflage coverings?" Facade asked.

"You mean the weird bark blanket things you somehow sewed together?" the main river pig said. "They're right here." A few more pigs had joined them at this point and dropped the coverings to the ground.

"Now, each of you will take one of these as I assign you places to hide before the meeting tomorrow," Facade said. "If even one of you is spotted at the meeting, it may spook the others and ruin everything. That's why I'll need to make sure your position and camouflage are complete."

"You ain't thinking of placing us in hiding spots at the logjam all night long, are ya?" the river pig grumbled. "It gets mighty cold here at nights and I'd like ta be able to count my gold at the end of this with working fingers."

"For now, I'm just showing you where you will be tomorrow," Facade replied. "As long as you stay together in one place and don't build a fire that'll give you away, you can rest off the river . . . but close by. We'll have one river pig of your choice keeping watch down by the lodge after we've established locations here. As soon as anyone leaves that lodge to head in this direction, the person on watch needs to immediately come back and report—I suspect it'll probably be sometime in the mid-morning. Then, you will take your hiding spots at once and wait until the meeting."

"Got it," the river pig grunted. He spoke to a short river pig standing nearby in a low voice, then turned back to the blackness where Facade's voice came from. "And we were told this is the final thing we need to do before we get the rest of our pay."

"Final thing," Facade answered. "But remember, there's no payment if you don't get the girl. She'll seem to come from out of nowhere, like some kind of Shadow Creature, so you'll have to be fast."

Tina heard Sally gasp at that statement before covering her mouth. If Facade or the river pigs heard it, they gave no indication.

A river pig behind the lead one grunted. "But if'n we're covered by these bark blankets, or whatever ya call 'em, then we won't be able to see when the girl shows up ta get out and catch her!"

The main river pig turned around and slapped him upside the head. "You got sawdust in those ears? Neech told us earlier that we'd know it was time when we heard the gunshot that he'd fire as a signal."

The river pig rubbed his head and muttered something about being on guard duty when Neech talked to the rest of them. Facade must have felt it necessary to follow up, "It's possible there won't be a gunshot at all, but either way, you'll know when it's time to move. I wouldn't worry about that."

The silence that followed showed that the river pigs accepted Facade's terms. "Now," Facade followed up, "let me show you where I want you placed and how we'll disguise you so that no one will suspect you're here. We'll start at the far side of the logjam."

It seemed to take forever to wait for Facade and the crew of river pigs to clear out of the area and find their way across the logjam, but once they were finally far enough, Tina and Sally crawled backwards into the forest and then stood up and turned southwards to make their way onto the path heading for the lodge where the others would be waiting for them.

"Are you okay?" Tina asked once they put enough distance between themselves and the logjam to feel comfortable speaking.

"More than okay," Sally responded.

"What was that gasp about?" Tina queried. "Either Facade said something that surprised you or you got bit by something."

Sally smiled in the moonlight. "Facade just told me that she would have the others out of their zip ties for our meeting tomorrow."

Tina raised her eyebrows. "Did you and I just hear the same conversation? Because I kind of got the opposite feeling."

"You know how sneaky she is," Sally replied. "Facade must've been the first to come across the logjam. Then she probably noticed us before we even saw the river pigs and placed herself close to where we were hiding so that we could listen in on what she told them."

"Okay, but even if that were true, how does that mean she's still on our side? Don't forget that she just finished telling them how to capture Charlotte."

Sally did not skip a beat. "Haven't I told you about the Shadow Creatures TV series yet? Well, settle in. It's a long walk, and I'm going to make the most of it!"

Chapter 6
HIGH NOON

By watching everyone else stirring, Luke figured that some sort of announcement had been made. Well, if it mattered at all, he would find out what it was one way or another. He strained his head so that he could see Haley. The dark fellow stood in earnest conversation with Neech. The position of the sun told him that it was getting closer to the meeting time, plus it allowed him to read Neech's lips. He was talking to Haley about the plans for capturing Charlotte.

This might come in handy, Luke thought. He tried to focus more but instead he felt someone tugging at his zip tie bonds. His peripheral vision told him it was that sneaky person, Facade. In a moment his feet were released from his hands. *Must be getting the captives ready for the walk over to the logjam.*

Suddenly, his hands were freed as well. *That's weird,* Luke wondered. *We don't need our hands freed to walk to the logjam. Seems like these guys would be more careful than that.* Then, he felt something bring his hands back together again. *Huh. Just replacing the old zip ties with a new one?*

But what he felt was not a zip tie. Instead it felt like . . . like some sort of leafy and fibery, sticky yet silky cord. Luke's eyes shot over to Dave Gardner who had stood up moments earlier in front of him. He looked and saw that Dave still had a white zip tie holding his hands together. A quick look to Mr.

Reeves, standing just to the left of Dave, showed the same thing. Then why did Luke's zip tie get replaced with something different? Something more earthy, and definitely more fragile—just feeling it, he knew he would be able to break it apart and free himself with very little effort.

Luke shifted and got a closer look at Dave's zip tie. Then he noticed. These were not zip ties after all. They only looked like them. He could see small wisps of bark fiber and leaf stems woven together sticking out from underneath some sort of white, silky wrapping.

Luke briefly wondered what the white covering could be, but then he realized that he felt it himself on his own wrists. Whatever it was, it was sticky. He considered this for a moment before suddenly remembering an abundance of moth or butterfly cocoons in the area as they walked through the forest. The silky threads were all over selected cocoon-laden bushes.

Another quick glance to Dave's wrists told him that Facade must have woven these new bonds and then wrapped them with excess cocoon threads from those bushes to make them look like the white, plastic, zip ties Haley used. The deception was clever enough that if Luke had not felt his own counterfeit zip tie around his wrists, he would never have thought the ones he looked at were anything but the zip ties that had been awkwardly holding them for the last few days.

But why would Facade do that? At this point, she had wandered away from him and headed towards Neech and Haley, but she turned for a moment and mouthed (at least, he felt pretty sure she was mouthing—people that speak out loud don't emphasize their lip movement as much as she was doing, plus no one else moved or reacted to any sounds that would have been coming from her): *Keep your hands behind you as if you're still bound. Wait until a signal at the logjam before you make your move to escape.*

Then, just like that, she turned and joined Haley and Neech to tell them the captives were ready for the march. Luke noticed Mr. Reeves and Dave glance knowingly at each other and then at Luke in a way that told him Facade must have whispered the same instructions to them when she cut their old zip ties and stood them up.

Thoughts flew through Luke's mind. He knew that Facade had orchestrated Eric's escape, as difficult as that was to fathom. Was Facade still in contact with Eric and working this out? Or with Charlotte? Or is this part of some bigger deception and he should not trust her?

He had plenty of time to think it through as they walked to the logjam, although he was unable to come up with any definitive answers. Other information that he was unsure of how or if it even related to these events was the fact that Felipe and the captured river pig stayed behind, presumably still being held by actual zip ties. And he, Dave Gardner, and Mr. Reeves were being escorted to the logjam by only Haley, Neech, Facade and two river pigs—kind of a small crew compared to the busy camp they had been among for the past few days.

By the time they neared the logjam, Luke saw that the sun nearly sat at its zenith. Once they stood at the bank of the river where it coincided with the logjam, Luke observed Neech ask Facade something. It looked like he wanted to know about the river pigs being in position or something. Facade looked at a few specific points along the logjam and then nodded.

Then, Luke saw two forms walk out from among the edge of the forest across from them on the opposite river bank: Sally and Tina. Neech must have just seen them too because he mentioned something to Facade and Haley while looking at them, and then turned around and informed the two river pigs to head back to camp and wait for them there.

Then, Neech waited. Luke could see he felt a high degree of confidence looking across the river and seeing little Sally standing next to Tina. Haley looked eager to cross the logjam and bring this to its obvious conclusion, but Neech needed only to position his body slightly in front of Haley to tell him that they were going to wait. It seemed obvious to Luke that Neech enjoyed making the amateur Sally take the initiative in this tense situation.

At some point, Dave must have said something snarky because Neech turned back and glared at him. Otherwise, they waited until they saw Tina get at the edge of the river and then slide in, catching her breath by the cold bite of the temperature change.

Neech turned to Haley and Luke caught him saying, "Looks like they are going to stay off the logjam and wade directly to the ferry point."

Sally, instead of getting in the river, stepped onto a grouping of logs that at first looked to be just a random gathering next to the bank, but as Luke scrutinized it, he could see that the logs were actually lashed together with some rope. Tina took the small raft and, with Sally awkwardly trying to keep her balance (all while wielding her precious Scribblings Diary), guided the makeshift raft towards the center of the river.

Neech watched the procession, amused. Then he mentioned something to Haley and motioned back to Luke, Mr. Reeves, and Dave Gardner. "Into the river," he barked.

Luke saw Facade eyeing him and Mr. Reeves carefully, clearly making sure they kept their hands behind them in order to keep up the pretense that the zip ties kept them bound—no easy feat considering the difficulty of descending the uneven and flimsy nature of the ground of the river bank. Dave, on the other hand, with his river pig/traceur feet secure underneath him, easily jogged down into the river. In fact, Dave had enough alacrity that Haley hurried into the river to slow him down, which had the happy side-effect of keeping the fugitive slave catcher from noticing anything funny about their zip ties.

Finally, Luke stumbled into the river and Mr. Reeves followed, but Facade did not breathe a sigh of relief until both were submerged past their waists and their hands hidden under the river's flow. Haley soon corralled Dave back to them and had positioned them so that they had the logjam on one side and him on the other. Clearly, this precaution kept them from having an open escape avenue downriver. Haley then motioned for Facade to flank their upriver side and Neech stayed close to Haley. Once positioned to Haley's satisfaction, they waded forward, towards Sally and Tina.

The two girls had not taken long to reach the ferry point mid-river. Once there, they waited. Tina stood on the downstream side of the small raft, facing the logjam, and held Sally steady. By the time Luke and the others were halfway to Sally and Tina, Luke noticed that Sally seemed ambivalent to the group coming towards them. Instead she held up her diary, opened to a specific page—as if glancing over a checklist—then nodding to herself.

A second later, Sally took her pen out of her pocket and started to write in her diary. *What a weird time to write something*, Luke thought. As she jotted down notes, she seemed to be mouthing out the words she wrote, something Luke had often observed people do unintentionally. Yet, something told Luke that even though she was not looking at him, she specifically intended him to see what she was saying with her mouth. Although her face was angled a bit down towards her diary, Sally had twisted it just enough to give Luke a fairly straight on view of her face as she said, "Don't listen to me when I'm speaking to the whole group. Watch Tina instead. Pretend to stumble to show me that you understand."

Luke had no idea what was going on, but he at least got her message. His next step had him stumble and nearly submerge himself in the river before getting his footing back and resuming his march to the middle of the river. Sally seemed satisfied and put her pen in her pocket, lowering her diary slightly, though she kept it open and facing up towards her.

Neech, for his part, kept a laser focus on Sally. Perhaps not even Sally, Luke decided as he attempted to follow Neech's line of vision, but to the area around Sally, the area where Charlotte was likely to appear. As they made their final approach, Neech motioned for Haley to come closer to him, presumably to be ready to make his move for Charlotte the moment Neech gave him the go-ahead.

Sally allowed Neech to get within a couple arm lengths of her raft, seemingly unconcerned by his close proximity. Then she started speaking. That was Luke's cue. He turned to Tina.

Because of Luke's position on the upstream side of Haley, closer to the logjam, and due to Tina's position facing upstream in that direction, her facial expressions were clearly visible to Luke. Also, her position compared to Neech and Haley would have made it difficult for either of them to catch her communicating with Luke. Not that it mattered. Luke could tell, even from his periphery, that they were only interested in seeing what Sally said.

Though Luke was also interested by what Sally said, he was even more interested by what Tina mouthed. "Group together as close as you can."

Mr. Reeves and Dave Gardner were both just off his elbows, but he mumbled to them, "Come close to me." He hoped his mumbling was not too loud. He did not get a chance to test it, but he sensed that the water trickling out of the logjam meant he would have to put a lot more effort into speaking up in order to be heard by Neech or Haley, especially since their attention was already on Sally. For a second, he even wondered if he had been loud enough for them to hear him, but moments later, both Mr. Reeves and Dave Gardner had shuffled close enough to touch him.

Tina spoke again, "Tell Dave to be ready to release the logjam on our signal."

Luke raised his eyebrows, but he passed the message along to Dave all the same. With Dave much closer, Luke barely needed to raise his voice at all. Dave's eyebrows also rose and he eagerly eyed the logjam wall. "Well, I'll be," Dave said quietly, "those crazy dudes somehow raised the river's water level. This sucker is ready to blow!"

Mr. Reeves, who had been listening in, must have asked Dave if he was sure it could be done, because the natural born river pig's eyes devoured the logjam wall in front of them before nodding with his eyes glittering. "Dude, I see the one piece it'll take. Once I get up on that wall, it'll be a matter of seconds before this whole place is an explosion of water and timber!"

Luke's eyes reverted to Tina. "Once we give the signal and Dave goes to release the logjam, you guys need to come close enough to Sally that she can reach out and touch you. And Dave should join us as soon as he has released the logjam."

Luke passed along the information. He could not tell if Dave's expression was skeptical or thrilled. Probably, he thought, knowing Dave, it was both. "Don't know if I'll have enough time to reach you guys after the logjam is released! Either way, I hope that Charlotte will be able to pluck the crew out in the blink of an eye."

For a second, Luke considered passing along this thought to Tina, but he knew she would not be able to read his lips as he could hers. This was one-way communication. And besides, Sally and Tina had to know the gamble they were making. He looked again towards Tina.

"The signal will be Dave's bridge," she mouthed.

Luke mentioned it to the others even though it made no sense. He just about shrugged to see if she could clarify, but that is when his eyes could no longer stick to Tina. All eyes suddenly turned to Neech. He had pulled out his gun and, while facing Sally, pointed it at Luke.

Sally hid her nerves as best as she could. On the one hand someone completely naive might also be nervous, sure, but not the sort of confident nervousness she felt. For one, she was confident that Neech underestimated her and was not expecting the complicated preparations she had scripted for this moment. For another, it was Neech and Haley, two ruthless and seemingly fearless opponents who may not act according to the expectations of a film character. Confident nervousness.

Luckily, once Tina guided the raft out to the ferry point, there could be no more getting lost in what ifs and failing scenarios. It was time for, as a director on a movie set would say, action! Immediately, Luke showed that he understood her instructions to watch Tina. That was one of her big what ifs that could be put to rest.

Now Neech, arrogantly confident, and Haley, broodingly bloodthirsty, stood in water just past their waists barely more than a couple arm lengths away from her.

Sally looked down at the diary, which remained open and facing up towards her. The words, "Not Yet" stared at her, and so far her other what if, what if Charlotte senses us and ferries here without first checking to see if it's safe, had not happened. Sally expected that Charlotte would first do her limbo-ferrying thing. If that were the case, then Sally hoped that the "Not Yet" from her diary would be clearly visible to that hovering seer and send her the message that it was not time.

But it was time to talk. That was something Sally could do well, and it only increased the confident part of her feelings as the nervousness took a back seat. "Gentlemen, welcome to our little rendezvous."

"Where's Charlotte?" Neech quickly demanded.

"And Eric," Haley scowled.

"Now, hang on just one second," Sally stammered. Again, she wanted to act nervous but not too nervous. Ugh. It was so much easier to write scenes for actors than to be one. "Why don't you send my friends to me first?"

"So that you can just grab them and get ferried, leaving us here until the moon reciprocates?" Neech shook his head condescendingly. "Little girl, I wasn't naturally born yesterday. I've more than held up my end of the bargain. I didn't need to bring more than one of the captives, but as you can see I brought them all and they are here without a single other river pig in sight."

Sally wondered if Neech knew that the smirk on his face as he mentioned the absence of river pigs would have given away his deception to even an inexperienced negotiator.

"Well," she said, trying to keep her voice tremulous, "how do I know that you'll give them to me once Charlotte shows up?"

"I guess you'll just have to trust me," Neech smiled. It was an oily smile, and Sally could not help but think that the guy was playing the bad guy part to a "T." This boded well for her plans.

Soon enough, Tina would give the raft a little bump that would tell her the message had been passed along to Luke and the others. To buy a bit more time, Sally put on a show of careful consideration of Neech's proposal.

While Neech seemed comfortable with the silence, Haley, on the other hand, was not. "You never answered me, girl," he gruffed. "Where is Eric? I've got a score to settle with that cheating scoundrel." Even below the waterline, Sally could see Haley's fists balled up in anger.

The whole tone bugged Sally, let alone the attack on her brother. Tina must be close to having passed along the info by now, she thought. Clearly, the best way to play this would be to not tip them off to her deception, but what kind of movie scene is it if the villain does not get a hint from the good guys that they have been deceived before their downfall?

"That 'cheating scoundrel' you're talking about happens to be my brother," Sally glowered, "and he made you look like an idiot when you had a gun and he had nothing." The barb clearly had an irritating effect on Haley whose eyebrow lowered. But Sally was not done yet. "And the closest you'll ever get to seeing him again will be in your nightmares, because neither of you will lay eyes on Eric or Charlotte again in your whole miserable lives."

Neech's smug face suddenly fell, something supremely satisfying to Sally. Without another moment's hesitation, he pulled out his gun.

The gun. The gun was not only one of Sally's what if scenarios, it was one that the theatrical side of her secretly hoped for. In fact, her last statement was most likely an unconscious affront with the idea of goading him into pulling it out. Didn't some storyteller guy once say that you can't introduce a gun in the first scene and not have it go off by the end of the story?

But now, with the gun pulled out, she immediately regretted her decision. This was real, not a movie, and guns are real killers not just the fake sounds and flashes from a prop.

Neech brought the barrel around, slowing as it came across Sally, but then continuing, to her surprise, towards their group of friends and stopping, leveled at Luke. "I don't know what game you're playing here, young lady, but it's over right now." The intensity of Neech's finger on the trigger spelled out his willingness to use it as much as anything. "I told you that I brought all of the captives to fulfill my end of the bargain, but really I needed some collateral to show how tired I am of back-and-forth scheming. If Charlotte does not show up right now, then Luke is gone first."

Sally now felt the true seriousness of the situation. "No! Please! What about me?" she tried, desperately, "You can make your point just as easily by shooting me."

Neech sneered. "I need you to get Charlotte here, so it'll be Luke. Then another. Then another. You have three seconds: three, two . . ."

Sally panicked. If she had more time to consider what she was doing, she might have made a different choice, but the urgency of the situation caused her to be rash. She flipped the diary page that said, "Not Yet" to the next page, which said, "NOW!"

Just like that Charlotte appeared, kneeling down on the raft, eyes fixed on Neech.

Neech smiled. "Finally," he muttered. "Charlotte, I've been waiting a long time for this, and to make sure you know how serious I am about this discussion, I'm going to finish what I started. You are going to want to blame me for it, but just remember that your parents are the ones that have been lying to you about who and what you are—and about who *they* are—this whole time."

"Blame you for what?" Charlotte asked.

"This."

Neither Sally nor Charlotte had time to digest Neech's statement before he pulled on the trigger of the gun.

Chapter 7
FERRY, EXPLOSIVE

As soon as Dr. Corinth had cleared out of the parking lot area, Charlotte sensed some movement at the ferry point of the river pig world. Even though her thoughts were clouded by plenty of things that she wanted to sort out, she knew that would have to come later. She hoped that whatever was happening right now at the ferry point would not already be the moment she dreaded.

Only one way to find out, she told herself.

Still kneeling, she let her mind zero in on the moon's position and the world around her disappeared . . . almost. Once again, she allowed herself to slip between worlds, still kneeling on the cold pavement of the parking lot and hearing the muted sounds of modern city life in the distance, but all around her she saw the world of the river pigs. This time it was broad daylight, and right next to her stood Sally, posted on some crude-looking raft. Below, in the water to Charlotte's left, Tina anchored the raft. Straight in front of them, Charlotte shuddered as she observed a seething Haley and a creepy Neech, the first time she got a real good look at either of them.

At an angle, towards the actual wall of the logjam itself, she saw Luke, her dad, and Dave Gardner. They were bunched together and seemed to be having a whispered conversation. Charlotte thought she saw the effervescent form of Facade just behind them, but she could not be sure.

Where's Eric, she immediately thought after taking in the scene. *He's got to be here somewhere, doesn't he?* Her thoughts reverted once more to the discussion she just finished with Dr. Corinth. In an instant, she was tempted to appear in Dave's world to interrogate everyone until she found out what had happened to Eric, but that is when she saw Sally's diary, which she held down at her waist, open and with the page angled in Charlotte's direction. The words, "Not yet," stared at her.

In spite of her concerns, Charlotte could not help but smile at Sally's cleverness. *This is your natural born element, isn't it?* Charlotte thought. *Staging some kind of dramatic entrance.* Charlotte dropped her hands on her thighs. *Fine, script doctor, I'll wait for your cue.*

She saw more whispered conferencing among Luke, her dad, and Dave. She saw Neech grinning like he knew he was the smartest person at the scene. When her eyes came across Haley again, she shuddered. This was a man with no regard for life. The fire in those eyes burned for blood, and Charlotte knew for whose. More than that, she knew how he would seek to satiate that urge.

Suddenly, Charlotte noticed Neech's grin dropped. The next thing she knew, Neech had a gun. *Where did he get that?!* An instant later and it was pointed at Luke. *What is going on?! Is it happening already? This isn't right!* She suddenly wished she had a chance to read the foreseer hieroglyphs leading up to the final one because she feared that it was not the only tragic one.

Do I ferry myself into their world? Charlotte raced through a thousand possibilities in a split second, but all of them just left question marks. The next thing she knew, Sally—herself seemingly nervous and antsy at the gun sighting—flipped the page of her diary. "NOW!" it told her.

Without considering the repercussions, Charlotte immediately completed her ferry to the river pig world. She felt her kneeling form settle in on the raft, her weight displacing it a bit. She felt the bright sun glaring down on her. She saw Neech staring at her with an ambitious passion.

Then she heard his voice: "Finally. Charlotte, I've been waiting a long time for this, and to make sure you know how serious I am about this discussion, I'm going to finish what I started. You are going to want to blame me for it, but just remember that your parents are the ones that have been lying to you about who and what you are—and about who *they* are—this whole time."

"Blame you for what?" Charlotte asked, her voice level but her emotions surging.

"This." Then he pulled the trigger.

Before Charlotte could even call out, she saw that her dad—his natural born bodyguard skills kicking in—had somehow managed to throw himself in front of Luke in the matter of a split second. But the sound of the gun firing never came.

She looked back to Neech, who eyed his weapon in confusion.

"Dude, you got it wet when Sally made you wade out here. What did ya expect?" Dave scoffed.

Charlotte's dad shook his head. "That kind of gun shouldn't have a problem firing after being submerged in water."

Neech made a few more attempts to fire, but the gun remained silent. While he was opening the chamber to check his cartridge, Charlotte heard Sally mutter, "Thank goodness. I was counting on Facade taking care of the gun. She even hinted to me that she had, but as soon as he pulled it out I panicked and couldn't be sure."

By that time, Neech had furiously extracted a spent casing that had been placed inside the chamber. He released the magazine, and emptied it into the river. It was filled with pebbles.

"Come out, pigs!" Neech shrieked. "Grab the girl!"

Scattered along the logjam, Charlotte suddenly saw sections of the wall of logs disappear and stout river pigs emerge from hiding places. They wasted no time in skillfully traversing the logjam on both sides, closing in on their position.

Neech nudged Haley, "Get her."

Haley, however, refused to budge. "Where is Eric?"

Neech was already irritated with the gun malfunction, but he kept himself from blowing his top. "You get the girl and you'll get Eric. Now, go!"

While this occurred, Charlotte suddenly saw out of the corner of her eyes, two logs drifting towards the logjam, one closer to them and one closer to the logjam. She did not even have time to voice the thought about where they came from before she glanced behind her and saw a head barely bobbing out of the water, blocked from everyone else's view by the raft.

Eric!

"Let's go home," he said, reaching to touch Charlotte's foot.

Charlotte suddenly felt Tina's hand reach out and grab her left hand. Sally grabbed her right hand. Then Charlotte saw that the two logs had now drifted close to Luke, her dad, and Dave. She heard Dave yelp, "The bridge!"

In a trice, the natural born river pig rocketed from the river and onto the first log, hopped to the second log, and from there managed a soaring leap to the logjam. Within seconds, he had scaled to a specific spot and then turned around.

The closest river pigs had almost completed their approach to the raft. Neech started to piece together what was happening. Luke and her dad had almost closed the gap from their position to Sally's extended right hand, her diary awkwardly placed in her mouth. Then Haley's keen eyes noticed the form just behind Charlotte holding onto her leg.

"Eric!" he spat venomously.

"Tiiiiiiimber!" Dave shouted, as if in a rapture. He shoved down on a log sticking out at about waist height, and then the world exploded.

Eric missed the initial breaking up of the logjam because his focus fell on the charging form of Haley headed straight towards him. Eric knew from Haley's obsessive look that Charlotte would be tossed aside in his fervor to reach Eric, and if that happened before they ferried, they would all be stuck in the middle of the exploding logjam. Already, Eric could sense the concussions of hundreds of logs being hurtled forward into the river as the repressed river water burst the interlacing log cage into smithereens.

Therefore, Eric went on the offensive. With a quickness rivaled only by Dave, he popped onto the raft and under Charlotte and Tina's arms. At this point, Haley's hands reached the raft, but they got no further. Eric swiftly pulled Haley's confiscated gun out from his back waistband, leveled it at Haley, and pulled the trigger.

This gun, too, refused to fire. Eric wondered what went wrong—had it been sabotaged too? Before he could reason it through completely, Haley swiftly snatched the outstretched weapon. In a flash, he flicked something and then reversed it.

"Pirate guns don't have safeties . . ." he growled. A sinking feeling hit Eric as looked down the barrel, realizing that he must have slipped the safety on when he first handled the weapon after subduing Haley.

Charlotte screamed, her voice somehow carrying over the rumbling crash raging towards them, "No! No! This isn't how it's supposed to happen!"

Eric watched Haley's spiteful eyes narrow and his finger slide to the trigger. But it never reached its destination.

A fist came crashing into Haley's head, knocking him sideways with a force that would have put a hurtling log to shame. Haley crumpled into the river and disappeared.

Charlotte's dad retracted his battering ram of an arm and then reached out and touched Eric on the knee, who, shocked as he was, still had the presence of mind to wrap his arm around Charlotte's torso.

Whitewater now rushed all around them, displaced logs started flying past them. "Now?" Charlotte called out.

Eric saw Tina gripping Charlotte's one hand and Sally gripping the other. Luke had Sally's other outstretched hand. He had Mr. Reeves and, of course, Charlotte. *Where's Dave?*

Eric looked upriver and saw the impossible. The logjam had disappeared, a wall of churning white water with the hidden shadows of logs scattered throughout replaced it—within seconds they would all be consumed by its inexorable advance. Somehow, navigating this broiling charybdis, Dave

Gardner danced towards them, finding logs invisible to the eye, dodging spinning projectiles that could easily decapitate him, leaping into voids that suddenly provided a landing spot in the form of a careening log.

In the split second that it took to take all of this in, Eric could not be sure if Dave would make it to them before he got taken out or they got overwhelmed by the onslaught. They had a second, maybe two, before getting slammed by the mad march of the released river.

Dave must have known it. His dance had taken him to a flanking position to the left of their location. Dave's eyes darted their direction, and Eric could almost see him embracing his mantra of moving first and letting his body figure the rest out. Dave took two steps on the flying log where he was and then sprang in their direction.

Eric decided they could put the same trust in Dave that he blindly put in himself. "Now!" he told Charlotte.

Dave shot towards them, "High five!" he yelled in the air.

The next thing they knew, Mr. Reeves's free hand flashed into the air and connected with Dave's passing palm. White spray overwhelmed them, Eric saw the butt end of a log streaking straight for his face, and then . . . and then . . . it all disappeared.

PART SIX

FORESEER FALLOUT

HOW TO BECOME A SEER

How strange it was. How strange to be in broad daylight, in the middle of a river, about to be consumed by an explosion of logs and foaming water, and then to find themselves kneeling or lying on the cold, hard, dry pavement of a parking lot enveloped in darkness save for a few weak lampposts.

Something sailed over Eric's head and he instinctively ducked. Did a flying log somehow ferry with us? His trailing eyes caught the form as it finished its trajectory over Charlotte's head and then tuck into a roll on the pavement beyond.

"Whoa!" Eric heard the dark form whoop. "Are you kidding me?! That was the most unreal and insane parkour experience ever!"

I guess Dave made it! This made Eric instinctively check on everyone else. Tina, Charlotte (of course), Mr. Reeves, Sally. Where was Luke? He saw a shadow shifting on the edge of their group past Sally. He looked closer and suddenly caught sight of a form move, still firmly attached to Sally's hand: Luke. Eric breathed a sigh of relief.

Sally was the next to speak. She had to drop her diary from her mouth. "Now *that* is how you give a story a climax!"

Eric laughed. "You did it, Sis. I mean, you really pulled it off!"

Sally let go of Luke and Charlotte's hands and then grabbed her Scribblings Diary. "It's all here if you ever want to review how I did it."

Eric smiled. "Sally, I will read your journal everyday just to show you how grateful I am for what you managed to just pull off."

Luke and Tina both stood up, grins plastered across their faces as they took in the gloriously boring Nibleton night scene. Dave laughed. Tina stepped over to shake Sally's hand. "Sally," she said, "wonderfully planned and perfectly executed!"

"Thanks!" Sally replied. "But I don't know about 'perfectly' executed. I think the gun spooked me more than it should have so I didn't quite—"

"We should go," Charlotte's voice interrupted.

Eric turned to Charlotte and saw her face troubled. He noticed that she looked past him, so he pivoted to check out Mr. Reeves. The bodyguard, too, held a disquieted expression.

"Yes," Mr. Reeves agreed. He scanned everyone else. "We're all accounted for." It seemed as if he felt more should be said, so he added, "I appreciate all you did to help protect my daughter in the process. Now that everyone is here, we should all go to our homes."

"Home?" Dave Gardner piped in. "You mean, you want us to just stroll into our houses, and if our parents ask, pretend like we just got done with another chill night out in Nibleton?"

"No." Mr. Reeves shook his head. "You should tell them that there were some suspicious characters up in this parking lot. Have them call the police."

"You think Neech and Haley survived that logjam explosion and they'll be able to ferry back?" Sally asked.

Mr. Reeves let Sally's question sit for a moment. "I don't know. But there's no need to take any chances."

"What would the police be able to do about it?" Tina followed up. "Unless we tell them an outrageous story about world-hopping, there is no proof that Neech and Haley have done anything illegal."

"I could get the dude in trouble by saying that they grabbed me downtown and brought me up here," Dave shrugged.

"That's right!" Sally chipped in. "I could be a witness! A courtroom drama. I've always wanted to be involved in one of those."

"I suspect Neech would have some innocent mix-up story to explain away the witness accounts of a few adolescents," Mr. Reeves replied. "At least enough to get out on bail and then disappear. But either way, he won't hang around a place that has police officers looking into his actions. This is not his first natural bornapping, so soon enough he could be connected to missing persons from other locations.

Mr. Reeves took in the whole group. "The best protection—for all of you—is to have him thinking he's being watched by authorities. He'll disappear fast after that."

"That should be the best protection for all of *us*—including you and Charlotte," Eric pitched in, not liking the way that Mr. Reeves did not include himself or Charlotte in the explanation.

Mr. Reeves did not respond. He simply glanced at Eric and then looked away. "Time to go home."

Eric looked to Charlotte. Surprisingly, she eagerly stood up. "Yes," she said, "let's go."

Mr. Reeves had driven Charlotte up to the parking lot on an adjacent street earlier that night. Even though Luke and Tina had also driven, he offered to give them a ride home and they could pick up their vehicles in the morning. The bodyguard in him did not want their group separated until he could see each individual enter the safety of their own home, Eric guessed. They all piled into the Reeves family car.

Underneath the chattering of Sally, with occasional bursts of exclamation from Dave, the car ride gave off a quietly turbulent tone.

First Dave waved goodbye as he popped out of the car and bounced off a couple trees, soaring over his porch railing before opening his front door. "Epic!" he called out before hopping inside.

Next, Tina took a bit more formal exit. Since she sat next to Luke, she looked him straight in the eyes. "Thanks for being there for me."

Luke lifted his pointer finger on one hand and twirled it in several circles. Tina smiled. "I know."

Then Tina thanked everyone else in the car before making a dignified walk to her front door. She only stumbled once on an uneven crack in the sidewalk, but she did not seem to mind—in fact, she even seemed to smile at the slip up.

Luke paused for a while once they arrived at his house. He seemed to be taking things in. Then his strong chicle gathering hand gave handshakes all around. He seemed to want to say something but paused as if unable to form the words. Sally interrupted, "Luke, you don't need to say anything. Sometimes people just understand each other without needing to talk."

Luke grinned. He nodded and then left the car.

Finally, they pulled up to Eric and Sally's home. "Sally," Mr. Reeves turned around in his seat, "you saved us all against incredible odds. Well done. You have a bright future ahead of you."

Charlotte got out of the passenger seat and ran around to Sally's side of the car, pulling her out and then embracing her in a long and hard hug. "You made the bravest choice, and you helped me to find myself when I was at my lowest point. You were huge to have as a script doctor, but most importantly you were my friend."

Eric had never seen Sally so affected. She wiped away some tears as they released each other, then she jumped back into another long hug with Charlotte. Finally, Sally released her and shuffled towards her and Eric's house, faithfully gripping her Sally's Scribblings Diary.

With just Eric and him in the car, Mr. Reeves turned around. He looked ready to say something, but Eric beat him to it. "Thanks for saving my life—I thought for sure Haley had me."

Mr. Reeves smiled. "I promised my little girl I would." He paused for a second, "But I would've done it anyway. I've been very impressed by your coolness under pressure, maturity in stressful situations, and fierce loyalty to my daughter, even when it requires sacrifice from you."

Eric almost thought he saw a shine in Mr. Reeves's firm eyes as he added, "I'm sorry that things did not work out differently."

And that was when Eric knew that he was suddenly facing the reality of Charlotte moving, and that this was where he said goodbye to Mr. Reeves. Worse, this was where he said goodbye to Charlotte.

Mindlessly, he shook hands with Mr. Reeves, who then wrapped his free hand around Eric's neck and drew him close. Their eyes met and Eric saw the appreciation that only a father and bodyguard can have for someone who helped him do his job. Then, he released him.

385

Eric stepped out of the car. In the distance, he heard Sally. "Don't worry, Eric. I know that this scene is just for the two of you! I'm going inside, and I won't even eavesdrop." The door to their house closed.

Dreading the moment, Eric grabbed Charlotte's hand as they trudged up to his porch. Once at the door, he turned. Charlotte had tears streaming down her face.

"I know," he said.

"No," she replied, "you don't." She wiped the tears but more took their place. "You can't possibly know the hurt I'm feeling right now. The pain. The feeling of being hopelessly trapped."

Eric suddenly realized that there was something deeper going on than even he realized. He saw the torture in her eyes, and it threw him off. "What is it?" he asked.

"Moving means losing you, but something deep down gave me hope that we would still find each other somehow, even if it were months or years or, well, years and years in the future," she said.

"Of course," Eric said.

"But losing you, really losing you, and having to watch it. I can't. I just don't think I can physically, emotionally, mentally handle it. It's too much."

Eric furrowed his eyebrows. "So you won't really lose me. Not really. You'll move, and we'll be cut off, but . . . but we'll find each other. It'll happen. I have to believe that."

"But you don't—"

"No, listen," Eric said. "Back in Tina's world when Facade held me captive, I hinted in that note that I'd be willing to stay in the aqueduct world if I couldn't be with you. And I've thought a lot about it. Part of that was to set Facade up with believing she had no leverage, sure, but then the whole idea took me back to the pirate hunter world where I had to choose if I wanted to stay or go back."

Charlotte tried to interrupt him, but Eric could not be stopped. He spoke without thinking, the thoughts coming out as if a logjam broke. "And it made me think back to my world, the world of pirate hunting. When I got

386

to choose to stay or return, I chose to return because of my family, and . . . because of you."

He gripped her hand tighter. "Now, things are different. I know that my family will be fine. I love them, I would miss them terribly—even Sally, maybe especially Sally after all this. But they don't need me anymore, and I feel as though I don't need them like I used to.

"But you, Charlotte? I have needed you since the moment you walked into my math class. And then after I discovered myself through you, I still needed you. Because there's more to you than just your ability—you taught me that."

Eric saw Charlotte's eyes twinkle under the streaming tears. "I guess what I'm saying, Charlotte, is that my letter was more accurate than even I knew at the time, because if there's not you, what else is there? I could have stayed in the world of aqueducts, or the world of pirate hunting, or here in Nibleton with you gone . . . and I would be fine in any of those situations because I would survive, maybe even thrive . . . but I still wouldn't be fulfilled.

"That's why, if circumstances were different and I got stuck on any of those worlds, or here with you gone, I still would find a way to get to you because . . . because I need you, Charlotte. I need you so much that worlds could separate us, and I will still find you."

Eric grabbed Charlotte's other hand and looked her full-on in the face. "I will find you no matter what happens to me or you. No matter how impossible, no matter what obstacles. Believe it."

The tears seemed to turn to rivulets at this point. "What if you're dead, Eric?"

Eric looked at her, bewildered. Because he got caught up in the fervor of his own speech, he had not expected such a blunt follow up question. "What?" he asked.

"I love your passion, Eric," Charlotte replied, "but you won't be able to find me if you're dead." Charlotte released one hand from his and reached into her pocket. She then placed Eric's phone into his open hand.

"My phone?" Her response just got more confusing.

"Eric," her voice focused, "you must *never* see me again. Ever. Because the next time you do, you'll be dead, and I'll have to watch it."

Silence, full and complete. Inside Eric came a growing realization where he finally understood the deeply embedded suffering in Charlotte's eyes.

"Eric," she could now only whisper, "this is goodbye forever."

The seer that had meant the world to him—no, who had meant *worlds* to him—closed her eyes and leaned into Eric. Her lips found his and the two kissed—not passionately, not intensely, but with a tender and heartbreaking firmness, full of yearning and loss.

In too short a time, the kiss ended and Charlotte, without opening her eyes for one last look at him, turned and stumbled down the porch. She clambered into her car, and Mr. Reeves—concern lining his face—backed out of Eric's driveway, taking his daughter away from Eric for the last time.

Epilogue
DISAPPEARING ACT

*I*t was not until the parking lot stood empty that Facade felt safe sliding out from underneath her trench coat.

In the chaos of the breaking up of the logjam, nobody noticed her staying low and following Luke and Mr. Reeves over to the raft with Sally. The real danger was being noticed after the ferrying took place, where she had to release her light touch on Luke's back and then duck into the darkness. As she emerged from her trench coat, however, it appeared as though that danger had passed and that she once again managed to hitchhike through another ferrying without being caught.

Now she watched the taillights of a car moving downhill and disappearing around a bend on one of the side streets near the parking lot. She knew she would not be able to follow them without a car of her own. She briefly toyed with the idea of taking Neech's car. She could manage to hot wire it, but even if she could do it fast enough to catch up to the already gone car, she knew that Charlotte's dad would have a keen eye out for someone tailing him.

No. As always, she would simply have to find another way. And, as magicians always do, it would have to be in a way no one would suspect.

A couple of hours later, she found herself scoping out a small house on one of the streets at Nibleton's edge, matching the address she had scribbled down on a scrap piece of paper held in her hand. The house, fittingly, was the only one with lights on at this hour of the night. Facade, blending in with the darkness, managed to bring herself under the window of the garage. She heard shuffling, hefting, shifting, and packing going on inside.

"Is that everything?" she heard Mr. Reeves query after a second's reprieve.

"It'll have to be," a female voice, not Charlotte's so probably Mrs. Reeves, answered. "From the sound of things, you would've liked to just take off as soon as the two of you got home."

"True," he said. "There's something about this that goes well beyond our normal precautions of avoiding seers, and not just because it was a natural bornapper. There is something else going on here, and I can't help but feel as if the whole situation started because of some specific knowledge of Charlotte, not just because of her being a seer."

"I trust your instincts," came the response, "but you need to trust mine, even for an extreme case like this. Leaving the house in disarray, as if there were foul play suspected, might cause more problems than it fixes. The more neat and orderly our middle-of-the-night exit, the more explainable it is when we call from a distance to wrap up loose ends tomorrow or later on this week."

"I do trust you," Mr. Reeves replied softly. "Besides, I think Charlotte needed some recovery time anyway. She's used to abrupt moves, but this time ... this one ..."

"He's a special kid," Mrs. Reeves finished. "We both knew that."

It was quiet for a moment before Mrs. Reeves picked up again, "I guess we always knew that something like this would happen eventually. She wasn't always going to be on board for every overnight move."

"I guess so," Mr. Reeves said. "I just didn't think it would be so hard on me too!"

"She's pretty special herself. That's why it's so hard to hurt her like this."

"You don't know the half of it," Mr. Reeves responded. "The natural bornapper suspected that we were hiding something from her, and before we got away he told her. She's hurt and probably doesn't trust us much right now."

"Then it's time to tell her everything. Let's get her in the car and we can tell her once we're on the road. Was that the last box?"

There was a pause. "Maybe five more minutes."

"For her . . . or for yourself?"

Mr. Reeves let out a short laugh. "Yes."

Facade was lucky to have caught them when she did. Now, she had very little time. She slipped around the back of the house and saw a light on in a small bedroom. She scaled a hose mount attached to the house under the window, slid the window open, and lightly hopped in.

"I've been waiting for you," Charlotte said, managing to surprise the usually imperturbable Facade. Charlotte watched her from near the door of the bedroom, sitting on a box. Her improvised seat was the only possession left in the room, which lay empty except for a bare bed. "But I did wonder how you were going to find my house."

"I had to sneak into your school and check for your address on one of the computers in the office. I'd tell you that the counselor keeps his password on a sticky note underneath his desk drawer, but it won't do you much good since you'll never be going back there again."

Charlotte nodded. Facade noticed for the first time that Charlotte's eyes were red. She had been crying. Charlotte followed up, "We don't have much time, but there's a lot I've been wanting to talk to you about. I think you've been wanting to talk to me too."

Facade jumped straight to the point. "The short version is that I need your help. I kept my end of the bargain by freeing Eric and helping you and Sally get the rest of your friends back safe."

Charlotte seemed to take issue with Facade's choice of the word "safe," but she still nodded. Facade saw that Charlotte fingered a small business card in one hand. "You definitely did your part, at great danger to yourself. I'm ready to help you."

Facade relaxed a little. She was not sure if there would be some difficult negotiations for this to work, especially considering she had been Charlotte's foe for half the night—or, by another count, at least a week.

"But first, I'm going to ask a favor from you," Charlotte said.

Facade looked at her carefully. "What favor?"

"I need you to perform a magic trick."

Facade's eyebrows raised, intrigued. "What kind?"

"One that can trick a natural born bodyguard."

Facade took a deep breath. "That's a tall order. What's the trick?"

"It's a disappearing act . . . for me."

ABOUT THE AUTHOR

Marty Reeder lives with his wife and five children in Smithfield, Utah. He teaches creative writing and Spanish at the local high school. Marty spends summers at a camp in New Hampshire where he ~~plays on~~ is in charge of the waterfront while irrationally forcing all the campers to address him as the "Admiral." In his off time he dreams of and writes about the far-ranging possibilities of the worlds of natural born talents.